HER

JANE JESMOND

Ebook ISBN: 978-1-80508-057-2
Paperback ISBN: 978-1-80508-058-9

Cover design: Lisa Horton
Cover images: Trevillion, Shutterstock

Published by Storm Publishing.
For further information, visit:
www.stormpublishing.co

ALSO BY JANE JESMOND

On the Edge

Cut Adrift

To all my friends, old and new.
Especially Alex, Caroline, Jane, Jonathan, Madeleine, Marion,
Mike, Stephen and, bien sûr, Anne.

1

Late September, but the summer heat still lingered. It was the worst drought for years, the weathermen said on the television, with farmers looking grave and muttering about ruined harvests, and pictures of long-submerged buildings revealed by the low water levels in the reservoirs. The grass in nearby Greenwich Park was yellow and worn, barely a different colour from the baked earth, but underneath its tired surface, I told myself, life dozed and waited. The first rain of autumn would turn the grass green again. The cycle of the seasons would take its course. It was just turning a little more slowly than usual.

But it didn't seem possible this morning. The heat of the sun had robbed the air of any freshness even though it was only twenty-two minutes to nine. The smell of damp that pervaded the shop when I first moved in had long disappeared and grit on the handle of my feather duster grated against my skin. Clay dust had crept through from my workshop like it did every night and settled. I cleaned the display of masks, poking the duster through the empty eyes that stared out of the shop window, and wished my brain was as empty, wished for a customer to distract me, but no one ventured up the alley to the shop this early in the morning and Amy, my assistant, wouldn't arrive until bang on the dot of nine and free me to retreat into my workshop and lose myself in sculpting and mask-making.

I checked the masks for flaws as I flicked the duster over them, but they were perfect. From the Venetian beauties, dripping with lace and sequins, and the horror faces of silicon painted to look like skulls or vampires, to the super-heroes for children's parties and the rest – all designed to turn you into someone or something beautiful, or mysterious, or comical or terrifying. My masks could make you into anything you could dream of.

Ironic, really, when I could do nothing to escape from myself and the treadmill of my thoughts.

My life was as dead as the scorched and withered grass, and I didn't think the autumn rains would revive it.

How different it had been when I moved into the shop and the flat above in Greenwich in early spring, encouraged by my aunt, Tilly – helped by Tilly and then left alone to find my feet by Tilly. And there, full of hope amidst the clutter of empty boxes and piles of clothes that had nowhere to live – wardrobes and shelving came later – I thought I might find a life. I thought I might find the person I used to be. Before marriage. Before Gavin.

Except my time with Gavin had locked me into solitari-ness. I'd lost the ability to make contact. Some part of me vital to the making-friends process had withered.

And I couldn't bring myself to contact my old friends. Not after Gavin's funeral. Oh, I was sure they'd be polite. No one would say anything to my face. But they'd have excuses if I suggested meeting up. They'd be busy at work. Or away. Or tied up with children. Or sick relatives. Even the ones who hadn't come to the funeral.

Word would have got round.

The years of silence came back and slapped me in the face. It was too late to explain what had happened. The complicated web of my marriage, that I barely understood myself, still held me tight. How could I tell my friends that all those times I said life was great were one big, fat lie? How could I explain that the rumours they'd heard were false when I couldn't tell them the truth? I could never tell anyone the truth. Never ever ever.

So I slipped into solitude, barely touched by the day-to-day exchanges with clients, the sparse chats with Amy, and Elizabeth's cheerful greetings as we passed on the stairs. I might even have been content if it wasn't for the terrors that woke me in the middle of the night and drove me out of my sweaty sheets to roam around the flat touching the walls and the furniture and letting their different surfaces reassure me that this was real.

Amy arrived at two minutes to nine, picked the post up from the mat and headed to the stockroom to get the cash from the safe, hang up the mackintosh she'd started wearing as soon as September arrived and leave the shopping she'd done on the way to work.

'Tea?' I asked as she took the duster from my hand and whisked it over the display.

'Please.' She smiled, a little widening of her mouth and a slight crinkle of her eyes. My fingers itched to touch her face and explore how such a minuscule rearrangement of her features could convey so much. Everything about Amy was efficient. The least effort calculated to produce the biggest effect. Her long straight hair scraped back into a ponytail. Low maintenance and tidy, she said. She never went to the stockroom for one thing but kept a list by the till and went when something was urgent or the list was long enough.

'Jamie's not well.' She looked up from the printout of orders that had come in overnight as I handed her the tea.

'Off school?' I asked. Her economy with words was contagious.

'My mother's looking after him.'

'Go, if you need to. I can cope.'

'I might have to leave early.'

Her voice was dull but brisk, like it was when I first met her, when she came in for an interview. Her just-getting-on-with-it voice – wary but determined. Not giving anything away. It had been weeks before I discovered anything about her. My fault probably because I'd never asked. It wasn't until I ran into her in Tesco that I realised she had children. A five-year-old and twins of eighteen months. For once, her face had shown some emotion as I made my way through the Saturday morning mothers and children fighting, negotiating and compromising over cereal choices.

The emotion I saw on her face was dismay.

'I didn't know you had children,' I said and cursed myself when I saw her face tighten even more.

'They're no problem,' she said, pushing one of the twins back inside the trolley where he sat down suddenly, crushing a family pack of crisps. 'My mother looks after them when I'm working.'

'I didn't mean... Look, I'm not bothered if you need time off because...' For the life of me I couldn't remember why parents needed time off, but I knew they did.

'Well, it won't be a problem.'

And it hadn't been.

Not even when Jamie, the five-year-old, had gone into hospital with a nasty chest infection and asthma, and Amy had told me quietly but firmly – pinching the end of each finger in turn, her little foible whenever she was stressed – that she wouldn't be able to come in for a while, and she'd understand if I replaced her.

I hadn't replaced her.

Something about the droop of her head and the curve of her mouth told me the job mattered to her. And I found she mattered to me. Besides, any time she'd taken off she made up for in spades. She took over the online orders that were the bulk and the most profitable part of the business, and stayed an extra half hour here and there when the shop was full of tourists over summer. We worked together well, chatted about day-to-day things and laughed privately at the more eccentric customers, though we'd never progressed beyond that. I didn't know how she'd come to be on her own with three young children and had never told her why I'd fled to London and immersed myself in work after my husband died.

'This looks personal.' She held an envelope out to me.

White envelope. Handwritten address. Ted's writing. Postmarked Guildford. Sent to Mrs L. Lyle.

For a brief moment I wanted to say no. To deny that Mrs Lucy Lyle had ever been me.

Amy knew though. 'It's my married name,' I'd said the first time Amy picked up the post with a letter from Gavin's mother, Moira, in it. Her eyes had been full of unasked questions. It would only have taken a few words from me to unlock them but all I said was, 'I don't use it.'

I took the letter from Ted and wondered whether to open it now. As I hesitated, Amy turned back to the rest of the post, darting me a quick glance out of the corners of her eyes. If I ever sculpted her head, I thought, that was the pose I'd use. Sideways on, but glancing at the onlooker as though giving them space to be private, a space that the full-on gaze from her face with its scraped back hair wouldn't.

I put the letter on my desk in the stockroom, then slipped away into my workshop.

The shop and the flat above were Victorian and, if I'm honest, a bit poky although full of what estate agents call 'period charm'. But the studio at the back, a modern addition built over part of the yard, was a complete contrast. Light poured in through the roof windows, even on the most sullen days, and the big table where I worked was right under them. And, best of all, both doors, the one through from the stockroom and the one that led out into the yard behind the building, had locks.

I sell and make masks for a living, but my first love is sculpture. I sculpt heads. I love heads. I always have. Since I was a child when I first rolled a lump of Playdoh into a ball then pinched ears, eyes and a mouth out of it and discovered that a smile doesn't always show happiness, and grief can be seen more in a certain inclination of the head than a facial expression.

I was perfectly capable of sculpting other things. Even abstract stuff. And of using other materials than clay. Three years studying sculpture at art college made sure of that. But it was always the heads and the clay that I returned to. Only the lucky few can make a living from sculpting so, when I discovered that all masks start with sculpture, I knew I'd found a way of doing what I loved and making a living.

There was a lot of work about for mask-makers. Masks have always been used in films and theatre, but the proliferation of music videos and theme parks had increased the demand for specialist work stratospherically so even a novice like I was when I started out got given a chance. I'd become the go-to designer and sculptor for a couple of small studios when their in-house staff couldn't cope. That, along with the bread-and-butter money from the shop and the website and the rent from my lodger Elizabeth meant I could survive. Just.

Besides, it left me time to sculpt heads that I'd never turn into masks.

And one of them was on show, on a block of shelves by the door. Along with a series of birds I'd made during the weeks at Tilly's after Gavin died when anything else was beyond me. The birds were exercises in form and space, but the head had forced its way out of me. On the surface it appeared normal but the more you looked at it the more you noticed that everything was slightly distorted as though some exterior force was squashing and pulling the features out of shape. I'd shown it at a small, local exhibition and something about it resonated with everyone who came. A German arts magazine had included me in an article about new talent to watch out for. Ironic, really, that it might turn out to be my best work – I hadn't done anything worth keeping since.

I was creating a series of masks for a fashion show in a month or so. The designer had sent me a sheaf of drawings and he wasn't up for me making any changes to his sketches, so the masks were largely technical challenges in construction. The one I was working on had spikes all over it. He claimed the thorns of the may tree inspired it, but it looked vaguely fetishist to me. I spent the day trying to make the spikes stand firm instead of flopping at different angles, only stopping for a quick sandwich with Amy at lunch. I was more or less successful, although I wasn't sure it would withstand his models tearing it on and off during the show.

Amy knocked on the door around five. I unlocked it and let her in.

'The orders are finished and picked up,' she said. 'And here's a list of the items we're running short of.' She paused.

'Go home,' I said quickly, so she wouldn't have to ask. 'See how Jamie is. I need a break from Spiky Joe.' I pointed to the mask. 'I'll sit in the shop and make some phone calls. Do the accounts. Update the website.' I sighed. Another exciting day was drawing to an end.

'If you're sure. Thanks.'

Once she'd gone, the building settled into the true quietness that meant it was empty. I retrieved the letter from Ted and thought about opening it. My grubby fingers left marks on its thick and textured envelope and brought the embossed pattern to life. It was probably only another document that needed my signature, Mrs Lucy Lyle's signature. Ted, who was also my father-in-law as well as the solicitor dealing with Gavin's estate, had looked away and muttered something about complications when I'd asked him if everything could be in my unmarried name from now on. Christensen, I'd said. Lucy Christensen, in case he'd forgotten. The months since had shown what a waste of time trying to be Lucy Christensen again was. Going back was impossible. I could call myself what I liked, but I'd never escape Mrs Lyle.

I stuck a finger in one corner and ripped it open. It wasn't a document. It was a cheque. And a letter from Ted at his most solicitor-like.

Dear Lucy,

The estate of Mr Gavin LYLE

I am pleased to advise you that I have now completed the administration of the above estate. Please find enclosed:

– A cheque in full and final settlement of your entitlement to the proceeds of the estate.

– A copy of the final estate accounts.

– Form of receipt.

Please sign and return the enclosed receipt to me as soon as possible.

Yours sincerely,

Edward Lyle

The amount written on the cheque in the blue ink of Ted's fountain pen was huge. Much larger than I'd expected. Paying Tilly what I owed her would barely make a dent in it. It was made out to Mrs Lyle. Of course it was. Not that it was a problem, I still had an account in my married name.

I wondered if the police knew how much I'd got from Gavin's estate. Was it published somewhere? Anyway, it didn't matter because Ted would have told them. All solicitors know their local police well and Ted's firm was no exception – plus, Moira played bridge with the detective chief inspector's wife.

My mind fled back to Gavin's funeral before I could stop it. Moira, for once silent. Her unceasing chatter stopped by the strength of her grief. She looked crushed under the weight of her slightly too large black hat – a rare sartorial error for her – clinging to Ted who was upright in the expensive suit that he wore like armour. Both of them welcoming Detective Inspector Cromer and his colleagues, their gestures stiff with grief.

2

Gavin's funeral took place in late November, a wild, wet end to the year with red berries on the holly in the churchyard and dark storm clouds scudding across the sky.

I'd expected a quiet funeral. Ted, Moira, close family and myself and maybe a few of Gavin's friends. I couldn't have been more wrong, and I nearly turned tail and fled when I saw the cars lining the road and the hordes waiting outside the church. Everyone in the village was there, along with Gavin's family down to the most distant cousin, colleagues and clients of the family firm of solicitors, the police and, worst of all, my old friends and Aunt Tilly. Moira had done a fantastic job of letting people know. She'd done a fantastic job all over.

The church was bursting with lilies and pictures of Gavin from a baby up to the week before he died, when we'd gone to a wedding in the village. Candles shone in every corner. The hearse was a horse-drawn carriage, the horses with black plumes, and the undertakers in top hats and tails.

At the sight of it, emotion overwhelmed me. Not sadness.

Not grief. Not even the rawness of loss. Nor the mixed emotions that the beauty of the magnificent horses with their gleaming black coats and intricately plaited manes might have inspired.

No.

It was laughter. Laughter at the sheer excessiveness of it all. A storm of hysterical mirth that shook my ribs until I could do nothing but bury my face in my hands and pray that everyone thought it was sorrow quivering through my body. Only Moira could have thought this magnificence was appropriate. Poor, poor woman.

The service was impressive. Moira had booked a string quartet, and the vicar's eulogy was long and detailed. I featured in it a lot. I was a beloved wife. Gavin and I had a romantic meeting. It was a fairy-tale marriage. Gavin had devoted himself to my happiness.

I switched off after that. It was the only way to cope. I shut myself away and thought of other things. Water rustling the pebbles on the tidal estuary where Tilly lived. Birds singing in the brambles. Children laughing and shouting in the park. The feel of wet clay guiding my fingers.

After the service, everybody filed past Ted, Moira and me as they left the church. They shook our hands and said kind words. I nodded and smiled until my jaw ached under the thick make-up. Beside me, Moira was doing the same. Except better. She found something appropriate to say to everybody. After a while, I realised she had about ten phrases that she recycled. Her face was puffy underneath the powder and her eyes tiny with grief and tiredness. Despite everything, my heart went out to her. At the end of the day, she was his mother. And she'd adored Gavin. It would – I thought, with the benefit of hindsight – have been better for him if that love had been diluted by the arrival of other children but, for some reason she never seemed prepared to discuss, Gavin had been an only child.

Moira and I had nothing in common. Never had. But she'd tried to be welcoming and pleasant to me even though she couldn't understand why I didn't want to lose myself in her life of coffee mornings, church fetes, dinner parties and bridge evenings.

'It was a wonderful service,' I said.

She took my arm. Her fingers felt hot as they pressed into my flesh. 'Ted,' she said. 'Go and make sure everybody knows they're expected at the golf club for tea.'

He nodded and moved off.

'I'm glad you think so. That means a lot to me.' She put her other arm round my shoulder and fought back the tears. Her embrace was stifling and her breath was hot and minty against my cheek and only the fiercest determination kept me from pushing her away. A couple of her friends who'd been approaching turned away to give us a few moments together. The bereaved wife and mother sharing a deep sorrow no one else could understand.

After this, I promised myself, I'd be free from the fantasy Gavin had spun out of our marriage. This was the last time I'd be Lucy Lyle.

'You'll come to the wake, won't you, Lucy?' she whispered in my ear. Her lips were so close, her breath tickled my skin. 'Please. I know how hard it must be for you, but we can do it together. I know you'll want Gavin to have the sending-off he deserved.'

'Moira...' I tried to find the words to explain how I couldn't face everybody. Couldn't face what they'd be thinking. Even if they didn't say it.

'Please,' she said again. 'Do it for my boy. My darling, darling boy.'

Ted hovered on the edge of my vision, clutching a huge umbrella ready to escort us through the gusts of rain to the car. I knew of old there'd be no hope of help from him.

I couldn't wound Moira by refusing. I knew how much it meant to her. Besides, I deserved this. I gave in. Yet again.

'If it's what you want.'

But at the hideous wake in the room at the golf club that overlooked the wind and rain lashing the trees into a wild jamboree, only my aunt Tilly would meet my eyes and her steady brown gaze was troubled. Even my old friends looked away.

The local network of gossips had done its job well. I caught snippets of the conversations, and what I couldn't hear I could guess.

'Broke his heart.'

'No one could find her.'

'...boyfriend in London...'

'Gavin did everything for her.'

'...police...'

'Look at her! Face plastered with make-up.'

'...no evidence...'

The stories whispered round the room differed only in details.

In the mildest, Gavin had been driven to despair by my behaviour, forgotten to take his tablets and his heart had failed.

Most were worse though. Everyone knew I'd been arrested on suspicion of involvement in his death. Most people thought I'd only been let go because of a lack of evidence.

In some of the stories, I'd hit Gavin. The news of the bruising on his face when his body was found had leaked out.

In most of them, I had gone off to London to meet my lover, having emptied Gavin's bank accounts.

In all of them, I was guilty of something, a wicked woman, an unfeeling bitch, as good as a murderess... a murderess who'd got off scot-free.

I suppose I should have been glad it was only whispered.

But my friends asked me no questions when they said goodbye. Some didn't even say goodbye. It had been so long since I'd seen most of them, I guessed they thought I must have changed. I knew they'd heard the accusations, but it's hard to fight against whispers and gossip. They're as elusive and uncatchable as smoke. And as choking. Anyway, what *could* I have said to them?

The truth?

Never. Never, ever. I could never tell anyone. So there I was, caught between the whispered lies and the truth I couldn't speak. Trapped. Once again.

I stuck the wake out until the bitter end. When the waitresses started clearing the remaining sandwiches and pastries from the buffet table and Moira was kissing the last guests at the main door, I headed for an exit that led out through the gardens.

Ted stopped me.

'Are you leaving, Lucy?'

I nodded.

'Won't you at least come back to the house for a cup of tea? It would mean a great deal to Moira. All this talk is upsetting her so much.' He paused. 'It will pass, but it would be better for all of us to put on a united front.'

A draught crept in from beneath the door behind me, promising fresh wild air once I stepped out of this stuffy, malice-choked room. Ted waited, his face, with its perfectly shaped eyebrows and clipped moustache, as smooth as his beautifully pressed shirts and as characterless. I never knew what he thought. Years of listening to clients pour out tragic or scandalous stories had schooled his expression into one of mild interest. In moments of high stress, I'd seen him run a finger over the cleft in his chin, but his hands fell loosely by his sides now.

'I don't think I can.'

'I see. But we will have to get together soon. There's a great number of practical details to be worked through in order to wind up the estate and obtain probate.'

The words meant nothing. I felt behind me for the cold metal of the door handle and turned it half an inch. It clicked.

Ted's eyes flared at the noise and the smile on his face became fixed. 'Of course, as executors, all the work will be carried out by us, but there will be decisions you need to make.'

'Decisions?'

'About Gavin's estate. There will be items you want to keep and some, I imagine, you want to sell. We'll need instructions about what you want to do with the house and the cars. Then there are all his personal possessions, such as clothes and his collection of pens. His stocks and shares and of course his life insurance. I can advise you, but the ultimate decision rests with you, his sole beneficiary.'

I'd have got little from a divorce, but it seemed I was going to benefit from Gavin's death. I suspected everyone who'd come to the funeral knew that as well. I turned the handle further round and felt the wind take the door, urging me to escape.

'Just sell everything, Ted. Or cash it in.'

'I see.' He didn't move a muscle, but his pupils swelled and darkened his eyes. I felt sorry for him.

'I can't bear any reminders of him,' I said. 'It's too painful.'

I only spoke the truth.

'Just send me a cheque,' I said and pushed open the door and went out into the wind and the rain.

Tilly found me in the car park, trying to get an Uber to pick me up, but unable to see the screen of my phone through the pelting rain.

3

A door slammed and feet ran lightly up the stairs to the flat above, startling me from my memories. Elizabeth, my lodger, returning from work early as she often did on a Friday. She was probably going to spend the afternoon getting ready to go out. She went out most nights at the weekend. Glimpses of short dresses in sharp, geometric patterns showed beneath her cream raincoat. Everything about Elizabeth was long and cream. Her legs, her hair, her fingers and the nose she looked down. Everything except for the short, tight dresses she wore when she went out in the evenings.

I scrunched the letter and the envelope into a ball.

I used to have fun, too.

I used to *be* fun, as well. I had pictures to prove it, stuffed in a box in a drawer somewhere. When I was a student at art college, larking around in the studios, clay smears on my face. A group of us in the early morning in Trafalgar Square, the last knockings of a night to celebrate something. And I'm the one laughing most, sitting on the edge of one of the fountains, my hands pushing a great arc of water up into the dawn sky.

And now the nearest I got to fun was the occasional drink in the stockroom with Amy after a difficult day.

God, how I wished I could go back and be that person. Before Gavin. Before marriage. How I wished I could be anyone except Lucy Lyle née Christensen. Stupid Lucy. Weak Lucy.

Stop it.

The top of my workbench was strewn with debris and bits of the mask I'd been working on. I tidied it back into the cupboard and slid the door tight shut, casting a look round the workshop. Sparkling white. Pristine. Not a thing out of place. Just like it should be. Just like the workshop Gavin built for me in our house and not at all like the glorious mess I worked in in Venice with bits and pieces of velvet and lace and gold and leather swept into corners of my table to make room for the work, sometimes splattered with paint and clay when the heat of an idea overwhelmed me.

How had it happened? How had I become Lucy Lyle who tidied up immediately, who cleaned every surface every time it was used, who changed her shoes when she came in through the door and who noticed every speck of dust as it landed on the polished surfaces of the furniture?

It had seemed so innocent at first. Gavin's pride in the new house he'd bought for us. He wanted it to be perfect for me, so I went along with his cleaning mania. I hated his look of hurt and disappointment when he came home after work and noticed a smear on a mirror, so I started cleaning the house before he arrived. A quick once-over first of all and then a more thorough going-over until it was easier just to clean everything as soon as I'd finished using it. After all, as he said, it was the least I could do given how hard he worked for us both.

The blandness of my workshop now repelled me. Even

the pale blue sky through the skylight was insipid, stained with heat haze. An idea came to me. I picked up the cheque and smoothed it flat on the empty table. I could do a lot with the money. Like go somewhere with colour. Deep blue skies, white houses with vibrant shutters, cliffs of white cascading down into aquamarine seas. Somewhere that didn't smell of bleach and takeaways and hot tarmac. Where I'd want to reach out and touch everything. Images whirled through my head, and I laughed. I could go somewhere where nobody knew me and start over. Europe. The US. A clean slate. A new beginning. I could even change my name. Leave Lucy behind as well as Lyle. Become someone else.

The money made everything possible.

An echo of Elizabeth's arrival and my other lodger burst into the workshop, clattering the cat flap behind her. She wound her narrow black body round my legs, and I bent to stroke her, feeling her smooth fur glide under my hand.

'You'll have to wait for supper, Talisker,' I said. 'Unless you want to go upstairs and ask Elizabeth.'

I'd shut the shop early, go out to pay the cheque in and spend the evening thinking how to spend it.

Talisker's yellow eyes stared at me without blinking as she waited to see what I would do. She followed me into the shop, but when I headed for the door that led out into the alley rather than the connecting door leading upstairs to the flat, she hastily cleaned her paws and shot out through the cat flap again.

The phone rang. I ran my hands through the folds of my skirt to remove the last traces of glue and rammed it between my shoulder and ear. Amy hated it when I left the handset sticky.

'The Mask Factory,' I said and saw that she'd left a packet of wet wipes by the till. I grabbed one and cleaned the dried glue from under my rings and nails. It didn't matter how short I kept them, stuff still crept under.

'Ah, Lucy,' the voice said. 'It's Luke Awuah.'

I stopped rubbing. Luke was my solicitor and no call from him had ever brought good news.

'Hi, Luke.' I heard the wariness creep into my voice.

He was straight to the point as always. 'The police have just called me in connection with their ongoing enquiries into Gavin's... um, into his death. Some new evidence has turned up and they want to interview you again.'

No. Please no.

I wondered if Luke ever sugar-coated bad news.

In the three months since DI Cromer had last called me back to that bland but horrible room in the police station in Surrey to run over my story once again, I'd begun to hope the enquiry was over. That even DI Cromer, with his hard, little eyes and the tic in his left cheek that jerked whenever his questions drove me into a corner, had given up.

'New evidence?' I asked.

'They didn't say what it was. Do you have any idea?'

I didn't want to lie to Luke.

'Why would I?' I asked.

'It's probably nothing. Just with Ted being a local solicitor and Gavin's father, they won't want to leave any avenue unexplored.'

I wondered again if Luke found it hard to be both my solicitor and know Ted so well. Maybe I should have changed solicitors rather than using someone in the same town as Ted and Gavin's firm? Except I liked and trusted Luke and I couldn't face having to tell the whole story to another solicitor.

'Has Ted said anything?'

I knew he and Luke met frequently at civic events and Rotary evenings.

'Ted? Of course not. We never discuss cases where we're...'

On opposing sides, I thought. But Luke saved himself.

'...cases we're working on.'

'I don't suppose I've got a choice,' I said.

'No. They suggested Monday at nine o'clock.'

'Fine.'

I hung up and noticed how my hand shook, rattling my rings against the phone. What a fool I'd been to think I could escape. I'd never escape Gavin. I'd always be tied to him. *Gavin's wife. Gavin's widow. Gavin's...* But I didn't let myself think the word.

I looked at the cheque in my hand. *Money made everything possible.* Ha-bloody-ha. It couldn't stop the slow grinding of a police investigation. It couldn't stop the buried truth forcing its way out of the hard ground.

I closed the shop anyway and thought about going upstairs, but I couldn't face Elizabeth. Not after the call from Luke. With her long-legged beauty, her dynamic job in the city, and her busy social life, she'd only remind me of everything I wasn't.

No, I'd head out into Greenwich. I hadn't left the flat and shop for days. Pay the cheque in anyway. Go to the park. Maybe climb the hill. Walk off the rising panic. The police had probably found nothing. As Luke said, Ted's involvement made them hyper-conscious of doing the right thing. And when I felt better, I'd come back to the flat. Elizabeth would probably have gone out. I'd have another evening in. Maybe sculpting, although I didn't think so. I wouldn't be able to with the police interview hanging over me. It would be a night for watching an old film. *Gone with the Wind*, I thought. Lose myself in Scarlett's battles.

As I locked the shop door behind me, Elizabeth came out of the front door to the flat beside it and the two of us jumped in unison, laughed in unison and locked the doors behind us in unison.

'Hey, Lucy. How are you?' She always sounded so pleased to see me, although I often felt she tried to avoid me as much as I tried to avoid her. 'It's such a fabby evening I'm going for a run,' she said, as though her shorts and vest and hair tied back and stuffed beneath a cap didn't give it away.

She was beautiful. I knew that because I'd examined her face many times. Studying faces is what I do. Trying to find the little bits of individuality that make each one different. But Elizabeth's face eluded me. It was perfect, but curiously empty, utterly symmetrical and devoid of quirks.

'I'm going for a walk,' I said. We laughed again.

'It's the park for me. How about you?' she asked.

'Along the river,' I said quickly. The path by the river was too busy for runners so she wouldn't come with me. She smiled. She was as pleased as I was. So we walked along the road, united in our pleasure at knowing we wouldn't be together for long and forcing the stream of commuters rushing in the other direction to part before us. Some flashed grumpy glances at us, their eyes lingering for a few seconds on Elizabeth, but most of them kept their heads down.

I'd seen her running once. I'd been walking back down through the park from Blackheath, strolling through the rose garden, when she tore past. She ran as if someone was chasing her. As if only speed could get her away. Her face grim with effort. She didn't look like the cool, beautiful Elizabeth I knew. I didn't tell her I'd seen her. Something about it was too private.

'What an utterly manic week I've had,' she said. 'And then this afternoon, it was suddenly quiet and I was like, "Wow, I so need to get my head together" so I slipped off early before the next crisis arrived.'

She chatted away as we walked. She did something in the city to do with insurance. She'd explained it when we first met, but it was all jargon and my brain had slipped out of pace with her words and thought about other things. Like how much I hated needing to have a lodger and was there any way I could stretch my income, but there wasn't, so I'd smiled at Elizabeth and asked when she wanted to move in.

Talisker had moved herself in. A couple of weeks after me. She sat outside the shop door waiting for customers to let her inside until I gave in.

I stopped outside the bank and paid my cheque in at one of the machines that lined the pavement. At least Tilly would get her money if the police charged me on Monday. Might they? My hands shook as I tapped the codes onto the screen and a sudden giddiness weakened my knees at the thought of what being charged would mean. I leaned on the keyboard, my skin flinching as it touched the hot metal.

'All OK?' The reflection of Elizabeth's head over my shoulder appeared on the screen. I jumped. I hadn't realised she was waiting for me.

Get a grip.

'Yes,' I said and stuffed the receipt into my purse as she hovered over me. 'A bit hot, that's all.'

The crowds thinned as we approached the junction where Elizabeth would go right to the park and I would turn left to the river.

I was caught up in my thoughts of the last year, like I so often was. The past is like a spider's web. The more you struggle to escape it, the more it wraps itself round you and all I can remember of those few minutes was wishing I could cut myself free of its clinging tendrils and move on.

I remembered very little after this. Neither did Elizabeth.

The police told us it was a car, caught in slow-moving traffic on its way to the Blackwall Tunnel. An impatient driver trying to escape by turning off onto a side road, misjudging it and hurtling straight into Elizabeth and me. It happened so quickly we didn't stand a chance.

The rest is caught on a teenager's phone as she videoed a message for a friend. The footage lasts thirty seconds but the accident takes less than one of them. It's so fast you can't see it happen. One minute Elizabeth and I are standing in the background behind the teenager's giggling face, the next the car shoots into us. If you slow it down and watch frame by frame, we start to turn our heads as the car approaches. The noise or wind must have warned us, but I don't remember. Then it smacks us together and up into the air. For a moment it's hard to tell which one of us is which. And then we fall onto the steps leading up to a café where we lie like litter blown up from the kerb, the car long gone.

The video carries on. The girl realising something happened behind her and turning. Her phone sliding over Elizabeth's white, still face, its eyes and mouth like dark holes, like the blank masks I make for drama schools. There's nothing to tell you what's going on inside her head.

4

I mop linoleum. A long, wide corridor of floor, grey with white streaks. Gleaming where it's wet. Detergent masking urine and the fusty sweetness of unaired spaces.

The nee-naw of an ambulance.

I walk down another long corridor. No, a supermarket aisle. One packet of crisps into the trolley. One into my pocket. Crackling in my pocket. Someone will hear. A guard walks towards me.

Lights. Bright lights. My eyes forced open.

The train pulls back out of the station and leaves me standing. The crowd of people drains in the other direction. I am part of neither. I am alone. The platform stretches away from me, lined with posters and adverts and maps and timetables. It is long. Longer. Miles. Its end invisible. I start to walk and a *hole opens up before me, so I turn and walk the way the train went. Another hole. I think they are illusions, drawn by pavement artists. I dare to tread forward. The surface holds. Then crumbles into nothing. I fall.*

I peer through the window of an upstairs room down onto the boys kicking the stones in front of a row of lock-up garages. Once, the doors were white, but now they look like yellowed, broken teeth. I run my tongue over my own teeth. Gap in the front wide enough for the ears of my stuffed rabbit to pass through. The sour smell of saliva rises from its fur.

Pain is all around me. Cold and hard. Pushing against my skin. A glacial block of hurt and harsh, white light. I push back but it holds me tight in its frigid embrace. I cannot move. I scream but my mouth doesn't open. I kick my legs, but they are encased in ice. I am trapped.

I woke up.

It was warm. Crisp cotton under my fingers. Softness all around my head.

Where was I?

A smell of clean. People breathing gently nearby and far away the tread of feet on linoleum. I'd heard all this before.

Where was I?

A bitter, metallic taste in my mouth. I knew that taste. Sleeping pills. More feet and the low murmur of voices off to my left. I opened my eyes. Except they didn't open. Heavy eyelids wouldn't rise. Tried again and slowly the curtain lifted.

Darkness. But a darkness dimmed by the warmth of lights somewhere I couldn't see. Thank God. I hated the dark. I was in bed. In a big room with other beds. A high ceiling and a blind-covered window on my right. All indistinct. A blur coated my vision like the faint fog that always softened the London horizon, but I knew where I was.

Hospital.

'Awake?' a voice said. Someone stood at the end of the bed. 'Already?' A woman. Fuzzy. I blinked my eyes to make them focus. For a brief second, they cleared. A nurse. A shaft of soft light tracked the wrinkles in her skin as she leant down, brushing against the bedclothes, and then my vision blurred again. 'You could barely keep your eyes open a minute ago.'

This was wrong. I knew this was wrong. But my mind failed to follow. It felt loose inside my head. Floating, as though the sticky tendrils of flesh that tied it against my skull had broken. I held it still. Forced it to settle. Let it reach out and anchor itself. Pain rushed down the connections, and my brain felt as though it was trying to break out of my skull.

I tried to cry but nothing came out.

Other bits of me woke up. Messages from my limbs raced in. Bits of pain everywhere and shakiness and heaviness. I couldn't move. I stared at the nurse and concentrated on words. They formed in my head but wouldn't transfer to my mouth. My tongue and lips lay still like lumps in the butcher's window, although my head roared with pain.

'Are you all right?' Her voice was kind, with a tinge of Scots. I felt the warmth of her skin as she took my hand and the warmth of tears rolling down my face. The barrier between my brain and my body slipped away. The pain receded and I shook my head. It was like a miracle. Thought and muscles worked together. I squeezed her hand and shook my head again.

'Delayed shock,' she said. 'Try and relax.'

Somewhere a door opened and a radio briefly played faint music as I fought through the fog and made myself speak.

'What happened?' Even to me my voice sounded strange. The ends of the words were clipped and vowels were softer and rounder.

'You mean, the accident?'

'Accident?'

'You don't remember?'

'No.'

She patted my arm and told me not to worry. Told me I was in hospital. Told me about the accident. Told me I was only unconscious for a short time according to passers-by, before standing up and staggering around, frightening them by screaming that my head was cracking apart.

'What's wrong with me?'

'Mild concussion,' the nurse said slowly. 'The doctor told you. Don't you remember?'

I hadn't seen a doctor. I was sure I hadn't seen a doctor.

'No.'

The patient in the bed opposite turned over and muttered a few words, then fell still again.

'Tell me what you do remember.' Her Scottish burr made the r's of remember lengthy and important.

I tried to remember. Vague images of people in uniforms and trolleys flitted through my thoughts, but no matter how hard I tried nothing fixed would come and I couldn't tell whether the images were real or imaginary.

'Nothing for sure.'

It was an effort to speak. My body still felt strange. I

panicked. Tried to move my feet. They wouldn't. Tried again and felt the sheet brush against my toes as my feet responded. But slowly. There was a delay. Like watching the picture and sound on the television when it's out of sync.

'Don't worry. This can happen with concussion. It's called anterograde amnesia. It just means that although you can remember everything up to the accident your poor shaken brain is struggling to make memories of new things so you've forgotten some of what has happened since. It will pass. The neurologist will check in with you tomorrow before you leave.'

'How long have I been here?'

She scratched at a spot on her tunic. 'Since yesterday evening.'

I stared at her. A faint mist clouded my sight.

'My eyes,' I said.

'Blurred vision?'

'Yes. From time to time.'

'It's normal. It will pass. Try and get back to sleep now. There's nothing to worry about.' She patted my hand again. 'Did you have a dream? Is that what woke you? Concussion can cause vivid dreams.'

I remembered fragments of things. Dreams. Were they dreams? They seemed as real as the memory of walking down the road in Greenwich talking to Elizabeth. *Elizabeth!* She was with me when the car hit. I wondered how she was. Tried to form the words to ask, but a great wave of drowsiness washed over me and dragged me back down into sleep. I felt loose again. Untethered. Like the thick strands of brown seaweed that the Venetians used to dredge out of the canals. A few pieces always escaped and floated for days on the surface, too light to sink and anchor again.

· · ·

*I am a small girl going to school. It's my first day. I stand
outside a red brick building with pointy gables. There are two
entrances. I try to work out which is the right entrance for me.
For a while I think it might be the colour of the shoes. Brown
shoes through one entrance and black shoes through the other.
Mine are brown and new, although slightly scuffed and they
pinch my little toes. I watch the children's feet.*

*A pair of large black boots with heels move towards me,
and I look up.*

I woke again. I was in bed in the hospital.

A flash of relief lightened my thoughts. I had remembered where I was.

I was eating cereal. Correction: the bowl was empty. I
had finished eating cereal. A few grains still clung to the
inside. My sight was clear and sharp. Did I remember eating
it? Maybe. The taste of it lingered in my mouth.

Something squeezed my arm tight. A nurse stood in front
of me, her face hidden as she stared at the blood pressure
gauge. Not the nurse from last night. Her hair was black with
a faint slash of brown at the roots.

'That's 120 over 80. All fine,' she said in a sing-song voice
and dragged the band from my arm, scratched the figures on
the clipboard at the end of my bed and bustled off. Fatigue
blurred my vision and I drowsed again.

*The teacher takes my arm and leads me inside. She talks to
me, but half of it is gibberish. I wonder if she knows she makes
no sense. Except the other children understand her. They
move to one wall, and I follow them. Along the wall, curved*

bits of metal protrude. Hooks. They're called hooks, I realise. I watch the other children take off their coats and hang them on the hooks. I pull my jumper over my head and try to do the same.

I was in bed again. In hospital. So, I was awake. If I was in hospital, I must be awake. But the dream still consumed me. Vivid. Immersive. Its dregs clung onto my consciousness. I fought to concentrate on the here and now.

Sunlight poured through the window and onto the crumpled sheets, warming my skin beneath them. Voices and laughter. *How long had I slept?*

A nurse talking to me. I turned my attention to her. High cheekbones like the head of a Greek Persephone, but a square jaw that showed her Anglo-Saxon ancestry. My vision was clear. My hands longed to explore the contours of her face and my fingers itched to drag it out of the clay.

Concentrate, Lucy. Concentrate.

'We need to get in touch with your friend's family,' the nurse said.

'I don't know her that well,' I answered without thinking. My voice worked much better though, although I sounded strange, my Liverpudlian flat vowels softer.

'She's badly hurt. A major head injury.'

Her face blurred. The dreams tugged me. Elizabeth was badly hurt. I should ask more but I couldn't stay awake.

I sit at an empty table. There are four tables in the classroom, but the rest of the children have crowded round the other three. I wonder if I've done the wrong thing. If some of the teacher's mysterious words have told us not to sit at the table near the window – the one I've chosen. But when I look to see if I can find a gap to insert myself, the children's bodies swell to fill the space.

I see the teacher through the glass in the door. The glass has a metal network running through it. She is talking to a man and then she turns and comes in. Her eyes sweep round the room and come to rest on me. She looks angry. I screw my eyes and wait for her to slap me, but the blow never comes. I look up. The teacher is over by another table muttering to the group of girls.

'She smells,' one of them says.

'It makes me sick.' This is another one.

'Well, Carly can sit by me,' the teacher says. She takes my hand and I sit next to her.

Amy sat on my bed talking to me. I struggled to focus. We were halfway through a conversation but she hadn't noticed that I'd lost the thread. That I had no memory of what we'd been talking about. In fact, no one had noticed that I dropped in and out of consciousness, diving in and out of my dreams and reality like a swimmer plunging through waves. 'I'll bring you some clothes tomorrow,' she was saying. 'The ones you were wearing are filthy and... and stained.'

I nodded my thanks.

'How are you feeling?'

'Fine.' The word came out easily. I wondered why I was lying.

'Well, better they keep you in another night. With the memory loss and everything.'

Bobbles of hair had escaped from her severe ponytail and

dark shadows hung under her eyes. Why was she so tired? I started to ask her, but pain clamped a band round the words and wouldn't let them out. Besides, there was a host of other questions demanding attention. Like how was the shop and how was she coping alone and had the gold leaf for Mrs Benning's half mask arrived? And a million others.

'See you tomorrow.' Amy smoothed the front of her hair as she stood but the loose loops sprang back after her hand had passed.

I wanted to say thank you to her. *Thank you for coming in. Thank you for looking after me. Thank you...* But the dreams reclaimed me.

I stand outside the school. It is the end of the day. The children take their coats off the hooks and I take my jumper. My head reels with all the new words I have learned – book, thank, jigsaw and a host of others I've worked out meanings for. I learn another new one as we stand in a line by our teacher.

'Is Mummy or Daddy coming to pick you up?'

Daddy is a new word for me. What is a Daddy? I guess it must be something similar to a Mummy. All the other children clearly know what one is, although they don't all know who is picking them up. So, it's OK when I shrug as answer to the question. I work out pretty quickly that a Daddy is a sort of man Mummy. I'm less sure, however, about pick up. I thought I'd learned pick up earlier today, as in: 'Pick up the pieces of jigsaw from the floor.' Many of the mummies and daddies do pick their children up, and a few bend down and wrap their arms round the children or push their mouths into their cheeks.

After a while I realise that we are waiting for my mummy.

I'm not sure that she knows she is supposed to come to the school to get me. I think she's probably asleep on the sofa. I wonder if I should try and explain to my teacher, but actually I'm quite happy standing in the playground on my own.

I woke up and the police were by my bed.

The *police* were by my bed. I was still in hospital.

Shit. I'd missed the appointment Luke had set up. They'd come to get me. To take me back to that horrible room with no windows and fire questions at me. Questions I had no answer to.

One on either side of the bed, their black uniforms sucked the light out of the air. Panic scraped the clinging strands of drowsiness away and I focused on the female constable sitting on my left. Someone had drawn the curtains round the bed. To give us a semblance of privacy?

'And the car,' she was saying. 'Can you remember anything about the car?'

The car? What about the car? I'd got rid of my car months ago.

'No,' I said automatically.

'You didn't see what type of car it was?'

What type of car?

I realised two things. One, she was talking about the accident. About the car that hit us. And, two, her mouth curved in a gentle smile showing the gap between her front teeth. She was giving me time to think. They must have told her about my memory lapses.

I relaxed and then I thought about the question. Had I seen the car? I had a vague sense of something dark and shiny.

'No.'

'You're sure?'

Clearly she'd never been hit from behind by a car moving at speed. I said nothing but stared at her mouth. It was a perfect shape. Exactly like the lips I painted onto the masks Venetian courtesans would have worn, and fate had given her a dark mole right above its left corner that only added to its allure. I wondered if she knew she had the mouth of a Venetian whore.

'They didn't stop, and no one noted the registration number.' I watched her lips form the words and struggled to take in their meaning. 'We're looking at CCTV footage but it takes time so all we know is it was a small, dark-coloured car. We'd like to find the driver.'

'Hit and run...' I'd watched enough crime series for the words to come to my lips without me searching for them.

'Failure to stop after an accident. Yes. It's a criminal offence.'

This I knew. It came under a range of offences that could best be summed up as crimes of not doing something. Not providing a specimen of breath when required. Not looking after your child. Leaving an injured person alone and dying.

'Witnesses said they were driving dangerously, far too fast – drunk maybe, because there was absolutely no need for them to mount the pavement at that point. You've been lucky, but your friend is seriously hurt.'

She rose and signalled to her colleague that they should go. He swept the curtains open. The lady in the bed opposite mine stared back at me. And the visitors clustered around her bed watched the police walk down the ward, then turned swiftly back to her. The low hum of excited chatter filled the space between us.

For the first time, sleep didn't reclaim me at once. The shock of waking to see the police had snapped my thoughts into some semblance of order. What exactly was wrong with me? Mild concussion, the first nurse had told me. In the middle of last night. Or was it last night? I wasn't sure. Mild concussion affecting my ability to make memories since the accident.

A bang on the head.

Nothing else hurt.

The bandages round my head felt tight. I reached my hand up to touch them but just the thought of it stabbed pain through my skull. I gave up and the pain subsided. At least I was awake.

I stayed awake all through the evening. Sort of awake. No strange dreams interrupted my consciousness, but I felt strangely removed from everything around me. Passive and yielding. Almost as though this was yet another dream.

I ate the food they put in front of me and answered their questions on autopilot.

'What would you like to eat tomorrow? Sunday roast or cauliflower cheese?'

Sunday. Tomorrow was Sunday. The accident had happened on Friday. I'd only lost a few hours here and there.

The light outside dimmed as day slipped into night. The ward quietened. Waves of tiredness started to drag me under. If I didn't concentrate, my vision fogged. I pulled the sheets round me in a comforting embrace and escaped back into my dreams.

I sit on the stairs and my mother sits behind me and grabs my hair and pulls it back until I can see her upside-down face and smell her breath. It reeks of the bottles lined up on the table in front of the sofa and the harsh odour of the ashtray.

I brought a piece of paper home from school this after-

noon. With a message on it. About nits. Little insects that live in my hair and must be killed. The whole class must get rid of them tonight and tonight only. That's what the teacher said when we left today. Remind your parents or carers. Tonight is hair wash and comb. But Mum seems to have missed the bit about hair wash and has settled down on the stairs with the shiny comb the teacher gave me for her. The teacher said to one of the other mums it was the only way to be sure my hair would be done. She gave me some shampoo too, but Mum left it behind on the wall outside the school. I didn't say anything because I could see today wasn't a good day.

Mum often says, 'Leave me alone. Can't you see I'm not having a good day?' But now I can tell without her saying when it isn't a good day.

Most days aren't good days.

On not good days, I play upstairs until she falls asleep, and then I go and get something to eat from the fridge and sit by her and watch television until I fall asleep. But even though today is not a good day, I made her read the note and told her the teacher said it had to be this evening.

She is rough, although I know she doesn't mean to be. It's what the bottles do to her. They stop her seeing properly and tire her out, so she falls over things and her words come out wrong.

I wait for the comb. Something tells me it will hurt. But it never comes. Instead she lets my hair go and there is silence. I wait and when nothing happens, I turn to look at her. A tuft of my hair is in her hand. I touch my head and feel the smooth patch of skin it's left behind. She slaps my hand away, seizes my head and tugs at my hair.

'No, no,' I cry as the hair falls onto the bare boards of the stairs around us. Afterwards she gets the kitchen scissors and

cuts what remains very short before staggering into the room
with the television and slamming the door behind her.

    I wait until it's dark and then look at my reflection in the
front door's cracked panes of glass. It's not good. When the
other children see me tomorrow it will be even worse.

5

I came to, with a woman sitting by my bed and talking at me. White coat. Papery skin that spoke of too much time indoors, as did the swoosh of acne on her shiny forehead.

No, no, no. It had happened again. I'd thought I was over the sudden memory lapses, the seconds when my brain shorted out and rebooted with no awareness of what had gone before. The sky was palest blue outside the window. Two women in pink overalls pushed a creaking trolley piled with cups and bowls and empty cereal packets. It was morning.

'You've got a prescription for painkillers and some ointment for the bruises, but they're healing nicely.' The woman fired the words at me in a soft but insistent rattle. She must be the doctor. 'The nurses will check the dressing on your head and remove the one on your face before you go. The bruising will take some time to fade, but it won't leave any permanent mark. You should take it easy for a week or so. If you experience any more periods of confusion, come back and see us straight away.'

I started to say that it had happened again, but she rushed away before I could get the words out. At least I'd seen her clearly. I made myself relax. My eyes were working better. A bit more time and everything else would heal.

'I've found you your dressing gown,' the nurse said as she came over. 'You don't want to go up to ICU in just your gown.'

ICU? Why was I going to ICU?

Nevertheless, I swung my legs out of bed and pushed myself up. I wobbled when I stood. My body felt like it didn't belong to me. My limbs functioned, but it was as though I was a puppet and a hidden puppeteer controlled the strings.

'Are you sure you're up for this? I understand you want to visit your poor friend but...'

I realised she was talking about Elizabeth. I wondered how she was.

'How is she?' I asked.

'No real change.' Her face creased. 'They're keeping her in a coma. But it's probably the best thing for her at the moment.'

A coma! Shock almost like excitement tingled over my skin, raising the hairs in an unconscious reaction to the news. I'd not realised she was this badly hurt.

'They'll be able to tell you more in ICU. Fifth floor. Go left when you get out of the lift.'

A cleaner held the door open for me when I reached ICU. It led onto a long corridor lined with doors. Nurses walked in and out of the swing doors to the ward at the far end.

The noise hit me as I went in. I'd expected it to be quiet. As if the seriousness of the patients' condition would smother every sound. But not at all. Over the bedrock of pumps whooshing, machines bleeping, and feet - sharp clicky feet on hard linoleum - and the rustle of clothing as nurses bustled around, rose the voices of people forced to speak a little louder to be heard. And there were a lot of people in the ward. Nurses at their station in the middle of the room. Talking to each other. Talking to relatives. Talking on the phone. And from each cubicle more voices slipped through the blue-green curtains and joined the hubbub.

Amy sat with a nurse at the end of one cubicle, head down and thumbing through a sheaf of papers. I padded up to them and looked beyond and inside at the figure in the bed. She lay unnaturally still, her mouth distorted by the thick plastic tube connected to the pump that drove her chest up and down and surrounded by a jumble of monitors, wires, plastic bags full of liquid and clear tubes. Her hands spread flat by her side and her hair swept up and over the pillow. Her brown hair. Loose curls of brown hair lying around her head as though she was floating in the sea.

Why was her hair brown?

Amy said something to me about nothing preparing you for the reality of it.

I took a couple of steps towards the bed as Amy returned to the form she was filling in with the nurse.

The figure in the bed wasn't Elizabeth. Not with hair like that. They'd made a mistake. Put someone else in here. Elizabeth was in another bed. I waited for Amy to tell me I was looking in the wrong cubicle. But she gave me a puzzled smile and carried on talking to the nurse.

I must be wrong. The figure in the bed must be Elizabeth. Some trick of the light had darkened her hair. And the thick tube and mask pressed into her face was distorting her features.

Because the other thing I was thinking – the horrible

thing that was making my thoughts break apart and judder with panic – couldn't be true.

But when I crept closer to the bed, I knew there was no mistake. The hair gave it away, and everything else confirmed it. The heart-shape of the face. The smattering of freckles along the bridge of the nose and the faint line of a scar running across the eyebrow – barely visible, but there if you looked hard enough.

I hated that scar. Hated what it said about me.

Me, me, me.

The figure in the bed looked like me. Exactly like me.

My thoughts banged in my head, beating out a jagged rhythm that fought against the steady whoosh of the respirator.

Amy's quiet words reached my ears as she replied to the nurse's questions.

'Age? Twenty-seven. No, she's not married. She's a widow, in fact. Quite recent. A year or so. No, no children. Her parents are dead, and there are no sisters or brothers. She chatted about her aunt a couple of times. Aunt Tilly. Matilda. Her father's sister, Matilda Christensen. I found her number in the flat and called her. She's on her way.'

My legs swayed.

'Full name is Lucy Frederica Christensen. No, that's her maiden name. She doesn't use her married name.'

The nurse got up and left and Amy came over to me.

'I brought you some clothes, Elizabeth, like you asked.'

Elizabeth, I thought. *She called me Elizabeth.*

And the meaning of the words I'd heard her say to the nurse penetrated my whirling thoughts. She'd given the nurse my details. *Lucy Frederica Christensen.* She'd called the motionless body in the bed Lucy Frederica Christensen.

She handed me a bag of clothes and pulled a chair

towards me. 'Spend a bit of time with her before you get dressed. I'll see if I can get us a taxi.'

My legs gave way and I sat as Amy went, then bent my head between my knees.

It was the concussion. That's what it was. Playing tricks with my eyes. I'd walked too far. Should have taken it gently.

But Amy called me Elizabeth... And called the body in the coma, Lucy.

Concussion playing tricks with my hearing. What had the nurse said? The impact had rattled my brain. Nothing was broken, but everything was loose and shaken. Not to worry if I felt confused or exhausted. It would pass.

I let the soft whirr of the machines calm me. My breathing slowed and I opened my eyes again and caught sight of the hands clenched in my lap, my hands clenched in my lap. This time I examined them without eyes clouded by the expectation that they would be as they always were. The fingers were long and the skin was clean and soft, the nails neatly rounded and polished. They stretched and uncurled as I watched. Elegant and lithe. Well cared for and mois- turised. No scars or rough skin. Expensive hands.

Not my hands.

My hands had short nails. Very short nails to keep the clay out of them and their imprint out of the clay. And the fingers were stubby with a multitude of small scars from scalpel and scissor slips. Exactly like the hands of the body in the bed. The hands lying palms down and unnaturally still on the crisp white sheet.

I must calm down. Think clearly.

I watched as the beautiful hands I knew belonged to Elizabeth reached out and caressed the hair of the body in the bed. The giveaway hair. Not only did it look like mine, but it felt like mine. Like it did in the morning when I ran my fingers through it, pulling out enough of the tangles to make it lie flattish round my head, and, as I bent forward, the sharp lavender scent of my shampoo rose through the odours of disinfectant and bleach.

It was my body.

My body lay in the bed.

Elizabeth's body sat beside it, her long fingers entwined in Lucy's hair.

Hallucinating. I was hallucinating. The accident had torn the connections in my brain, and now the filaments fluttered loose, colliding and sparking strange visions. I was hallucinating.

It had to be a hallucination.

It didn't feel like a hallucination. It felt real. Lucy's hair. My hair. I felt each separate strand with Elizabeth's hands. Through Elizabeth's skin and nerves.

Some strange exchange had taken place when the car hit us.

I was in Elizabeth's body, sitting by Lucy's bed.

And Elizabeth must be in my unconscious body.

My thoughts scattered and for a while I knew nothing.

Elizabeth's hands grasped one of Lucy's and it was only then that I was sure. The skin of Lucy's hand was cold. I felt it through the warmth of Elizabeth's skin. The nerves in Elizabeth's body transmitted the sensation to me. I was touching Lucy's skin. There was no doubt.

But as Lucy's skin grew warm in my grasp, the sense of separation lessened. I stopped feeling the difference between her skin and mine. Between Elizabeth's skin and Lucy's. I couldn't tell which one of us was touched and which was doing the touching.

A new sensation. It started as a nudge. A sense of something woken. And then a gentle tug. Something pulled me. Like a magnet dragging me to itself. Enticing me. Was it Lucy's body? *My* body? I thought so. I thought it might be calling me. Luring me home. If I relaxed, whatever had happened would be undone. I'd return to my body and Elizabeth would return to hers. I dragged a deep breath in and let it trickle out over my lips, shut my eyes and drifted. I started to slip. The shapes of things became liquid. I floated in the sounds. Drifted through the hiss of the pump and danced over the blips and whirrs of the machines.

A touch on my shoulder snapped me back. Our hands fell apart.

A nurse spoke. 'Nearly asleep?' she said.

I opened my eyes – Elizabeth's eyes opened. Lucy lay on the bed before me, motionless apart from her chest driven up and down by the respirator.

'We need to change your friend's drip shortly so you'll have to leave in a minute.'

She slipped out, swishing the curtain shut behind her. I had a few minutes at most before she came back. My hand, Elizabeth's hand, reached out for Lucy's hand again and stopped.

Pain spiked through my head.

I wasn't sure.

Not sure at all.

The inertness of the body in the bed frightened me. What if my body never woke up? What if the brain injury was catastrophic? I'd be trapped inside as my body slowly died.

But my hand moved again and touched Lucy's. The force pulling me back towards my own body grew stronger. I was loose and untethered in Elizabeth's and it grasped me, sucking the struggle out of me. Inch by inch.

The nurse came back into the cubicle, dragging a trolley, squeaking over the lino. The force dragging at me faded.

'Here we are,' she said.

I looked around. I was still in the chair. I was still Elizabeth. The nurse's arrival had broken the connection.

I stood up and walked out of the ward and to the lift. Or at least I thought I did. I felt very weird. The ward noise was distant and distorted as though thick blankets were wound round my head and my vision blurred and sharpened spasmodically. I pressed the lift button and leaned my head against the metal panel as I waited. Far below me, the mechanism rumbled and wheezed on its way up. The metal was cold. Its chill and the vibration grounded me. I felt the breath sweep in and out of my lungs. My thoughts steadied. Hearing returned to normal.

What was I doing?

I should go back to Lucy's cubicle. Immediately. I should go back to my own body. Release Elizabeth from it. I was sure we only needed to touch again, alone and undisturbed, for Elizabeth to return to her body and me to mine.

But part of me refused. I didn't want to lie paralysed and trapped in Lucy's unconscious body. I didn't want to die there.

Even if it meant being someone else?

Yes.

Because I'd like to be someone who the police didn't want to interview. I'd like a bit of a holiday from Lucy and her problems. Oh God, I'd like to be free from it all. I'd like to have a life and some fun.

And Elizabeth had fun. She was out several nights a week, creeping back in the early hours, while I lay awake reliving every moment of my marriage and its end. I'd like to be Elizabeth. With her long legs that gleamed and her neat nose with a slight up-turn at the end. With her perfect skin and her elegant voice.

Her elegant voice! That's why I didn't sound like myself. Elizabeth's lips and tongue and all the rest of her mouth were used to producing her honeyed tones. They couldn't distort themselves to produce my flat vowels.

But what about Elizabeth trapped in my body?

I hoped she was unconscious. She must be unconscious. My body in the bed seemed so empty and whitely transparent, like a chrysalis after the butterfly has flown. I wouldn't leave her there for ever. Of course I wouldn't. I just needed time to think. The lift arrived. The door opened.

'Elizabeth! There are you are. I've got a taxi coming in half an hour.' Amy pressed the button to keep the doors open.

She didn't like Elizabeth. I could hear it in her voice, in the flatness of her tone, although she was taking great pains to hide it.

'You need to get a move on.'

No I didn't, I thought. There was no rush. I didn't need to decide now. Lucy wasn't going anywhere. I could come back any time.

I stepped into the lift and nodded.

Amy talked to me briefly on the way down, telling me Lucy had some trauma to the brain and swelling. She didn't think they'd know much more until they tried to wake her up although she didn't know when that would be.

I couldn't speak. The emotions raging through my mixed-up head put paid to that. Not that Amy seemed to find it strange. I caught her flicking Elizabeth a glance through narrowed eyes and wondered if she thought Elizabeth's silence was normal.

Back in the ward, I saw the things I should have noticed

before. If only I hadn't been so confused and tired. Elizabeth's neat little backpack sat on my bedside table. Not my raggedy tapestry bag. The label on my wrist said Elizabeth Hughes and the dressing gown I was wearing was Elizabeth's.

A curly-haired nurse came over, with a plastic bowl of scissors and forceps. She snapped a pair of sterile gloves over her hands. 'Now, let's have a look at that head of yours.'

She snipped away at the bandages until they fell in a white coil onto my lap. I put up a hand to touch my naked head and realised something was missing. My hair. Elizabeth's hair. Her long, smooth blonde hair that slipped over her shoulders like a shampoo advert – it wasn't there. Not at all.

No hair. What? I wasn't Elizabeth. I was someone else now. This wasn't real.

I seized a handful of crisp sheet and crushed it in my fist. It felt real. They must have cut her hair. *Of course.* My thoughts calmed.

The nurse made an approving sound. 'It's very tidy and healing well. No need for a dressing. And your hair is growing well. Alopecia, is it? A recent attack?'

Alopecia, I thought. It was when your hair fell out in chunks. For no apparent reason. *Elizabeth had alopecia.*

'Well, the regrowth isn't too patchy,' she continued. 'So your hair looks fashionably short.'

She explained to me what I could and couldn't do with the dressing. How to shower and so on and I replied mechanically.

'Your wig is in the bag.'

Wig? An image of Elizabeth, walking down the street next to me, flicking her hair over her shoulder. Her smooth blonde hair that I envied so much. Never untidy, never greasy, never ruffled when she got up in the morning.

Elizabeth wore a wig.

'I'm afraid it was sodden with blood, you know. Head wounds bleed a lot. Even minor ones like yours.' Her blue eyes creased as she smiled at me. 'It was an expensive one, wasn't it? The nurse who stitched you up has a lot of experience with chemo patients, and she said yours was top quality. She thought it would wash out, but we didn't like to try in case it needed specialist treatment.'

She opened the bag and took it out. It was bloodstained and tangled, but even so I could see it was blonde and straight, very straight. It was Elizabeth's. I was Elizabeth. I stroked my fingers over its hair, trying to smooth it out. It was soft. It looked like real hair. Very expensive. Elizabeth's hair.

'That's everything,' the nurse said. 'You're free to go home. It's healing nicely. You've been lucky.'

I emptied the carrier bag of clothes Amy had brought in for me. For Elizabeth. Because never in a hundred years would I have chosen these things. Tight black ski pants that moulded to Elizabeth's legs and sat comfortably round her narrow waist. A soft cream T-shirt and a beige scarf.

I hate cream. I hate black. I loathe beige. Gavin had the house decorated throughout in shades of cream and beige, with accents of black. Sleek leather sofas and shiny kitchen cabinets. He employed an interior designer and spent hours poring over pictures and samples with her. To save me having to do all the work. And when I muttered that I didn't like cream, the lines of his mouth drooped. He knew it was bland, but the decorator had thought it would be the perfect backdrop to my Art. Gavin always spoke as though it had a capital A. What could I say? That I didn't want to live in an art gallery? That the space he'd created would stifle me? I knew I'd sound sulky and ungrateful and immature, so I said nothing and smiled and kissed him until he smiled back, and then he bounced around the house, showing me the wonder of the fitted wardrobes in the bedroom and the beauty of the kitchen tap that produced boiling water at the swivel of a lever. And so the first part of me was eroded away. Invisible to the eye. Like the soft caress of the sea on a spiky and rough stone that eventually becomes a smooth, round, featureless pebble.

I drew the curtain tight shut and dressed. Elizabeth's hands found the zips and buttons instinctively and knew exactly the right tweak to make the pants sit straight and the clever twist to make the scarf look elegant round her neck.

'Your hair. Oh, Elizabeth, your hair,' Amy said, when she came to pick me up from the ward. 'I didn't notice because of the bandage. They shaved your head.'

'They had to.' Even to my ears, my voice sounded cold and the words weren't at all what I meant to say to Amy but the impossibility of telling her who I was – she'd whisk me straight back to the ward – had taken my voice away and I'd spoken without thinking.

My curtness stopped her talking though. And maybe that was a good thing because it meant I didn't have to reply. When we reached reception, my eyes met my reflection in the glass on the entrance.

I saw a figure. In cream and black. With very short hair. Shaved short like Sinead O'Connor singing 'Nothing Compares 2 U'. But even shorn of her hair, I recognised Elizabeth's face staring back at me.

The bruising wasn't bad. It stained the top of her cheek. The woman in the reflection reached up a hand and touched the bruise. She whisked a finger over it as though to wipe it away. It was a feather touch. Then her eyes crinkled with concern, and her mouth made a little pout. I recognised the pout. It was what Elizabeth did when the bin in the kitchen smelled or when the Wi-Fi bugged. How strange that my feelings should translate on her face into something that was unmistakably Elizabeth's expression.

The woman in the mirror and I, we gazed at each other. Short hair suited Elizabeth. The long hair of her wig distracted the eye from the glorious lines and planes of her face. With it, she dissolved into anonymous prettiness... but without it, her beauty screamed at you. Alopecia was something that came and went, with times of respite when your hair grew back. Like Elizabeth's had. Her hair was sleek over her whole head, and the parts that were slightly shorter were barely visible. So why would she wear a wig now? I saw no reason for it.

6

By the time the taxi dropped us at the end of the alley it was late afternoon but still warm, with the sun large and red, low in the sky as though its weight was pulling it down to the horizon. I staggered as we climbed out. My balance was still not great, and Elizabeth's body thrust her legs out of the taxi first whereas I normally stuck my head out and let my limbs follow. Her muscles had their habitual way of doing things and my head started to pulse with pain from the strain of keeping up with it.

It was better if I didn't try to direct her body. Left to its own devices it managed well. Only natural, really. Babies took years to learn to coordinate until the control became second nature. I was trying to impose a way of moving onto Elizabeth's body that it wasn't used to. I relaxed and went with the flow.

Amy followed me up the stairs and I had the presence of mind to turn left into Elizabeth's room rather than struggle up the last flight of stairs into my attic bedroom.

'Are you going to bed?' she asked.

'Yes.' I realised I was.

'Shall I bring you tea?'

'Please,' I said, although I didn't mean it.

I thought of asking her to make it strong with milk rather than the milk-less weak stuff Elizabeth drank, but I was too tired to find the words, and the headache had become a raging battle in my head. I put on Elizabeth's silky pyjamas, hating the way they slid round my legs, and thought longingly of the old T-shirt I normally slept in.

Elizabeth's bed was an old divan I'd picked up cheap from a second-hand shop but the mattress was new and comfortable and the pillows soft beneath my head. My thoughts started to drift. Amy startled me by putting a cup of lapsang souchong down on the old tea chest by Elizabeth's bed. I really ought to have replaced it with something new by now, but Elizabeth hadn't complained. Not about that, nor about the sparseness of furniture. An old table, a wobbly chest of drawers and a rail for clothes had been all I could afford. She'd said in that gratingly cheerful way of hers that it was a blank canvas and she'd enjoy getting it how she wanted. Except, I realised, she'd done nothing. Except hang some clothes on the rail – far fewer than I'd have expected – and cover the table with cosmetics.

Amy hovered at the door. She wanted to go. She probably needed to go. I ought to tell her to go, but when I tried to speak the pain twisted the insides of my head.

'I've got a few things to do in the shop,' Amy said. 'I had to close early yesterday afternoon to come to the hospital and it's easier to catch up when it's shut.'

I must have looked blank because she added, 'It's Sunday, Elizabeth.'

Of course, it was.

'And then I'll be off. I'll buy you some bits and pieces,

shall I? There's nothing much in.' Her voice was gruff, and her hands plucked the doorframe.

'Marvellous.' It was not what I wanted to say. I wanted to thank her for being so nice to Elizabeth, who she didn't really like. I was seized by the desire to tell her what had happened. That I was Lucy. That she didn't need to be so awkward with me, but the pain in my head made speech impossible.

I lay in Elizabeth's bed and drank Elizabeth's tea and listened to Amy treading up and down the stairs to my own bedroom. Drawers opened and shut and her footsteps moved over every inch. I'd never realised how much Elizabeth could hear from her room. Even when Amy moved down into the shop below, the squeak of the door between the shop and the stockroom and rattle of keys filtered up through the white-painted floorboards and rugs.

The tea didn't taste as bad as I remembered. Less harsh and tarry. The smokiness was sweet. Maybe I was tasting it with Elizabeth's taste buds. In any case, I should probably try to eat and drink the sort of things Elizabeth did. I was only a tenant in her body, after all. And a short-term one, I reminded myself. I ought to hand it back in reasonable condition and without any newly acquired tastes for red wine, fruit gums and suppers of toast and jam.

But I'd think about all that once I'd had some sleep.

I laid the empty mug back on the tea chest and snuggled down amongst the covers, wondering if I'd dream again of Carly. As my thoughts began to dissipate, it struck me how strange it was that I had dreamed of the little girl losing her hair and then discovered that Elizabeth's hair was false. Maybe my sub-conscious had guessed? Something else tugged at my thoughts, but I was too tired to follow it and it vanished.

I woke with a bang. Sweating. And sat bolt upright. The street lamp in the alley shone straight into Elizabeth's room, gleaming off the white floor. My breath came in rasping gulps, but otherwise no noise broke the silence. I was alone. The flat and the shop were empty. I was safe.

Of course I was safe. What had I been dreaming about? Not Carly. At least, I didn't think so. It was hard to remember and the harder I tried, the more my dreams slipped out of my grasp. *Running.* I'd been running. As fast as I could. To get away. To escape.

No surprises there.

Although this time I had the impression my flight had taken me through streets of houses. Through the city. Through London. Rather than through dark fields and woods.

But the terror was the same.

I was thirsty.

I flung my legs out of bed and went to the kitchen, remembering to let Elizabeth's body guide me, and drank some water.

A shopping bag sat on the table and a note with a couple of receipts. I looked inside: salad, fruit, water – the sort of things Elizabeth liked. Amy had kept her promise. *Here's your things,* she'd written. *Leave me a list if you need anything else and I'll get it tomorrow. Lucy's aunt is going to come and stay. She'll use Lucy's room.*

Tilly was coming. Of course she was. She'd be worried sick about me. I needed to think about this. It would be very weird sharing a flat with her while I was Elizabeth. The doubts from yesterday resurfaced. Had I done the right thing?

I pushed them away and looked at the receipts. I had some idea of how precarious Amy's finances were, so I needed to pay her back fast. But that was going to be difficult. My bag with my purse and cards must be in the hospital. It felt wrong to use Elizabeth's cash, although I might have to.

A picture came into my mind. A wad of cash nestling in a multicoloured scarf. Upstairs in the wardrobe in my bedroom. The money was Elizabeth's rent, paid in cash at the beginning of each month. I kept it there, automatically transferring it into my purse as needed. I'd use that. It was mine. I was Lucy, after all. Nevertheless, I felt like a thief, tiptoeing up the stairs and stepping over the one that creaked.

I opened the vast wardrobe the previous tenants had left behind and reached up to remove the money stashed on the top shelf but my hands stopped en route to touch the glowing fabrics of my clothes. Through Elizabeth's eyes they looked different somehow.

They were organised by colour. I'd got into the habit of doing it when I was married and never shaken it off. On the left, red going into yellow, the fire colours, softening through green, deep emeralds and the fresh colour of new leaves, into the blues and indigos I secretly loved best. All the things that I'd bought since Gavin's death.

And on the right the other clothes. The black essentials and the chestnut browns that Gavin said suited my colouring, fading through beige and twenty shades of cream to white.

The first few times Gavin and I had gone out after our marriage, I'd noticed he'd winced when I'd come down the stairs all dressed up and, finally, one evening, when we were heading off to a Rotary dinner, he'd laughed at me.

'It's not fancy dress, you know,' he said.

'What do you mean?'

'Oh no. I've upset you. I didn't mean to upset you. It's

just... Lucy, you know I think you're beautiful whatever you wear but, honestly, you do look a little strange sometimes. And people don't like it. It reflects on me and, Dad and I, we can't be too careful, you know. Local solicitors and all that. Why don't you put on that lovely grey wool dress that I bought you for Christmas?'

And before I could say anything, he'd taken me upstairs, found the dress – a garment I'd hated as soon as I unwrapped it – and watched me while I put it on.

'Wow,' he said. 'I thought it would suit you, but I never realised quite how well. You look beautiful and stylish and classy. I've got fantastic taste.'

I looked at my reflection. Those weren't the words I'd have chosen to describe how I looked, but at the dinner that night I received so many compliments – Moira gushed over me – that I began to wonder if Gavin wasn't right. And the next time I went shopping, he came with me. He wanted to treat me, he said. And after that he always came. He enjoyed it so much. And the assistants loved him and always agreed he was right, especially when the clothes he chose were eye-wateringly expensive.

My hands ran through them, letting the coolness of the silky fabrics and the soft touch of the woollens brush my skin. Why hadn't I thrown them all away?

A wave of exhaustion overwhelmed me. I should get back to bed. I shut the wardrobe door and realised I hadn't taken the money. Never mind. I needed to sit down. I felt giddy and disorientated. Coming up here had been a mistake in the state I was in.

I slumped into the chair in front of my desk. My computer stared back at me. I might as well check a few things. I turned it on and put in my password. Slowly and deliberately. With a pause between each key. My own fingers knew the keys to hit without me thinking, but Elizabeth's didn't and, in my spaced-out state, I didn't want to make a mistake.

The bank balances for the shop and my personal accounts appeared on screen, both small but solid and irritatingly out of my reach. Amy's wages were due in a couple of days. I could pay her easily. A few taps on the keyboard and the money would whizz from the shop account to hers, but she'd wonder how the money had got there, with Lucy unconscious in hospital.

I'll find a solution, I told myself.

The cheque for Gavin's estate that I'd paid in before the accident had arrived in my Lucy Lyle account. It hadn't cleared, but by the time the monthly repayment of Tilly's loan was due, it would have. Thank God I'd set up a standing order so that the money would flow out automatically. I couldn't have Tilly losing her house.

Not many new emails. A few suggestions of books I might like to read from Amazon. My phone bill. And a message from the solicitors about the shop and flat.

Tilly had first heard about the shop, during the winter weeks after Gavin's funeral when I was holed up in her lonely house overlooking a great swathe of the Wash, always full of birds, some passing through, some living on the wide, flat sands of the estuary. A birdwatching friend of hers had known the elderly couple who'd owned the shop. William and Eileen Cooper. They'd run it as an electrical store with her selling and him repairing, back in the days when people mended stuff, until William died and Eileen rented it out.

She was looking for a tenant for the shop and the flat above it, but it was off the main streets and up an alley so there was little in the way of passing trade and therefore of little interest to most retailers. It didn't matter to me though.

The bulk of my sales came from my website or special orders, and most of the people who visited the shop came on purpose or wanted to discuss a commission face to face. Plus, it had the workshop I needed and the flat above. And it was cheap.

But not cheap enough.

The costs of fitting it out and for basic stock, for solicitors and accountants, for minimal advertising, computers, expanding the simple website I already had, were huge. The small inheritance from my parents would barely cover a third of it. The bank turned me down for a loan. I didn't have enough commercial experience. There were too many unknowns in my business plan. Plus, I had no security. Just at the point where I was ready to give up, Tilly stepped in again. She borrowed the money from her bank with her house as security. Her beloved but ramshackle home that generated the bulk of her income from the hordes of bird-watchers who came to stay. It would only be a temporary thing, after all, she said, until the money from Gavin's estate came through. Then I could pay her back.

My hands rummaged through the loose papers on my desk and arranged them into neat piles automatically as I remembered back to those early days in the shop when, in the excitement of preparations, of painting and building display units, of cleaning and choosing materials, I'd thought the past might be over and the future might be round the corner.

Eileen had died a couple of months ago and her solicitors had written saying that the building was for sale – with me in situ, of course – and the Coopers' son, another William, would be happy to give me first refusal.

I duly refused.

But now they'd come back suggesting a price well under

market value. Clearly, with a sitting tenant, William was struggling to find a buyer. The money I'd received from Gavin's estate would nearly cover it. If things had been different, I might have been tempted.

I stared at the screen for a long moment as I thought and then my eyes glanced down to the pile of papers I'd been fingering: birth and marriage certificates, driving licence and so on, plus Gavin's death certificate along with a copy of his will. I didn't remember leaving them out but no matter. My eyes fell on an old polaroid photo that had fallen from the pile.

It was a photo from Venice. Inside one of the dark workshops at Ca'Maschera. Of me. Holding up hands with bits of velvet and paper stuck all over them and laughing. I remembered it well.

7

I'd been happy. So happy. I loved Venice. From the moment I'd come out of the station and walked down the steps towards the Grand Canal, seeing the ripples of the lagoon glinting in the early March sunshine, exactly as they did in the pictures, I'd known it would be OK.

There were four of us apprentices, the lucky four chosen from hundreds of applicants. We'd come from all over the world to Ca'Maschera. The tiny mask workshop down a back street in Venice, run by Pietro Bondesan, was known to be the best.

There was Elodie from France, with her dark hair sliced round her face and a slash of red on her lips, and David from the US, who liked to make faces from metal plates, springs, bolts and screws. And there was Jonty, from Denmark, with fine blond hair that clung to his narrow head, a beaky nose and hooded eyes. Elodie said he looked like a Viking who'd just removed his helmet. But there was nothing very Viking-like about him. He was the quietest of the four of us. The last to laugh and the first to say goodnight every evening. He and

I fell in and out of love with each other throughout the year but never managed to feel the same thing at the same time, whereas David and Elodie got together straight away and said a loving and unregretful goodbye to each other when the year was over.

We lived in each other's pockets, working and studying long days. Every evening we'd dive into the bar on the corner and spend a couple of hours there until the alcohol and laughter loosened our muscles, knotted from bending over the workbenches. And we'd dance to the collection of CDs belonging to the bar owner: compilations of hits from the sixties and seventies, bought for their length rather than their quality; famous opera arias; a recording of The Who playing live; and some jolly Italian folk songs that I can still sing along to without understanding a single word.

And then the news about my parents arrived. They were returning home on a foggy November day from a holiday in the French Alps in a coach speeding towards Calais. A moment's inattention from the driver. The coach left the road and rolled over. Most passengers survived with a few cuts and bruises. My parents died.

I met Gavin a couple of months later in January when Venice had turned cold and damp. The sky permanently grey. Not that I saw the sky. I passed every daylight hour buried in one of the windowless back rooms at Ca'Maschera, sticking things on masks. Sequins, glitter, gold leaf. You name it, I stuck it. Feathers, lace, fringing, crystals. All efforts to train us four apprentices in the finer arts of mask-making had been abandoned at Christmas and would be until the Carnival was over in February, when our year of study came to an end and the next four apprentices arrived.

For now, we were just pairs of hands. Cold hands. The damp penetrated them after the first couple of hours in the morning. I tried everything to keep warm. Half-fingered gloves, but their wool got caught in the glue. Fine leather gloves, but they made my hands clumsy, and besides, their thin material was no barrier against the cold. In the end, like all the others, I snatched a few minutes each hour in front of the stove in the accountant's office.

The end of my studies loomed nearer and nearer, and the moment when I'd have to decide what I was doing next approached faster and faster. My parents' deaths had robbed me of everything. My childhood home – rented because they always planned to move back to the country – and the two people who'd loved me and supported me while letting me find out about myself. With them gone, I'd lost the ability to see my future, and I was too young to realise that a couple of days off for their funeral before escaping back to Venice was not enough to process what had happened. I'd stored up problems and they were catching up with me.

The others were sorted. David had a job with a film company that made animated short films and was already sketching ideas for metal characters. Elodie was returning to Paris and freelance work for a company that made prosthetics and masks. And Jonty was heading out to China to work and study at a traditional mask factory. They were so sure of themselves, so ready for the next steps, and I was lost. I wanted someone to rescue me and was too young, too immature, to know that the only person who can save you is yourself. The others tried to help, but their practical suggestions were not what I wanted to hear.

And then one night Gavin was there.

He was on holiday, with a girlfriend who'd laughed in his face when he asked her to marry him as they sat in a gondola going up the Grand Canal. He'd leapt off at a convenient mooring and stormed up the narrow *calle* until he came across our bar.

I found all that out later.

That first evening I only knew he was English, very drunk and couldn't dance. His movements were clumsy and soft. And he himself was almost pudgy, with squashed, dark curls of hair sitting on his head like a tea cosy. Even his ears, poking through, seemed limp.

Later he'd say I was a flame flickering and leaping in the dark bar and as soon as he saw me, he knew I was the one. He was a moth unable to escape from my aura and I lit up his life from that moment on.

That's not how I remember it.

I remember him trying to dance with all the women. Even the owner's mother, a thin, intense woman in her sixties, who did her best to slip out of his grasp as he lurched around the tiny space, knocking empty chairs over and making the sour old men put their hands between him and their grappas. He only latched on to me later when he discovered I was English.

And I let him. Story of my life. It was nice to speak English with an English person and anyway I was pretty drunk, too. Somewhere during the evening I poured my heart out to him. It was easy. He was a stranger. I'd never see him again. A stranger with a sympathetic look rather than the glazed expression that froze the others' faces when I started talking about my problems.

I thought I'd never see him again, but he came back the next night.

And the night after.

With flowers.

He took me out to restaurants, prepared to wait for hours until I finished work. Always ready to listen to me. Always ready to hear the same old story, the same old problems, again and again. And after a while, sitting on a bridge overlooking the moonlight-flecked waters, he seemed less of a buffoon and I let him kiss me. Besides, I thought he would only be there for a few more days, for the rest of his holiday, and then he'd go back to the UK and we'd never see each other again.

But Gavin had other ideas.

He went home, but came back to Venice every weekend. Helped by the proliferation of low-cost flights and the fact that he worked as a solicitor in the family firm, so bunking off early on a Friday was allowed. And he treated me like a queen. Nothing was too much bother. In my nervous state, exhausted and frayed by the long hours and the continual pressure to work faster, it was wonderful and Jonty's sour expression every time Gavin turned up made it even sweeter.

Gavin was there on the last Friday before the Carnival. God knows how he got a flight! Waiting outside the workshop, a rose in one hand and my favourite shampoo from the UK in the other.

'Too tired for food?' he asked.

I nodded.

'Then I'll walk you home.'

Jonty and David came out of the shop, and I was sure they sniggered.

'No,' I said. 'I'm not ready for sleep. I need to walk the day away. I feel restless.'

'Then let's be restless together. Come on. We'll go and explore.'

I think I loved him that night. We ran through the narrow streets and dark alleys and rippled our fingers through the fountains in the middle of deserted squares. We swung round the columns of the façades of crumbling churches and kissed in the middle of the bridges over the canals. It felt like every romantic dream I'd ever had come true.

We watched the sun rise over the lagoon and, even though it was only the lightening of a grey sky and a few silver rays fluttering over the restless water that nudged the gondolas into their wooden mooring posts, it felt special and significant and symbolic. Every laugh I breathed and word I sang, every gesture that danced from my limbs and every expression that flowed across my face, felt imbued with the magic of the place and the moment.

Venice is a city on the move. Shifting. Elusive. Illusory. Water and boats. Tides and people. Even the houses seem to dance... The light changes. The weather changes. *La Serenissima*, they call her, because she floats on the lagoon, but she is no more serene than any boat on the sea and that night I felt part of her.

He asked me to marry him.

And Venice beguiled me, so I took the easy way out and said yes.

8

The phone rang in the shop below and Amy answered it. The clock beside Elizabeth's bed said ten past nine. I'd slept late.

Or had I? My brain felt clearer than it had since the accident, but Elizabeth's body felt restless and edgy with gritty eyes and dry lips as though I'd been lying awake for hours.

I turned to my right to get out of bed and a finger of pain flicked my skull. Elizabeth's body turned to the left and stood. Clearly this was what it was used to doing. I relaxed and obeyed its routine impulses as it dressed in the nearest clothes that came to hand.

Now what?

The phone rang again and Amy answered it once more. I went down the stairs and stood by the internal door that connected the flat to the shop. I still felt weird and spacy, but my brain had settled during the night so that my thoughts followed a more logical path. Should I go and talk to Amy? But I shrank from playing Elizabeth in front of her.

'Intensive Care. Yes. Since Friday.' Her voice was clear. The door let every sound through.

'No, no. Her aunt is with her. Yes, I'll let you know if there's any news. Give me your number. Awuah, you said? Luke Awuah.'

Of course, it was Monday and this was Luke phoning to find out why I hadn't turned up at the police station this morning. Amy had told him I was unconscious in hospital. Seriously injured. No one could blame me for missing the interview. No repercussions. No police car sent to haul me in.

Maybe I *should* stay as Elizabeth? It was tempting.

Except, of course, it wasn't so easy. Elizabeth had a life I knew nothing about. She had a high-powered job doing something I couldn't do. She was always out so she clearly had an active social life and, I guessed, lots of friends. And a family.

I didn't have a clue about any of them.

Bad idea, Lucy. Very bad idea. Only someone whose brain was befuddled with shock and concussion would have thought otherwise.

I wondered if someone had let Elizabeth's office know about the accident? Probably not. No one would have seen the need. Not with Elizabeth herself apparently functioning as normal. I guessed that also explained why her friends hadn't been in touch to find out how she was. They didn't know anything had happened.

But that wasn't going to last for long. And when they did start calling and arranging to meet... When I had to go into her office... This charade was all going to fall apart.

I heard Amy walk towards the door. Was she coming into the flat? To see how Elizabeth was?

I grabbed a hat and slipped out of the front door into the

alley before I had to find out. Some fresh air – if that was possible in the middle of this heatwave – would help me think clearly about what to do.

I loved the secrecy of the alley, lined on one side by the shop and the houses next to it and on the other by the backs of the buildings on the adjacent road. I loved that I could sit by the little table in the kitchen and see who came up and down. In the early days, when my brain couldn't quite get used to the fact that Gavin was dead, I'd spent hours there watching.

A frisson of something like fear shivered along the skin of Elizabeth's body at the end of the alley where it met the streams of people on the High Street. How strange. There was no breeze to speak of. Maybe the noise of cars on the main road had sparked a memory of the accident.

A moment's hesitation, then I let Elizabeth stride out. The strangeness that I'd felt in hospital was still there. The sense that her body and my thoughts moved to a different rhythm. But I understood now. In fact, I wondered if she... if *we'd* had concussion at all. I wondered if the confusion, the unsteadiness, even the memory loss was just the strain of learning to function together.

I reached the park and stopped in the shade under the trees along the wide path leading up to the Observatory, its bulbous dome dominating the southern skyline. The leaves were taking on their autumn colours, shrivelling at the outer edges and yellowing along their veins, obeying some inner clock despite the lingering summer heat rising from the sun-battered earth.

I noticed how stiff and achy Elizabeth's body was and started to stretch. Her body slipped into a routine, and I felt the exercises liquefy the tight muscles in her legs. The warmth of the day penetrated them. I felt alive. Correction:

Elizabeth's body felt alive. There was an energy in it I hadn't felt in my own body for years. And I knew we would go running. Elizabeth's body and I would run.

We started at a brisk walk up the hill towards the Observatory, and then eased into a slow, loping run. It was steep, but Elizabeth's body didn't care. It felt fabulous to run so easily. The muscles in Elizabeth's legs whipped us smoothly up the slope, and her body supported them like a perfectly tuned machine, sucking air into her lungs and filling her blood with the oxygen needed to provide their power. No wonder she was so sleek. A little part of me exulted in the admiring glances other runners darted at her.

At the top, I circled, jogging on the spot for a moment, admiring the view. The park ran down to the crisp white buildings of the Queen's House and, beyond, the Old Royal Naval College, rigidly symmetrical with its two domes framing a glimpse of the Thames, while above them, on the far bank, rose the jumble of towers that was Canary Wharf.

I made myself a promise: I was going to do this every day. Even on rainy days. I was going to get up every morning early and run. It would be hard at first because I wasn't used to it. Because Lucy wasn't used to it.

And then reality burst the bubble of my thoughts.

What was I thinking? I wasn't going to be running whether I was Elizabeth or Lucy. Lucy was in a coma and if she emerged from that it might well be into another prison. Elizabeth wouldn't be running if she lost her job. Her friends and family would probably have her committed to a psychiatric hospital once they found out how strangely she was behaving.

I trudged back down Greenwich hill, feeling the energy drain out of my limbs as the impossibility of my situation caught up with me once again. I really needed to come up with a plan. The heat was deadening now. Sweat scratched Elizabeth's scalp under the thick woolly hat. Why had I put it on? I thought about removing it, but a trickle of pain stopped me. Odd how Elizabeth's body would go for ages feeling fine and then all of sudden stab me for no apparent reason. Maybe it had been a mistake to run so soon after the accident.

Back at the flat, tiredness overwhelmed me and, rather than thinking, I spent the afternoon switching between dozing in front of the television and picking the stuffing out of the hole in the sofa arm. The noise of people in the shop below disturbed me every now and then but Amy didn't come near me.

Finally, I woke up properly. The television had turned itself off, and the shop was shut. All was quiet and somewhere during the afternoon I'd reached a decision.

I was going to have to go back to the hospital, wasn't I? Back to the inert body in the bed. No choice. I might have no future as Lucy but I had even less as Elizabeth. And I couldn't condemn Elizabeth to a life trapped in my body. Not after everything that had happened.

Tomorrow, I thought. I'd do it tomorrow.

I showered. It felt odd. Almost as if I were a voyeur spying on Elizabeth from close quarters because I couldn't stop myself examining her body. It was immaculate. Smooth, taut skin covering and softening the lean lines of her bones. She reminded me of the Barbie dolls Granny gave me for Christmas. Before I broke them up to make my first sculptures, turning them into powerful monsters by gluing twigs and adding Playdoh. But beauty had its own power, I thought, staring at Elizabeth in the mirror.

I snatched a bottle of scented oil and poured it into the palm of Elizabeth's hand. A spicy, citrus smell rose. I smoothed the oil over her skin and into every nook and cranny, glorying in the feel of it, warm and smooth, and the dull gleam of the reflected light from the mirror on her body.

The long dozing afternoon had rejuvenated us and restlessness itched its way through her body and into my mind. I'd go out. Go out and have some fun. I could get away with it for one night. Just for one night and then tomorrow I'd be sensible.

I looked at the clothes hanging on the rail in Elizabeth's bedroom. There weren't many, but then she'd said she hadn't had time to move her things down from her old flat. Somewhere up north, I thought it was. Her promotion to the head office of wherever she worked had been unexpected and she was rushed off her feet at work.

Only one possible dress hung on the rail for tonight. Short but with a tight bodice and a flared skirt, blurred squares of hot pink and green on black. It looked demure until it was on, and then it wasn't demure at all. The shortness of the skirt and the way the bodice was cut tight saw to that.

We turned the radio on and jiggled a few steps, found a pair of thin-heeled shoes and slid them on. Some part of me hated myself for enjoying all this. For letting the thrill of Elizabeth's allure take me over. But the rest of me screamed it down. I needed a break. There'd be time enough in the future to be serious.

We were going out and I knew just the place. A bar round the corner with a small dance floor. I'd passed it a few times, and it always seemed full of beautiful people, sipping cocktails and dancing to a DJ. A less confident thought put its hand up timidly. *On your own*, it said. *Are you sure?* Oh, but I was. When you looked like Elizabeth did, you could do anything. Anyway, it would only be for a quick drink. Just the one. And then I'd come home and rest.

But first I needed to cover up the bruise staining the skin round her eye and cheekbone. An amazing array of foundation creams and liquids, eye shadows and liners, and lipsticks and glosses covered every inch of the table, all arranged in neat lines, according to colour and shade. Many of them were far darker or lighter than the honey tones of her skin. Her hands wandered over them and automatically picked a thick creamy liquid that hid the bruise with ease. Her perfect but bland face stared back at me from the mirror. God, she was beautiful. And the smoky eye shadow and dusting of glitter on her cheekbones only added to her allure. I hadn't worn anything except the creamy powder and pale lipstick that Gavin had considered suitable for a solicitor's wife for years.

I wondered about her hair. As well as the long blonde wig she'd always worn when I'd seen her and which now lay bloodstained and tangled in a carrier bag by the door, she had two wigs in boxes under the table. One a reddish bob and the other straight and dark. Clearly Elizabeth liked to ring the changes, although I guessed the two in boxes were used for fun only. Neither of them was as good quality as the blonde one. I know about wigs. Some of my masks have hair. If it's simple, I'll thread it in myself, but if it's complicated I get a wigmaker to do it. Elizabeth's long blonde wig was top quality, real hair and, I thought, made to measure for her. It fitted perfectly. The other two were off the peg, still good quality but not real hair and without the naturalness that meant I'd never suspected she wore a wig.

In the end I left them and slicked her short hair even shorter with a dab of gel so that nothing detracted from her smoky eyes and high cheekbones.

I flung the big hood of Elizabeth's cream raincoat over

her head as I stepped out into the alley. A car screeched as I turned into the road, and a wave of fright shot through her body, but the car passed us. Just an impatient driver.

The lights from the bar splashed pink and purple onto the pavement and the thud of bass vibrated through the air. A group of laughing people spilled out of a taxi and I followed them in and stood for a moment letting the wave of colour and music wash over me, stirring forgotten feelings to life. Then I handed over my coat to the attendant and walked over to the bar. No, I sashayed over to the bar. I'd never sashayed before and, if you'd asked me, I'd have said I didn't know how, but Elizabeth's body did. It slipped automatically into a high-stepped movement with a slight sway of the hips and I knew that eyes swivelled as I passed.

The barman pushed a drink towards me. A margarita. I hesitated and my eyes travelled up from his hands over his unbuttoned pink shirt to the suntanned face with the floppy, Mexican bandit moustache. He was smiling. The drink was for me.

Shit. They knew Elizabeth.

A margarita. Not something I'd have chosen myself. The acid taste of the citrus and the salt round the rim was too powerful. But it tasted fine. *Elizabeth's taste buds*, I thought, and knocked it back, smiling a thank you. He winked. Another arrived as promptly as the first. And as free. Clearly the barman liked Elizabeth. I hoped her body had better resistance to alcohol than mine. I tried to drink it slowly, but the alcohol was sparking ripples of happiness. God, I needed this. There'd be plenty of opportunities to be sensible and responsible later. For now, I just wanted to have fun. I drank faster and felt the edges of my consciousness blur.

'You've not been in for a few days.' It was the barman,

leaning in close and breathing rum all over me. 'Everything OK?'

'Sure thing.' My voice rose to combat the shrieks of laughter from the group gathered round the far end of the bar.

The beat of the music thudded, and lured me onto the dance floor, echoing in the throb of the blood flowing through my limbs. I surrendered to its rhythm and lost myself in the dance. Riding the rise and fall of the songs and driven by their relentless pulse, the music and I were one. I was one of the cool girls. A babe. A princess. Everybody noticed me. Many eyes lingered on me. I drank some more. No, I wasn't a princess. I was a queen.

And finally my king arrived.

He wasn't what I expected.

Trainers, jeans, a striped shirt open at the neck and with a hint of softness at the waist. He was young. Younger than Elizabeth. And scruffier. Cleaned up, showered, and smelling of aftershave. He watched me without connecting. As if I was a film. But Elizabeth's body moved towards him and put her empty glass beside him. The barman came over and took the glass.

I smiled at the youngster but the alcohol racing through my blood turned it to a giggle. 'Oh sorry, you were here before me, I think.'

What else could he do but order his beer and pay for my drink? He pulled a battered wallet stuffed with cash out of his back pocket.

Somewhere I knew how drunk I was but I didn't care. I'd let whatever was going to happen, happen.

His name was Pete. And he'd only been here a few weeks. Staying with his sister and her husband who had a flat down by the *Cutty Sark*. Bit squashed though and he liked to give them some space in the evenings, so he'd popped out for a quick beer. Not really his sort of place, this, but the pubs were closed and he really wanted that beer, you know. And who was I?

Good question.

Because I didn't feel like Lucy and I didn't even feel like Elizabeth. The classy and cool Elizabeth wouldn't go round picking up strange men in bars like I was doing. Like I seemed to be doing. But it was wonderful. I felt free. Everywhere glittered and glowed.

'Cathy,' I heard myself say. 'I'm Cathy.'

And it felt right. Tonight I was Cathy. Cathy who just wanted a good time. Who didn't care about anything else.

He nodded towards the dance floor and the thinning crowd. Somehow the best of the night had passed and it was the dregs that remained: the students, the uncool and the no longer sober. But we made the best of it. And I drank more and more until the alcohol broke the rest of the night into fragments. As sharp and disparate as shards of glass.

Outside, down by the river, a sweet wind lifting the dead leaves and circling round our legs, we moved closer and his hands slipped under my coat, clumsy at first and uncertain, but Elizabeth's body slid beneath them like a soft silky snake, and he began to gasp.

An anonymous hotel room, the sheets white in the light from the street lamps outside. Two half-clothed strangers writhed round each other. And I was one of them. Unthinking and carefree. I forgot my past and existed only in the now. I forgot I was Lucy, with all her problems and her worries, and lost myself in the rhythms stirring in Elizabeth's body. I purged myself of Lucy like a snake shedding its skin. It seemed to me that all my wishes had come true. I was free.

9

I trudge up the steps in a high-rise block of flats and along the outside corridor, switching my school backpack from shoulder to shoulder. My eyes are fixed on the floor as I step round the litter. At the door to the flat where I know I live, I stop and take a deep breath. I've done this so many times and still a feeling of apprehension makes me hesitate. Instead I look out at the view. At unending rows of small, cramped houses, punctuated by more high-rise blocks and smaller church steeples.

I take out a key and open the door. The hum of the television seeps out from the living room. I ignore it and head for the stairs, but another noise stops me. A banging and yelling. I peer in.

Every inch of floor and corner of space is crammed with detritus: old clothes, empty cans, plates of cigarette ends. The grey-faced, dirty-blonde-haired woman on the floor looks like one more heap of discards, but I see her at once. My mother lies on the floor.

'Fell,' she says. 'Can't get up. Hurt my ankle.'

I drag her up and dump her on the sofa then turn to leave but she seizes my hand. Her skin is hot.

'You'll have to go out for me, love. I couldn't get out.'

'No.'

'Please, love.'

'No.'

But later when the noise of her cries and muttering gets too much, when it soaks through the walls between us and roams around my bedroom, I know I'll have to do what she asks.

So I take her money and go out into the dusk to the park nearby, like she told me to. To the man standing by the recycling bins. I say the words my mother told me to say and give him the notes, take the plastic bag with the crumbly white rock in the corner and walk back through the park, past the swings where a few errant children scream and laugh, along the road of houses where the gleam of light in back kitchens flickers through the empty windows, and trudge up the steps to the flat. I feel a wetness on my face as I open the door, but I scrub my cheeks with the edge of my coat and go in.

10

I woke up. It was still dark. Even with my eyes closed, I could tell. Pete was beside me, an arm flung round my neck, but as I tried to move, he turned over and pulled the covers over him. I grasped for the excitement of the night before, but it slipped through my fingers like the fine sand on the beaches of my childhood. My head hurt. The after-effects of alcohol and the present effects of regret, as bitter and unpalatable as the grounds of coffee at the bottom of the cup.

What had I done?

The whole thing seemed tawdry, like a chipped and cracked mirror ball when the lights are turned off and the reality behind the glitter is clear. A one-night stand. Just sex. Nothing special. He'd have probably slept with anyone. The room smelled musty. The bed was lumpy. I wanted to go home, but when I tried to open my eyes and slide to the edge of the bed, I couldn't. My body, Elizabeth's body, wouldn't. Nothing worked. Her eyelids were glued shut. Her head wouldn't turn. Her arms wouldn't lift. Her legs lay motionless. I began to panic. Somehow, during the mad night, I'd lost control. The link between my consciousness and the pathways of her nerves had broken. I was paralysed. Was it the alcohol? Visions of ambulances and paramedics passed through my mind. Of pitying looks tinged with disapproval. I couldn't, I really couldn't let myself be found here with nothing but a gaudy dress and a coat.

And to add to my misery, I wanted to pee. The urge became stronger and stronger until I worried the muscles would give way and I'd wet the bed. I couldn't bear it. I forced my consciousness to grope for the connection, like running your hands over the floor trying to feel a dropped contact lens that your eyes can't see. Praying that somehow or other I'd find it. And success. Sort of. Suddenly I felt a great surge of wakefulness. My legs, Elizabeth's legs, swung round and sat her body up. It leaned forward and headed to the loo.

We must have both been searching, I thought, my Lucy consciousness at one end and Elizabeth's body at the other, and the urgency had snapped the connection back into place, although it felt as weird and distant as it always had. No matter, though. It was working.

I peed, slipped into my underwear and dress and covered them up with my coat. I was still unmistakably someone returning from a night out, but who cared? I edged round Pete's side of the bed to the door. He was deep, deep asleep. I bent over and picked up his jeans.

My dream of the girl still clung to me as though I was half in her world and half in this dark hotel room. I was sure it was the same girl as other dreams. Just a little older. Carly. That was what the teacher had called her. It had been surprisingly coherent for a dream. Nothing illogical happened. No strange time and place jumps. No old friends wandering in. It was more like a slice of real life than a dream. As real as this room felt now with the carpet harsh against the soles of my bare feet and my hand reaching in the pocket of Pete's jeans for his wallet.

The money, shoved in hastily, stuck out, and I took it. It was a lot. More than a week's worth, I thought. Stupid to carry so much around with him. In one swift movement, my hands stuffed it into the pocket of my coat and picked up my shoes, before I could register what they'd done. My legs took me out of the room, my hands closed the door noiselessly behind me and I crept out into the night. Like a thief. Exactly like a thief.

Disbelief caught up with me out in the street. What had I done? But I didn't stop. Elizabeth's ridiculous shoes still clattered on the pavement. Our shadow shrank then stretched as I sped under the street lamps, her hands thrust in her pockets, the left one clutching the wad of money. The paper was smooth, but the edges of the notes cut into her skin, like the thoughts slicing into my brain.

How could I have taken his money? I must still be drunk. Or the concussion was making me behave strangely.

The thoughts grew faster and louder and pain stabbed her temples. I stopped underneath one of the lamp posts and put Elizabeth's hand to her head. *Go back*, I said to myself. *Go back and return the money. He's probably still asleep, and if he isn't you can make up some story about how you found it on the floor outside the room. Tell him he must have dropped it.*

But I didn't move.

The headache grew worse, stabbing the inside of her skull.

I wanted to get home. Above all else I wanted to get home. I didn't want to stand under a lamp post, I wanted to be in bed, burrowing my head into the pillow, letting sleep smother the awful suspicion raging through my mind.

We clattered off again, and before we turned into my little alley, Elizabeth's head swung round and we looked up and down the road. No one was there.

My brain made one last lunge.

Go back and return the money.

Pain wrenched my brain cells apart and I could do nothing but stagger into the flat and pass out on Elizabeth's bed.

11

It was morning.

I knew that because light poured in through the kitchen window and on the table in front of me was a bowl containing muesli, a carton of soya milk, a spoon and a plate with an apple cored and sliced into even crescents by the knife lying beside it. One of the knives from the magnetic strip on the wall. A complete set. Top quality. Very expensive. A wedding present from one of Gavin's family. The kettle hummed.

Nothing abnormal about any of it. Except I had no memory of waking up nor of slipping out of bed. No memory of coming into the kitchen and preparing this immaculate little meal. And worse still, I was on the phone and I had no idea what I was talking about. I didn't even know who I was speaking to.

Either the concussion had struck again and wiped my recent memory or...

Or what?

The suspicion I'd had last night returned and I grappled

with it, trying to understand what it was telling me as the voice on the telephone wedged against my ear droned on.

'You should receive it in forty-eight hours. You're very lucky we've got it in your size. I'll get it packed and sent. We've got your address on file, haven't we?' The voice waited for an answer to the question.

And my mind whirled. *Who was I speaking to? What had I ordered?*

My voice, Elizabeth's voice, answered, without any help from me, and a cold trickle of acceptance chilled my thoughts.

'Actually, I've moved,' Elizabeth said. 'Please send it to Elizabeth Hughes,' and gave them my shop's address, finished the conversation and hung up.

I was almost sure now. I cast my thoughts back over everything that had happened since I woke up in the hospital. The strange gaps in my memory. The sense that Elizabeth's body acted of its own volition. Stealing Pete's money. Only one thing made sense of it all.

When the kettle boiled and Elizabeth's hand took down a thin china mug with poppies on its outside and reached for the box of organic green tea, I knew this was the moment. The tea tasted like weeds. Even Elizabeth's taste buds couldn't disguise it. I wanted proper tea, hot and dark and fragrant with a good dollop of milk. Now was the moment to test if what I suspected was true.

I took a deep gulp of air. A virtual gulp of virtual air because Elizabeth's body carried on breathing lightly and gently. I raised her left hand to the shelf above to close round the box of Darjeeling.

Nothing happened.

Try again..

I concentrated very hard. Pictured the instruction

forming in my brain, firing a spark that travelled along nerves, leaping the gap between synapses, and snapping the muscles into life. Elizabeth's hand twitched on its way to the green tea.

But that was all.

I screwed myself up for one last try. Concentrated on the image of gleaming tea with a light steam rising from the cup, imagined my hands curling round its heat and lifting it to take the first sip, the one you feel travel down your body and revive you.

This time the hand stopped and shook, then fell back to the worktop. Pain ignited in Elizabeth's head. She stumbled a few feet to the sink and a great squeezing in her body emerged as dry retching. She wasn't sick, but for a few minutes her vision went fuzzy as if it was a television covered with static.

I let her be.

Her retching and the headache subsided and her vision returned to normal, although she stood over the sink for quite a while clutching its sides for support, too giddy to let go.

My thoughts reeled, too. I was sure now. There could be no doubt.

I was inside Elizabeth's body.

But I wasn't alone.

Elizabeth was here, too. Inside her own body. Inside her own head. Controlling every action her body took. I was simply an observer. A passenger. Everything I thought I'd done since waking up in hospital had been done by Elizabeth. Elizabeth had come home from hospital. Elizabeth had gone running. Elizabeth had gone out last night, picked up Pete and stolen his wallet.

How had I not known?

I thought back over the days since the accident. I'd been

so dazed and confused in the hospital, and the diagnosis of concussion with its resulting strange amnesia had seemed to make sense of how I felt so I hadn't questioned the weirdness of the gaps in my memory. But now I realised I hadn't forgotten anything. The gaps had occurred because I was asleep or unconscious while Elizabeth was awake and in charge. Looking back now it was easy now to see how much of a passenger I'd been without realising.

After all, who would have suspected the truth?

And when we'd got home, I'd let what I thought were the routines her body was used to dictate our actions. The headaches, the sudden stabs of pain were when my wishes contradicted Elizabeth's, like when I tried to get out of bed one side and she tried to get out of the other. And, of course, hers won every time. Hands down. No contest. I was powerless. Yet again.

And I hadn't noticed. But then often our wishes had been the same. So much of life was automatic. Someone asks you how you are. You say 'fine' without thinking. They make you a cup of tea, you drink it.

Elizabeth let go of the sink and sat down heavily on one of the chairs at the kitchen table by the window. She opened the window and let in the cool morning air. She was as shaken as me by the fight over the tea. Her fingers trembled as they traced the rim of the plate of apples.

I might be a passenger, but my presence affected her. Her body reacted if I felt anything strongly. I thought a little more about what had happened since the accident because there had been moments where I thought I'd been in control.

Like when I first woke up in hospital. The initial conversation with the nurse. That had been me. I'd asked questions Elizabeth wouldn't have asked because she already knew the answers.

And the night before last, when I'd woken and gone upstairs to my bedroom, checked my mails and my accounts. That must have been me.

Maybe, when Elizabeth was asleep, when her brain switched off, maybe then I was in control? I certainly hadn't been in charge last night though. At least I hoped not. My behaviour made me cringe now and I couldn't use the alcohol as an excuse for the early part of the evening. No, that had been wish fulfilment. My desperate longings to be someone else had chimed with Elizabeth wanting to go out.

I felt sick at how pathetic I'd been.

12

The flat doorbell rang. I glanced at the clock. Correction: Elizabeth glanced at the clock and I saw what she saw. Then her eyes went back to the knife and the apple. I tried to see if I could flick her gaze back to the clock. Just a gentle nudge as a test. But nothing happened. I had no control over her eyes. No control over her body. I could only do what she did, and I was sure that if I tried any harder the conflict would cause debilitating pain. For both of us.

The bell rang again and Elizabeth peered out of the window.

It was the police. Two of them.

Fear scattered my thoughts but I gathered them together. Whatever the police were here for, it couldn't be me. I felt the echo of my fear in Elizabeth's body though. It tightened her muscles and pumped blood faster through her arteries. Very odd. Unless it was her own feelings? Did she fear the arrival of the police? Maybe she worried Pete had reported her? Maybe he had. Maybe she was about to be arrested. How very, very ironic.

I thought it was unlikely though. Pete didn't even know her real name.

Elizabeth drew her dressing gown tighter round her body and went downstairs.

Taking me with her.

Now that I knew I wasn't in control, it was the weirdest sensation. I saw what she saw and heard what she heard. I felt what she felt: the cool hardness of the stair rail, the slight give of the old stair boards as the weight of her legs settled on each one in turn. And I felt her body move. I felt her lift her arm, grasp the bolts on the door and slide each one open.

And, honestly, if I hadn't known it was Elizabeth making it happen I'd have thought it was me.

The friendly police constable from the hospital with the gap in her front teeth and the perfect smile stood in front of a colleague in the open door.

'Ms Hughes. Police Constable Evans. Good morning. We're sorry to disturb you but we have a couple of follow-up questions about the accident. Would now be a good time for my colleague and I to discuss them?'

'Sure. No problem.' Elizabeth relaxed. The blood racing through her arteries slowed and the electrical impulses fizzling along her nerves stilled. She smiled and opened the door wide for them.

PC Evans trudged up the stairs, but the second police officer waited.

'After you,' he said and the tic on his left cheek jerked into life.

I recognised him.

It was DI Cromer, the detective inspector who'd interrogated me after Gavin's death and who I'd been supposed to see yesterday in Surrey. What was he doing here in London?

Elizabeth ran up the stairs in front of him and into the

sitting room, where they settled themselves on my mismatched chairs and sofa. As DI Cromer lowered himself, the throw fell off the back of the chair and draped itself around his shoulders. He pushed it away and shifted to avoid the spring that stuck into your bottom if you didn't sit carefully enough. His knees bent awkwardly in the low chair and he rubbed them with a glimmer of a frown. Even though my thoughts were full of worry, I found room for a whisper of satisfaction at his discomfort.

'We now have a video of the accident.' PC Evans handed a tablet to Elizabeth. 'We hoped watching it might help you recall a few details.'

A girl's chatting, laughing face filled the left half of the screen, and behind it, cars crawled past while the occasional bus and cyclist moved faster in their separate lane. When the accident came, it was fast. Too fast to see anything really. One minute Elizabeth and I were walking, tiny figures, then there was a swoosh of dark, a confusion of blurs, and the next second we were a heap on the steps, with the car speeding away. And all to the side of the girl's smiling face mouthing messages to her friend. They'd cut the sound.

'Sorry,' Elizabeth said eventually. 'But I can't see anything. I mean, I can barely tell it's me and Lucy.'

For a moment I thought it was me talking because this was exactly what I was thinking. But it was Elizabeth who'd had the same thought.

'It is difficult. We were particularly interested to get hold of this because it supports one of the witness statements.'

Elizabeth raised her eyebrows.

PC Evans continued. 'The witness was waiting to cross the road and actually watching the traffic at the time of the incident. The road has two lanes at that point, one for traffic heading to the Blackwall Tunnel, which was congested and slow-moving, and the other, a bus lane that becomes a lane for traffic turning left into the streets leading down to the river. That one was empty. We had assumed, and earlier witness statements appeared to corroborate this, that the driver who hit you was stuck in traffic, had become impatient and pulled out into the empty lane, accelerated away and misjudged the corner.'

Elizabeth nodded. I felt the hair on the back of her neck prickle.

'However, this later witness said the driver was perfectly in control of the car. That they had slowed and straightened after changing lanes and then appeared to accelerate and aim for the kerb.'

The tablet slipped out of Elizabeth's hands and clipped the table. The noise echoed in the sudden silence. Sweat broke out on her palms, and she rammed them between her knees, rucking the silky material of her dressing gown.

'You mean...' she said. 'You mean that he was aiming for us?' The edges of her vision crumbled into black dots and her ears buzzed. She put her head down onto her knees. The possibility that someone had tried to kill us had shaken her.

DI Cromer hauled himself out of the chair. 'Let me make you a cup of tea.'

For a moment I forgot Elizabeth was in charge. I didn't want DI Cromer in my kitchen. I tried to say 'No', to say I was all right. But, of course, I couldn't. All I succeeded in doing was making Elizabeth's hands tremble as she gestured towards the kitchen.

I thought I knew why he was here now. He must have been in touch with the London police when Luke had told him I'd been in an accident. And when they'd told him they were interviewing Elizabeth today, he'd seized the chance to look round my flat without me knowing.

'I'm afraid we have to consider it is possible that someone deliberately drove into you,' PC Evans said as DI Cromer slipped out. 'Especially as we've also had reports of a similar car parked up along the road, with the driver inside and the engine running.'

I attempted to take it in. And Elizabeth asked the question I wanted to put.

'A car parked up? You mean watching... for us?'

'Possibly? They were there for a long time. And it wasn't the first occasion. One of the local shopkeepers said the driver had been hanging around for a few days when we went asking for CCTV.'

'And has that shown anything?'

'Nothing conclusive.' She waited for Elizabeth to say something, and when she didn't, carried on. 'You see, the pavement is particularly high where they left the road, so the car must have had considerable force behind it to mount the kerb so fast.'

The rumbling of the kettle in the kitchen penetrated the thin wall and the chink of china told me that DI Cromer had found the mugs. Clever bastard. I suspected he'd made full use of the opportunity to look through all my cupboards.

'We wondered though if you were aware of anyone who might bear you a grudge. Or Ms Christensen?'

'What...?' Elizabeth forced a laugh and tossed her head. 'I really don't think so. Of course, I can't speak for Lucy, for Ms Christensen, but for me, no way.'

But I wondered. There was something strained about the light tone of her voice and the feeling of something tamped down inside her.

DI Cromer came in with her tea, and I thought I saw him give a nod to PC Evans.

'How is Ms Christensen?' he asked. He avoided sitting down again.

'Lucy. Oh. Not great. I mean...' Elizabeth took a deep breath and forced herself to breathe out slowly. 'In a coma.'

'So, she's been unconscious since the accident?'

'Completely.'

Yes! You tell him, Elizabeth. Make him see that I'm beyond his reach.

He asked Elizabeth a few more questions about my injuries and then they left with instructions to get in touch if she thought of anything else.

Elizabeth didn't drink the tea DI Cromer had made. She went into the kitchen and poured it down the sink then sat down at the table and stared out into the alley for a long time, clearly thinking, although I had no idea what about.

I focused on the edge of her vision and counted the knives on the magnetic strip next to the hob. They were all still there. But a couple of them were slightly out of alignment as though someone had moved them. As though they'd been looking for something that should have been there – the sharpening steel that completed the set – but wasn't.

The new evidence Luke, my solicitor, had mentioned. Had the police discovered what I least wanted them to? I hoped not.

I might be better off staying where I was. Because with Elizabeth running her own life, all my previous worries about dealing with her job and her friends were solved. I could lie low. Have time to think.

Elizabeth picked up the coat she'd slung over the back of a chair last night, took Pete's money from the pocket, counted it and shoved it in her purse in her bag. And then the big question that had been waiting its moment to step on stage pushed through my thoughts and took the spotlight.

Why? Why had she stolen Pete's money? A sudden impulse? Because she was a thief? An uncontrollable kleptomaniac? For fun? Because she needed the money?

There was nothing much else in her bag. Some paracetamol and what looked like sleeping tablets. None of the everyday detritus of receipts and leaflets, used tissues and old tickets. Her purse was new and held little except the money she'd stolen. No bank cards, no store cards, no library membership. In fact, nothing except an Oyster card. I knew she was neat and ordered but this was extreme.

I began to feel uneasy.

I wondered what else I was going to find out about her because, of course, I didn't have much choice. No. I didn't have any choice because I was trapped here. Trapped until I could get back to my own body. And I wasn't going to be able to do that unless Elizabeth went back to the hospital. But she'd have to want to. I couldn't make her.

A vision of my future life as an imprisoned passenger inside a woman I knew nothing about rolled out before me and I realised how stupid I'd been to think, even for a second, this might be the answer to my problems.

13

Elizabeth showered, while I tried to think what to do. I had the impression she was as lost in her thoughts as I was. Afterwards, she washed her blood-stained wig in the sink, letting the running water loosen and carry the blood away. She put it on a polystyrene head to dry and dressed herself in taupe trousers and a cream blouse.

Amy called up the stairs.

'Elizabeth. Are you there?'

'Yep.'

'Lucy's aunt is here.'

'I'll be right down.'

But she didn't rush. She checked her face in the mirror, still lost in her thoughts. I wished I knew what they were but they were shut off from me. When she started down the stairs, Amy's voice, talking to my aunt, rose to meet us.

'I'm fine keeping the shop going for the moment,' she was saying.

Tilly said something indistinct in reply.

'It's the least I can do,' Amy went on. 'She, Lucy, has

been very good to me. I took a lot of time off when my son was in hospital, and she paid me for every—' She broke off as Elizabeth pushed open the door.

Tilly – my aunt Tilly, my father's sister and my only remaining family member – stood in the centre of the shop surrounded by a paradise of feathers, sequins, gold leaf, laces and velvets. Rumpled and creased, she appeared totally out of place. She belonged outdoors in jeans with an ancient jumper or a shirt depending on the weather, rather than the skirt and blouse she wore in clashing shades of green. Her so-called smart clothes were always green. So much easier, she'd told me. That way she could be sure everything matched. But the dark bottle green of her skirt fought with the leafy hue of her blouse and her clothes were even more crumpled than usual, while her grey-streaked hair, flattened round the sides but spiky on top, bore witness to her sleeping in a hospital chair.

It was good to see her.

We'd spoken on the phone but never face to face in the months since she'd said goodbye and left me surrounded by boxes and cases when I'd finally moved into the flat in Greenwich. She'd hugged me and driven off in her battered car back to her ramshackle house to look after the stream of summer visitors who gave her the bulk of her income and the huge and shifting array of wild birds they came to observe. Some were exotic creatures passing through or only staying the summer months, but the others were the local birds that lived in the brambles on the hills and in the reeds on the marshy land down by the strand of river winding its way to the sea.

She'd taken me home with her after the funeral, looked after me and given me time to begin to heal, and when she'd thought I was ready to fly she'd let me go. That was how she worked with the injured birds she cared for. I wasn't sure it had worked for me. Not the flying away bit anyway.

'Elizabeth.' Amy's voice interrupted the flow of memories. 'This is Ms Christensen, Lucy's aunt. Elizabeth is Lucy's lodger. I can't leave the shop right now, so she'll take you to Lucy's room.'

'Oh please, Elizabeth, call me Tilly. Everybody does.'

Tilly shook Elizabeth's hand awkwardly. The strangeness of her skin touching Elizabeth's caught me by surprise. It had the same warm but slightly rough feel that I was familiar with, but it made me uncomfortable. Some quality of Tilly's flesh called out to me. Something about the DNA we shared maybe loosened whatever tied me to Elizabeth's body.

Tilly dropped Elizabeth's hand and I wondered if she felt it too.

'It's kind of you to let me stay,' Tilly said, rubbing her hand against her skirt. 'It's very uncomfortable in the hospital and hotels are so expensive. I don't suppose I'll be here much, but it would be good to have a bed to grab a few hours' sleep in and a proper bathroom. I'll try not to get in your way.'

Talisker burst through the cat flap. She went straight to Tilly and wound herself round her legs, purring. I realised I hadn't seen her since I – we – got back from the hospital. Tilly bent and stroked her. 'I'm not normally all that keen on beasts like you,' she said. 'I've seen too many casualties caused by your ilk raiding nests. But since you're being so friendly... although I suspect it's cupboard love.'

'How is Lucy?' Elizabeth asked.

I listened hard.

'They're going to wake her up,' Tilly said in a rush, folding her arms over her chest as though holding herself tight, 'this afternoon. It's such a relief. The swelling on her brain has gone down a great deal so they think she's ready. They'll stop the drugs keeping her in a coma and... I'm so sorry. I'm babbling. It's just...'

Amy's voice was soft as she spoke over Tilly's stuttering. 'Tilly is trying to say that when Lucy wakes up, we'll start to know if the head injury was serious.'

Tilly's face looked pale beneath the broken veins on her cheeks and the weather-beaten skin. Anxiety had painted mauve shadows under her eyes and robbed them of their gleam.

I began to worry myself. What would happen when they tried to wake me up and found no one there?

'Do you have to go straight back?' Amy said to Tilly. 'No time for a bit of a rest?'

'I can't let her wake up on her own...'

'I'd come with you if I could,' Amy said. 'But there are orders to get out and—'

'I'll be fine. I'd rather you managed the shop and kept it running ready for... for when Lucy recovers and comes back home.'

'I'll come with you,' Elizabeth said, startling me.

'Yes,' Amy said. 'Let Elizabeth go with you. You shouldn't be on your own. She can help you with the buses.'

'That would be very kind,' Tilly said. 'I'm not sure I'm up to dealing with buses, and I certainly don't want to drive in London any more. Thank you, Elizabeth.'

Yes, thank you Elizabeth. Thank you for going to the hospital.

Because it was even more urgent now.

'Park your car in the yard behind Lucy's workshop,' Amy said. 'It'll be safe there behind the big wooden gates. If you don't mind leaving me the keys in case I have to move it for a delivery.' She reached up to the little shelf above the till where we kept the key that unlocked the gates and held it out to Elizabeth.

'Will you unlock it, Elizabeth?'

'I've got a key,' Elizabeth said.

'Yours unlocks the little door in the middle of the gate. There's only one copy of the key for the big gates themselves.' She handed the key to Elizabeth. 'Could you give me the money you owe me too?'

Elizabeth peeled off some notes from Pete's stash in her purse and then we walked through the storeroom and into my workshop at the back of the building, behind the shop. Tilly stopped.

'The birds,' she said, reaching onto the shelf where I kept the birds I'd sculpted when I'd stayed at her house. 'I'd forgotten how wonderful they were.'

She picked up a swift. A bird that spends its life in the air, swooping and curling in its currents, its body ill-adapted to the ground. I'd tried to convey something of its dynamic shape but it hadn't worked. The bird had remained a thing of clay, heavy and lumpen, but now as Tilly turned it round in her hands and the light caught the sheen of the glaze I caught a glimpse of how it might have been and I longed to pull out some new clay, dig my hands into it and try again.

Elizabeth picked up one of a group of sparrows, drab and brown in colour, but bustling and bickering with life. It felt weird though. Normally when I touch a finished piece I sense a ghost of the excitement and pleasure I'd experienced as I pulled and pushed the clay into life. But Elizabeth's hands felt nothing.

14

The bus emptied at the hospital as most of the passengers headed towards the main entrance. Heat rose from the baked pavement, radiated from the walls and reflected in the gritted teeth and fixed looks of the people around us. I watched Elizabeth's feet and noticed the way she sent unconscious signals to her body. Slow down or you'll bump into the woman in the red blouse who isn't looking where she's going. Step round that patch on the ground that could be dried vomit. For the first time I began to sense the impulses vibrating along her nerves as they transmitted commands to her muscles.

Tilly hesitated at the bottom of the steps, took a cotton handkerchief out of her pocket and dabbed the perspiration on her upper lip. But Elizabeth pulled her woolly hat further down her head and wrapped her coat tight round herself.

'Let's get inside,' Elizabeth said.

'Of course. Are you cold?'

'Kind of.' She smiled at Tilly. I felt the skin across her lips stretch and the corners of her mouth dig into her cheeks, but I had no idea what provoked the smile. Nor why she had wrapped herself up in the coat and hat. She wasn't cold. In fact, her skin was damp with sweat. I might be able to sense the instructions her brain sent to her body but I still had no access to her thoughts.

We joined a cluster of people shuffling through the revolving doors at the entrance. Once we were inside, the muscles across the back of Elizabeth's shoulders released, her jaw unclenched, and she stopped darting glances around. She pulled her hat off and ran her fingers through her short hair although it was cooler inside the building than outside. Maybe she was slightly agoraphobic?

I didn't see Moira until she stepped in front of us as we waited for the lift.

What was she doing here?

'Matilda,' she said, seizing Tilly's arm.

'Moira—' Tilly stepped back, nearly treading on Elizabeth's feet, and knocking the flowers clutched in the hands of the young man waiting next to us. 'Sorry. I'm so sorry. I don't think they're damaged.' And turning back to Moira, 'What *are* you doing here?'

'Luke phoned Ted and told him Lucy was in hospital, injured in an accident. I called you but you didn't answer so I came straight away. How is she? What happened?'

A sneaky feeling of relief that I wouldn't have to deal with Moira washed over me. That would fall to Tilly. Like she had after the funeral when I was staying with her. Moira rang every day for a while although I only spoke to her once: when Tilly told me I'd have to because she couldn't make any more excuses to the poor woman.

'She's lost her only son and you were his wife. You're the closest thing to him she's got left,' Tilly had said. 'I know you don't want to but...'

'She still wants to talk to me? Even after the whispers at the funeral?'

'It was very unfortunate. But it was just a storm in a teacup. Stupid, stupid people. And you can be sure Moira feels the same way as I do.'

But there was a note of uncertainty in her voice and I thought she was more concerned about the gossip than she let on. Nevertheless I gave in. And next time Moira rang, I let Tilly pass the phone to me. Moira talked. She was always good at talking. She could maintain a conversation for ages with very little input from the other person. She talked about Gavin. Gavin as a little boy. Gavin at school. How happy he'd been when he met me. And then endless 'Do you remember when' stories. The time he'd driven all the way to Hampstead to get me some special materials I needed so I wouldn't have to waste a day going there myself. The time he'd worked all through the night so he could take the day off work to go with me to an exhibition I wanted to see. And on and on. Gavin this and Gavin that. And I listened. I listened until my head was full to the brim of Gavins. Until I thought it would explode with them all cramming themselves in there.

Tilly took the phone away from me when my nails, digging into the palms of my hands, had drawn blood. I didn't hear what she said to Moira but it was enough to stop her calling me although she'd written every week after that and still did.

I never opened the letters.

'Oh, Moira,' Tilly said. 'It was an accident. A car hit her. Her and Elizabeth.' She turned to me. 'This is Elizabeth. She's Lucy's lodger.'

Moira nodded. Elizabeth smiled back.

'But Lucy has been badly hurt,' Tilly continued. 'A head injury. She's been in a coma since.'

'That's terrible. So terrible.'

'I'm sorry. I should have called you but it's been... Well, you can imagine. But I promise you I will keep in touch. We're just on our way to see her now so I should know more soon. I'll call you as soon as do.'

'Oh no.' Moira seized Tilly's hand and patted it. 'I couldn't possibly leave you to cope on your own. I told Ted not to expect me back until late. Mrs Jenkins can do the church flowers for once and I'll stay here. The flowers will be a horror, but never mind. You haven't forgotten I was a nurse, have you? Or maybe I never told you. Quite a senior one, though I say it myself. I ran my own ward back then until Gavin arrived and then, of course, I stopped working to look after him. But you never forget so I can help you deal with all of this.'

The crush of people waiting for the lift forced us close together and Moira's sweet perfume hit Elizabeth's nose. It twitched.

'I couldn't ask you to do that, Moira.' Tilly sounded fraught. 'Besides, Elizabeth is with me.'

'I'd like to.' Moira said. 'Very much. Gavin would have wanted me to make sure Lucy was properly looked after.'

The lift doors opened and Tilly bowed to the inevitable and nodded.

It was quieter in ICU today. Machinery still whirred and hissed but there were fewer people around so less chatter and the background noise was almost soothing.

'Ms Christensen? Could I have a word?' A nurse raised himself off the desk he'd been leaning against, straightening long, skinny limbs until he towered over Tilly. She went with him into a wide-windowed office off the ward without speaking, and Moira followed.

'I'll go and sit with Lucy,' Elizabeth said to their departing backs and headed straight towards the curtains round Lucy's cubicle.

This was it.

I hadn't expected the opportunity to come so quickly and easily. In a few seconds Elizabeth and I would be alone with my body. The transfer would happen. I was sure of that. And although I felt sick at the thought of my future I knew I had to go back. If they were going to wake me up, I had to be there. I couldn't run the risk of them finding out my body was an empty husk.

Elizabeth pushed back the curtains round the cubicle and we went in.

The bed was empty.

My body wasn't there.

What had happened? Had it died? Had I left it too long without its consciousness, its spark, its driving force? Had its systems shut down one after the other, deprived of the impulse to keep functioning? Was that why the nurse wanted to speak to Tilly?

As my thoughts raced, Elizabeth's eyes looked round the cubicle and her breathing quickened. She pulled the curtain completely shut behind her, edged past the array of equipment and cables to the cabinet by the bed, bent down and opened it. My tatty, tapestry bag was inside. She unfastened it, saw the jumble of contents and muttered an expletive, but her hands were fast and she found my purse, grabbed it as well as my phone and rammed them into her pocket.

What was she doing?

Then she rummaged deeper, unzipping all the pockets

and plunging her fingers into them, but whatever she was looking for wasn't there.

She was quick and by the time Tilly entered, the cabinet door was closed, Elizabeth was standing by the bed fingering the sheet and I was not even sure if what I'd seen had really happened.

'Where's Lucy?' Elizabeth asked. A faint tremor unsteadied her hands as they smoothed the sheet.

'They've taken her for a final scan.' Tilly darted a look over her shoulder. 'Just to check everything, before they wake her.'

I wasn't dead. Thank God.

'Elizabeth,' Tilly continued and dropped her voice to a rapid whisper, 'could you take Moira away? I've told her only one of us can stay. Can you do that?'

'Of course,' Elizabeth said. 'No problem.' She reached her hand inside her pocket and stroked the worn leather of my purse. 'I'll go and head her off.'

No. I need to stay. I need to transfer.

I fought Elizabeth's legs as she tried to turn and leave. She sat down on the edge of the bed suddenly.

'Are you all right?' Tilly's forehead wrinkled with concern. 'You're very white.'

'Yes. Just shook me up being back. I'll be fine in a minute.'

'They've told me Lucy probably won't wake up immediately. That it might take quite a while. But if it's quick I don't want Moira's face to be the first thing she sees. It's complicated and I don't want to upset Moira so if you could just keep her occupied until I know what's happening and then I'll find a way of getting rid of her.'

I relaxed as Tilly spoke. I still had time.

The lanky nurse came in pushing a trolley, followed by

Moira telling him how the NHS had changed since she was a sister. He didn't reply but snapped rubber gloves onto his hands and put a mask over his face, tying it underneath his small ponytail.

'Moira,' Elizabeth said. 'Only one person can stay. Let's get a coffee?'

'Good idea,' Tilly added.

Moira looked unsure and as she hesitated Elizabeth's eyes flitted between her and Tilly. Both around the same age, but so different. Tilly's skin had crumpled into fine wrinkles made all the more obvious by their paleness against its weather-beaten surface, while Moira's face, plumped up with expensive creams and make-up, was a study in artifice, although a tiny smudge of lipstick stained her front teeth. I'd always wanted to sculpt her, but as she'd have seen the result I never dared.

Eventually she nodded her head.

15

The coffee bar was in the corner of a great echoing atrium, crossed continuously by fast-moving staff, visitors walking slowly as they deciphered the myriad of signs overhead, and an endless stream of injured on crutches, in wheelchairs, or on trolleys. I reckoned we weren't far from Accident and Emergency.

Someone had tried to separate the café area from the general thoroughfare with screens of flowery material, but the overall effect was lost beneath the wallpaper of posters exhorting people to have a regular mammogram, to wash their hands and so on and so forth. Elizabeth chose a table behind a screen and asked Moira what she wanted.

'A pot of tea please, dear. The coffee in these places is undrinkable.' She dusted the seat with a handkerchief and smoothed the box pleats of her skirt into parallel lines as she lowered herself onto it.

I could have told Elizabeth she'd choose tea, and that if Elizabeth bought some biscuits she'd eat them too, but only after protesting that she never did. She must have eaten enough packets of biscuits to fill an average-sized Tesco's during my marriage to Gavin.

I could also have told Elizabeth, as she squeezed her way between the tables, balancing the tray, that she should have brought more paper napkins. Moira liked to place one under the cup and use another to wipe the handle before she picked it up.

'So you're Lucy's lodger?' Moira said.

'That's right.'

'Are you an old friend of hers?'

'No, actually. I've only known her a few weeks. I was looking for a room in Greenwich and she had a room to rent.'

'Lucy always liked Greenwich.' Moira wiped the handle and the rim of her cup.

'Sorry, did I spill some of it?'

'No, dear. You never know how well they've washed it and...' She gave a meaningful swish of her eyes to indicate the other people sitting in the café area with us, many of them in hospital gowns and attached to drips, their faces grey and drooping with illness. 'I don't know who might have touched it before.'

She took a sip and sighed.

'So how is Lucy doing? I mean, how was she doing before the accident?'

'Fine, I think. We don't spend that time much together.'

'And how is her new flat and the shop?'

I felt Elizabeth try to form a reply but Moira spoke again before she could.

'I'm sorry, my dear. You must think it's very strange me asking all these questions but the truth is I know nothing at all about Lucy's life. She had some sort of breakdown after Gavin— after my son died – and she can't face any reminder of him. Being with me or even talking to me makes it worse.'

Moira's voice had risen as she poured out her heart to Elizabeth and a young man in a hospital gown at the table by us looked up from his crossword.

'Gavin. He was Lucy's husband.'

'Yes. Gavin was my son.'

'Lucy never talks about him. I guess it's still very painful?' Elizabeth said.

Moira caught the young man with the crossword staring at them and sniffed. He reddened and wrote something on the paper.

'Very painful,' Moira said. 'They were everything to each other. They did everything together. I don't think we ever saw them apart. Lucy barely left the house without him. But sometimes when she was doing her sculpture Gavin would pop in to see me on his own. Don't get me wrong; I love Lucy but I treasure those times when it was just the two of us. Gavin was a wonderful companion. Always full of good advice. And funny little anecdotes about his day. And ready to give me a hand. No mother could have asked for a better son.'

She paused. Lost in her memories as smiles and sadness chased each other across her face.

And I felt nothing but guilt.

'So being cut off from Lucy is a double blow. It would be so lovely to be able to share memories with someone who loved Gavin as much as I did. And I worry about her. I know Matilda said she was better left alone. But you can be too alone. I've asked around – delicately, of course – and no one has seen anything of Lucy for months. Not even Matilda or Lucy's arty friends.'

'She does seem very alone,' Elizabeth nipped in when Moira paused for breath.

There was a tension in Elizabeth's body. Just a light

holding of muscles that revealed itself in the way her thumbs circled the tips of her index fingers below the table. Where Moira couldn't see.

'You think so too! That's terrible. I so hoped she was recovering. I should have tried harder to keep in touch. Gavin would have wanted us to look after her, you know. He would have expected us to, so I can't help feeling that I'm letting my boy down. You see, Lucy has never been very capable. Gavin lavished care on her and, believe me, she needed it. He bought the house and furnished it and organised all the alterations. He even built her a studio for her little sculpting hobby. Nothing was too much trouble if it kept her happy.'

'It must have been tough for Lucy. Losing her husband and having to earn a living all of a sudden.' Elizabeth's voice was casual, but she leant forward to hear Moira's response and I thought she was genuinely interested.

Moira put her cup down on the saucer. It clinked with the force of the movement and her expression would have made me laugh if I'd had the means to do it. Didn't Elizabeth realise how offended she'd be by any suggestion that Gavin's management of our life was anything less than perfect?

'Gavin left her well provided for. Very well provided for. In fact, Lucy is a very wealthy woman. As I said, he was a deeply responsible man. Always conscious of his role as a provider for her. Always aware that she'd struggle without him.'

The tea had diluted the smudge of lipstick on her teeth and spread it like a pink veil staining the white enamel.

'And that worries me too. I asked Ted if we could set up some kind of trust for her so we could make sure the money was used wisely. And keep Lucy safe from...' She leaned forward and whispered to Elizabeth, 'Safe from predators.'

'Predators?' Elizabeth wasn't as careful about keeping her voice down and Moira wrinkled her lips in a little moue of alarm.

'Men,' Moira muttered. 'Men after her money. I don't suppose there are any men...'

Was that what this was all about? Men?

Did Moira want to know if I'd found a boyfriend? Ha! If only she knew what my life had been like since Gavin died.

Elizabeth ducked the question with a forced smile. 'I wouldn't know.'

A couple walked slowly behind the screen at the end of our table arguing about which floor orthopaedics was on. Elizabeth and Moira sipped tea and waited for them to pass.

'I think Lucy is managing fine,' Elizabeth said. 'She's always busy with work and the shop seems to be doing well.'

'That's wonderful news. Ted and I were so worried about her borrowing all that money from her aunt to set the shop up. I wondered if we should offer to advance money from Gavin's estate, provided she'd let Ted run an eye over the figures and advise her, but when I suggested it to Matilda, she didn't think it was a good idea. In view of Lucy's mental frailty, you understand.'

I might have ignored Moira but clearly Tilly had kept in touch. I felt guilty again. Really, I should have made more of an effort. Phoned Moira. Or at least read and replied to her letters. She'd lost her only son who she'd adored. Tilly was right, she just wanted to talk to someone who she thought had loved him too.

None of it was her fault.

'Of course, she's always dabbled in making masks.' Moira patted her lips with a serviette. 'Pocket money, you know. Gavin said there was no real money in it, but Lucy liked to think she was pulling her weight. He'd have preferred her to concentrate on her sculpture but there was no persuading her. He did the accounts, of course, and, if she asked, he always assured her it was going well and that they'd be able to retire and go round the world on the proceeds. So, you'll understand why Ted and I were so concerned when she opened the shop.'

Elizabeth shrugged.

I seethed.

Moira had told the truth. Gavin did the accounts for my business, of course he did. He was good with figures, and I was an arty, creative type. And the money went into some account I never saw, and if I asked him, he'd tell me the business was doing fine, I was making lots of money, but in the tone of voice that made me think he was lying to be kind.

And he never let me see the accounts. He told me I wouldn't understand them. And when I said I'd like to try, he looked taken aback.

'Well,' he said. 'If you want.' His voice was cold. 'They're in the office. I'll bring them back next time we have a day free so I can take the time to explain them properly. But if you don't trust me...'

And of course I rushed in to assure him it wasn't that I didn't trust him. Of course I did. And it didn't matter. I merely thought I should make an effort to understand. So the next day he came back with a book on accounting and a big smile and suggested we worked through the book together, so he could explain everything to me.

We did too. A couple of times anyway. The book was dull but reasonably easy to follow. It was Gavin's explanations that confused me. So I gave up and the next evening he pulled the book out, I asked if maybe we could leave it this time. And he said, sure, and put on his 'anything I wanted was fine with him' face but I could tell I'd upset him again.

And, of course, I didn't want to do that because of his heart. So I never asked about the accounts after that.

But when Gavin died, I found them. Not in the office like he'd said but in a box under the bed in the spare room. They weren't difficult to understand and they told a different story to the one he'd told Moira. And the one he'd implied to me. Don't get me wrong, the business wasn't hugely profitable, but my mask fabrication made money and with a few minor changes it would make more, especially if I had an outlet and streamlined the range of designs I made myself, bought some masks in and concentrated on my better-paying clients.

'We did our absolute best for her after Gavin died, of course.' Moira's voice dragged me out of the swamp of the past. She sipped from her cup again. 'Ted offered her an allowance while the estate was being sorted but she refused and, of course, he dealt with all the probate. I organised the funeral and I packed up the house for her and sent everything off to be sold. We began to realise then that she was having some sort of breakdown. She told Ted to cash everything in. I mean everything: the house; all the furniture; all of Gavin's carefully chosen stocks and shares; all the jewellery he'd given her; his pen collection.'

She rummaged around in her bag and produced a handkerchief, a small one with a lace-edged corner and an embroidered initial M.

'We bought his pen collection, of course, and a few of his more personal things. I couldn't bear the thought of them going to a charity shop.'

I realised how unwittingly cruel I'd been. I should have asked Ted and Moira if there was anything of Gavin's they wanted. I swore that if I ever got out of this mess, I'd make a bigger effort with them.

Elizabeth watched Moira dab her eyes. I wondered if she was trying to reconcile Moira's picture of a wealthy and spoilt wife with the paucity and cheapness of the contents of the flat.

'She told Ted, she couldn't bear any reminders of Gavin. Nothing at all. But the thing is...'

I watched her lose the battle against discretion.

'She did take one thing from the house,' Moira whispered. 'She took a set of knives. Very expensive. Very sharp. A wedding present from a dear friend who'd wanted to give them something that would last for ever. I noticed they were missing and I can't tell you how much I panicked. Why would they be the one thing she'd take?'

'You thought she might kill herself with them?'

Elizabeth was quicker than me. I hadn't had a clue why Moira was worried. All I could think was how stupid I had been. I should have taken other things as well as the knives. To make it less obvious.

'Well, what would you think?' Moira went on. 'She was falling apart with the grief and there was a lot of unfortunate talk around the time of Gavin's death which didn't help. Poor, poor Lucy. I can't tell you how awful it was. I told Ted but he said Lucy had gone to Matilda's after the funeral and that she was being looked after. And then she moved to Greenwich and her life looked as though it was back on an even keel. But when Luke rang and told us she was in hospital... I wondered...'

'It was an accident. A car accident. I have seen the knives though. They're in the kitchen. Very nice.'

'Such a strange thing for her to take. Because she and Gavin nearly fell out over them. It was the only time I've ever seen him a little impatient with her. Lucy burnt the handle of the sharpening steel that came with the set. So stupid. She left it out on the counter top, you see, and she must have nudged it when she answered the phone because the handle rolled onto a gas burner that she was using to boil some rice and slipped underneath. Gavin was very upset and Lucy was distraught when she realised.'

I remembered it well.

Except I hadn't been boiling rice, I'd been warming milk for coffee for Moira and Ted and a couple of their old friends who were paying a courtesy call to meet the new bride. I'd learned enough by then to know that you didn't serve morning coffee with cold milk and that you prepared everything in the kitchen and took it, on a tray, through to the sitting room where Gavin would be entertaining the guests with talk about the weather and the latest goings-on in the village.

I don't recall who rang but they distracted me for long enough for the milk to boil over and, in the confusion, the sharpening steel handle rolled onto the burner. When Gavin came out to see what was happening, I'd already found the steel and was running the handle under the tap. Moira remembered him as upset but I didn't.

A look of ice-cold rage wiped his face clean of all other emotion. He seized the sharpening steel from me roughly and for one brief second I thought he was going to carry the gesture through in a big circle and smash my hand with it. But Moira bustled in and he put the steel down.

'It left a huge burn mark. Like a sort of spider's web over the whole handle. I've never seen anything like it.'

The full implication of Moira's words took a few moments to sink in. But even before it did, I knew this wasn't good news. Not good news at all. And as soon as I understood how clearly she remembered, I realised just how bad it was.

'I don't recall seeing the steel,' Elizabeth said.

She wouldn't. Because it wasn't there. It was at the back of one of the kitchen drawers as I couldn't face seeing it every day. But ready to produce if I ever needed to. Although I wished now I hadn't hidden it. I wished I'd thrown it away. I wished I'd thrown the whole set away.

Because if the police asked Moira about the burnt handle, I was in trouble. And, I thought, Tilly was too.

16

During the dark days after Gavin's funeral when I was staying with Tilly, the ones where it was a struggle to get out of bed, when anything but the most basic of conversations was beyond me. Even then I'd known the sharpening steel was a problem – whether it stayed missing or was found – but I couldn't see a solution.

Then, Luke, my solicitor, rang. The police had finished in the house. They no longer thought it was a crime scene. I could go in and get my personal things any time I wanted to. I allowed myself a glimmer of hope that they'd found nothing and the investigation was coming to an end.

'Ted asked me to let you know he'd like to go in and take Gavin's papers whenever it's convenient,' Luke told me. 'He needs to start preparing the paperwork for probate. He'll have to make an inventory of Gavin's property too and I thought you might want to remove your belongings before he did that.'

'An inventory?' I said. 'Is that necessary?'

'Ted will want everything to be done by the book. He asked me if I wanted to be present as your representative. Do you want me to?'

'God, no. I mean, I have complete trust in Ted's... er, integrity.'

And in his thoroughness. His damned, pernickety, thoroughness.

'When you say "personal things", Luke,' I asked. 'What does that mean? What about household things? Like ornaments and kitchen stuff? What can I take?'

'You can take anything you want. Just make a note and let Ted know so he can decide if it is part of Gavin's estate or not. It's only for valuation purposes and he'll put a nominal sum against all the household goods anyway.'

If only I could be sure Ted would be the sole person to look round our house. I didn't think he'd notice the missing steel. Moira might though, and she'd be longing to spend time in our house. In Gavin's house.

What could I do?

The next day, Tilly and I were in the high street of a nearby town. Tilly had dragged me there saying she wanted to get a pair of binoculars mended at a specialist shop and it would be a change of scenery for me. I wandered up and down the high street while she was inside and came across a kitchen shop. A very expensive and chic shop that sold knife sets exactly like mine. Tilly found me there staring at them and wondering if I'd found a solution to my problem.

'Would you go in and buy me that steel?' I said to Tilly and pointed to it. 'That one there. Only that one.'

It was more words at once than I'd spoken in days.

She hadn't asked any questions. Just taken the cash I'd handed her. I guessed she knew I'd said all I could. I watched her through the window as she chatted away to the assistant, admiring the steel as he held it up to the light and listening as he tapped away on his computer and spoke to her. But she came out empty-handed.

'They can't sell me the steel they have in stock because it would mean breaking up the set, but that very charming young man has organised for the manufacturers to send me one direct. It should only take a few days.' She put the cash back in my hand. 'I paid by card.'

I couldn't tell her that she'd blown it in every way. Because I needed the steel now so I could replace it before Moira went to the house and that I'd wanted an anonymous elderly lady to buy it with untraceable cash. I managed to produce a smile and thank her.

When I went to the house to pack up my workshop and collect my clothes, I took the knife set too. Maybe I should have left it. Maybe no one would have noticed the steel was missing. But I couldn't be sure.

And when the steel arrived, I burned the handle. It wasn't the same mark – not at all – but I thought no one would remember. And as the months had passed, I'd begun to think I was safe.

But now I thought the police had found the original. It was the new evidence they mentioned. It was why they wanted to see me. Now there were two steels. Both with burnt handles. And Moira knew which one was which. Would they ask her? It was very possible.

If the police looked hard enough, they'd find a trace of Tilly's purchase. The knife set was super-expensive and only sold through specialist kitchen shops. I didn't think there'd be many sales of a replacement steel to hunt through before they came across the record of Tilly buying one for me.

Tilly. Had I got Tilly into trouble? An accessory after the fact or whatever it was called? Because if Ted ever thought there was more to the police's interest in me than routine questioning, he'd leave no stone unturned in his quest for legal revenge.

17

'Tilly!' Elizabeth's voice knocked me out of my turbulent thoughts and back to the hospital coffee bar. Elizabeth had stood up. Moira had pivoted her head round so I could see where a stray, but perfectly coloured, hair had slipped from her head onto the collar of her pink jacket.

Tilly walked towards us, closely followed by the same nurse who had spoken to her earlier. Her arms were wrapped round her chest and she seemed not to notice the steady stream of people cutting across in front of her.

'What's happened, Matilda?' Moira asked. 'Didn't she wake up?'

Tilly swallowed. 'No. But we knew that she might need time. I'm probably overreacting but I think I'd hoped she might and when she didn't—' Her voice cracked and broke.

People turned to look at us and just as quickly looked away. Another mini-tragedy playing out in a space that I suspected had seen many.

Elizabeth looked at the nurse. He shook his head slightly.

Despite his thinness he didn't stoop like so many tall people did but stood shoulders wide and feet rooted in the ground.

'I'm Sean,' he said. 'I'm going to be the lead nurse looking after Lucy. And you are?'

'Her lodger, Elizabeth.'

'Well, Ms Christensen needs—'

Moira cut him off. 'And I'm Lucy's mother-in-law, Mrs Lyle. We'd like to know what's going on.'

'Ms Christensen needs to go and get some rest,' Sean continued as though Moira hadn't spoken. 'She's been here almost non-stop for forty-eight hours, talking to Lucy all the time. It's very tiring and she must have a break. We're moving Lucy to a side room where it will be quieter for her, and it will take a bit of time to get her settled.' He turned to Tilly and patted her shoulder. 'Come back tomorrow when you've had some sleep. We'll run some more tests and talk through it all again.'

Tilly looked wrung out and her clutching hands had pulled her blouse out of the skirt waistband so it hung in folds of crumpled material. 'Thank you, Sean.'

He loped off towards the lift doors, stopping to give directions to an elderly lady clutching a small child by the hand.

I could only think of my empty body and Tilly sitting by it and forcing words out of herself to try to make the connections in my brain snap together again. Tilly, who didn't chat much except when she'd seen a rare bird visiting her garden. Tilly, who belonged in the silence of the outdoors, staring into the sky, with only the cries of the birds and the rustle of little creatures in the undergrowth, rather than in a cramped, noisy and airless ward.

What had happened?

'What's happened?' Elizabeth asked. 'Can you tell us,

Tilly?' She passed her a serviette and Tilly scrubbed her face and blew her nose.

'Nothing,' she said. 'Which they warned me about. But they were a little surprised. I could tell. Something about her brain activity, or lack of it.'

She pushed the hair out of her face. Her skin was pale except where the broken veins ran in faint purple lines over her cheeks.

'I didn't really understand what they were saying. They talked about different kinds of unconsciousness... they were very kind. Explained it several times. But I can't remember it all.'

'You need sleep,' Elizabeth said. 'I'll take you back to the flat.'

No! We couldn't leave now!

Moira nodded, for once quiet.

This wasn't a disaster, I told myself. I still had time. No one had expected me to wake up immediately. But I couldn't help feeling the first fingers of fear touch my thoughts. Getting another chance to be alone with my body might be very difficult.

Outside, the day had become heavy, as though the air itself was sick of the heat and too exhausted to do anything but flop onto the ground. The three of us stood on the steps in silence.

Moira broke it first. 'Will you call me and let me know what's happening, Matilda?'

'Of course.'

'Let me know if there's the slightest change. It's too dreadful. Poor Lucy. Both Ted and I will be praying for her. When you get the results of the tests, I'll come back or pop by the flat and explain them to you. Whatever is easiest. And you must call me if there's anything we can do. Anything at all.'

'I'm sure I'll be fine. I just need some sleep.'

'You mustn't think twice about asking. I know how hard it can be for people without any medical training to understand these things.' She took a rose-coloured scarf out of her bag, wrapped it round her hair and snapped her bag shut.

We watched her go until her pink jacket disappeared round the corner.

'She's upset,' Tilly said. 'I can tell. But having her around won't help Lucy.'

'She said Lucy couldn't bear anything that reminded her of Gavin.'

'She is right.'

'And that she'd had a breakdown because of her grief.'

'Did she say that?' Tilly sighed. 'I don't think it's true. Lucy is suffering but I don't think it's grief. I think she tried to leave Gavin the night he died. And that brought on a heart attack and she blames herself. He had a heart problem that meant he had to be careful. Long QT syndrome. Have you heard of it?'

'I think so. There was a footballer died recently from it, wasn't there?'

'Yes. Your heart starts to beat incorrectly in response to exercise or stress. Most people don't know they've got it, but Gavin did. It runs in the family. On Ted's side. So Gavin had pills for it. Beta blockers. And he knew he needed to be careful. Lucy knew he needed to be careful. Knew he mustn't get too stressed. It upset her too much to talk about his death. And I didn't like to force her.' She put her hand to her forehead and rubbed it leaving a sharp, red mark that contrasted with her tired pallor. 'Despite what Moira thinks, I wasn't sure it was ever a very happy marriage.'

18

I was on a train when I first realised I had to get out of my marriage. In between Carshalton and Hackbridge, to be precise. Going up to London.

I'd escaped. Just for the day. To see a Spanish sculptor I'd long admired, Alfredo Aznar, talking about his work at the Tate Modern. I was excited, willing the train to go faster, begrudging every stop at every station. Congratulating myself on how clever I'd been.

Gavin thought I had a gynaecologist's appointment so he wouldn't ring me from work. Medical appointments were one of the few things I went to alone. To be safe I had actually made an appointment but cancelled it that morning, saying I'd been struck down by a stomach bug. And that's what I'd tell Gavin when he got home. In case he checked up.

I'd lied through my teeth because I couldn't bear going with him.

When we were first married, we went up to London and caught up with my old friends, saw exhibitions and visited galleries, but it was difficult. Gavin always tried too hard. He read up on the exhibitions beforehand and made comments all the way round instead of just letting it speak to him. And he'd go on and on to my friends about how he wasn't the least bit arty or creative, so they'd have to forgive him if he didn't understand their conversations.

It's hard to discuss anything in front of someone who says that.

So our visits tailed off. I tried to see my friends on my own a couple of times, but it upset Gavin. He said he knew they despised him because he was different but he couldn't bear it if I felt the same way. I promised him it wasn't like that although part of me knew there was an element of truth. My friends didn't despise him but they didn't find him easy either.

The last time I went to visit a friend on my own, Gavin wasn't in the house when I got back. He'd left a note saying he couldn't stand being home on his own and he'd gone out. He didn't come back until the morning.

'Where were you?' I asked. After a night of no sleep, with visions of him dead from a heart attack, my voice was thin with exhaustion.

'At my parents'.'

'I was worried.'

'Well, now you know what it's like.'

Some part of me knew this wasn't fair. Gavin had known where I was. He always knew where I was. And I'd come home on time. But I didn't have the energy to argue.

He mistook my silence for lack of understanding.

'I said, now you know what it's like.' He yelled the words at me this time.

And he stormed out and slammed the door after him

with such force that the handle fell off. He came back and picked it up.

'Now look what you've made me do.'

I knew this was ridiculous but I couldn't find the words to calm him as he walked around the room and told me how much I'd hurt him. He was beside himself with misery and after a while, I began to feel dreadful. How could I have been so thoughtless? He did so much for me. Surely letting him come with me was the least I could do. After all, it wasn't as though I couldn't see my friends. He was always happy to go with me even if they did make him feel inadequate. And anyway it was normal, wasn't it, for married people to do things together? They shared their life in every way. Gavin didn't go off with his friends and leave me alone. And on and on, until I no longer knew what were my thoughts and what were Gavin's words as they slowly aligned.

After a year of marriage, I rarely saw my friends.

After two I'd completely lost touch with all but the closest.

And in the third year, sitting on the train, stopped at Carshalton station, I couldn't remember the last time I'd seen any of them, nor the last time I'd been out for a trip alone. It was dreadful to feel so happy to be out of the house by myself, but I did. It wasn't Gavin's fault though. He couldn't help it. He didn't understand art and he didn't understand my friends. He was a wonderful man in every other way.

'Tickets, please.' An inspector stood by my seat, holding out his hands.

'Sorry,' I said. 'I was miles and miles away.'

'I could tell. Up to London for the day, are you?'

'Yes. That's right.'

'Hope you're going somewhere nice.'

'I am. Actually, I am. A really fascinating exhibition. On

sculpture. It's a bit of a treat for me, in fact.'

'Nice to see a smiling face, for a change.'

He handed me my ticket back and went on down the train. I watched him go, aware that I still had a smile on my face. I traced it with my fingers. Honestly, I couldn't remember the last time I'd felt so relaxed. Nor, I realised, the last time I'd had a conversation without being conscious of Gavin standing by my side and listening to every word I said.

He wouldn't have liked you chatting away like that to the inspector.

I didn't know where the thought came from. Surely it wasn't true. Of course it wasn't true.

My eyes wandered over the platform. Sandwiched between a day-glo yellow advertisement for a local auction and one, with a shocking face of some poor, battered wife, asking for funds for a local refuge, I saw a poster advertising the exhibition and talk I was going to, with a picture of a recent sculpture Aznar had done of his daughter. It was a glorious piece. My fingers longed to touch it and feel the shapes he'd made. Maybe if I lingered after the talk, introduced myself, maybe he'd let me have a closer look? I'd done the right thing coming alone. I could never have talked to Aznar afterwards if Gavin had been there. I'd done the right thing escaping him for the day.

Escaping him.

The rattle of the train picked up the rhythm of the words. *Escaping him. Escaping Gavin.* All I could think about was how much I wanted to escape and the word shocked me. Did I really feel trapped?

I realised I'd started to feel uneasy the moment we were married and back in the UK. The moment he gave me the keys to the house we would live in and told me he'd bought it as a surprise. I thought he was joking at first, but no. He told me he wanted me to be free to do my Art (with a capital A) and he would deal with all the boring things.

So, he'd bought the house. In a Surrey village, near his parents. And when I muttered something – half-heartedly in the face of his overbearing happiness – about thinking we'd live in London, to be near galleries and exhibitions and my friends, he looked hurt and asked me if I realised how good the train service was. How I could be in London in under an hour. After all, I wouldn't want to go up every day, whereas his work was in Surrey. I probably hadn't thought of that, had I? It would be tiring for him to commute. But he was prepared to do it. For me. Of course he was. I mustn't think he wasn't.

So, we stayed in Surrey. It wasn't the same. It could never be the same. But I thought I could cope, and I couldn't bear the hurt on his face. I couldn't bear the thought of all the disruption and grief it would cause if I asked him to sell it. And, by then, Moira had told me all about his heart and how he had to avoid being stressed.

The house had a massive garage that he planned to convert into my studio. That was a mistake, too. I should have insisted on renting a space in London and going up to it every day, but Gavin threw himself into the design, consulting me on every detail, telling the builders it had to be perfect, fretting over the plans. So that when it was finished I was stuck with it.

Stuck with having to show Gavin what I'd been up to every evening when he came home and each weekend when he popped in to my workshop every hour or so. He never understood that sometimes I was in the middle of something. I tried to explain that it wasn't always easy for me to stop and chat, that sometimes I was following an unconscious flow of something; he said I should ignore him. Coming home from the office and seeing what I'd been up to or watching me work was the highlight of his day. Surely I didn't want to spoil that for him?

I didn't. Of course, I didn't. I knew how much pleasure it gave him. He told me all the time.

Except even his presence was distracting. And he couldn't keep quiet. He couldn't stop himself asking questions. Questions I couldn't answer because when you're making something with your hands, words don't come into it.

And he never knocked before he came in. Why should he? It was his house, his workshop built with his money... his wife. So I was always on edge waiting for him to appear.

Anything I said sounded like the whining of a spoilt child because, let's face it, I had what every artist dreamed of – the time and freedom to sculpt without having to make money. Except I couldn't. My ideas dried up. The heads I forced myself to produce were dull and lifeless. They had nothing to say. *I* had nothing to say.

So, I did less and less. And I started the mask business. Partly for something to do. Partly because it was fun. Partly because I had no money.

Except Gavin's.

He was generous. Lavishing me with presents. Always telling me to get whatever I needed. To buy myself nice things. Except Gavin's idea of what was needed and what was nice wasn't the same as mine, and as he balanced the joint bank account every month and asked me what each amount was for – just so he could categorise it, you understand – and, well, he couldn't help his face. I saw when he didn't like what I'd bought, and my life was all about doing what Gavin liked by then. Because he deserved it. And in case I upset him, because of his heart. I must never upset him.

I thought if I had my own money, I could escape the questioning. I could have a bit of privacy, carve out a space in my world that was only mine.

Of course it didn't work out like that.

I sat on that train and thought how tired I was. How tired I was of everything Gavin did. How much I hated everything Gavin did. How I hated everything he said at the awful dinner parties we were always being invited to. When Gavin would describe what I was working on and show them pictures I didn't know he'd taken. He never let me get a word in as he told everybody how wonderful I was and how exciting my work was, but with a slight look of worry on his face and a deprecating 'not that I know anything about it' note in his voice.

I could tell his friends didn't think much of my work anyway. They never mentioned it and swerved the conversation away if I touched on anything related to it. I asked Gavin but he assured me that wasn't the case.

'Maybe,' he said, 'they're concerned you might start talking about things they don't understand. All that creative stuff you and your friends go on about. Not everyone finds it as fascinating as you do. My darling.'

After that I made sure I never said a word about my work or about anything creative but no matter how hard I tried to get to know people and make friends, none of my overtures ever led anywhere. And the only time I ever saw people was when we were both invited to dinner or some other social event. I guessed they put up with me for Gavin's sake.

So on that train to London, staring out of the window at the speed-and-tear-blurred suburbs going by, I thought about escaping my marriage. Even though it was entirely my fault that it wasn't working. Even though Gavin was the perfect husband: love, patience and understanding personified. Even

though I was an ungrateful scrounger. Somewhere I knew
that if I was to survive, I had to leave my adoring husband.

But how?

That was the question.

I tore a piece of paper out of the notebook Gavin had
given me a few days ago. It was a beautiful thing with a thick
leather spine binding and marbled paper cover.

'It's gorgeous,' I'd said to him. 'I'll have to find something
special to use it for.'

'That's not what it's meant for. We need to start getting a
bit more organised. Mum said there was no milk when she
came over to make you lunch the other day.'

I bit my lip and fingered the thick paper pages of the
book. I hated Moira coming over to make me lunch. She'd
started doing it when Gavin had told her that I didn't eat
properly if he wasn't there. *Surprise*, she'd trill, as she opened
the front door. *I've come to cook you a proper meal. We can't
have you wasting away. Just pretend I'm not here.*

As if.

'So,' Gavin continued, 'I thought if you had a fixed place
to make notes and lists, we could look in it every evening and
decide who was going to do what. It's a great idea, isn't it?'

'Fantastic,' I said.

Well, there was no time like the present. I found a stubby
pencil in my bag and started making a list of things I'd need
to do to get away from Gavin because I'd never succeed
without planning and organisation. Gavin was absolutely
right. It was the key to achieving anything.

Leaving G, I wrote. *Things to do.*

And I wrote a list.

And then I sat there and knew I could do everything on
the list but I wasn't sure if I could actually leave. For some
reason the thought of it terrified me.

19

The shop was busy when we arrived back from the hospital. A group of children, overseen by a parent distracted by the messages she was receiving on her phone, laughed as they tried on the cheap witch, werewolf and vampire masks I'd bought in for Hallowe'en. A couple of tourists fingered the Venetian masks and a man inspected the photos on the back wall. They were shots of some of the more outrageous film work I'd done, along with blow-ups of a couple of articles about me in the local press and one from a German art magazine running a series on young sculptors.

Amy took one look at Tilly and asked Elizabeth to keep an eye on the shop while she helped Tilly up to the flat.

'Sure,' Elizabeth said. 'No problem.'

I noticed it all automatically because my mind was preoccupied with wondering when Elizabeth would return to the hospital. Or if she would...

Maybe she wouldn't. She was only my lodger after all. Tonight, I thought, tonight I'd test my theory that I was in control when she slept. Maybe I could get us there then. It was impossible while she was awake. I was sure of that now.

The children and the tourists grew bored and left, and Elizabeth started poking through the shelves below the till. Hunting for something. Sending up little explosions of dust as she rifled through the piles of paperwork. Amy had, I guessed, been too busy to clean.

Only the man looking at the photos remained in the shop. Elizabeth wandered through to the stockroom, leaving the door between open, and picked up a cloth. I thought she was going to clean the shelves, but she only wiped the dust off her fingers and her jacket, gazing round at the shelves and drawers, neat and ordered, everything in a box or bag. She opened a couple of drawers and peeked in. Greek lace and flowered lace.

The Italian names sprang straight into my mind as Elizabeth fingered them gently.

Punto Gotica and *Punto tagliato a fogliami.*

Our first job, Pietro told us when we arrived in Venice in early March, was to tidy the atelier. Someone, probably Elodie, snorted at this. Definitely Elodie, because she followed it up with a mutter in swift French. None of us understood a word, but we all knew she was complaining. We'd paid a lot of money to be here, and tidying wasn't what we wanted to do. But Pietro had his reasons. Every year the new apprentices started in March when the Carnival had finished. The staff were on holiday, and the atelier was empty but devastated from the chaos of the final weeks leading up to it. It was as though an explosion had scattered everything, not only over every surface and corner of the stockroom but throughout the whole atelier.

Over the next couple of weeks, we slowly reduced the gaudy mountains of frippery into drawers and cupboards and counted and labelled and became familiar with the materials we would use to make masks. Jonty and I did the bulk of it, while Elodie and David sneaked off to explore Venice.

English was the lingua franca at Ca'Maschera and I learned only a little Italian during my year in Venice – enough to order what I wanted in bars and cafés, a few words to rebuff the street pedlars – but a huge vocabulary of terms for the adorning of masks. Even now when I flick through a haberdashery catalogue, the Italian names for the different types of lace come back to me.

The man in the shop called through to Elizabeth and interrupted my thoughts. She shut the drawers of sequins and paillettes she'd been examining and went back out.

'Excuse me, but are the photos for sale?'

Elizabeth's eyes met his. His short hair confused me, but his voice, with its distinctive Danish lilt, offered a shock of recognition.

It was Jonty.

Unless my memories of Venice were playing tricks with what I saw through Elizabeth's eyes.

Elizabeth glanced at the photos and then back to him. It *was* Jonty. Now he was in profile, facing the photos, his nose and jutting eyebrows were unmistakable.

'I don't know,' Elizabeth replied. 'I don't think they're for sale. Let me check.'

She headed to the door between the shop and the staircase to the flat.

'Is she around, then? Lucy?'

Elizabeth turned. His hands were thrust into the pockets of his beige cloth jacket. It had seen better days. As had his jeans, torn on one knee but not in a way that was fashionable. Jonty never cared about his appearance and, the shorter haircut notwithstanding, it didn't look as though he'd changed. He smiled at Elizabeth as though aware that she was sizing him up. What was he doing here? After all this time? And how had he known where to find me?

'You know her then?'

'Yes. That is, I used to. But I live in Denmark, so we haven't seen each other for a while. For quite a while.'

He was right. It had been over three years.

The second-to-last time I'd seen him was at my wedding.

Gavin and I got married the day my year at Ca'Maschera finished. In Venice at the Municipio, presided over by the fat mayor with his tricolour sash, who kissed us both afterwards with wet smacks on each cheek. I don't think Gavin liked it much. In fact, I don't think he liked anything about the ceremony at all. At the time I thought he was doing it because it was romantic and much easier for me with my lack of family, but now I think he knew he'd have trouble getting me to the altar once I got back to England.

Jonty didn't make the ceremony. David and Elodie had to play the roles of witnesses, guests, bridesmaid and best man, but afterwards, as we walked down the steps outside, husband and wife, Gavin clutching my hand so hard that the slightly too-big ring dug into my finger while my ribs ached in the too-tight dress he'd bought, Jonty was waiting for us. He was drunk. Very drunk. So drunk he fell into the water as they pushed the gondola that was taking Gavin and me to the Gritti Palace for our one-night honeymoon.

And now he was here.

Facing me.

Although he didn't know it.

'I knew Lucy in Venice,' he said to Elizabeth. 'I thought I'd look her up while I was in London.'

Ah, but that was a different Lucy and she has long gone.

The one who lives here is a poor and feeble thing compared to her.

'She's in hospital,' Elizabeth said. 'A car accident. Dreadful.'

Jonty stilled for a few seconds, then listened to Elizabeth explaining without interrupting. God, it was so familiar. Where someone else might have rushed in mouthing empty words, Jonty always waited. The hollows under his slanting cheekbones deepened as she told him I was in a coma, that so far I hadn't woken up, that they were concerned I might have a serious brain injury. His face took on its familiar dark look.

In the old days I'd have shoved an elbow in his ribs and told him to lighten up. Like I did when his Nordic gloom became too heavy for the rest of us. And most of the time his face would crack into a smile and he'd complain that I was too, too frivolous but he'd relax and laugh and knock back small glasses of the foul-tasting grappa made by the bar owner's *nonna* and kept under the counter out of sight of the local police. The dynamic between us only failed when my spark of fun had been smothered and I was the one who needed elbowing out of despondency, which Jonty couldn't do.

'Is she going to be all right?'

And that I remembered, too. The hesitation on the double L of *all*. As though it weighed too much to free his tongue without an effort.

'We don't know. Her aunt is here. I'll get her if you like.'

Elizabeth was being very helpful, and a nasty suspicion that she found Jonty attractive darted into my mind.

'No. Please don't disturb her.'

There was an awkward pause. Neither of them made the first move to end the conversation, and an even nastier suspicion took shape. He found her attractive, too. Of course he did. What man wouldn't? But I really couldn't, I really couldn't bear to watch while they circled round each other.

He picked up one of the Venetian masks, a glorious confection in gold and blue with a cascade of peacock feathers shooting out of its top.

'Fantastic, isn't it?' Elizabeth strolled over to stand close by him.

'Indeed.'

Frippery, he'd have called it in the old days. A concoction for the tourist market. Somewhere in the years since I'd seen him, he'd learned tact.

'Are you in London long?' Elizabeth asked.

'I don't know yet.'

She took the mask out of his hands and held it up to her face, tilting her head coquettishly. She was taller than I was and her eyes were on a level with his. It was a strange feeling staring directly into them and for a moment I wondered if the mask concealing Elizabeth's face would somehow cancel her out and reveal me hiding inside. Elizabeth laughed and put the mask down. The moment passed.

'Maybe I could visit her?'

'Family only. Sorry. But, hey, come back later or tomorrow, and I'll update you.'

'Please. If you could give me your phone number. I will call. If that's OK?'

'Sure.'

A faint smell of pine cologne was all that remained of him when Amy shoved open the connecting door with her shoulder, her hands grasping the rubbish sacks from the kitchen and bathroom. 'Did he buy anything?'

'No. But he liked the photos.'

'They're not for sale. Bin day tomorrow. I think Tilly's asleep.'

I waited for Elizabeth to explain that Jonty was an old friend of mine, but she merely said that she would have brought the rubbish down if Amy had asked and tiptoed up the stairs to the flat. She hovered at the bottom of the steps leading up to my bedroom for a few seconds. If Tilly was asleep, it was a restless sleep. The bed creaked the floorboards as she tossed and turned. Elizabeth sighed and slipped into her bedroom and picked up her phone.

My thoughts were full of Jonty and his strange reappearance so I looked at the screen of the phone without paying too much attention at first. Elizabeth was flicking through her bank account. Or, at least, I thought it was hers until I noticed the name at the top. *Ms Sophie Leonard.* The bank account belonged to a Ms Sophie Leonard and it was empty. The balance was zero. Before I could look any closer, Elizabeth disconnected abruptly. Something had disturbed her. She grabbed her phone, tapped in a number, and rammed it against her ear. It rang. Someone answered it. A man. A light whispery voice.

'Not now,' he said. 'I'll call you when I can.'

She threw the phone onto the bed and paced up and down the room. I felt her brain race. Vessels dilated to carry oxygen to feed the teeming sparks tearing around her head.

My own thoughts were confused. Elizabeth had been looking at someone else's bank account!

A nasty doubt dug into my head. I remembered going upstairs to fetch the cash hidden in my wardrobe, when I'd fingered all my clothes and checked my bank balance. Was I so sure I'd been in control then? Or might it have been Elizabeth?

No. It had been me. Elizabeth wouldn't have known the codes and passwords for my computer and my accounts, even if she'd poked around the flat in my absence. The only place they were written down was in a locked drawer in the workshop.

Still, there was something very odd going on. She hadn't called her office and apart from the strange phone call she'd just made she hadn't spoken to anyone, or at least not while I was awake. No friends. No family. You'd have thought someone would have phoned to find out how she was. Even I had Tilly and, I supposed, Moira looking out for me.

I thought back over the weeks since she moved in and realised I'd learnt very little about her other than what she told me when we first met.

I'd put an advert in the local online forum. *Lodger wanted.* Although I didn't. I desperately didn't want one. I wanted to be on my own. To burrow down into the flat and hide. But I'd always known I'd need one while the business was getting established.

Elizabeth replied straight away and suggested we meet for a coffee. I was quiet, contained, polite and unsure. She was quiet, contained, polite and unsure, too. And I was drawn to her because of it. We drank our coffee and she told me about herself. Good job in insurance. Just been moved to London from somewhere up north. Not sure how long for. She didn't want anywhere too permanent. It was all ideal.

She was currently living with three younger girls in a shared house. All she could find at such short notice. They were nice but... well, noisy and a bit intrusive. She liked them, but she wasn't the sort who enjoyed gossiping about her life and, really, she was tired of knowing everything about their work colleagues and who fancied whom and so on. So, she'd like a change. Preferably with fewer people. She worked long hours and had an elderly aunt with Alzheimer's whom she often visited in the evenings, which was tiring. I mustn't think she was being unsociable if she wanted to be quiet while she was at home. If I was happy for her to move in, that is. But I should take my time. It was a big decision. Although she didn't think she'd be able to wait very long. But there were lots of people out there looking for rooms to rent, so I wouldn't have any trouble finding someone.

Of course, I didn't wait. She was keen. I could tell that. Trying not to be over-eager. So, unable to believe my luck that I'd found someone so close to a perfect lodger with my first try, I asked her to move in. She was so perfect I didn't ask for references. I didn't even check she was who she said she was.

And, of course, she wasn't. Neither of us was. Neither of us was quiet, contained, polite and unsure in reality. For me it was a shell created by years of living with Gavin. For Elizabeth it was a veneer too, painted on, I realised now, in response to what she saw I wanted.

I'd felt some unease after she moved in. Somehow, I hadn't noticed how beautiful she was at our first meeting, and she never mentioned the elderly aunt with Alzheimer's again, but I accepted what she'd told me as the truth. I didn't question her or check up on her. I took it all at face value, believed the story of her life that she told me. You'd think I would have learned by now not to believe the stories people weave about themselves.

20

I tried to stay awake, but Elizabeth was tired and a wave of drowsiness, slowing her heart rate and lightening her breathing, engulfed us as soon as she put her head on the pillow and I drifted away too.

I am on a train with the countryside flashing past. My eyes flick back and forth as the spire of a church or herd of cows catches and holds their gaze for a fraction of a second. Mascara stiffens my eyelashes and long legs stretch out under the table of the train. The letters inked on my knuckles spell Carly, although I am a teenager now. Two women sit behind me, talking about their sister-in-law and the amount of money she spends on her kids. I smile, but it isn't a nice smile.

The green spaces between villages and towns grow smaller and smaller, and then melt away to become a continuous vista of terraced houses and shopping centres. Roads fill with cars and buses. The train is entering the outskirts of a city. London. The engine whines, the train slows, and the railway lines multiply at the approach to Euston. I reach into my bag and take out my make-up, check my eyeliner in the mirror and wipe away a smudge at the corner of one eye, then I pull the mirror back to examine my whole face.

A sudden noise of brakes squealing from the road disturbed Elizabeth. Her legs kicked. Her arms threshed and she sat up and opened her eyes. Carly's face disappeared. Like a reflection on a bubble that burst. But not before I'd recognised it.

Carly's face was Elizabeth's face. The girl on the train was Elizabeth. Carly was Elizabeth as a child and now a teenager. Unmistakably Elizabeth. Blonde hair framing a face whose beauty even the coarse dark eyeliner round her eyes and the loose flakes of skin on her bitten lips couldn't hide. A younger Elizabeth. Much younger. Mid-teens, I thought. But the face of the woman she would become was present in the sharpness of the cheekbones and the delicate hollows beneath them.

Elizabeth inhaled, deep breaths. She drank from the water at the side of her bed and made herself continue with the slow breaths, putting her hands to her mouth to feel the air go in and out.

So Carly was a dream that Elizabeth and I had shared. A dream with her younger self taking centre stage. Or was it? Strange things happen in dreams. You shift from one place to another in the blink of an eye. You hunt for things you cannot find, driven by a need that never seems clear when you wake up. No, not a dream. A memory. One of Elizabeth's memories.

Carly. Elizabeth. Who exactly was this woman I'd invited into my home? Who exactly was this woman whose body I floated in?

She'd had a rough childhood. Deprived and neglected. Who'd have thought all that lay beneath her charming and confident exterior? She'd made good, although I thought a past like hers left traces deep in your bones, in the DNA of your character. Maybe it was this that prodded her strange actions into life. Maybe it was this that made her steal...

She was calmer now. Her legs heavier. She lay back down and closed her eyes. She was going back to sleep. My mind wanted to follow, but this time I resisted. I had to stay awake. I disconnected from her body bit by bit and created a little space inside her head where her slowing heartbeat and the languor of her blood couldn't touch me. I needed to be patient, wait an hour or so to give her time to reach the most profound sleep before I tried to control her body.

And as she slipped away, I kept hold of the little spark that was my own self and let it float freely. At first there was nothing but dark. I saw nothing, heard nothing, felt nothing. It was a strange sensation, like floating through space must feel, a black void with nothing but the whispers of ice-cold interstellar winds carrying me along.

And then I felt something. Little nudges at first. Elizabeth's memories floating around me. Just a few. I waited. Stayed very still. More and more appeared. Clustering around me, pressing up against me. I reached out and touched them. They opened and showed me the scenes of Carly's childhood: her near-empty but tidy bedroom and the squalor in the rest of the house; the endless quarrels between Carly and her mum; the tiredness overwhelming her as she sat in a warm classroom at school and couldn't, but couldn't keep her eyes open. I searched until I found Carly on the train, the memory I'd been floating in before Elizabeth and I woke up.

· · ·

Carly, with blonde hair pulled back into a tight ponytail and thick make-up, telling the world to keep its distance. She passes the mirror round her head with practised gestures and tugs at any loose strands. There are no gaps. No hair comes away in her hands. For now. She smiles.

The train pulls into Euston. She drags her bag from the rack and slings it over one shoulder, marches off the train and up the steep slope onto the station forecourt. She stalks past the queue of elderly day-trippers waiting to hand over their tickets. Carly doesn't wait. She pushes through the patient line, chucks hers at the guard and strides off. A few murmurs from the queue. A grump from the ticket collector but no one stops her.

Once in the forecourt though, she hesitates, lost in the waves of people going places, parting round the others waiting for their train to appear on the overhead boards. She finds a wall and leans against it, dropping her bag to the ground. An ache behind her eyes meaning tears are not far away. Tears and tiredness. She's left home. Run away. Something has finally pushed her over the edge, and she's made the grand gesture. Packed up her meagre belongings. Taken the train to London. Telling herself she'll get a new life. A better life. Only it doesn't seem so easy now that she is here. She's got to London, but she doesn't know where to go now.

So she waits, anonymous in the shifting crowds. She watches people and eats an apple. Time passes. New trains arrive and leave, but nothing changes. After a while, I notice the man at the edges of her vision. The only person neither going anywhere nor staring at the boards. Carly's gaze rests on him for a few seconds. He's good-looking in a swaggering sort of way. She likes that. I don't, and I don't like the way he surveys the outskirts of the crowds, finding the youngsters like Carly hanging around. He takes his time, eyeing them from *afar and circling closer the longer they remain. Sometimes the person they're waiting for appears and they peel off together. I see him approach a girl who's been hanging around for half an hour, nibbling the skin on the end of her forefinger and then plunging her hand into her pocket. Her eyes darting between the crowd and the exits. He saunters up to her and says something. Her head leans towards him, and for a moment they almost touch but she breaks away, grabs her rucksack, and pushes through the crowd towards the escalators going down to the Tube.*

Then he focuses on Carly, and he circles round her. She can't help but notice and she laughs. He ambles over and leans against the wall next to her.

'Piece of gum?' he says and offers her one end of an open packet. 'You can't smoke in here, and I'm desperate for a fag.'

She looks at him properly for the first time, but she doesn't notice the calculating expression, the looseness of his mouth, and the faint aura of grubbiness: the smell of clothes not washed often enough and the dirt round his bitten nails. She sees the cocky allure and the confident moves.

'Ta,' she says and takes a piece of gum.

They chew for a while, leaning back against the wall and watching the train times and destinations flicker over the black boards. It's a companionable silence and she relaxes. He asks her where she's from.

'The sticks,' she says. 'Somewhere I'm never going back to.'

'Trying your luck in the big smoke, then?'

'Sort of.'

'Like me. You could be me five years ago.'

'For real?'

'Sure,' he says. 'Things were pretty crap at home. Decided

to cut and run. Came here. Best thing I ever did. I'm Joe, by the way.'

'Carly.'

'Pleased to meet you, Carly.' He takes her hand and sweeps an extravagant bow. She giggles.

'You waiting for someone?'

She hesitates. Some fleeting suspicion tells her to be careful. To say that, yes, she is waiting for someone and to move away. Go anywhere. Disappear into the labyrinths of the Tube whose escalators rattle and whirr behind her but despite everything, she wants to believe this new adventure is going to turn out well and she's done the right thing by running away.

'Not really,' she says.

'Got somewhere to stay?'

He's pushed her too far now and she lies.

'Friends,' she says. 'They said I can sleep on their sofa. For a while, you know. Just waiting for them to get in, like.'

He nods. They chat more. About bands they like. He tells her about gigs she should go to. Good clubs. Places where you can pick up work. I almost begin to think he means well. He cracks jokes about the people around them. She laughs. He buys her a coffee. And a sandwich. She thanks him.

And then he makes as though to go. To leave her. He must get going, he says. Spent far too much time chatting to her, but it's not every day you meet a kindred spirit.

She doesn't want him to go. Of course she doesn't. Because then she'll be back at square one. Just arrived. Alone. Friendless. Wondering what to do next.

He watches all that pass over her face.

'Look,' he says. 'I share a house not far from here. Come back if you like? Wait for your friends there.'

He holds out a hand. She takes it, and I feel him grasp it.

Tight. Too tight. Carly holds back for a second and then stumbles after him as he strides towards the exit.

A figure runs up to us, stretches his arms out and barges into Joe, who staggers a few steps, letting go of Carly's hand. She stares. A young lad, not much older than Carly, stands beside them. Plumpish. Spectacles. Hair flopping into his eyes. The effort has made him slightly breathless and he wheezes.

'Get out,' he says to Joe. 'The police are over there. I'll call them. They know you, don't they?'

The people around us turn, and we become a little pool of quiet amidst the relentless anonymous bustle. Under their gaze Joe moves away. Floppy-hair boy watches him leave, legs apart and hands on hips. Then hitches his bagging trousers up. He is a most unlikely rescuer. Geeky. Halfway between boy and man. With the bravado of a bantam cockerel. The sort more likely to be picked on than to see someone off.

He looks at the small crowd. 'That's all, folks,' he says. 'Show over.' They move off or turn away to stare at the train information boards. We slip back into anonymity.

'He's bad news, you know,' the boy says to Carly. 'Hangs around the station picking off arrivals. Kids like you. With nowhere to go. You OK?' His words disappear into wheezing. He frowns and swears, fumbles around in his pocket, and pulls out an inhaler.

A prickling round Carly's eyes that means she's close to tears. A tough girl but not tough enough, learning that running away doesn't mean your problems stay behind you.

'I'm OK,' she says.

He sucks on the inhaler until his wheezing stops.

'Don't hang around at the station. He's not the only one.' He hands her a card. 'Go here. It's a hostel. I volunteer for them. That's why I'm here. We keep an eye out for new arrivals. *They'll take you in for a few nights, while you get yourself sorted.'*

She looks at the card and back at him.

'Where is this?' She takes a deep breath and continues. *'I don't know London, really.'*

He gives her a shy smile. *'I'll take you. If you want me to.'*

She nods.

'I'm Reuben, by the way.'

She gives him a long, hard look. *'I'm Sophie.'*

21

I woke. Elizabeth was examining herself in the full-length
mirror in the hall, patting the black wig she wore and
slumping her shoulders forward until her posture made her
seem older and less confident.

It was morning. I'd fallen asleep while moving among
Elizabeth's memories. I'd missed my chance to see if I could
control Elizabeth's body while she slept. In fact, all I'd
achieved was to make myself so tired I'd overslept. The last
thing I remembered was the moment Carly became Sophie.

Sophie whose bank account Elizabeth had been looking
at. Carly and Sophie. They were both Elizabeth. When had
Sophie become Elizabeth? There'd be a memory of it somewhere. An important moment still intact in Elizabeth's mind.
I wondered if I could search through her memories while she
was awake. Probably not. Everything in her head felt fenced
off now.

Her wig and her choice of outfit today surprised me; a
navy-blue raincoat and a muted tartan scarf with a large
cloth handbag. All of them had seen better days. They were

clean, but the raincoat's elbows and cuffs had lost their gleam. It wasn't the sort of thing I imagined Elizabeth wearing to work although I guessed that must be where we were going. Not that I often saw her going to work. Her hours were flexible and she normally left the house before I got up or after I'd started work in the shop.

Tilly's coat hung on a hook. She must still be asleep upstairs.

Elizabeth left the flat and slipped into the stream of commuters on the high street but caught a bus that meandered through the districts of south-east London rather than the railway to Canary Wharf. We got off in a high street somewhere, full of smallish shops, and walked to a doorway that led up to offices above the shops. A brass plaque showed the name Grand & Brown Solicitors LLP with a bell below that Elizabeth pressed. A crackle and then the door clicked. Elizabeth pushed it open, kicked the pile of flyers advertising special offers on takeaway pizzas and beauty treatments out of the way and walked sedately up the stairs.

What were we doing here?

She knocked on a door with a sign saying Reception and went in. The woman at the desk, mid-fifties in a blouse with a floppy bow and a sparkly brooch, looked up from her computer and peered over the top of her spectacles.

'Can I help you?' Her smile was kind and grew kinder as Elizabeth hesitated.

'I really hope so.' Elizabeth's voice was lighter, more uncertain than normal, and she clasped her hands in front of her letting her bag bang awkwardly against her knees. She gave a little laugh. 'I'm buying a flat, you see, and I need a solicitor.'

The woman laid her glasses on the table, massaged the bridge of her nose, and gestured to her to sit.

'Well, you've come to the right place,' she said. 'People normally ring us first, but now you're here we can discuss it.'

'Would you? You see, the estate agents just called me to tell me my offer has been accepted and they want to know who my solicitors are, and five minutes later I saw the plaque on your door. It seemed like it was meant to be. I've never bought a flat before. Or a house. Or anything like this. So, you'll need to tell me exactly what to do. I haven't a clue. I'm sorry. I must sound very inefficient. I'm quite excited.'

She pulled the chair out, sat down, and gazed at the woman who was maybe older than I'd thought but winning the battle with her careful hair-do and make-up.

'So, tell me, what do I do now, and how long will it all take? Will you be the person doing it? I don't even know your name. Are you Grand or Brown?'

Elizabeth didn't sound a bit like she normally did but her gushing enthusiasm made the woman laugh.

'Neither,' she said. 'I'm their assistant, Pamela Harkins. You'll be mainly dealing with me on a day-to-day basis although Mrs Brown will do the actual conveyancing.' She pulled a notepad towards her with fingers whose ends were shiny with clear nail varnish, put her glasses back on and rearranged the stiff curls of her hair over her ears. 'Let me take a few details.'

Elizabeth had never mentioned to me she was buying a flat, and she certainly hadn't just had a call from any estate agents.

'So, your name is?'

'Susan Elias.'

For a moment I thought I hadn't heard correctly, but then Elizabeth spelled the surname out without a pause. No nervousness tensed her muscles or made them twitch. She was lying, but with practised ease.

'Address?'

The address Elizabeth gave was in Dulwich. I recognised the postcode.

'Email and telephone.'

'Shall I write it down?'

'Please.'

As Pamela held a notepad out to her, Elizabeth retrieved a spectacles case from her bag and put the glasses on, tidying the hair of her wig with a similar gesture to Pamela. I looked down at the pad through her eyes. Nothing had changed. The lenses were clear glass. 'It's such a nuisance having to wear them, isn't it?' Elizabeth said. 'But I'm as blind as bat without.'

I was sure now. Elizabeth was playing a part for reasons I could only guess at but I suspected the worst. The cheap trick with the glasses was designed to make Pamela warm to her. I was horrified but part of me was also fascinated by the cool bravado of her actions and when Pamela smiled, I felt a hint of excitement tingle along Elizabeth's skin. She was enjoying this.

'And what's the next step?' Elizabeth asked.

'We will send you a Letter of Engagement – basically a contract between us. You need to sign it and send it back to us, along with a deposit payment to cover our initial costs and various documents, copy of your passport and so on. Your estate agent will give you a memorandum of sale once you give them our details, and we'll take it from there.' She handed Elizabeth a business card. 'Have you got your mortgage arranged?'

'I don't need one,' she said. The words tumbled out. 'An aunt, my mother's sister, left everything to me and my cousin. It turns out she made some canny investments, and I've enough to buy a little flat. I never thought I'd be able to own my own place. Not in London. Not with property prices like they are. It's a dream come true. I can't wait to move in and make it my own. So how long do you think it will take?'

Pamela relaxed into her chair as she listened, and her eyes stopped glancing towards her computer screen and whatever work she'd been in the middle of when we'd walked in. She'd softened towards Elizabeth and I wasn't surprised.

Pamela explained how the conveyancing would work. Elizabeth nodded and smiled, made suitable comments, and encouraged Pamela. But she wasn't paying attention. Most of the time her eyes were fixed on Pamela's face, but every now and then they darted to the back of her computer screen following the cables down to where they disappeared into a hole at the back of Pamela's desk. Elizabeth's hand dipped into her coat pocket and closed round an oblong plastic object. She ran the tip of her finger over its metal top.

'Could I possibly see a draft contract?' she asked. 'Just so I know what to expect when we come to exchange.'

'You really don't need to worry about that. Mrs Brown will explain all the relevant parts of it when you come in to sign. Most of it is standard anyway.'

Elizabeth tapped her fingers on the desk in an edgy arpeggio. 'I don't like to sign anything without understanding it. I know that's very old-fashioned, but it's stood me in good stead, and I don't want to waste Mrs Brown's time.'

Pamela nodded. 'I understand. We've got some printed contract templates that we adapt. Let me go and find one of those to set your mind at rest.'

She stood and smoothed down the pleats of her skirt. Elizabeth's eyes followed her until she shut the door and the click-clack of her shoes receded up the corridor. Her smile dropped and in one fluid movement she rose from her chair, slipped round the front of Pamela's desk, and bent over the computer. I felt the short hair beneath her wig prickle but the rest of her was as cool and calm as ever. Her heart pumped steadily. Her lungs pulled the air in and out in an unchanged rhythm, and her hands didn't shake as they took out the plastic object from her pocket. A USB stick. She inserted it into one of the computer's USB ports, while her ears listened to the silence outside the door. I heard her whisper – counting to ten – then she ran her fingers over the keyboard too fast for me to register what she pressed. Bars appeared on the screen, filled up with green from left to right and then disappeared. She hit a few more keys, and the contents of Pamela's hard drive appeared on screen. A surge of blood warmed her skin.

I'd read stories about people being scammed out of large sums of money because of intercepted emails between them and their solicitors and I guessed Elizabeth was up to something along those lines. She was cool and efficient, but I was terrified. What if Pamela came back and found her? I desperately didn't want her to be caught but I couldn't let my fear disturb her. I focused on the silence beyond the clatter of her fingers on the keyboard and the hum of the hard drive working to keep up with her, praying that she'd be quick.

Her ears screamed a warning. Footsteps clipped back down the corridor. A few more keyboard taps and a whirl round the desk, snatching the USB stick as she dashed. And when the kind and trusting Pamela Harkins pushed the door open, Elizabeth turned from the seat Pamela had left her in and gave her a grateful but slightly anxious smile. She told her how sorry she was to have been such a bother, thanked her for being so understanding, then she glanced at her watch and exclaimed over the time.

'I'd no idea it was so late,' she said. 'I'm sorry to have taken up so much of your time.' She stood and waited while

Pamela stapled a business card to the draft contract, took it, shook her hand and left.

Several solicitors later, I'd worked out how she operated. She chose small solicitors in the high streets of south London. Taking long bus rides in between. They were mainly fronted by a secretary who manned the outer office alone. Elizabeth muttered an excuse and left when the office in one solicitor's contained three chattering youngsters.

Her objective was to gain some time alone with the computer, and mostly it wasn't as easy as it had been with Pamela Harkins. Sometimes Elizabeth didn't get an opportunity but often she did. A couple of times the assistant was called to an office by one of the solicitors. One particularly trusting assistant uploaded whatever was on the USB stick onto the computer herself when Elizabeth told her the file was the details of the flat she was buying.

I was fascinated by her skill. She took her time to get the measure of the person she was dealing with. Then, like a chameleon changing colour to slide unseen into a deep green bush or hide against baked sandy rock, her body took on the persona of her prey. She mirrored the women facing her, crossing her arms and fiddling with her hair as they did. Softening or sharpening her voice and gestures. If they wore glasses, she took hers out and put them on. If they had pictures of children on their desk, she dropped some mention of hers into the conversation. If they were motherly, she was disorganised and confused. If they were dynamic and efficient, she was grateful and obedient. It was impressive how quickly she could penetrate their defences, gain their trust and disarm them. A master class in entrapment.

22

A couple more solicitors and Elizabeth took a bus back to Greenwich. We were going home. I felt nothing but relief. My fear that Elizabeth would be discovered hadn't diminished and each time she worked her magic with the solicitors' computers, I found it hard to stop my panicking thoughts unsettling her. I really didn't want her to be arrested. I needed her out in the world so she could take me back to the hospital. And soon. Clearly the high-powered job in the city was another lie and this was how Elizabeth spent her days.

She sidled up the alley, unlocked the front door to the flat quietly, then tiptoed up the stairs. I supposed she didn't want Amy to see her with the black wig on. In the hall, she glanced at the empty hook where Tilly's coat had hung. It was empty. Poor Tilly must have left for the hospital and her patient vigil by my bed long ago.

Elizabeth flung the wig and coat onto her bed, grabbed her normal handbag, and ran her fingers through her hair, scratching away the itchy dampness. Then she slipped back into the hall and called up the stairs quietly.

'Tilly?' She waited. 'Tilly? Are you there?'

No answer. Not a rustle or a murmur. I was sure Elizabeth had realised Tilly had gone.

'Tilly, I'm making a cup of tea. Would you like one?'

Still nothing.

Elizabeth crept up the stairs and into my bedroom.

The door was ajar, but she tapped all the same.

'Tilly,' she said. 'Tilly?' and knocked again. When there was no possibility Tilly was there, she slunk in.

She turned my computer on, typed in my password rapidly and opened my emails.

Shock blanked my mind for a few seconds and then my thoughts whirled.

I'd been wrong, hadn't I? Wrong, wrong, wrong when I assumed I was in control the night we'd woken, gone into my bedroom and looked at my mails and bank accounts.

Or maybe I'd started it. Maybe my wanting the cash in my bedroom had chimed with some desire of Elizabeth's and so she'd carried through what I'd started. It was possible. She'd been sleepy.

But once we were there, she'd been the one who'd turned my computer on. I hadn't planned to. I'd done it automatically when I'd sat down. Or so I thought.

I watched as Elizabeth scrolled through my mails until she found the one from the solicitor asking me if I wanted to buy the shop. I watched as she hit the reply button and started typing. I watched. There was nothing else I could do except wonder how she knew the password to my computer and try to work out what she was up to.

Dear Mr Halvin

Thank you for your mail and apologies for taking so long to respond. I have given Mr Cooper's offer to sell the premises I currently rent serious consideration, and I am writing to tell you that I am interested. However, I feel that due to prevailing market conditions and the situation of the premises away from the High Street, a lower figure would be more appropriate and with that in mind, I would like to offer

Her fingers hesitated over the keyboard and then she pulled my purse out of her bag – the purse she'd stolen from the locker by my hospital bed – and found the receipt for the cheque I'd paid in on the day of the accident. She typed an amount for a few thousand less and carried on.

I understand that Mr Cooper is keen on a speedy completion. I would be too. I have no need of a mortgage and, should Mr Cooper accept my offer, would like to exchange contracts at your earliest convenience. To that end, please would you send me the draft contract as soon as possible?

Yours sincerely

Lucy Christensen

She reread the mail then pressed send as my thoughts reeled. Why was she pretending to buy the shop and the flat? She couldn't be seriously planning to go through with the purchase. How could she? Surely someone would check up and discover I was in hospital?

Or would they?

I'd dealt with the same solicitors when I signed the lease. They'd done all the background checks on me then. And even if they did them all again, would they necessarily find out I was in a coma in hospital? I didn't think so. Not with Elizabeth intercepting my mails and my letters. Not unless they phoned but, of course, they had my mobile number. And Elizabeth had my mobile phone. She'd taken it at the hospital when she took my purse. This must be why she'd stolen them, why she'd wanted to accompany Tilly.

Luck had been on her side too when Moira had talked about me to her. She'd told Elizabeth where the money had come from and how solitary I was. Elizabeth must have been thrilled to discover there were no hordes of friends checking up on me. Only Tilly, preoccupied at the hospital, and Amy, struggling to balance her family life with keeping the shop going.

If I needed any further confirmation that she was an adept crook I got it straight away as she logged without hesitating into my Mrs Lucy Lyle bank account where the money from Gavin's estate was. The cheque had cleared and a quiver of emotion stirred her blood as she scribbled the account details in looping strokes on the back of the receipt and logged out.

I knew she was going to rob me. This was all part of some plan I didn't understand. My brain raced. Could she transfer the money into her own account? I didn't think so. A small part of it online maybe, but there were limits. And what about the solicitors and the sale of the shop and flat?

None of it made any sense.

Not to me, anyway, but I was sure Elizabeth knew what she was doing. She'd have a plan I hadn't thought of. Something too clever for a person as stupid as me to have worked out. She'd take the money, empty the bank account and disappear.

And then I thought of Tilly and the money she'd borrowed for me against her house and the payment that went out of my account every month without fail to repay her. The repayment that I'd thought would be safe while I lay unconscious in bed because it was a standing order. If there was no money in the account, the payment wouldn't be made and the bank would seize Tilly's house. They'd left me in no doubt about that when I'd gone to see them with her and sign the papers. They hadn't wanted her to put up her house as security, but she'd insisted.

Shit, shit, shit and double, triple shit.

I'd messed up big time. I should never have seized the opportunity to hide from my own problems in Elizabeth's body. Tilly loved that house. It perched on the edge of the estuary where she could sit at her upstairs sitting room window with her binoculars and watch the migrating birds arrive year in and year out. She'd be lost without it. It was her home and her livelihood.

Elizabeth reached behind my computer and unplugged a USB stick. So that was how she'd gained access to my computer. I'd never noticed it but then I didn't think I'd looked at the back of my computer since I'd set it up. I wondered if she'd been spying on my life for a long time. And what had started out as curiosity and an ever-present open eye to the chance of a quick buck had become, with the arrival of the cheque from Gavin's estate and my convenient absence, a plan to rob me. I remembered her staring at the cash machine screen when I'd paid the cheque in just before the accident. Clearly she'd seen the amount then.

A sound on the stairs made her jump, and she shut down the computer quickly and stood. Talisker put her head round the door and stopped still at the sight of Elizabeth.

'Get out,' Elizabeth hissed. And when the cat slid round the door and headed for the cat-hair-covered window seat she must have been sleeping on, Elizabeth threw a paperweight at her and she ran away.

I gave Elizabeth a stab of pain as punishment as we skulked back down the stairs. A quick instruction to her legs to stop moving was all it took. And another contradictory instruction in the kitchen as she spooned coffee made her wince.

She hummed a tune while she waited for the kettle to boil. I recognised it. ABBA. 'Money, Money, Money'.

I thought my rage would explode into the kitchen and drown out the bubbling of the kettle and Elizabeth's soft crooning. I wanted to stamp my feet, clench my fists, shout at Elizabeth and scream my fury to the world. Except, of course, I couldn't. I was locked in Elizabeth's body and my fury had nowhere to go.

It affected Elizabeth, though. She stopped humming and swallowed several times like you do when you think you're going to be sick. I felt the muscles in her legs soften and sag and she braced herself against the worktop. Her hands curved into claws and gripped the black-speckled melamine, while above them the knife set stared back at me. Pale wood and silver, with the movement of Elizabeth's heaving body glinting in its shiny surfaces, they were beautiful objects, hand-crafted, burnished and utterly desirable, yet threatening Tilly with prison and shame.

The bin was under the worktop by Elizabeth's legs. If I could only get the steel and drop it in, Tilly would be safe. Rubbish would pile on top of it. Amy would put the black bag into the big bins in the yard. It would be collected and disappear into the tons of London waste. I could do this. I made myself calm down. Elizabeth stopped rasping. Her dizziness passed. Her body relaxed.

I pounced.

I snatched at her arm and moved it towards the drawer where the steel was hidden. Not gently. Not gradually but hurling my own desire down into her muscles. For a microsecond I thought it would happen. Then her consciousness sprang into action, raced down her nerves, and broke the connection between her body and my thoughts. I fought for control, and pain jagged through us both. I pictured my hands in her head, digging my fingers into her brain, pulling it apart and pushing my orders down its pathways. Forcing the muscles in her arm to lift. But she squeezed me tight, wringing every bit of strength out of me. I fought on, long after I knew it was hopeless and that I had no chance of winning. The connections between her brain and body were too many, too intertwined, too embedded. I fought even as the pain overwhelmed me. A heavy black cloud spiked through with flames, beating me down bit by bit by bit...

'...and then I vomited in the sink.' It was Elizabeth's voice. We were in the shop. At the counter. Elizabeth sitting on the tall stool while Amy ticked off a delivery. 'It was really awful, and then the pain went and I felt completely shattered.'

'Something you ate?'

'Surely that wouldn't have given me a headache?'

Amy shrugged. She was only half-listening to Elizabeth, her shoulders slumped as she leaned on her elbows over the delivery note. Her breathing disturbed the fine film of dust that lay over the glass top of the counter and the odour of clay, dry and earthy, crept into Elizabeth's nose.

What had I been thinking of? Even if I'd succeeded in throwing the steel in the bin, Elizabeth could have picked it out again as soon as I released her. The fight for control had been ten minutes of madness.

'I had terrible headaches after the accident, really bad,' Elizabeth continued. 'And I kept on forgetting things when I was in hospital, too. I had a conversation with a nurse, you know, that I've never remembered. A Scottish lady. They told me it was only concussion. And then when I visited Lucy in ICU, I had a very strange experience.'

She paused and I wondered what she was going to say.

'One of those weird out-of-body type things. I can't really explain.'

'Maybe you should go back to the hospital and get them to check you over?'

Amy finished ticking her list and rubbed her eyes. The shop lights, I realised, were on. It must be early evening and Amy was working late. She gathered the papers and rapped them on the counter to straighten them. Elizabeth winced.

'Maybe,' Elizabeth said. 'I feel utterly exhausted. I think I'll go to bed.'

A flash of derision flickered in Amy's eyes. I guess she thought Elizabeth didn't know what exhaustion was.

I was shattered, too.

It had taken every ounce of strength I had to fight to control Elizabeth and I'd failed completely. Only one glimmer of hope remained. She'd told Amy she couldn't remember the late-night conversation with the Scottish nurse. She'd put it down to concussion. I knew now I hadn't been in control when Elizabeth had searched through my computer in my bedroom but maybe I had when I spoke to the nurse. And if I'd succeeded then, I could now. Once she was asleep. So I had to stay awake tonight to try to get her back to the hospital and me back to my own body.

Elizabeth hauled herself up the stairs to bed, stripped her clothes off and left them in a pile on the floor, all the more untidy because the rest of her room was pristine in its neatness. Tiredness dragged at her body as soon as she flopped into bed and pulled the duvet up round her. Waves of fatigue lulled me towards sleep too, but I withstood their drag. Elizabeth closed her eyes tight against the gleam from the street lights bouncing off the white painted floor and slipped into a deep sleep, leaving me trapped in the dark behind her eyes.

No going searching through her memories this time; I needed to keep awake.

Ninety minutes was the average time it took someone to

fall into deep sleep. Ninety times sixty was five thousand four hundred. I made myself count the numbers slowly. In the dark.

I hated the dark anyway. And this was absolute dark. Pitch-black smothering dark. It was both an absence and a presence. A hole you could fall into for a million years and lose yourself, and a weight pressing down and squashing the little spark of consciousness that was me into a million shreds. If only it wasn't so dark. If only I could see.

Somehow.

If only...

And as I counted the last numbers, I tried.

I reached out and into her body. Slowly. Gently. I mustn't wake her. I focused on her eyes. On the lids of her eyes. I imagined they were mine. And I told them to open. Over and over again, I sent messages to the little muscles that control the eyes. I dragged up the anatomy I learned at art school that explained how the body moved. And used it. Over and over again. And just when I was ready to give up, just when I thought that the moments in the hospital when I'd used Elizabeth's body to talk and move were a one-off, only possible because the connections in her brain had been shaken and bruised by the concussion, just then, I felt Elizabeth's eyes respond. The lids lifted, the pupils rolled forward, and I saw the glass of water on her bedside table, gleaming softly as a stray beam of street light hit it. The glass was tinged with blue, half full of water that glimmered and reflected dim fragments of light onto the walls and ceiling. It was beautiful.

23

It took me until two in the morning to get as far as the kitchen. It felt much longer. Each little action, each inch travelled, was the tiny victory of a hard-fought battle. All the tougher because each time I sent a message down a nerve or coaxed a muscle into life I had to do it softly. I had to caress Elizabeth's body into action so she stayed asleep. I got better as the hours passed – practice makes perfect – but I felt her consciousness surge a couple of times when I tried to move too quickly. If she hadn't been so shattered by the fight we'd had in the kitchen, I thought she would have come to.

It was nothing like it had been the first time I woke in the hospital and spoke to the Scottish nurse. Sure, I'd felt a disconnect then and it had taken time to make her body work for me but I'd never sensed a conflict or even a presence. I didn't know how I'd done it but I could only assume her brain, concussed by the accident, had been deeply unconscious.

We sat by the window that overlooked the alley while I worked on manipulating her hands. The rest of her body was relaxed and inert with her palms flat on the chipped black and white Formica table as I slowly made each finger lift in turn.

I'd learned quite a few things.

Elizabeth's body knew how to walk, for example. I didn't need to tell it to lift one leg and place it in front of the other while coordinating the myriad of muscles that shifted her weight and controlled her balance. All I needed to do was visualise where I wanted to go and send a general command, but it had taken me ages to discover how to do that and it still required constant monitoring to make sure she didn't bump into any of the furniture.

Little movements were difficult. Especially when hand—eye coordination was involved. And doing two things at once was impossible. I hadn't been able to put her dressing gown on and I wouldn't be threading any needles in the near future. Talking was beyond me. The intricacies of controlling and coordinating the muscles involved too complex. So, I didn't know how I'd managed to talk in the hospital. Somewhere I was missing something.

But I had hope and a plan.

If I could get this far in a few hours, then with practice, with time, I could take her to the hospital. There needed to be no jolts, no loud noises, no sudden changes of light or temperature. It was going to be hard to master the intricacies of her clothes and dealing with the buses. I saw long hours of work while she slept ahead. But I didn't care. I was going to do it. I was going to escape.

Tonight my one aim was to get rid of the steel. I'd have liked to change the password on my computer but Tilly was asleep in my bedroom. Besides I didn't think I'd have the time. Even getting rid of the steel was going to be a challenge. I needed to be able to lift one arm, open the fingers of one hand, grasp the drawer handle and pull it towards me. Then let go, reach my hand inside, grab the steel and lift it out, move the arm to the bin and let the steel go, while all the time controlling the muscles that kept her body upright. Normally it was simple but for me it would require more determination and concentration than swimming the Channel and doing fine embroidery at the same time.

'Elizabeth.' A voice called me back to the present.

I raised Elizabeth's eyes from the table and turned them to the figure standing in the doorway, one hand reaching for the light switch. It was Tilly, a deep red dressing gown belted round her waist and her hair tangled.

'Are you all right? Sitting in the dark like this.'

She turned on the under-cupboard lights.

I concentrated hard and nodded.

'I can't sleep, either,' Tilly shuffled towards the kettle. 'I'm going to make myself a cup of tea. Do you want one?'

From somewhere inside Elizabeth I produced an 'mmm' sound and nodded her head again. And I did want a cup of tea. A cup of normal tea, hot and strong, with milk. The sort Tilly drank.

'I've had a dreadful day.' Her hands dropped teabags into mugs and poured water using only the light under the cupboards, while the rest of her was a shadow in her bulky dressing gown. I was glad she hadn't turned the main light on, because Elizabeth was also in shadow, so Tilly couldn't see the absence of expression on her face. 'Terrible news. I should have guessed as soon as Sean said they wanted a meeting to discuss Lucy's treatment.'

Elizabeth should react to this. She needed to say some words of comfort or ask Tilly what had happened but I couldn't make her. Her silence didn't seem to disturb Tilly.

She carried on talking with her head turned away as she waited for the kettle to boil.

'They're worried because she hasn't woken up yet. She's not even breathing on her own.' She paused and picked up the mugs of tea.

Elizabeth's face was blank but my thoughts raced behind it. What did it mean?

Tilly turned and put a mug of tea on the table before me. I triggered the movement that would make Elizabeth's hand reach forward and clasp it, and watched as it obeyed my command and wrapped itself round the blue and white china. Except it was hot. Too hot. Reflexes pulled her hand off the burning china and knocked it over. Nerve ends sent shock messages to her brain – and Elizabeth woke up.

Tilly thought it was her fault and fussed around with cloths and apologies while Elizabeth stretched out and pushed herself into every corner of her body. I retreated before the waves of her presence, and made myself small and quiet. Very quiet.

Elizabeth stared at Tilly. 'Shit,' she said.

'Are you OK?'

'I was asleep.'

'You fell asleep in here?'

'No. No. I went to bed. I remember going to bed. I remember going to sleep. And then I was here.'

Tilly mopped the last of the spilt tea and dropped the cloth into the sink. She tore some sheets of paper from the kitchen roll and passed them to Elizabeth.

'Here you are. Most of it went on the table, but there's a bit on your sleeves.'

Elizabeth dabbed at the pale brown spots, her hands trembling slightly.

'You mean you've been sleepwalking?'

'I guess so.'

'Has it happened before?'

'I don't think so.'

I felt the questions in her brain show themselves in her body. Neurons sped along pathways, flexing muscles, testing sensations and the hair on her skin pulled upright. Something stirred in the deep parts of her head. Something searching to understand what had happened to her. Something cold and suspicious.

'You should go back to the hospital and get it checked out.'

Elizabeth's finger traced the pattern on the table. 'Maybe I will. Were we talking?'

'Yes. Well, I was. Now I come to think about it you were very quiet. I'll make you another tea.'

'Please. Ginger though. Use the ginger and lemon teabags.' She waved towards the cupboard above the sink, and I envied the casual grace of the gesture. I wanted to go into her arm and feel the muscles contract, learn how she did it and copy the movement, but I needed to stay unnoticed.

Tilly made the tea and sat down opposite Elizabeth. A curl stuck out of one side of her head where she'd been winding it round and round her forefinger. I wanted to reach out and smooth it.

'The thing is,' Tilly said quietly, almost as though she was talking to herself, 'if Lucy is...' She stared into her tea.

'Lucy is?' The sharp smell of ginger rose between them.

'Oh, Elizabeth. It's brain death. That's what they think. They haven't actually said it yet but I know that's what they mean. They're doing more tests, but I can tell they're preparing me for the worst. I've got a meeting with the consultant in the morning.'

I saw the moment Tilly's thoughts sped towards. The

moment when she was asked to take the decision that would end my life or, in their eyes, merely let my body go where my brain had gone before. I knew what she'd decide.

How long did I have? How long before they pulled the plug or did whatever they did? Withhold food and drink. Starve my body to death while it stubbornly clung to life. Or just switch off the pump forcing air into my reluctant lungs. How long had I got? That was the question. Enough time to learn to control Elizabeth's body? To dress her? To take her to the hospital and to the room where my body lay? And all without her waking up. I didn't think so.

'But you don't know that for sure, do you?' I felt an echo of my fear in Elizabeth's words.

'No. But I can't stop thinking about it. It was particularly difficult this evening. I'd been chatting to her about home and my birds, and when I ran out of thing to say about them, I started asking Lucy all the things I wished I'd asked before. About Gavin and the funeral and if she was ever happy with him.'

'It must be dreadfully hard.' Elizabeth's voice was soft and she rearranged her face into an expression of sympathy. Her thoughts were elsewhere though. She was twitchy with them, her left hand rubbing her pyjama material while her feet arched and dropped and arched and dropped. 'Listen, you absolutely must sleep. I've got some sleeping tablets I use for emergencies. They knock me out cold for six hours. How about it?'

'I don't think so. I've never taken anything like that.'

'Are you sure?' Elizabeth stood with a fluidity of movement I'd never achieve. 'I'll put them by the kettle, just in case. You can take up to two. Let me know what the consultant says, won't you?'

She fetched the tablets and then went back to her

bedroom where she sat on the bed for a few minutes, before running her hand through her short hair. When she took it away, a few tufts clung to her fingers. She sighed.

Her phone lay on the bedside table. She'd had a couple of texts.

One was from someone called Reuben. The same Reuben, I supposed, who'd rescued her at Euston Station.

Don't call me again, Sophie. Text if you have to.

She texted back.

Need to see you. Tomorrow?

Ok. Free at 11. But not here. Where?

She thought for a few seconds and texted back the name of a pub on the river down from the old Royal Naval Hospital.

The other text was from Jonty, asking if there was any news about me.

Not much. Want to meet up tomorrow and I'll fill you in?

But Jonty didn't reply. He, at least, was asleep.

Elizabeth slipped her body back into bed, twitching the covers straight and plumping the pillows in a tour de force of coordinated activity that left me despairing, but she didn't lie down. She hugged her knees and rested her chin on them. I felt suspicion roil through her brain, stirring her thoughts and unsettling her blood. I wondered if some unconscious part of her had become aware of my presence and was seeking me out.

Time was running out, slipping through my hands like sand on a beach. The nights I'd hoped I had were gone, snatched away by Tilly's news. I thought of waiting until Elizabeth slept and coaxing her out of bed again, practising making her move but, even asleep, there was something watchful about her. Something stalked the corridors of her mind, alert and ready to wake her.

I should never have stayed in Elizabeth's body in the first place. I should have slipped back into my own at the first opportunity. But hey, my life was littered with *should haves* and *should never haves*.

I should never have married Gavin. I should never have stayed married to him. As soon as I realised, on the train going up to London, that I needed to escape the trap that was my marriage, I should have told him. I meant to but, that evening, when he came through the door, he looked tired and white. He asked me for a paracetamol and a cup of tea, because he had a headache like you wouldn't believe.

My resolve weakened. Instead, I made tea and lied in answer to his questions about the gynaecologist. He was grateful for the tea and for the omelette I made. So nice of me to look after him for a change. And my cooking was wonderful. He'd never had such a nice omelette. I should do it more often. I began to feel guilty and wonder if I was mad. Mad to have a problem with such a kind and giving man.

It was only after he'd gone to bed, apologising again for leaving me so early, that I started to feel the desperation again. The cream walls of the house with its tasteful black and grey contents closed round me, and I knew I had to find a way to escape.

It was like that for the next few months. I alternated between thinking there was something wrong with me, that no one in their right mind would want to leave someone as kind as Gavin. And knowing that living with him was squeezing the life out of me.

And so I split myself in two.

Part of me – well, most of me really – played the wife he wanted me to be. I kept the house immaculate, wore the sort of clothes he liked, socialised with his friends and parents, worked at the masks and produced lifeless but tasteful sculptures that even Gavin quite liked.

But while the surface me was doing all this, the tiny core of resistance beneath the polished exterior worked towards leaving him. You see I knew I'd need to disappear. I refused to think how I knew, but I did. I had to go somewhere where he couldn't find me. Out of reach of his words. Out of reach of him.

From time to time, the two parts of me would collide, and I'd spend an hour locked into a treadmill of thoughts. I was being stupid. Gavin was a wonderful husband. Everybody said so. It was me. I was wrong. Gavin did everything to keep me happy. I had everything I could want. I was selfish and self-centred. And on and on until I managed to rip my two different selves apart again so that they wouldn't question each other.

Sometimes I caught Gavin staring at me with a brooding look as though waiting for something to happen and I'd wonder if my raging thoughts showed on my face. Wonder if he sensed I was desperate to escape him and I'd find myself being ultra-nice to him to make up for the hurt I wanted to cause.

Yet I kept on preparing. I opened a bank account, my Mrs Lucy Lyle bank account that I still had, slipping to London when I knew Gavin had all-day meetings and wouldn't be able to call me at home. I squirrelled money away but it wasn't easy because Gavin kept such a tight eye on my spending. I found another solution. A couple of new clients I didn't tell Gavin about. I sent them invoices with my new bank details on and slowly the money grew. I found a block of studio flats rented by the week in an anonymous part of London. They were expensive but they had a twenty-four-hour concierge and security entry. I filled out all their forms and went through all their formalities until I was approved. I could book a flat whenever I wanted.

Finally I rented a tiny but very cheap storage unit not far from our local Waitrose. Gavin had started monitoring our petrol consumption to make sure the cars were giving the correct mileage to the gallon so it was tricky to go further afield. Not that I went to the supermarket very often. Gavin and I did a big shop together at the weekends and he picked up anything else we needed on the way home but I did go from time to time. And each time, I took a few, a very few, clothes with me and a few precious items – my mother's jewellery and some photos of my childhood – and put them in the unit. The closer I inched to the point where my new life was ready for me to step into, the harder it became to screw myself to the moment of telling him I was leaving. Of facing the storm that would follow and, then, going. And so I dallied, mired in deceit and trapped between the voice telling me I should be happy with my lot and the one screaming at me to leave.

24

I finally left Gavin on a Saturday. Thanks to a pot of plum jam. We'd not long had breakfast, not that anything in the kitchen would have told you that. Everything was washed up and put away. Gavin thought it was so much better to do it straight away. And, of course, he was right. It was so much better to keep everything clean and tidy. Much easier to find things when you needed them.

Gavin wasn't there. He'd gone to see his mother like he always did on a Saturday morning, while I did the laundry, when the doorbell rang. I assumed it was the postman or a delivery so I was startled when I opened the door and saw Veronique there. She was one of Moira's crowd of friends, mainly memorable because she wore her hair in intricate chignons and her nose had a kink in it whose origin I'd never dared enquire about plus she was the only friend of Moira's who could match Moira word for word in a conversation. She'd come round to drop off a pot of the jam I'd expressed polite interest in at a dinner party.

'I hope you don't mind my coming round uninvited,' she

said. 'I was visiting a friend just up the road and I only remembered as I rang your bell that you hate being disturbed when you're working.'

'I wasn't working. But I wouldn't have—'

'I nearly left the pot on the doorstep and ran away. So stupid of me. Gavin – your lovely husband – is always reminding us not to call round uninvited. Bless him. But, you know, when you reach my age, you forget these things.'

'Gavin said that?'

'Oh no. I shouldn't have told you, should I? I know how hard you try to be sociable. I'm so tactless. But, you know, we do all understand. We might not be artists like you but we all have moments when we want to be undisturbed.'

I didn't quite know what she meant and I gazed at the yellow jam as I thought.

'It's an old recipe of my mother's,' she said. 'Made with Mirabelle plums. The best ones come from Lorraine, where she was brought up.'

I'd forgotten her mother was French. Maybe she'd misunderstood Gavin. No, of course, she hadn't. She spoke English perfectly.

'A cousin of mine brings a few crates over for me every year. There's nothing to beat the Mirabelle plums of Lorraine.'

'Come in,' I said. 'And have a coffee.'

She narrowed her eyes.

'I'm not being polite. Honestly, I'm not. I'm doing the laundry, not working, but even if I was—'

'Well, I would love to but I truly don't have the time now. But I tell you what. You come and have a coffee with me sometime. That way I'll be able to resist the temptation to ask you if I can see what you're working on.'

'I don't mind that. I'd happily show you. I'm not always very good at explaining but—'

'I'd never ask you to do that. I know you hate talking about your work.'

Her words surprised me and she startled me even more by taking my hand and squeezing it.

'I understand you're busy and that your art requires huge amounts of concentration and energy but it's not good to be so solitary. I feel as though I hardly know you, although you've lived in the village for quite a while.' She laughed. 'You tell that husband of yours he needs to stop protecting you so much and force you to socialise a bit more. It would do you good to get out and about.'

The voices started arguing in my head as I watched her go.

Gavin had told her I hated being disturbed. That I hated talking about my work. He'd painted a picture of me as an egotistical recluse. Of course Veronique was right and he was only trying to protect me but I couldn't bear it. I couldn't bear to stay here. And I couldn't bring myself to tell Gavin I was leaving.

Maybe I should just go. Forget about telling Gavin first. Of course. A sense of overwhelming relief flooded through my body. Why hadn't I thought of that before? I phoned the studio flats and told them I'd be arriving later, slipped to the lock-up, picked up a bag of clothes then thought again.

Gavin didn't deserve this. I'd have to tell him first. Otherwise he'd hunt for me and, when he couldn't find me, he'd call the police. He'd be stressed and panicked and I needed to remember about his heart.

Maybe I could leave him a note?

And then it struck me how unfair I was being. Maybe Veronique had misunderstood. And even if she hadn't, he'd meant it for the best. I couldn't just walk out. Not without discussing it first. It was childish and unkind to even think about doing it. So I hid the bag in the garden and waited for the right moment.

It didn't come until that evening, as we caught the news before we left for dinner at his parents. I was ready and dressed in a smart frock with too-tight belt, beige court shoes and light brown tights. And wondering if the pearls I'd chosen were right for the outfit while the screaming inside part of me demanded to know why I cared.

Tell him now, it said. *Stop putting it off.*

'Gavin.'

'Uh-huh.'

'Veronique came round today.'

'Did she? Why?'

'With some jam.'

'What jam?'

'The jam doesn't matter. It was something she said.'

He sighed and turned the television off.

'What did she say, my darling?'

'Well, she didn't say it exactly but she suggested... That is, I got the impression you'd told her that I didn't like being disturbed when I was working.'

'But I thought you didn't.'

'Well, yes. It is true that sometimes, if I'm in the middle of something, it's not easy to break off.'

'Well, there you go then.'

'But have you told everybody that?'

'I might have mentioned it.'

'But, Gavin—'

'Why are you going on and on about it?'

'I'm not.'

'Well that's OK then.'

He turned the television back on and we watched pictures of a flood in a far away place. But the screaming part of me screamed a bit louder, until I couldn't bear it.

'Gavin. Might you have told people I don't like talking about my work as well?'

'What?'

He gave me an irritated look and I started to repeat the question.

'I heard you the first time. What is this all about, Lucy? Because the truth is you don't much like talking about your work. At least not with the likes of me. You can talk the hind leg off a donkey when you're with your arty friends but you'll never discuss anything with me. God knows I've tried. I've tried and I've tried. I've gone with you to every exhibition and art gallery there is and asked you to explain things to me but you just look down your nose and mutter something about it not being so easy.'

His voice had risen and grown hard as he spoke and I remembered how he mustn't get upset because of his heart.

'So yes,' he went on, 'it is possible I've told a few of our friends that it's best not to talk to you about your sculpture. I absolutely don't want them to feel as put down by you as I do. Nevertheless, I apologise. I apologise if I have said something I shouldn't.'

He clenched his fists and regained control.

I forced the screaming part of me down. It was childish and self-centred. Everything Gavin said was true. I did hate it when he tried to discuss sculpture and art and anything creative with me. I loathed it.

'It doesn't matter,' I said.

But it does. The screaming inside part of me fought back.

He smiled and patted my hand. 'We ought to go, darling. I told Mum we'd be early so I could give her and Dad a hand with moving the table in the back room. You go and get your coat and I'll get the car out of the garage.'

The screaming part of me burst its shackles. *Shan't*, it shouted in my head. *Shan't, shan't, shan't.*

'Come on, sweetheart.'

He nudged me but I couldn't move. I couldn't speak.

'You're not still annoyed with me, are you?'

Or I thought that's what he said because his words were drowned out by the screaming voice.

Shan't, it said again. And, *No more. No more. No more.*

And then before I could stop it...

'I'm leaving.'

Did I just say that out loud?

'Good. Don't be long. And don't forget to turn the television off properly.'

I did say it out loud.

He stood up and headed towards the door.

'No, I mean I'm leaving you.'

He froze mid-step. Just like in a cartoon. It would have been funny only it wasn't.

His face, when he turned, wore the expression of a child whose parents have just told him his dog has died. Eyes wide and shocked. Mouth quivering. But for once it didn't move me and the words I'd rehearsed so often reached my lips and before I could stop them, they fell out of my mouth again.

'I'm leaving this house. I'm leaving this marriage.'

All the old arguments about how stupid I was to leave him clamoured in my head. But the screaming inside part of me strangled them. It was a relief. A huge relief. I didn't care if I was making a mistake. I probably was making a mistake. I only knew I'd die inside if I had to spend one more hour in this house, with this man.

He laughed and let the silence between us stretch.

'Lucy?' he said in the end.

'I'm leaving.' Now I'd found the words, they were a life-line to cling onto.

The expression drained out of his face leaving it white and pinched and somehow I found some more words.

'I'm sorry, Gavin, but—'

'You're leaving me?'

Something shifted deep inside me and I nodded.

'You're sorry?' He stretched a hand towards me and I shivered – it must be getting chilly – but he picked up the remote and switched the TV off. Then turned it off at the mains. Like he always did.

Then we both stood and avoided looking at each other. His breath came in short sharp pants. I couldn't hear mine. Maybe I wasn't breathing.

'Listen, Lucy,' he said eventually. 'I suppose I have been a bit busy recently. Not had time to go and do anything. I know it's boring for you being stuck with a dullard like me, who has to go out and earn the money and is too tired in the evenings to do much apart from eat and watch television. Look, I can take a few days off next week. Dad won't mind. He can run the office without me. What do you say? Shall we go somewhere? Just the two of us? Spend some time together and sort things out. We could go to Paris. You'd like that, Lucy. Wouldn't you? I only want to do what you like.'

I nearly gave in. I nearly opened my mouth and told Gavin that I'd go to Paris and that, yes, we could sort everything out, but I held the words tight in my mouth and refused to let them out.

He took my silence for agreement.

'Paris it is, then! I've always wanted to go. You can show me round the Louvre. Explain everything to me.'

From somewhere inside me I dredged up a *No*. It was quiet but he heard it.

'That's fine, Lucy. You don't have to show me round. In fact, if you'd rather, you can go to the Louvre on your own. I can wait outside, have a coffee, read the paper. I can see I've been rather selfish expecting you to devote a bit of time to me.'

'No,' I said again. 'No, Gavin. I'm not going to Paris. I'm leaving.'

He sat down on the sofa heavily, as though his knees had given way, and lowered his head in his hands.

'I'm sorry,' I said and a host of meaningless words came to me. The sort of things people say in television dramas. I said them all the same. 'It's not you. It's me. It's my fault but I just can't be the person you want me to be. I never could.'

He said nothing.

Was this it?

I'd thought there would be endless questions. Questions I couldn't answer. I'd expected drama and misery, but it seemed as though my marriage was going to end quietly.

'I'll get my stuff then,' I said.

Everything I needed was already in the storage unit or in the bag I'd hidden in the garden. I could have left there and then, but there were things I wanted to take if I could. A couple of coats. A pair of boots. A painting from Venice. Things he would have noticed if I'd removed them before.

When I came back downstairs, he was waiting for me in the hall.

'Give me those,' he said. 'I'll put them in the car for you.' He'd been crying. I felt like crying, too. Our marriage hadn't been all bad, I thought. He'd done his best. Just we were totally incompatible.

I held my bag and keys out to him and—

I slipped and fell. Just like that. With a thud. *Hard. Hard floor. No breath.* My ribs seized a great lungful of air. Pain flared across my chest.

I replayed the moment in my head. Saw the fist heading for my middle.

He'd punched me.

'You're not leaving.' His voice was calm. 'I don't like having to put my foot down, Lucy. You know that, but you've given me no choice.' He dropped my keys in his pocket and moved my bag to the bottom of the stairs. 'I'll take that back up later.' He marched towards me, grabbed my arm, and hauled me up.

The screaming inside part of me found her voice. I screamed.

He slammed one hand over my mouth, driving my teeth into the soft flesh, and seized my hair with the other. 'Don't be stupid.' Anger cracked through his voice as he yanked my hair. 'You need a bit of time to calm down. That's what you need. We're married, Lucy, and that should mean something. Even today. You can't just walk out.' He shook my head with each word. 'You can't just walk out. Not now. Not after everything I've done for you.'

My chest hurt more with every jerk, and I tasted the salt of blood in my mouth. I wrenched myself away from him and staggered into the sitting room, but he ran after me, spun me round and grasped my upper arms. Squeezed them until I thought the bones might crack. The only noise was his hoarse breathing. My legs gave way and we tumbled onto the floor where he knelt over me, pinned my hands above my head and slapped me.

The force of it knocked my face to the side, and my eyes fixed on the sofa. On the black leather, with the sheen, buffed to perfection once every six months by a special product we bought online.

Gavin drove his fist into my ribs. Then into my arm.

I'd missed a bit of dirt on the sofa. In the bottom right-hand corner. A trace of mud. *Mud. No shoes in the lounge. Who brought the mud in?*

A slap to my face drove it away from the sofa. Away from the mud. *I must look at the mud. Whose side of the sofa was it on? No. Don't. He might notice it. Better pretend it's not there. Wait till he's gone and wipe it clean.*

He grunted. Each time his fist or hand hit me, he grunted, but his eyes were empty. Empty with the deep concentration of someone focused on doing a good job. Gavin was doing a good job. Gavin always did a good job. A thorough job.

He punched my ribs, and a crack whiplashed through the room.

I had to go. I couldn't sit through this.

I never liked the violent bits on TV. Couldn't bear them. Always went and made a cup of tea and left Gavin to watch alone. Shut the door behind me in the kitchen blocking out the thud of bone hitting flesh and the screams of pain and fear. Except she wasn't screaming. Why wasn't she screaming? Because she couldn't breathe. His weight ground into her with every grunt and punch. She had to breathe.

I had to breathe. I grabbed the air and croaked.

'Gavin, stop, please, stop.'

Someone came back behind his eyes. Blood flooded into his white cheeks. His mouth opened in a gasp. The person behind his eyes looked at me.

'Christ, your face.' He struggled to his feet and stumbled over to the window. Stood there for a while, resting his head against the glass, and then went into the kitchen.

It was over.

Pain woke and sent spasms rippling through me. I didn't care. It was over. Besides, it felt right. I deserved it. A price that had to be paid. For causing Gavin so much pain and misery. And now it was over.

Was it over?

In a minute, I thought, *I'll get up. I'll just lie here for a while first. Catch my breath. Let the worst of the pain die away.* And then I'd fetch a cloth and wipe that mud away. Before Gavin came back.

Was it over? Where was he? What was he doing?

Could I get up? How bad was the damage? I tested my arms. They hurt, but I could move them. One more minute and then I'd stand up.

Footsteps up the stairs. His tread was slow and measured. Now would be a good time to move, except I wasn't ready to stand. A few minutes more lying here, I thought. Footsteps down the stairs and stopped in the hall. Silence.

Was he coming back?

I whimpered.

Pain flared along my ribs, and I breathed as lightly as I could for fear of waking it again. The soft swoosh of the door opening over the carpet and the tramp of his feet echoed in the thud of my heart pumping.

'I'm sorry.'

He knelt down and stroked my face. A gentle whisper of a caress and my treacherous flesh betrayed me. Tears trickled down my face.

'I'm so sorry, Lucy. It was so awful thinking you were going to leave me. I lost it for a few seconds there. But you won't, will you?'

I shook my head.

'Oh, thank God.' Tears rolled out of his eyes. 'Look what you've done to me,' he said, pointing to them. 'Good thing I brought some tissues down from upstairs.' He blew his nose on one and forced a laugh. 'I haven't cried for years. Not since a cricket ball smashed into my face at school.'

I forced my lips into a smile as he reminisced about the incident. How he'd had to have his chin stitched and an emergency repair on his front tooth. How upset Moira had been, taking him to a specialist dentist, saying nothing was worth more to her than his smile.

He pushed himself to his feet. 'Mum will be expecting us, so I'll head off then. Don't worry though, I'll explain that you've got a bit of a headache. She'll understand. Oh, my darling. You've bitten your lip. I'll leave you the tissues to clean up. What a palaver about nothing. I suppose all married couples have their difficult moments, but you do love me, don't you? I couldn't bear it if you didn't.'

'I love you,' I said and I pursed my lips and blew him a painful kiss.

He whistled to himself in the hall, opening the drawers in the chest and rummaging for something. What was he doing? The front door slammed and a sort of hope prickled the hairs on my skin.

Silence.

More silence.

He'd gone.

I sat up and felt my legs. They were fine. I didn't even think he'd touched them. I rolled over, wincing as fire stabbed my ribs, and stood, leaving watery bloodstains behind me on Gavin's beautiful silky grey carpet. *Shit*. Nothing removed bloodstains completely, but some carpet cleaner might help. There was some under the kitchen sink.

I walked stiffly into the kitchen. I was OK provided I

didn't move more than absolutely necessary. Passed the mirror. Cast a glance to check my hair was neat. And stopped.

The mirror reflected a dreadful sight. An illustration for an article on domestic violence. How strange. Like the poster I'd seen on Carshalton station. Next to the one advertising Aznar's exhibition. Red marks all over my face. Patches of blood with carpet marks imprinted on them. A drying trickle from one corner of my mouth and a cut the length of my eyebrow.

An abused wife.

I couldn't let anyone see me like this. They'd think *I* was an abused wife. And, of course, I wasn't. It was all a mistake. I'd pushed Gavin too far. Poor Gavin. He'd been so upset.

An abused wife.

The words wouldn't go away. They rang round my brain, as I rummaged through the cupboard under the sink for the carpet cleaner. Their accusing tones distracted me as I sprayed and scrubbed at the stains, gently, at first, then with increasing anger. Why wouldn't the blood come out? I'd done everything the cleaner said on the instructions. I'd done everything right. I started to cry and as my tears pierced holes in the surface of the mounds of white foam hiding the blood on the carpet, my blood on the carpet, the screaming inside part of me stopped cowering.

Get out, it said. *Get out now*.

Ten minutes later, I realised I couldn't.

Gavin had locked the front door and the back door. And the connecting door into my studio. The windows in the sitting room were locked and the ones in the kitchen and the hall. And the ones upstairs. And he'd taken my keys and the spare sets from the kitchen. He'd locked me in and taken the keys.

Only the window in the downstairs toilet was unlocked, but it was too small for more than my head and faced away from the neighbours. No one came when I forced myself to shout out for help.

I'd have to phone. I'd have to phone the police. I couldn't think of anyone else.

There was an empty place on the chest of drawers in the hall. An empty place where the phone normally stood with its cable running to the phone socket in the wall. The phone wasn't there. Nor was the one in the kitchen. Nor, I realised, as I clung onto the banisters along the upstairs landing, dizzy with the fear running through my body, was the bedroom phone.

I stumbled back down the stairs and rummaged through my bag for my mobile. It was gone too.

I sank onto the ceramic tiles in the hall. The ones that looked like a hardwood floor. Much more hard-wearing, you know, exactly like luxurious wood but with all the advantages of tiles. This house. I was still trapped inside this house. Still trapped inside this marriage.

I had to get out.

Back in the kitchen I picked up everything heavy I could find: the steel for sharpening knives, a skillet, an iron casserole, a hammer for tenderising steaks, and stood in front of the big window in the sitting room. The triple-glazed, extra-tough, super-insulated window. *Only the best for you*, Gavin had said.

The hammer just bounced off it, and I couldn't get enough strength behind the weight of the casserole for it to make a dent. My arms were sore and shaky from the beating and the impact of each blow was agony in my chest. I gritted my teeth and ran at the glass and whacked it with the skillet. Still nothing. I tried bashing it all over with the hammer, and a crack appeared in one corner. I smashed at the glass a bit harder. A few more cracks appeared. But it was going to take hours at this rate. My fear ratcheted up a notch, and sweat made the hammer handle slippery. I made myself stop and think.

I taped the steel to the end of a broom, stood at the other side of the room, raised it like a weapon over my head and charged at the window, screaming to vent the pain. It holed the first pane and spread a misty network of cracks over half the window. The broom handle broke with the force of the blow. I knocked the shattered glass out and charged again. I holed the next pane on the third attempt. And the last gave away easily. I bashed round the edges of the holes with the steel, ignoring the splinters of glass shooting out with the force of each jab until I could clamber through. Then I tiptoed round to the drive, clutching the steel taped to the broken broom handle. I thought Gavin had driven away, but I couldn't be sure.

I staggered to my car.

No car keys. I had no car keys.

I wept.

I'd done the impossible. I'd got out. But I kept my car keys on the same ring as my door keys. And now I was stuffed. I could walk, but I wouldn't get far enough away. I could call a taxi, except I didn't have a phone.

Salt from my tears stung my cheeks, and I reached up a hand to dash them away. Little flakes of glass scratched my fingers. The movement of my reflection in the car window caught my eye.

My reflection was clear in the clean windows. So clean. Gavin liked the cars to be clean. He took them to the carwash every fortnight. He never asked me for my keys. He must have a spare set. Had he remembered to take them?

I climbed back through the window and tore the house apart. I emptied Gavin's drawers. In the bedroom. In the office. Hunted through his pockets – not that Gavin would leave anything in his pockets. Searched through his bedside table. Nothing.

I trudged down the stairs. Slowly. Hope draining away. And remembered something he'd said about scammers accessing fob keys from outside the house. Unless they were kept in a metal box. A metal box. He'd bought me a neat little box for the keys in my bag. That I tried to remember to use. A metal box.

I found it. In his study in the back of a drawer. A box that used to contain biscuits but rattled when I seized it. Rattled with the sound of metal against metal. The sound of keys.

I drove away. Towards London. Towards safety and freedom and my future. But slowly, because I could see little through my tears and the blood dribbling from my eyebrow. I didn't care. I only wanted to put as many miles between me and my prison as possible. And when I stopped to wipe my eyes, I told myself it was over. I'd never have to see Gavin again. Never have to go back to the house again. I'd escaped.

I was wrong on all four counts.

25

I will escape, I told myself, as I waited for Elizabeth to go back to sleep. But she spent most of the hours after our middle of the night conversation with Tilly watchful and awake, sometimes pacing up and down her bedroom, sometimes sitting with her eyes fixed on the far wall but seeing thing I couldn't see, sometimes exploring exotic foreign destinations on her phone.

Around five, just as the night was starting to lighten into the long wait for dawn, Elizabeth drowsed into sleep. I thought about trying to get her back to the kitchen, but she slept uneasily. Her muscles were tensed and her brain listened to her ears as though expecting an attack at any moment. What would be the point anyway? I needed weeks and I only had days or maybe even hours. I needed a better plan.

And as I lay with Elizabeth, fighting against the horror of the dark I hated so much, a desperate idea came to me. I couldn't take her to the hospital. But maybe I could get someone else to take her there. Maybe I could injure her.

Badly enough so an ambulance would be called. But not badly enough so she couldn't walk. I'd need to use her legs to get her into the lift and up to Lucy's room on the fifth floor. Make her fall down the stairs? Too risky. She might break a leg. Step out in front of a car? Same problem.

My thoughts chased after one another while outside a delivery truck for the butchers in the next street along rumbled over the dirt at the back of the flat with the men shouting instructions to each other. The day was beginning.

I gave up on the injury plan and dipped in and out of Elizabeth's memories, searching for something that might tell me what she was up to, but they were chaotic and disordered. Sometimes the most tedious days remained unedited and long in her head, while other moments were fragmented and meaningless.

In the early months after her arrival at Euston Station, after she became Sophie, Reuben was often present. I saw him meet her at the hostel where she'd passed a restless night, unused to sleeping surrounded by other people. He helped her find a job. Contract cleaning for employers who asked few questions. There were long stretches of memories of over-brightly lit, early-morning offices with windows showing night outside and hoovers passing over miles of cheap grey carpet.

Interspersed were the small triumphs. Moving into a shared flat. A tiny room but her own and with a lock on the door. Finding a permanent job. Only cleaning in a retirement home, but the regular hours, the holiday pay, the security, removed an anxiety that ate up her concentration. I saw her research evening courses. Move into a tiny studio. Start to cook for herself. Join the local library.

And then there were memories that tried to slip by without letting me see them. Things Elizabeth didn't want to remember. After a mind-numbing flow of days and weeks mopping linoleum and emptying bins, during a bitter winter when the early morning starts were hard. When the cold made her sit as far away from the doors on the bus as possible and blow on the fingers of her gloves to keep warm. When the heat at the retirement home and the endless drone of voices made her sleepy. Every evening back to the chill of her flat, with its thin walls and ill-fitting windows leaking heat. A couple of hours in bed and then out to an evening class or a shift in the local pub or sometimes waitressing at a gala dinner, dressed in an ancient black dress and thin flat shoes.

A memory hid among the difficult days. I nearly missed it but something about its feel caught my attention. It was dimmer, surrounded by a thick shell that made it hard to see inside. I forced myself in.

The gas heater in her shower has stopped working. There's no roar as she turns on the tap. She sticks a hopeful hand in the stream of icy water, despite the silence. She knows it won't be warm, but she can't stop herself testing it. Not that it produces much hot water when the weather is this cold, but even a warm trickle might entice her in because she is chilly yet damp with sweat after the day at the retirement home. She gives up.

She scrambles into her black waitressing dress, then takes it off and pulls on the thick T-shirt she wore earlier. The dress goes on top and zips up. Just. The tights she washed last night aren't dry, so she finds a pair under the bed, worn before but they're black and the grime doesn't show.

She picks up her brush. In the mirror her hair is shortish, about three inches long. Except for the gaps. Her alopecia is back. She slicks gel through it and arranges the strands so they hide the white patches of scalp, but as she smooths it, more hair slides out. She swears and grabs a black scarf, ties it round her head and goes out.

It's hot at the hotel. The guests, some two hundred gathered to celebrate a wedding, are in evening wear: tuxedos or lounge suits for the men and off-the-shoulder, backless numbers for the women, who sit and talk about nothing and compare dresses and jewels with their eyes. Sophie is boiling. And her feet hurt. It's a long walk from the kitchens to the dining room. And in the pause between the main course – chicken chasseur with a brown sauce that has left a greasy trail on the skirt of her dress, and dessert, some kind of cake with layers, yellow and pink – she slips out onto the fire escape to let the icy weather shock her body back to coolness.

Another group of waitresses are outside smoking. They've climbed down the metal stairs to the next landing so the smell won't slip in through the door and give them away. They don't see her. Which is fine. They're mostly students earning a bit of pocket money to pay for nights out, and their lives are as different to hers as those of the sleek guests at the wedding.

Snatches of their conversation mingle with breathy laughter and the clang of the metal staircase as they move around. She hears her name.

The memory shrinks. It becomes nothing but the cold iron of the handrail beneath her hands and their voices wafting up to her with the smoke from their cigarettes.

'Smelly girl, you mean... With the filthy hair! Ooh yes! Eau de piss and bleach... Can't even carry a plate without spilling it... What a derp.'

She grips the icy rail as the words echo in her head. They merge into older memories. Of Carly at school. Of children refusing to sit next to her. The biting cold of the metal starts to burn her palms. She wants to cry but she won't let herself. A fire starts inside her. She pushes away from the handrail, stomps down the steps to confront the girls. Their laughter fades as they see her.

All except one. There's always one. And this one has long blonde hair with a perfect little curl at the end. Like Sophie's hair would be if she didn't have to keep it short all the time. If it didn't have bald patches that she knows make her look like a mangy cat. The girl gives a little laugh and a toss of her head that ripples down through her hair. 'Sorry, sweetheart,' she says. 'But you could take a shower from time to time.'

The others smother giggles behind their hands and Sophie explodes. Runs down the last few stairs between them and pushes the taunting girl. A brutal shove with the force of twenty years behind it. Years of never fitting in, of being the butt of every joke, of half-heard insults whispered behind hands. It knocks the sneering girl over, its strength flattening her and clattering her head against the metal balustrade as she tumbles down the steps of the fire escape to the frosty ground where she stops and lies still, although the shrieks and gasps of the other waitresses keep echoing into the dark.

But as we stare at the girl on the ground with the light from the open door hitting her white face and casting a dark shadow round her, the scene flickers. It flickers between night and day, between the smell of cigarettes and the sharp reek of fear, between icy cold and smothering heat. Another image, a different image, stamps itself, off and on, over the sight of the girl lying there until it takes over and suddenly we're somewhere else.

It is daytime. A man lies halfway down a metal fire escape but this one is rustier and battered. He is old. Balding. With a belly that flops over his half-open trousers. He is as motionless as the girl was but he doesn't lie on frosty-white ground. A fast-growing pool of red blood pillows his head.

· · ·

The memory cuts to yet another scene. Reuben sits in front of Sophie. We're not at the hotel, but Sophie is still dressed in her waitressing outfit with the T-shirt underneath and the grease marks on the skirt. We're in a café. One that's open all hours with a patch of waste ground outside, crammed with minicabs and delivery scooters, while the drivers hunch over cups of tea and listen to their radios or watch their phones. Reuben's helmet and keys are on the table between us, among the cup marks and the cigarette burns. Someone is smoking despite the signs.

'There has to be something better than this,' Sophie is saying.

'Not at this time of night,' Reuben says. *An older and paler Reuben, with the skin of someone who doesn't often see daylight.*

'Not the café,' Sophie hisses back. 'Life.'

'Oh, life.'

'Yes. Life. That thing you're supposed to make something of. Get some fun out of, even. I'm sick of just getting by. Sick of never having enough money. Sick of smelling of the old people at the home.'

'You don't smell.'

'Only because everything stinks in here anyway. Look at my hands.'

She thrusts them out onto the table and splays her fingers over the dirty Formica. The nails are cracked and the cuticles fraying, while the rest of her skin is red and rough.

'Look at them. The state of them. And look at my head.' *She pulls the black scarf off and with it comes a handful of hair.* 'The doctor told me it could be stress-related. Told me to take things easy. Ha-bloody-ha. It's enough, Reuben. I've had enough of playing by the rules. By their rules.'

'Yeah, yeah, yeah. You've lost a job. You've had a bad night.

But it could have been worse. At least the girl is all right. Go home, get some sleep. Things won't look so bad in the morning.'

'No, they won't look so bad in the morning. You are so right. For once, you are absolutely right.'

Something in her tone warns Reuben. 'Sophie?' he says.

'In the morning, I'm going shopping for a new coat. One that might keep me warm. And then I'm going to the posh wig shop on Oxford Street, and I'm going to buy myself a wig of real hair. Not like the crap you get on the NHS.' She stands, and her fury hardens and settles. 'I'll nick the coat. And I've got enough money to pay the deposit on the wig. They take weeks to make, and when it's ready I'll have the money. Believe me, Reuben, I'll have the money.'

The alarm on Elizabeth's phone blared out an ear-piecing tone. No one could sleep through that. Elizabeth fumbled to turn it off and saw the time.

She muttered an expletive. It had just gone ten.

For a moment I was lost, caught between Sophie in the café in the past and Elizabeth in my flat in the present. Both had the fire of determination running through their blood. It ran coldly through Elizabeth now though, more like liquid steel than raging flames.

She sped through her shower and threw some clothes on. Just jeans and a T-shirt today. And a different wig. The bob-cut reddish brown one that changed the shape of her face dramatically. Especially with the beret, adjusted to exactly the right angle in the mirror. She'd come a long way, I thought, from the angry girl in the café and from her squalid childhood. Part of me couldn't help feeling a sneaking admiration for her. Part of me understood the forces that had driven her to push the girl down the balcony stairs. Although I didn't understand the end of the memory when the girl had become a man.

She picked up her phone and saw that Jonty had replied to her text, suggesting they meet that evening in the pub in the market. She sent a quick text saying yes, around seven, and I felt less charitable towards her.

She gulped a glass of water in the kitchen. Tilly had already gone. Her breakfast dishes drained by the side of the sink. The sleeping tablets lay unopened by the kettle. Tilly hadn't taken any and I wondered if she'd had any sleep. Probably not. She'd probably lain awake all night, worrying about me. All my fault. Everything was my fault. I had to put things right. I just didn't know how.

26

Reuben was sitting outside the Cutty Sark pub when Elizabeth arrived. At a table littered with empty glasses by the Thames, alone apart from a couple of elderly men a few tables away. I recognised him straight away from Elizabeth's memories, although he was older. His plumpness, once so round and tight, had sagged into folds, and some spark in him had died. I couldn't imagine him rescuing Carly now.

The tide was out and he was gazing at a group of people trundling along the shore hunting for treasure. Mudlarking. Searching for history in the river mud. For hundreds of years people have chucked their detritus into the Thames. Their broken pottery and ornaments, spoons and shoes and knives. Twice a day the tide shifts the soft mud and brings new things to the surface. Nothing stays buried for ever and each item is a little window into the past.

Elizabeth didn't go and join him, though. Instead, she slipped into the café next door, ordered a coffee, and watched him through the window. She observed him for a long time, and only when he started to get restless and glance at his phone and reach for the threadbare green jacket on the bench beside him, did she get up and go out to meet him.

'Reuben.'

He scrutinised her through his little round glasses and his mouth opened. 'Sophie, I wouldn't have recognised you in that wig.' He'd lost a tooth at some point and the replacement was white against the faint yellow of the others. 'You're late. I was just leaving.' He clamped his pale lips shut again.

'You surely didn't expect me to come looking like myself, did you? I'm not that stupid. Sophie's gone, anyway. I'm Elizabeth now. Remember that. Elizabeth. Anyway, I got held up.'

She sat down across the table from him, pulled her beret down over her head and leaned on the wall to cast a glance at the mudlarkers below.

'I can't stay much longer.' Reuben's irritation showed in the curtness of his voice. He picked up his drink and knocked it back in one long swallow.

'Please, Reuben.' Her voice shook and for once the tremor felt sincere. I'd learnt there was a cold, hard centre to Elizabeth that very little reached and touched. 'I wasn't sure if you'd be alone.'

'Well, I am.'

'I know. They'd have grabbed me by now if you weren't.'

A shout from below. They both twitched but it was only one of the mudlarkers.

'They won't give up, you know,' Reuben said. 'Never. They've put the word out everywhere.'

Elizabeth was cold. Despite the coat and the beret and the heat of the day, she shivered.

'What happened, Soph? I warned you not to mess with them. But to do this!'

'No, be truthful, Reuben. You told me not to get involved with them in the first place.' Her voice was like a whip.

'Yes,' he said. 'And I was right.'

'What was I supposed to do then? You and I both know that it's the only way for people like me to make money. They seemed a classy outfit.'

Faced with her anger, Reuben was silent for a long moment, running a finger along the gaps between the wooden slats of the table. 'Or so you thought,' he said quietly and I saw a glimpse of the youngster who'd saved Carly at Euston Station.

'Do you think I *wanted* to do it?' There was no pretence in Elizabeth's vehemence. No conscious shaping of her expression nor careful choice of word and tone of voice. She was angry Sophie once again.

Someone called out to them from the pub doorway. 'No table service. You'll have to get your drinks at the bar.'

Reuben raised his near-empty glass in acknowledgement and one of the elderly men sitting three tables away from us stood up.

Elizabeth ignored it all. 'Do you think I didn't hate every last minute of it? The only way I could do it was by shutting off. Pretending I wasn't there, that I was someone else – the person they wanted me to be. You get good at going through the motions after a while, you know.'

Bubbles of memory burst in her head. I saw a hundred men scan her up and down. I saw doors shut behind her. I saw bodies and beds and felt flesh slap against flesh. I saw things I didn't want to see. Things *she* didn't want to see. These were the dark, slippery memories that skulked in the corners of her mind.

I shut off from the clamour in her head and focused on the sun sparkling on the Thames and the cries of the gulls circling above the mudlarkers and the voices of the old men discussing types of beer. Elizabeth's hands clenched and unclenched on the table. She pushed the memories back down and her hands stilled.

'Most of the girls take something to help them get through, you know.' Elizabeth wrapped her arms around herself. 'I never have. But the last time they offered me something, I caught myself thinking, why not? The other girls said it made it easy, and I just wanted a bit of easiness.'

'You didn't, did you, Soph?'

'No. Nothing except the occasional sleeping tablet afterwards, when I needed to forget... but I knew I would someday. Everybody does.' She bit her lip and I was sure she was thinking of her drug-addicted mother.

The shadows in Reuben's eyes darkened and he went back to brushing his finger along the long table slats.

Neither of them spoke for a while, although it was not an uneasy silence. Elizabeth slouched over the table and sank her face in her hands in a most unElizabeth-like way. Normally she held herself tight when she was with anyone else. Reuben had been a thread in her life since she arrived in London and, I realised, he was the closest she had to a friend. Was that why she was here? To spend time with a friend. I thought there was more to it than that. She wanted something. She was keyed up.

'How did it happen?' Reuben asked. 'You didn't tell me much when you came round.'

'When you told me to get out, you mean.' She grabbed his restless hand. 'Don't, you'll get splinters.'

'I was right. They weren't far behind you, you know. They know we're friends.' He pulled his hand away from her, took his glasses off and wiped them with the bottom of his T-shirt. One arm was held in place by Sellotape.

'Reuben?'

He blew on the glass and rubbed hard on the grease marking the inner side of the lenses.

'Reuben?' Elizabeth's voice was urgent.

'I told them I hadn't seen you but if you get in touch with me, I'm to let them know.'

Elizabeth whipped her gaze round the tables and along the road in both directions but no one was there apart from the mudlarkers below and the two old men, one still at the table and the other crossing to the pub. A group of youngsters shouted insults at each other but they were far away.

'But I haven't and I won't. You know that, Sophie.'

Elizabeth nodded but her muscles retained their readiness to run.

'Tell me what happened.'

'Don't you know?'

'I know old man Petraitis is dead and you're involved.'

'He is dead then?'

'Yes.'

Her breath left her body in a long-drawn-out sigh that left her empty.

'I knew he was really but I guess I hoped he might not be. Not that it would have made much difference.'

'How?'

Elizabeth didn't want to tell Reuben. Her breathing was shallow and rapid and her skin twitched but she forced calmness into her body and words into her mouth.

'I was in a hotel with – let's call him Max,' she said. 'He's a regular. Always asks for me because... Well, never mind about that. But this one was "off the books", so to speak.'

'But you were bound to get found out.'

'I wanted to stop, Reuben. And to stop, I needed money. Real money, much more than I could get doing a few scams for you on the side. Seeing a few of my clients privately was the only way. I was careful. I only did it with the ones I knew well, the ones I could trust. Or thought I could. Max and I met in a hotel I hadn't used before, in Paddington, one of hundreds. And we did the thing.' She shrugged and laughed. It wasn't a nice sound. 'Maxie boy made sure of that. He got what he wanted first. And when I asked him for the money, he laughed at me, and the next thing I know he's grabbed me and told me they're waiting downstairs.'

Oh God. Part of me couldn't believe what I was hearing. Couldn't believe this hid beneath Elizabeth's aloof and composed exterior. But part of me realised how horribly inevitable it all was.

Now it was Reuben's turn to glance uneasily around. 'And?'

'I kicked Max where it hurt, punched him in the face, and smashed one of the hotel chairs on his head. Flung my clothes on, snatched his wallet and scarpered, but down the fire escape.'

Her breathing had quickened as she spoke, and memories of terror leaked chemicals into her blood. She quivered. Deep inside herself.

'Old man Petraitis was already there. They must have guessed I might take that way out.'

Her voice cracked and at the same time so did her mind. Memory flooded through.

She is two floors up on the fire escape. Beyond the leering face of the old man with the greasy comb-over blocking her way is the jumbled mass of backyards, alleys and outbuildings that lie behind the streets of grand houses now converted to seedy hotels like this or thin-walled flats. Not that she sees them.

Her eyes are fixed on the man before her although she hears the other men burst through the door behind and come to a halt at a nod from him.

He laughs, unbuttons his trousers and points down.

In case she hasn't understood, one of the men behind her gives her a shove forward.

She is on the point of kneeling. On the point of giving in. When a wave of fury surges through her veins. It's powered by swirling scraps of memory – of her childhood, of sniggering children and scornful girls, of the seedy encounters in cramped bedrooms.

Another nudge from behind but harder this time.

And the rage takes her over. She scarcely knows what she's doing as she raises her arms and lets the force of the push propel her forward. She thrusts her hands forward and shoves the old man away. His mouth opens and his hands flail but miss the rail and he tumbles. He tumbles down. Down one flight of steps and comes to a sudden rest. His legs dangle over the next flight and beneath his head a slowly spreading pool of red makes the dark metal gleam.

A short moment of stillness, then the men behind race down the steps.

Quick as a flash, Elizabeth turns. Runs back into the hotel, down the main stairs, through the reception and out into the street. She runs and runs and runs. The roads, the passers-by, the cars, everything is a blur.

'I pushed him out of the way,' Elizabeth said. 'And he fell. I knew it was bad, so I ran. And I've been running and hiding ever since.'

I was shocked. And horrified. And a whole host of other things. But most of all I was struck by how bloody funny it was! Elizabeth was on the run. Hiding from men I didn't want to meet. I'd discovered someone whose life was worse than my own and I was stuck with her.

The barman sauntered over and cleared their table, establishing that none of the drinks belonged to Elizabeth and Reuben and slopping the remnants of someone's beer over Reuben's battered trainers. They waited while he gave the table a cursory wipe and left. I wished I could get up and leave, too. Leave Elizabeth and the mess she was in behind.

'I went back to my flat,' she said. 'Eventually. I wasn't stupid. I hung around and watched for a while. And they were there already. I knew it was all up for me then. So I walked away. Kissed goodbye to all my stuff. Got on the first bus and ended up in Greenwich. Bought a few things with Maxie's money, stayed at a hotel for a few nights, and then I found a place to rent. Some dumb girl with a shop selling masks looking for a flatmate.'

Yup, I thought. *Some dumb girl who took you at face value, who never thought to ask for references, who fell for your glib story*.

I didn't blame her though. I wished I'd never met her, but I didn't blame her for all the lies she'd told me.

No more, I realised, than I blamed her for killing a man.

Rage and fear had made her lash out. I understood that.

'Where *are* you living?' Reuben asked. Then as she went to answer, he interrupted. 'Don't tell me,' he said. 'I shouldn't have asked. I'd rather not know.' He swiped a lock of hair out of his eyes. 'Do you think we should buy a drink?' He gestured to the empty table.'

'No. Look, I've fixed some computers for you,' she said rapidly.

'Solicitors?'

'Small ones, who mainly do conveyancing. Like we used to.'

'I wished you'd asked me first. I'd have told you not to bother. They're getting wise to it now.'

Nevertheless he took the piece of paper and USB stick she held out to him and put them in his wallet.

'Rubes, could you give me some money now?' Her voice was different. Less sophisticated. Less knowing.

Reuben didn't reply.

'I'm utterly skint. I'm reduced to going out at the weekends and picking up anyone who looks like they might have money on them.'

'I can't, Sophie.'

'Please. Rubes. *Please.*'

'You said you had quite a stash already.'

'I did. My rainy-day money.' Her voice sharpened. 'But someone got into my bank account and cleaned it out.' She held his hand tight and twisted his little finger. 'Someone good with computers. With IT skills. Someone like you.'

He jerked his hand away. 'Not me, Sophie. You know I wouldn't do that. Not to you.'

They stared at each other.

'Did you leave your computer in your flat?' Reuben asked.

'Of course I did. Do you think I take it with me when I'm seeing a client? I had nothing except what was in my bag.'

'Easy for them to get at your account then.'

'I suppose so.' She relaxed. 'Sorry. I should have known it wasn't you. I'm paranoid.'

He touched a faint trace of bruise round her eye. His fingers were damp on her skin, and she pushed them away. But gently.

'That wasn't them. I wouldn't be here if they'd got me.

You know that. At least, I don't think it was them. A car crashed into me. The police thought it was suspicious.'

'Not them,' Reuben said. 'Not personal enough. You've killed his dad. Matis will want to watch you suffer. And film it.'

A late summer wasp buzzed between them and landed on the table close to a splash of beer the barman had missed.

'Please, can you give me some money? Lend it to me if you like. I've got some coming in soon.'

'How much?'

'How much can you spare?'

'Fifty?'

'Fifty pounds! But you'll get much more from those solicitors.'

He laughed. A sour little noise with no hint of amusement.

'I thought you'd have understood by now. The likes of you and me, we don't get the big payouts. We're just the mugs who do the legwork. I write the little bugs that slip into their computers and explore all their secrets, find their codes and pass them back. But I don't get the big money. Or I didn't. I've stopped. Thought better of it after what happened to you. I'm back delivering on my bike. The money's shit but I'm not looking over my shoulder all the time.' He took his glasses off and wiped them again on the bottom of his T-shirt.

More shouting from below. The mudlarkers had dug a hole in the sand and hit black mud. A pile of it sat beside the hole. They'd moved away from it though and stood beneath the wall under us, laughing and exclaiming. Elizabeth sniffed and the smell of rotten eggs made her gag. Hydrogen sulphide. The mudlarkers had uncovered something less pleasant.

'Urgh. What's that?' Reuben asked.

'Something rotting in the mud.'

He covered his nose and sighed. 'I could maybe spare you a couple of hundred, Sophie, but that's all.'

'Thanks. It'd help. Anything would help.'

He put a tatty pile of notes into her hand and squeezed it shut over them. He must have known she'd ask for money and come prepared.

The smell grew stronger.

'Let's move,' Elizabeth said.

'I should be going.'

'Not yet. There's something else.'

'What?'

'Not here. Let's get away from here. It's too hot to sit outside anyway.'

He shrugged but followed her along the path that led along the Thames back to the centre of Greenwich.

By the time they came to the Old Royal Naval College, with its twin domes and symmetrical white buildings opening to the Thames, the underarms of Reuben's T-shirt were wet with sweat and he was wheezing. Elizabeth slowed.

'Let's find somewhere to sit,' she said. 'There are benches.'

'It's the grass,' Reuben said. 'There's too much pollen. I'll head back to the high street and get a bus.'

'Not yet. Let's go in here. It'll be quiet and we can sit down.'

She dragged him up the steps into the Painted Hall, paid for them both with Pete's money and pushed him into one of the wooden chairs scattered around the lower hall. He leaned his head between his knees and took deep, rasping breaths. She stared at the back of his head. At the loose flecks of dandruff contrasting with the dull sandy hair. At the faint glimpses of scalp poking through the gaps between the congealed locks. At the hunched frayed green collar moving up and down as he gasped. One of the most spectacular painted spaces in Europe soared above her, but she kept her eyes fixed on the lines of grime where Reuben's neck had met his coat for many years.

Reuben found his inhaler and puffed it into his airways. She waited until his breathing had calmed and then spoke quickly.

'Reuben,' she said, 'I need something from my flat.'

'No way.' His breathing grew hoarse again. 'No way, Sophie. Someone will be keeping an eye out.'

'Go early. In the morning. Before seven. When no one's about. Go up the fire escape and in through the back door. I've got the key.'

He rested his head against a pillar. 'No. It's too much. You're asking too much.'

'Please.' She took a deep breath. 'Look, we've never talked too much about the past, about our families and stuff like that. But I've got no one, you know. No one. You're the only person who's ever done anything for me.'

She stopped and her eyes filled with tears. She dashed them away with a finger. I couldn't for the life of me tell if they were real or if they'd come from the part of her, the chameleon part of her that knew what everybody wanted from her and played along with it. But I could tell this was important. This was the reason for meeting Reuben. Everything had been leading up to this.

'They'll have been in your flat. There won't be anything left.' Reuben's voice was gentler.

'There will.' Elizabeth dropped her voice so that not even the vast hall's echo picked up a whisper of it. 'I've got a hiding place and I don't think they'll have found it.'

'Where?'

'Will you get my stuff then?'

Reuben didn't answer. His gaze shifted beyond her and up into the building.

'What is this place?'

'Some old hall.'

'It's amazing.'

He heaved himself up and wandered into the Upper Hall with its vast painting covering the far wall. She followed him.

'Incredible,' he said. 'From a distance I thought the steps and arch were real.'

Elizabeth stared at the painting of George I and his family seated on the steps of a great building with pillars and arches, St Paul's Cathedral in the background.

'I guess so,' she said.

'What do you need from your flat, Sophie?'

'It's an envelope, Sellotaped to the underneath of one of the kitchen units. The one under the sink. If you pop out the plinth and put a hand underneath, you'll feel it.'

'And...'

'It's got a passport and some cash.'

'Your passport?'

'No. A false one.' She switched her eyes from George I's face, somehow so ordinary-looking despite the magnificent figures and glorious architecture that surrounded him, to Reuben. 'I need to disappear.'

'For sure.'

'I mean really disappear. No more Sophie. I need to get out of London, maybe out of the country, give it some time and come back as someone else. Someone new. Someone no one knows.'

Reuben raised a sceptical eyebrow, and his gaze wandered away from her and back to the painting.

'Plus I need a bank account. A new one. And I need a passport to open one. I can't do anything without some ID. Not these days. It used to be easy, but it isn't any more. I'm this close to getting my hands on some money.' She held up the thumb and forefinger of her right hand. 'But I need a bank account.'

His eyes never shifted from the painting.

Silence.

'All right,' he said in the end, and he gave her a quick smile but he held up a warning hand. 'I'll try. I'm only saying I'll try. And I'll have to think about how to do it.'

'I need it soon. The money's just waiting. Nobody's looking out for it. But that will change. I need to act fast.'

Something told me Elizabeth was talking about my money. And I realised it was my death that might change everything. If I died, my bank accounts would be frozen. She was as short of time as I was.

Voices drifted in from the entrance. More visitors. Their footsteps on the stone floor echoed through the building. Elizabeth's shoulders tensed and she darted a look left and right. There was no way out except back through the main door. The steps and arch leading to a sunny sky and open air before them were a painted mirage. She grabbed Reuben's arm. I felt the question in her eyes.

'It's just tourists, Sophie.'

She risked a glance over her shoulder.

A family strolled towards them. Mum and Dad poring over a guidebook with teenage daughter behind, bored and wearing headphones. Elizabeth's shoulders dropped a little, and she smiled and nodded at the parents as she and Reuben slipped past them to the open door, where they both stopped and scanned the green lawns and arcades from the top of the steps, then said a curt goodbye and separated.

I realised she was always tense and watchful. Especially when she was outside the flat. It hadn't registered as odd before. Maybe because it was a feeling I'd been used to. Eternal watchfulness. Always present. I'd never managed to get rid of it entirely. Even though Gavin was dead.

27

Elizabeth walked back to the flat, head down, as though the weight of her thoughts pressed on it. Mine were turbulent, horrified by what I'd learned. So many things made sense now. The clothes Elizabeth wore when she ventured out of the flat. She was unrecognisable in the hats and the bulky coats. Her uneasiness every time she went out; she was always looking over her shoulder for the people after her. Extremely nasty people, by the sound of it. I absolutely didn't want to experience how nasty they might be. The way her body shrivelled when she thought of them told me it would be beyond anything I could bear.

The alley leading to the shop was dark and the air felt different. Thundery clouds crept over the sky, and the dry leaves clustered in the corners twitched as short gusts of wind blew over them. It was still hot though. A heavy heat that squeezed the energy out of you.

Elizabeth stopped before she reached the shop and tugged the wig off her head, put it into her bag and opened the flat door. The connecting door between the shop and flat was open and Amy called through to her.

'Elizabeth. A package arrived. It's addressed to Sophie somebody, care of you.'

Elizabeth's heart beat a rapid tattoo then calmed. I wondered if this was the package I'd heard her ordering over the phone.

'Oh yes,' she said. 'Someone at work who's on holiday asked if she could have it delivered to me.'

Outside, a gust of wind spattered flakes of dead leaf over the window.

'I guess summer's finally over,' Elizabeth said. 'Where is my package?'

'I put it in the stockroom on Lucy's desk.'

'Thank you. I'll get it.'

She nipped into the back room and picked the package up from the old table I used as a desk. Its drawer was slightly open. Amy must have unlocked it for something. Quickly and quietly, without a second's hesitation, Elizabeth rifled through the contents. She found what she was looking for. I knew because she couldn't contain a breathy gasp.

My passport.

She curved her lips when she saw the photo. Taken just after I returned to England, married to Gavin, I'm wearing my best Surrey village lady pearl earrings and looking uncomfortable. What did she want with my passport? Was she thinking she could use it to go abroad if Reuben didn't manage to get hers?

Elizabeth shoved it in her pocket as Amy came through the door. She picked up her parcel.

'You found it then?'

'Oh yes. Sorry I was just looking at...' Her eyes fell on a

silicon mask I'd made for a local amateur film group. Elizabeth pointed to it.

'Albert,' Amy said.

'Albert?'

'Einstein.'

'Is that who it is?'

'Yes. An early version anyway. No hair. The finished one had hair. Lucy keeps it to show clients.'

The shop bell rang, and Amy peered through the door.

'Tilly,' she called through. 'We're in the stockroom. You're back early.'

No reply.

'Are you OK?'

Tilly came into the back room and sat heavily on my office chair. Her face was empty although her jaw was clenched and her torso rigid. Only her hands twitched, rubbing her fingers together in furious circles and plucking at the cloth of the jeans she'd gone back to wearing.

'Tilly? Has something happened? Was it the meeting with the consultant?' Amy's voice was soft.

Elizabeth fingered my passport in her pocket and glanced at the door. She was itching to get away.

'If you don't mind talking about it, that is?' Amy added.

'No. It's fine. I need to anyway because it's going to affect you both.' She took a deep breath. 'There's no easy way to say this. They think Lucy is dying. She has no higher brain activity. The consultant explained it to me, but it just means that there's nothing left of her inside her body. It's a shell. An empty shell.'

'Dying?' This was Elizabeth. Amy reached out a hand and touched Tilly's shoulder.

'If they're right, it's only a matter of time. Her body, her reflexes are shutting down and there's nothing they can do.

They'll test again tomorrow but sooner or later...' She tried to swallow but the effort was too much and a great sob snatched her breath away. 'Sooner or later, there'll be no point carrying on pumping oxygen into her lungs. They wanted me to be prepared.'

When? How long? That was all I wanted to know. Elizabeth's eyes fluttered with the speed of her thoughts.

'Have they said how long?' she asked. She wanted to know too.

Amy winced at Elizabeth's question. 'It doesn't matter,' she said quickly.

'Yes, it does,' Tilly said. 'Of course you need to know. However no one can be sure. Maybe tomorrow—'

'Tomorrow?' Amy and Elizabeth spoke at the same time.

Tomorrow. Tilly had said tomorrow. My thoughts reeled, undetected beneath the turbulence of Elizabeth's which were making her fingers twitch and her eyelids flicker. The thought they might pull the plug on me as soon as tomorrow perturbed her too.

'I've got another meeting with the consultant tomorrow to review the... the situation. But he told me to come home, to speak to family and friends...' Tilly fingered the papers on my desk. 'I should ring Lucy's solicitor really. And I suppose I should call Gavin's parents.'

'No.' Amy and Elizabeth spoke together again, but Elizabeth let Amy continue with a flick of her wrist.

'Don't. It can wait. Go back to the hospital. Take this time with Lucy for yourself.'

'Leave the solicitor and the paperwork until later,' Elizabeth added. 'Be with Lucy.'

Tilly sighed and sagged against the desk like a balloon puckering as the last gasp of air left it.

'I'm going to shut the shop,' Amy said. 'It's lunchtime anyway.'

She marched away and the sharp clash of the bolts closing was followed by the noise of the cupboard door under the till opening. She came back holding the bottle of grappa Pietro had sent me from Venice when I'd written to tell him about the shop.

'I think we should have a drink.'

Amy's eyes were bright and blinking rapidly. Tilly nodded. 'Why not.'

Amy pulled three mismatched glasses out of a drawer of odds and ends and sloshed a large measure of grappa into each.

'Sometimes,' she said as she stoppered the bottle back up with a sharp push, 'if we'd had a difficult day, Lucy and I would close the shop early and have a quick drink.' She passed a glass each to Tilly and Elizabeth. 'So... so... well, it just feels right.' She raised her glass. 'To Lucy.'

She knocked the glass back and gulped the clear liquid.

'To Lucy,' Tilly said and repeated her action, although her gulp was more of a large sip.

'To Lucy,' Elizabeth echoed but she too took a cautious mouthful. As well she might. Pietro's grappa was not for the faint-hearted and when I'd had a drink with Amy, the glasses had contained a fraction of the amount she'd poured.

The grappa burned a trail down to Elizabeth's stomach and she discreetly placed the glass down on the table.

Amy pulled a tissue out from her pocket and scrubbed her face, leaving marks round her eyes. She downed another mouthful. 'Sorry, but I can hardly believe it. It doesn't seem right. Lucy, I mean. I can't take it in. She's been so good to me.' The tears welled up in her eyes and she attacked them with the tissue again.

God, I thought, *I'm present at my own wake.* The warmth of Pietro's grappa radiated into Elizabeth's stomach. Some part of it that had been clenched since the meeting with Reuben relaxed and she picked up her glass and took another mouthful, enjoying the blaze as it hit her insides.

'What a waste,' Tilly said. The grappa had stained her cheeks red and relaxed her voice. 'Such a waste. Lucy was only starting to have a life.'

If only that was true.

'I mean, since Gavin died.' Tilly gripped the glass with both hands as she spoke and swirled the liquid slowly round so it slopped against the sides. 'She was in a dreadful state after his death. But I hoped once she opened the shop and got back to work that some of the fun that had been crushed out of her would return. Even if it took time.'

'Losing her husband like that must have been awful.' Elizabeth's voice was sympathetic, but her hand patted the outline of my passport in her pocket and her eyes slipped out of focus. Her thoughts were elsewhere.

Tilly took another mouthful of the grappa and shuddered as she swallowed.

'I think it started long before his death,' she said. 'Did she talk to you about him?'

'Never.' Amy gripped her glass and leant forward. 'She never mentioned him. She never said his name. Not once. Never even told me she'd been married until she had to.'

The two of them each took another gulp of grappa. Tilly's was less cautious this time. Then they looked at each other. I recognised the moment. It was an invitation to take the next step and confide in each other. I hoped they would. I wanted to know what they thought.

Tilly started.

'It was such a strange marriage,' she said slowly. 'Gavin

adored her, clearly, but I was never very sure she felt the same and she sort of disappeared under the weight of his love, if you know what I mean. God knows why I'm telling you all this.'

She broke off and I willed her to go on. Elizabeth took another sip of the grappa, then put it back on the table. She held her package tight.

'I didn't see that much of her after she got married and came back from Venice. Somehow it was never very convenient, but I went to stay for a few days, not long before Gavin died. Anyway, it was difficult. How can I explain? Gavin had taken time off work and thrown himself into plans for my stay. So, we were always going somewhere or doing something. When all I wanted was a quiet time to speak to Lucy and catch up. Sometimes he'd tell us he was leaving "his girls" to chat, but you always knew he was around and that he would come in soon and offer us a drink, or ask if we were warm enough, or how we liked our steak done. So there was never a chance to really talk.'

Time alone with Tilly. That was all I'd wanted. But Gavin had put so much energy into making Tilly's visit a success. I couldn't bring myself to suggest it. I knew how upset he'd be. How much of a heel he'd make me feel. And, above all, Gavin mustn't be stressed. Anyway, husbands and wives did everything together. That was the norm. I was the one being unreasonable.

But now a quiet voice asked me if spending a few hours alone with my aunt would have been too much to ask.

'And then Gavin invited me into her workshop. Without her. He showed me what she was working on and pictures of what she'd made recently. Told me how privileged he felt to share her artistic life. It all seemed marvellous on the surface. But...'

Amy pulled the top off the bottle again and waved it at
Tilly and Elizabeth but they both shook their heads. She
poured herself another glass, then leaned against the wall of
drawers and sipped as she listened to Tilly with eyelids half-
closed.

'Lucy was different,' Tilly went on. 'She looked different.
She dressed like someone thirty years older and all her
laughter and quirky grace seemed to have been sucked out of
her. It was as if the Lucy I'd known had disappeared behind
the exterior of a polite, Home-Counties wife. She didn't even
sound the same. The lovely Liverpudlian lilt to her voice had
gone.'

My accent. I was brought up near Liverpool, and you can
hear it in my voice. Especially when I swear. Don't get me
wrong, I like my accent. But occasionally it made people
laugh. They called me Cilla and Our Kid and repeated what
they thought were typical Scouse phrases and words. It could
get a bit wearing. I moaned about it once to Gavin, saying it
was difficult to be taken seriously because of it.

He agreed, said he'd often thought that, and threw
himself into helping me eradicate it, kindly telling me each
time I sounded Liverpudlian, even recording me and playing
it back. The final straw was the elocution lessons he bought
for our first wedding anniversary. He was devastated when I
was upset. Told me he hadn't realised how hard it was for me
to get rid of the accent. That he loved me just the way I was.
That it made me individual. That he'd never have started if I
hadn't said I disliked the way I spoke. I should have told him
I'd changed my mind. How was he supposed to know? And
his breath became irregular and noisy, so I remembered his
heart. And I said I was sorry. Again and again and again.

And he never said another word about it.

But he'd wince when I dropped into my childhood

accents and, after a while, I trained myself to speak with the rounded Surrey tones of his mother when he was with me.

Amy leant forward and spoke. She bit each consonant tight and I wasn't sure if it was the effort of speaking through the alcohol or something else. 'Whatever went on between Gavin and Lucy, it wasn't good. Believe me. She had a way of flinching when I went into the stockroom sometimes, when she hadn't heard me coming. A way I recognised.'

Amy stopped, and Tilly said nothing. I was sure they were looking at each other, but I couldn't tell because Elizabeth had picked up the Albert Einstein mask and was staring at it with unfocused eyes, turning it round and round in her hand. The way you do when your mind is elsewhere. When it's fixed on working something out.

'Be careful with Albert Einstein, Elizabeth,' Amy said. 'He's quite fragile.'

Tilly smiled. 'Is that who it is?'

'An early version.' This was Amy.

'I know so little about what Lucy does.'

'It's really clever – look.'

Amy took the mask from Elizabeth and pulled it over her head, easing the silicon into place. The effect was staggering, though I say it myself. Amy disappeared and, in her place, an elderly man with heavy brows stood in the tiny stockroom.

I felt Elizabeth's mouth open, and Amy laughed. The mask moved with her face, so the old man laughed with Amy's deep gurgle.

'Amazing,' Elizabeth said with a trill of a laugh as she stood up. I'd have liked to stay, but Elizabeth wanted to get away. 'Thanks for taking my parcel in.'

Back in her bedroom she tore the package apart and revealed yet another wig. A long brunette one. She slipped it on and admired herself in the mirror, flicking its ends back-

wards and forwards over her shoulders, and laughed. Not an
affected trill this time but a burst of real pleasure. But my
thoughts were downstairs. With Amy and Tilly in the stockroom, downing grappa and sharing stories about me. And
about my marriage.

28

Elizabeth was full of energy. The alcohol and finding my passport had unlocked an excitement in her I hadn't felt before. The passport must be what she'd been looking for in my handbag in the hospital, in my bedroom and in the shop. Some other emotion also fizzed through her blood.

I thought it might be hope.

She sat on the bed and grabbed her phone. And went through the process of opening an online bank account. In the name of Charlotte Patricia Morgan.

My thoughts boiled. *What was this? What could it possibly have to do with getting her hands on my passport?* I stared at the screen as she filled out the details on the form.

Charlotte Patricia was a first-year student at University College London. Just arrived, I assumed, as it was the beginning of the academic year. She lived in my flat in Greenwich. She was several years older than the average first-year student, because her date of birth was close to what I thought Elizabeth's must be.

Elizabeth's fingers sped through the form. God knows it

was simple enough. At the end, the bank congratulated Charlotte Patricia Morgan. Her account would be open as soon as she provided them with proof of her ID and address. Elizabeth clicked on the option of taking it into a local branch and chose the one in Gower Street, near the university.

The noise of the shop door opening and closing came in through the open window. Elizabeth looked out. Tilly and Amy were leaving. Amy to go home, I guessed, and Tilly back to the hospital.

Elizabeth watched until they disappeared, then ran up the stairs to my bedroom and turned my computer on, whacked in the password and clicked straight through to my emails. The solicitors had replied. They were, they said, delighted to inform me that Mr Cooper had accepted my offer for the premises mentioned above. The draft contract was attached and they would be grateful if I would give them the details of my solicitor. They looked forward to a speedy and satisfactory conclusion to the sale.

She sent the contract to the printer in the shop and tore down the stairs to collect it, pinching one of the office envelopes to put it in. Then jogged back up to the flat, her nerves quivering with adrenalin.

I felt nothing but depression. Everything was hopeless. There was every chance they were going to discuss stopping my life support tomorrow. I was stuck. Trapped in Elizabeth's body. I'd have to watch as she stole my money and made Tilly at best homeless and possibly imprisoned for helping me cover up Gavin's death.

What a huge, huge mess.

I had to do something. I wasn't going to give up. I'd done that too often. I thought back over my plan to injure Elizabeth to get her back to the hospital and I thought I knew how to do it. Maybe because the knife set loomed large in my mind. Would it work? And more importantly, could I bring myself to do it? I wished I'd paid more attention to the basic anatomy we'd studied at college. Not that it had dealt much with arteries and veins. We'd learned about muscles and bones.

Elizabeth paced up and down her bedroom for a while, then sent a text to Reuben.

Desperate for stuff from my flat. Please Reuben.

He didn't text back.

She went into the sitting room and turned on the television. Her excitement was draining away along with the effects of the grappa, and she was tired after the disturbed night and meeting Reuben. I could feel it in the way her head lolled on the back of the sofa and her hands drooped on her knees. I kept as still as I could. It would be much better if she went to sleep while it was still day rather than the middle of the night. So much better to go to the hospital now. I thought of soothing things. Of gentle waves whispering against sand. Of soft pillows cradling her head. And faint summer breezes washing the heat off her skin. Maybe some of them would seep through the barrier that kept my thoughts and hers apart. Maybe she would go to sleep.

At first, the constant checking of her phone to see if Reuben had replied kept her awake, but gradually her limbs grew heavy, her eyes closed, and sleep captured her. I waited until I was sure this was more than a doze and tried to take control.

Her body resisted me at first. It was weighted down with sleep and didn't want to move. But I coaxed it to obey, careful to be smooth and calm. She wasn't deeply asleep and the slightest thing would wake her.

Everything was quicker this time. The things I'd learned

before worked straight away. We stood and walked out of the sitting room, each step gliding into the next so she would think she was dreaming of walking. We picked up the phone in the hall. Went into the kitchen. Headed to the sink and slowly stopped.

The knives on the wall glinted as I decided which one to use. The smallest would be best. Its weight would be the easiest to manipulate and it was super-sharp. Able to slice through the toughest meat with ease. It would have no problem with Elizabeth's soft flesh.

I laid her left hand, palm upwards, on the edge of the sink, lifted her right hand, curled its fingers round the smooth wood of the knife's handle and gripped it. Then held the blade a millimetre above the pale skin of her left palm with its fingers curved upwards as though begging. And I hesitated.

What if I cut too deep? What if I nicked an artery and she bled out on the kitchen floor? What if she woke and panicked and didn't see the phone I'd brought in from the hall and left beside the sink for her to call an ambulance?

There were endless flaws in my plan, but I couldn't think of a better one. Nevertheless I couldn't quite bring myself to plunge the knife into her flesh. The muscles in her right hand started to tremble with the effort of gripping the knife. Now or never. I pulled a deep breath into Elizabeth's lungs and turned her head away, readied the knife in her right hand to cut and... I saw her sleeping tablets, still lying by the kettle.

Sleeping tablets.

A memory stirred.

The bitter taste in her mouth the first night when I'd spoken to the Scottish nurse. I'd recognised it immediately. Sleeping tablets. Elizabeth had taken sleeping tablets. Maybe it was their effect that made it easy for me to control her body. Maybe they'd shut her deep into the paralysis of sleep and left her body empty for me to move into. Because it had been easier that time. So much easier. My control hadn't been perfect. Movement had been sluggish and uncoordinated but everything had been possible - even speech.

I laid the knife down and lifted the tap lever gently until water trickled out. Picked up a glass from the draining board and filled it halfway to the top. Thinking of streams rippling over rocky beds through a forest. *You're dreaming, Elizabeth.* Turned the tap off. Careful. Mustn't let the water spill as I placed the glass onto the work surface and took the bottle of sleeping tablets.

How many should I give her? She'd said up to two to Tilly but I'd give her one more – to be sure.

The bottle was hard to open, needing a push down and then a twist. I couldn't do it. Or, at least, I couldn't get Elizabeth to do it. It needed muscles in both hands to coordinate with each other and that was beyond me. I tried and tried and failed and failed. Until my frustration forced her lips apart in an explosion of air. And her hands opened the bottle. My anger had broken through and woken some muscle memory and it performed its task obediently.

But it had woken something else.

The desperation I'd felt had stirred something deep inside her.

I didn't have time to be careful. I chucked three tablets in her mouth, raised the glass, poured water between her lips and closed them. I couldn't get her to swallow. There were too many muscles involved, and my control was slipping as panic electrified her nerves.

Alarm rushed through her body. Elizabeth woke.

She started to swallow. A reflex action. Then choked as some of the water slopped into her airway. The glass tumbled out of her hands to smash on the floor and she whirled round, spluttering and coughing, with fists clenched and her eyes raking the air around her for an attacker. Then a long still-ness as she froze. There was no noise apart from the sounds of cars passing at the end of the alley.

Had she swallowed any of the tablets? Some water had gone down, but she'd coughed most of it onto the floor and work surface. I couldn't see the tablets, but they could be anywhere, rolled into a corner or under the table.

Her body sagged as she realised where she was. I felt her lips mouth, 'No.'

But she exhaled and forced herself to relax, picked up the bits of broken glass and placed them carefully on the worktop. And as she mopped up the water from the floor and squeezed the cloth into the sink, the roiling suspicion tore through her body again. I felt it as a brooding in her blood and a tension in her nerves quivering like the infinitesimal vibration of a tuning fork. It was hunting me again.

I shut down. Made myself transparent and forced my thoughts to echo back her feelings. I could do nothing except wait and see if she'd swallowed any tablets.

Her phone bleeped. She snatched it. She hoped it was Reuben, so I hoped it was Reuben. It wasn't. Disappoint-ment made her body sag. I focused on my own disap-pointment.

The text came from Jonty. *Where are you?* I remembered she'd arranged to meet him at seven. It was far later than I'd realised. Waiting for her to fall asleep, then getting her from the sofa to the point of swallowing tablets had taken a couple of hours. Some of the darkness outside was evening. Some, I thought, was an approaching storm.

On my way. Sorry, Elizabeth texted back. Her mood brightened. The suspicion and fear settled once more to its normal background hum. I wondered why, in the middle of everything else, she was so keen to see Jonty.

She grabbed her coat, rammed a woolly hat on her head and left the flat, walking down the dark side of the alley where the trees cut the light from the street lamps.

The pub was quiet. The traders had all packed up and gone. No visitors or tourists passed through and only locals came in. Most were inside, but Jonty sat at one of the tables outside under the market's glass roof, surrounded by empty stalls and black rubbish sacks. He raised his hand, but he didn't stand when he saw Elizabeth.

'Sorry,' she said, as she slid into the high-backed bench seat opposite him.

Wearing jeans and an ancient black T-shirt, clean but faded, he'd made no effort to dress up for her. Typical Jonty.

'Busy, busy day,' Elizabeth chatted away in her normal vivacious manner. 'And I hoped Lucy's aunt would be back before I set out, so I'd have the latest update for you.'

'How is Lucy?' he asked.

'Not good,' she said and told him everything Tilly had told her earlier. The likelihood I might never wake up. The decision Tilly was facing. I barely listened. I watched Jonty instead.

His face had always been difficult to read, but the years spent watching Gavin for signs of stress had changed me. I'd learnt to recognise the small clues that gave emotions away. And Jonty was upset. It showed in the breaks in his quiet breathing and the flick of his eyes away from Elizabeth. Things I wouldn't have noticed when I was younger in Venice. When I was Lucy the party girl, always in a rush, always looking for fun, like a moth fluttering towards the brightest light and never thinking that the glow of something dimmer might be better.

'Drink?' Jonty said when Elizabeth had finished telling him how I was.

'Yep. Sauvignon.' She smiled. 'And then you can tell me all about Denmark. I'm mad to visit it. It's been on my bucket list for years and I thought I might organise a trip very soon.'

He disappeared into the pub and I wondered if an invitation to Denmark was what she was after. A chance to hole up and hide where no one knew her. Or maybe she just planned to rob him blind. Like me. She pulled a little mirror from her bag and touched up her lipstick before blotting most of it off with a tissue. She thought he liked her. I could tell. But I wasn't so sure. I thought he'd gone inside because he wanted a break from her. Time to think about what she'd told him. When things were mad busy at Ca'Maschera, he'd slip outside for ten minutes to escape the noise and people.

He was a long time and the quiet in the market was only broken by the background murmur of other customers chatting. Elizabeth's eyelids grew heavy and her head fell forward from time to time. She rested it on her arms and I began to hope. And when she leaned her head against the bench's high back, I was sure. She had swallowed some of the tablets and they were taking effect.

Her consciousness relaxed its grip on her body and retreated. It went a long way away, further than ever before, like the lowest of low tides ebbing to leave expanses of wide, flat sand. I slid into the places she'd deserted and settled there. I took over her limbs and stiffened them, raised her head and opened her eyes. The links snapped back into place. It felt exactly as it had in the hospital. Her body was mine. A little slower than usual. A little strange at times. But obedient and controlled.

It was fabulous and fantastic. And thrilling and amazing. I stroked the table and tapped the table and pretended to play the piano on the table. Suddenly I was desperate to dance and jump and run to experience the sheer bliss of freedom.

Jonty walked back out carrying a glass of wine and half a pint of beer. He put the wine down in front of me.

'Thank you.' Elizabeth's voice slurred as I spoke and I coughed to explain it away. Not that I cared. It was wonderful to speak. To think of words and to hear them said. After days of being dumb.

I lifted the glass of wine and drank a mouthful. It wasn't elegant but everything worked. Jonty looked at me as though he hadn't noticed me before. Had he sensed the change?

'Hey,' I said and I couldn't keep the lilting cadence of happiness out of Elizabeth's voice. 'Would you mind if I left you for five, maybe ten minutes? It's been a long old day, full of battles and strangeness and rushing around, and I could do with ten minutes of nothing. Would it bother you?'

Unless Jonty had changed completely, I knew he'd understand.

'Sure.' He smiled at me, and I wanted to kiss him. 'You go.'

'Promise me,' I said. 'Promise me you'll wait.'

'No promises, but I need more than ten minutes to finish my beer. If you come back soon, I'll be here.'

I stood and walked away, but as I left the tables around the pub, something came back to me. I turned and called to him.

'*Vi ses snart*,' I said. '*Vi ses snart*.'

'See you soon, too,' he replied, raising an eyebrow.

I left the market, went out into the street, and walked fast towards the Thames.

It was heaven. Elizabeth's limbs moved without me

thinking. I only had to fix on the idea of looking out over the dark water of the Thames and we were on our way.

We reached the esplanade surrounding the *Cutty Sark*, the fastest ship of her day, who ran before the wind, speeding cargoes of tea from China back to England but now lay trapped in concrete only a few yards from the surging waters of the Thames. I felt for her. On nights like this with the breeze off the water rushing past her masts, did she dream of the old days when she raced through the ocean? And I was possessed by the idea of running. There was no one much about. The storm-filled clouds had driven them indoors and, anyway, I didn't care what people thought.

I strolled around the great ship, alongside the sheets of glass that surrounded her hull and tied her to the ground, her masts and rigging lit up against the lowering sky, and walked faster as the wind blew ever stronger. And then I ran and ran. It still wasn't perfect. When Elizabeth was in control, her body ran in a smooth sinuous dance. With me, there were breaks, moments when her limbs moved in a way I didn't expect, hesitations when the instructions got lost somewhere along the unfamiliar pathways of her nerves. But it was good enough. For someone who'd been trapped, unable to move for days, it was more than good enough.

I caught sight of us reflected in the glass. We looked OK. We looked great. I laughed and she laughed back at me, and for a few moments we ran together, laughing into the night and giving each other thumbs up signals. Until a few drops of rain spattered the paving and I saw some passers-by had stopped to stare at us. One of them was holding up his phone and filming us. I slowed. I was being stupid. There were people searching for Elizabeth and, though I couldn't believe they had watchers on every street in London, it was mad to draw attention. Anyway, my ten minutes was nearly up.

I did some calculations as I strode back to the market and the pub and Jonty. I had six hours. That was what Elizabeth had said when she left the pills out for Tilly. The pills put her to sleep for six hours. And even if I called it four, allowing room for error, allowing for the fact that Elizabeth might be less deeply unconscious as the pill's effect reduced, I had three and half to go. It was eightish now. I was safe until eleven thirty. Enough time to talk to Jonty before I hurried to the hospital. I really should go straight to the hospital, but I couldn't. There was too much unspoken stuff between Jonty and me. Too many unasked questions, still unanswered.

My body might never wake up. Kept functioning by drugs and drips and pumps it might already have passed the point of no return. And I wanted to understand what had happened the last time I'd seen Jonty. On my final day in Venice, the day after my wedding, when I slipped back to Ca'Maschera to collect the remnants of my stuff after waving goodbye to Gavin at the airport.

The flights were full, and Gavin hadn't been able to book us on the same one. He was keen to get back to finalise the house purchase, although I didn't know that at the time, so he took the first flight, leaving me to follow the next day.

I was tired. Shocked and full of disquiet at what I'd done now that the excitement of the wedding and the honeymoon night were over. When I dragged myself into the great mess that the atelier had become over the last couple of months, every surface buried in the beautiful stuff we used for the masks, as though a tsunami had swept through it, carrying the people away but leaving debris everywhere, I felt as though time had ceased to function. It could have been the first day when we arrived and were set to work to tidy the place up.

I wished it was.

Jonty was in the side room where the four of us had worked together, clearing his table. Not that there was much for him to clear. Jonty's space always stayed tidy, an island of clarity in the chaos.

It was just the two of us. I said nothing and went to my table and started sifting through the wreckage to find the tools and sketches that belonged to me. We worked in silence, ignoring each other. His drunkenness at my wedding the day before had left him, but he looked cold and shivery and wore a huge cable knit pullover despite the mildness of the afternoon.

He put his last few bits and pieces in a cardboard box and headed for the door. I couldn't let him leave without speaking.

'*Vi ses snart*,' I said.

He stopped. 'That doesn't seem very likely.'

'You never know.'

'That, at least, is very true. With you, you never know.'

'Keep 'em guessing. That's what I always say.' I tried for a mocking tone, but I only heard echoes of uneasiness in my voice.

He must have heard them too, because he turned back. 'Why did you do it, Lucy?'

I couldn't meet his eyes. The fragments of cloth and sketches on the table blurred into one mass of colour as tears welled. I couldn't answer because I didn't know why. I only knew that it was a big mistake.

I heard Jonty dump the box on a pile of sample books. He wrapped his arms around me and buried his face in my hair. And I had a moment of utter clarity.

I disengaged myself from his arms. 'Why did I do it? A moment of madness, I guess. But it's over now.'

'The madness? The marriage?'

'Both.' Although my heart sank at the thought of what I'd have to do to separate myself from Gavin. 'Both,' I repeated and turned and swept my pile of belongings into an old carrier bag. 'When are you leaving?'

'Tomorrow.'

'China?'

'No. Home first. Denmark for a couple of weeks. Then I go.'

'Me too. Back to England.'

We stood on the steps outside that led down to the small canal and hesitated.

'A drink?' Jonty said. 'In the bar. For old times' sake?'

'A last drink. Yes, I'd like that.' The same question had been on the tip of my tongue, but I was glad he'd asked first.

One drink led to another. Another drink led back to Jonty's room, where we slept together for the first time. And the last. But despite the alcohol, we were sober. I remember it as a sober occasion. Both of us tentative but sure.

And the next day we travelled to the airport together and said goodbye. He didn't ask me what I was going to do. He didn't ask me to come to China with him. Or even to Denmark. He didn't offer me a refuge from my problems. At the time, in the airport, rammed close to him by the pressing crowds of travellers and feeling the warmth of his presence, it didn't matter. I was going to England to sort everything out, and then I'd be a free woman.

But Gavin and his parents picked me up at the airport and took me straight to a party of his friends and family to celebrate our marriage, complete with Champagne and speeches. Gavin wasn't even dismayed that I'd turned up in jeans, having forgotten his instruction to wear the blue frock he'd bought. He was just relentlessly pleased to see me. To

show me the house he'd bought for us. To describe the workshop he was going to build. And all the other massive
surprises he'd prepared to welcome me. Me, the woman of
his dreams. The love of his life.

I couldn't do it to him. I couldn't hurt and shame him in
front of everyone he knew. Not for the insubstantial something that lay between Jonty and me. The might-have-been.
The *Vi ses snart* he'd mouthed at me when we waved goodbye. It wasn't enough.

Weeks later, when I unpacked the carrier bag I'd swept
my things into on that last day at Ca'Maschera, I found
scraps of material and sparkly threads intertwined among my
possessions. I unpicked every single one of them and threw
them away.

29

Jonty was waiting when I returned to the pub.

'Hello,' I said. 'You still here?'

'Yes,' he replied. 'I have half my drink remaining. You could have taken longer.'

I took a sip of mine and reminded myself to be careful. The grappa still fired Elizabeth's blood and I couldn't afford to get drunk.

'Might you visit Lucy?' he asked. He'd been doodling, I noticed. While he waited. He'd always carried a notebook, an old school exercise book, filled with sketches of faces, but also used for the scribbles he did to keep his hands occupied while his mind was elsewhere. The page was covered with bits of Venice: the tiny window in the backroom at Ca'Maschera where we worked, too high to look out of and too small to give any useful light; the old juke box in the bar; and a dozen images of a girl dancing with hair flying and glimpses of laughter between her curls.

'Yes. Funny you should ask, because I'm going to the hospital this evening. In half an hour or so.'

The rain started. A spattering on the glass roof first, building to a steady drumming and the gush of water running through gutters and down pipes. Finally summer had broken.

'In half an hour?' Jonty jerked his head upwards.

'Or maybe a bit longer,' I raised my voice. 'I might wait until the rain has died down.'

'Perhaps I could come with you?'

He leaned forward to hear me over the drops drumming above.

'No,' I said. His presence might stop the transfer happening. 'Only one person allowed.'

Our heads were close. Like they often were in Venice, looking together at a sculpture for a mask one of us was working on, discussing the way the face muscles contracted to produce expressions, Jonty drawing marks on the clay with a fork to illustrate what he was saying. The memory was overpowering. I could smell the earthiness of the damp clay and the mustiness that lingered in every corner of the atelier.

There was so much I wanted to know. How had he been? What was China like? What had he been doing since he returned? Why had he waited so long to get back in touch?

The clatter of the rain drowned out the noise of other people's conversations and built a bubble around us, daring me to question him.

'You met Lucy in Venice, didn't you?' I asked.

'Yes. We were both apprentices at one of the big mask-making workshops.'

'Ah, you must have been there when she got married.'

'I was.'

I waited to see if he'd say anything else. But he seemed to be thinking.

'You know her husband's dead?' I said.

'Yes. I went to their house in Surrey looking for her. It was the only address I had. The neighbours told me Gavin had died. They didn't know where Lucy was, but they gave me Gavin's parents' address and Gavin's parents gave me her address in Greenwich.'

He didn't say anything about them, but I could imagine what they'd thought of him and what he'd thought of them. Was his turning up out of the blue behind Moira's questions about a boyfriend at the hospital?

The barman came over and lit the outdoor gas heater above us.

'First time we've had to do that for quite a while,' he said, as it hissed into life. 'Wonderful summer we've had.'

We both nodded and waited for him to go.

'There seems to be some...' Jonty hesitated. 'Some mystery about his death.' His eyes shifted away from mine. I could have let it go and pretended Elizabeth knew nothing but I found the truth was easier.

'You mean that Lucy'd left him and gone to London the evening he died, and the police found her there and arrested her for murder.'

None of this was a surprise to him. I could tell.

'I expect the neighbours told you,' I said. My bitterness coloured Elizabeth's voice. 'It was the talk of the village for weeks. People thought there was no smoke without fire.'

'You seem very angry,' he said.

I was, I realised. I was sick of the half-truths and the silences. God, but it was tempting to pour everything out to Jonty. Except he thought I was Elizabeth.

'I've been a victim of small-minded gossip, too,' I said quickly. 'It's difficult to deal with. You're caught in a sticky web of other people's words, but the spider never confronts you, so your life just leaks away while you're trapped.'

Especially if you feel guilty too, I thought to myself. Guilt traps you as much as gossip. But I didn't mention that.

'But surely nobody believed Lucy had anything to do with Gavin's death.'

I stared back at him without saying anything.

'No,' he said in the end. 'How could anyone think that – of Lucy of all people? I haven't seen her for a while, but she can't have changed that much.'

Tears prickled at the back of my eyes. Jonty didn't know how much I'd changed. How I'd turned out to be made of malleable clay that Gavin had shaped into his idea of a perfect wife.

I shivered. Elizabeth shivered, despite the warmth of the patio heater. It wasn't really cold, but the rain had made the air damp. I reached for Elizabeth's coat and shrugged it over my shoulders.

'Are you going?' Jonty asked.

'Soon,' I said. Thinking of Gavin's death had destroyed the magic of the moment. 'The rain is less ferocious now.'

As if to spite me, the storm hurled a gust of water against the roof above.

Jonty laughed.

'I'll get a taxi,' I said.

'Finish your drink.'

I couldn't. I pushed the glass away.

'I'm sorry, but I can't drink it. White wine belongs to hot summer evenings.'

'Something else?'

I shook Elizabeth's head and the strangeness of the situation struck me.

'Why are you here?' I asked and added hastily, 'If you've been out of touch with Lucy for years?'

Jonty stared at me, the light from the heater above casting

a yellow glow on his hair and skin. His face was impenetrable. As ever. And it drove me mad.

'Lucy was hurt, you know, that you hadn't kept in touch,' I said. 'She thought there was something special between you both.'

'She talked about me. To you?' Jonty folded his arms tight against his chest, bunching the faded logo of some obscure Danish band on his T-shirt. His eyelids lowered.

'Yes,' I said quickly and searched for a reason why Elizabeth and I would have talked about him, but I couldn't think of one. Jonty would just have to accept it. I couldn't stop the words pouring out of me any more than I could stop the rain cascading on the roof.

'She thought there was something between you. Something important. That, at the very least, you were friends.'

Jonty put his head in his hands and muttered something.

'She told me you got together,' I said. 'The two of you, on her last night in Venice. It meant a lot to her. And then you never spoke to her again.'

Jonty's head shot up. 'What did she expect?' A frown of quiet anger creased his brow. 'She was married to Gavin. Two days married to Gavin. I didn't know what she was doing, and it sounded as though the marriage was over already, as though she'd woken up and realised what a mistake it was. She was like a loose stone hurtling down a steep path during those weeks after she met him. There was no stopping her. I thought she needed some space and time to sort herself out.'

'Sometimes people dig themselves into a hole and they need help to get out.'

'She couldn't have doubted what I felt for her.'

'Really?' I said. 'Are you sure?'

His eyes narrowed at the force of my voice. He must have

wondered why Elizabeth felt so strongly on Lucy's behalf, but he answered.

'Look. She went back to England and to Gavin. I thought she'd let me know what was happening, but I never heard from her. I waited and waited. When I couldn't bear it any longer, I asked Pietro if he had her address. And he told me she was Mrs Lyle. Mrs Gavin Lyle. Living in Surrey. It all seemed so wrong. I wrote anyway. I sent her a couple of letters. But she never replied.'

I never got the letters. That was all I could think. *I never got the letters.* My thoughts raced and then I knew.

Gavin intercepted them. It was the only explanation. And my understanding of our marriage finally flipped the full one hundred and eighty degrees. He'd started cutting me off from my friends from the start. I'd sort of realised that he'd isolated me but some part of me still thought it was a misguided attempt to protect me. To shower me with love. But not this. Not stealing my letters. The knowledge blew oxygen onto my anger until it burned white-hot. I opened Elizabeth's mouth to tell Jonty that Lucy had never received his letters, but a sudden surge of rain made conversation impossible. The months of dryness were ending with a storm of water. Jonty leaned even closer and spoke into my ear.

'I had an email. An email from her that worried me. Just over a year ago.'

He'd got my email.

The email I'd sent the night of my epiphany on the train, when I'd realised I had to escape my marriage.

Dear Jonty,

I don't even know if this is still the right email address for you, but I hope you get this message. Where are you, and what are you up to? Still in China? Do you ever hear from David or Elodie? I saw that the company David works for won an award for a short film about a creature living in a rubbish heap, and I thought David must have had a hand in the creation of that.

Things aren't great with me. Sorry to burden you with it, but I need to write it down and somehow you seem like the right person to tell first.

I'm going to leave Gavin. I feel as though I've been going round in never-ending circles since I left Ca'Maschera. Maybe I'm right to do it or maybe I'm wrong. It doesn't matter, because I have to get away. Otherwise I'm going to lose myself completely. I already feel as though I've been slowly disappearing under the pressure of keeping Gavin happy.

Anyway, I'm sorry we lost touch. Let me know how you are. I'll try and be more cheerful next time I write. I promise.

My fingers had hovered over the keyboard as I tried to decide how to sign off. *All the best* felt too businesslike, although I wished nothing but the best to Jonty. *Love* was too presumptuous after years of silence. So in the end, I just wrote, *Lucy*, and, after a couple of minutes, added *xxx*.

I hesitated over sending it, but I heard Gavin's footsteps coming down the stairs, and my hand pressed the mouse button and away it went. And afterwards I was pleased. Until Jonty never replied, and I hoped it was because he no longer used that address. I prayed he'd never received it. Because I couldn't bear to think he'd ignored it and me.

'And you left it for over a year before you thought to come and check she was OK?' The words exploded from Elizabeth's mouth before I could stop them.

'I replied immediately. I told her if she needed to get away, to cram a few things into a bag and get on a flight to Copenhagen. She only had to tell me when and I'd pick her up. We'd sort it out together as friends. I wasn't expecting her to be anything else. Just friends. But I never heard back. And, you know, marriages are complicated things. I thought she'd changed her mind again. I thought she'd decided to stay so I left it. But, a couple of months ago, there was an article about her in a German magazine. It called her Lucy Christensen. It talked about her living in a flat above her shop in the centre of London. So, I thought... I didn't know what to think. But I decided to come and see for myself.'

I knew we were going to cry, Elizabeth's body and I. I could feel the ache round her eyes, and there was nothing I could do to stop it happening. My feelings had infiltrated her body.

I wasn't upset, though. Not at all. They were tears of relief. Huge overwhelming relief. Breaking over me like the waves of water the dark clouds were emptying onto the roof.

Gavin was a monster. I needed no more confirmation.

Even before the night our marriage ended, he'd been a monster.

I could be sure now. I had my proof. He'd intercepted Jonty's letters and monitored my emails, deleting Jonty's reply. It was easy for him. Because it never occurred to stupid, trusting Lucy to be careful. If only one communication had gone astray, I might not have been sure. But not both. Not the letters and the email. Gavin was the monster I'd begun to think he was.

The email. If he'd read Jonty's email, he must have known I was planning to leave. No wonder I'd thought he looked at me oddly from time to time. Oh God. That shed an entirely different light on the beating he'd given me. Maybe it hadn't been the reaction of a provoked and desperate man. Maybe it had been planned. Maybe he'd been waiting for the moment to come.

The thought was unbearable.

I grabbed Elizabeth's coat and stood, turning away swiftly to flick away the water from my eyes. I wanted to hug Jonty. To tell him everything. Except I couldn't. Not as Elizabeth. And anyway, I wanted to touch him with my own fingers and speak to him in my own voice. I needed to be Lucy. I needed to go to the hospital and get back to being Lucy. There were awful things waiting for me when I woke up – police and questions and maybe prison – but I still had to be me again.

'Got to go,' I shouted at him over the battering of water on glass. 'Otherwise, I'll be too late for the hospital.'

'You're leaving? Now?' He stood, too.

'I'll text you,' I said. 'Let you know how she is.'

'You can't go like this. We were halfway through our conversation. Lucy!' Shock stopped my tears. He broke off and shook his head. 'Slip of the tongue,' he said. 'You sounded so like her just then.'

'It doesn't matter. I have to go. Look, come round tomorrow. Tomorrow evening and I'll tell you how she is.'

I hoped it would be good news. I hoped Tilly or Amy or even Elizabeth would tell him I'd woken up. I'd still be in hospital but maybe he would come and see me and tell me everything he'd told Elizabeth this evening.

I left him standing there and raced into the street. Rain pelted down and I was soaked in seconds. I didn't care. At least nobody could tell I was weeping. Not that anyone was looking. Most people were heads down and rushing by. In a useless attempt to shelter, a few held bags or newspapers above them while some just stood, heads up and facing the dark sky roiling with clouds, glorying in the rain tumbling down.

I tore towards the taxi rank as though demons were after me. I didn't think I'd run that fast since the night Gavin died.

30

I thought I was safe the night I fled Gavin and the house in Surrey and checked into my studio flat.

I was still confused about what had happened. Despite the pain in my body and the cut on my face, I shrank from labelling myself a battered wife even when the reflection in the dark windows showed me the truth. The cut above my eye had bled again and mingled with the mud that covered my face, my hair, my clothes.

I stripped the filthy clothes off and winced my way into the shower taking care not to disturb the pain in my ribs and arms. Streams of dirty water drained away and once it ran clean, I soaped myself all over and let the suds remove the last traces of Gavin. Afterwards, I looked better. The cut on my face barely visible above my eyebrow and though my body hurt, only a few red marks showed on my skin. No one would guess what had happened. No one need ever know. I'd tell them I'd tripped and fallen. I couldn't bear anyone knowing.

For the little that remained of that night, I lay on the bed, shivering and aching, and gloried in being alone. The knock at the door broke the silence.

At first, I thought it might be Gavin and I lay quivering, as my carefully spliced strands of composure dissolved into abject fear. I wouldn't answer. I'd wait until they gave up. But the knocking didn't stop. And finally a voice announced that they were the police, and I needed to come to the door.

There were two of them. A youngish constable with blond hair and acne-marked cheeks and an older sergeant, quite a bit older, with streaks of grey in her dark hair, and a white mark round her wedding ring finger. I noticed it when she held out her ID and realised I was still wearing my ring. I was possessed by the urge to rip it off, but it stuck against my knuckle, and I had to be content with twiddling it round and round.

I knew their arrival wasn't good news.

'Mrs Lyle?' the sergeant said, her eyes narrowing as she scrutinised my face.

'Yes. I mean, no. Ms Christensen. Lucy Christensen. I don't use my married name.'

'Could we come in, Ms Christensen?'

'Could you tell me what it's about? There's not a lot of room in here.'

'Inside, Ms Christensen, please.'

We squeezed in. The flat was tiny and filled by the bed. I bundled the sheets and duvet out of the way and turned the bed back into a sofa. The constable tried to help but I shook my head.

'Sit down.' I gestured to the newly made sofa and pulled the stool out from the counter that served as kitchen work surface and table. We sat uncomfortably close to each other.

'Your husband is Gavin Lyle.'

'Yes. That is, he was. I've left him.'

'I see. And that would be a recent event?'

'Last night.'

Her eyes narrowed again. She took a deep breath.

'We have found a body that we believe may be that of Mr Gavin Lyle.'

Gavin was dead.

Part of me couldn't believe it. The last time I'd seen his face. Distorted with rage. Towering over me. He'd never seemed more alive.

Part of me was relieved. Whatever happened now, Gavin wouldn't come after me.

Part of me was terrified.

Something snapped and a flood of emotions broke through. My body shook. I couldn't speak.

I suppose the sergeant had been trained in how to break bad news, because she wasn't at all perturbed by my reaction, but repeated the words several times until they started to take on a reality.

'But how?' I asked.

'We were hoping you might be able to help us with that.'

Help them? What did they mean?

'Me? He was fine when I last saw him.'

'And when was that, Ms Christensen?'

Something told me to be very careful.

'Yesterday evening.'

'And where was that?'

'At our house. His house.'

'I see. And he was fine, you say?'

'Well, he wasn't happy. I'd told him I was leaving.'

'And then you left your house and came to London.'

'No.'

The questions were coming so fast. I wanted her to stop so I could get a grip on myself.

'That is, he left first, actually.'

'And where was he going?'

'His parents. He drove off... Has he had a car accident?'

It was a reasonable question. He drove too fast all the time, patting my knee and laughing at me when I flinched. It was exactly the sort of question a wife would ask. Even one who'd left her husband.

'Like I say, Ms Christensen. We're not sure. Could I ask what happened to your face? It looks very painful. Have you seen a doctor?'

I didn't want to talk about my face. 'I fell over.' I couldn't tell them Gavin had done it. I wasn't sure I would ever be able to tell anyone what he'd done to me. In any case, a hard edge had sharpened her voice and I wasn't going to reveal anything until I knew what was going on. 'Look. This is ridiculous. Please will you tell me what has happened to Gavin?'

She flashed a glance at the constable, and he jumped and pulled a notebook and pencil out of his top pocket, flicked through to find a blank page and waited, pencil poised, for me to speak. I realised the interview had changed from a house call to inform a relative they were bereaved to something entirely more sinister.

'I'm going outside to make a phone call, Ms Christensen.' The sergeant's voice was cold. 'I'd be grateful if you'd bear with me while I do that. PC Derring will wait with you.'

'Well, actually I'd quite like to have a shower and get dressed, so maybe you could both wait outside.'

'I'd rather you didn't do that.'

'Why? Please tell me why.'

But she pressed her lips together and left the flat.

PC Derring and I shifted around uneasily. Under my pyjamas the places where Gavin had punched me hurt and when I surreptitiously rolled up a sleeve I saw the red marks on my arms were tinged with blue. I guessed the bruises on my face had done the same. PC Derring sniffed and cleared his throat. I wondered if I smelled. I wondered if the flat smelled. I leant over and opened a window. He jerked his arm forward as though to stop me and then thought better of it.

'Don't worry,' I said. 'I'm not going to jump out.'

He wrote something in his notebook.

'How did you find me?' I asked. No one knew my address.

'ANPR.'

'What?'

'Automatic Number Plate Recognition. Cameras picked up your car and traced it to the car park here. Were you trying not to be found, ma'am?'

I didn't bother to answer this but sat and stared at him, trying to work out how much trouble I was in. If only they'd tell me where they'd found Gavin. None of this seemed very real. I wondered if I was dreaming. Was I still lying in the sitting room in Surrey, bleeding gently onto the carpet? But there was something deeply authentic about the police officer facing me, from his hands with the specks of white paint (had he been decorating?) to the way the ends of his blond hair curled as though it wasn't cut quite short enough.

And there was nothing dreamlike about his senior officer when she strode into the flat, snapping the fastener on her jacket pocket shut.

'Ms Christensen. I'm arresting you in connection with the death of Mr Gavin Lyle.'

My guts churned as she launched into the words so familiar from crime series on the television about not having to say anything but how anything I did say might be given as evidence.

This couldn't be happening.

'At least tell me what's happened to Gavin.'

'For operational reasons, I'm not at liberty to discuss your husband.'

She made no effort to be pleasant but bit the words out curtly.

'OK, I'll get ready,' I said.

'That won't be necessary.'

My pyjamas and dressing gown were new. Bought for my new life in London. Peacock blue and green. I loved them, but no way were they suitable attire for an interview with the police.

She gestured towards the heap of clothes on the floor by the sofa bed. 'Are those the clothes you were wearing yesterday?'

'Yes. I haven't had time to—'

She nodded to PC Derring who snapped on gloves, went over and held them up. Damp and muddy, they dropped bits of twig and grass on the floor as he placed them inside a large plastic bag and sealed it.

'I fell,' I said. 'In the mud.'

He wrote my words down assiduously and I realised I'd be better keeping my mouth shut.

After the indignities of taking my nightwear off while standing on a plastic evidence bag, and shivering from cold and fright while blank-faced officers swabbed different parts of my body and snapped photos of the red marks slowly turning to bruises, they gave me a paper suit to wear and escorted me to the interview room – a windowless square box decorated in cream many years ago and now a dirty porridge colour. There was nothing except a table in the middle and four scratched chairs, one of which lay on its side on the floor. The thin paper I was wearing wasn't enough to counteract the chill.

Luke was waiting for me. A young go-getting solicitor with a practice in the same Surrey town as Ted and Gavin. He handled mainly criminal cases. The kind of thing Ted and Gavin didn't want to touch. They respected him though and I liked him. He was a breath of fresh air with his skinny-cut suits and sardonic smiles at the ghastly civic events we had to attend. He'd been the only solicitor I could think of when the police had asked me if I wanted one. The awfulness of the forensic searches had made me sure I needed someone. Besides, he was a good solicitor. I knew that, because he'd never have survived in our whitest of white neighbourhood if he hadn't been outstanding.

Today his face wore a schooled expression of polite enquiry as though assisting a fellow solicitor's wife with a police investigation into the death of her husband was an everyday occurrence. An older police officer in plain clothes stood behind him. A skinny fellow with broken veins on his cheeks and wearing a tweed jacket with leather patches at the elbows, curiously out of place in the airless interview room.

'I'd like a word with Mrs Lyle, before we start the interview, DI Cromer.' Luke pulled one of the chairs out and gestured to me to sit. He held the door open for DI Cromer then closed it firmly.

I started to shake, rustling the paper suit so that it scratched the tender skin on my ribs. Luke sat down next to me. The nutty smell of the oil he used to groom his hair wafted over me, familiar and reassuring. The trembling calmed.

'Lucy, I know this all feels awful at the moment, but I need you to hold yourself together and tell me what happened.'

My teeth rattled when I opened my mouth and all that came out was a shaky moan.

'OK. You take a minute and I'll tell you what I know.'

He told me how Gavin's body had been found in the fields between our house and his parents' early that morning by joggers. His voice was soft but nothing could dilute the awfulness of the news. It was exactly what I didn't want to hear. The police had identified him quickly then discovered our house looked as though someone had broken in, and there was no sign of me anywhere. There had been some considerable concern as to what had happened to me. Hence the search.

'And that's all they've told me.' Luke waited.

I reached for threads of words, but they disintegrated into the silence when I tried to grasp them.

'How did he die?' I asked in the end.

This was the right question.

'I don't know,' Luke said. 'The police said nothing.'

'Could it have been his heart? He had long QT syndrome.'

'I really don't know.'

'He was very upset last night.'

Luke cleared his throat. 'Lucy, do you think you could tell me exactly what happened between you and Gavin last night, so we can work out why the police think you might be involved?'

'It's complicated.'

'It doesn't matter. Just start and I'll ask questions if I don't understand.'

Lack of sleep and the aftershock from the night before had robbed me of the ability to think clearly. I knew that. My thoughts strayed and fell into holes in my mind. I wanted desperately to forget everything, but Luke was waiting.

The truth was the only thing I was capable of. The truth. So I told him the bare minimum: I'd broken the news to Gavin I was leaving; he'd hit me – a lot; then locked me in and left; I'd escaped.

Luke said nothing while I spoke and the pauses while I searched for the right words were filled with the scratch of his pencil on paper. He sat next to me and I fixed my eyes on the stains on the wall opposite rather than see his expression as I told him Gavin had beaten me.

He let a long silence unroll when I'd finished, then stood and walked round to the other side of the table, picking up the chair on the ground and sitting in it to face me. His eyes were sombre.

'And that's everything, Lucy? You've told me everything?'

I lied. 'Yes.'

'And was this the first time Gavin hit you? Or hurt you in any way?'

'Yes,' I said.

But, I realised, I hadn't been surprised. It was as if I'd always known he would. The knowledge had been stored inside me, in a corner of myself that I hadn't allowed to penetrate my consciousness, but I'd been frightened of it all the time. No, he hadn't hit me before, but he hadn't needed to. Because I'd spent every waking minute of my marriage being the perfect wife.

'OK. We're going to tell DI Cromer what you've just told

me. Every bit of it, Lucy. Don't leave anything out. I'll interrupt you if I think it's necessary.'

'I told the police I got the injuries from falling over.'

'Ah.' He tapped his fingers together in front of his mouth and thought. 'I don't suppose they believed you for a second. You look as though you've been in a fight. But they'll understand when you explain. Sadly women often lie at first about being abused. It's an instinctive reaction. So don't worry about it.'

He thought a bit more.

'I wonder if that's what's behind them bringing you in. That and the fact that you had most to gain from Gavin's death.'

'Me?'

He raised his eyebrow. 'You'd have got little from a divorce, Lucy, but I imagine Gavin's death will leave you with money.'

His words punched the air out of my body.

He stood.

'Let's get them back and tell them everything. And I mean everything, Lucy. We don't want you to miss any little details that come back to bite you later. I'll make them wait until you've finished before they ask questions. Don't let them upset you and, above all, don't respond to them unless they ask you a direct question.'

They trooped back in. DI Cromer and yet another police officer. The thought of telling the whole story again made me tremble.

'Does your client need a doctor, Mr Awuah? She seems very upset.' DI Cromer settled himself opposite us on the table and signalled to his sidekick to start recording.

'She's doing the best she can, DI Cromer. Her husband has just died following a particularly violent incident of domestic abuse as you are about to hear. She wants to get this over and done with so she can go home. She'd like to tell you everything that happened last night. I'll stop the interview if I think it's getting too much for her.'

DI Cromer nodded and leaned back in his chair, arms folded and legs stretched out underneath the table that had been bolted to the floor with the worn carpet tiles cut clumsily to fit round the metal supports. I tried to keep my eyes away from him as I retold my story, easier the second time round – Luke knew what he was doing when he made me tell him first – but my gaze slid back to DI Cromer over and over again and one part of my brain started noting each flicker of his eye and twitch of his lips and analysing whether he believed me or not. Parts of my story sounded mechanical and unreal, as though I wasn't connected to it. As though it had happened to someone other than me. Occasionally it all became too much and I ground to a halt, Luke stopped them interrupting me with questions, and when I'd finished, insisted on a short break.

'Was I OK?' I asked when they'd gone.

'You were fine.' Luke saw the doubt in my eyes. 'It was fine.'

The breath left my body in a deep shudder.

'But be careful, Lucy. I'd say there's something still bothering them. We're not out of the woods yet.'

He was a comforting presence by my side throughout the next part of the interview, interrupting when he thought they were haranguing me rather than asking questions and referring them back to my statement when they asked the same questions, time and time again.

What time had I left the house? I didn't know. I hadn't looked.

Had I spoken to Gavin after he'd left? No.

Tiredness started interrupting the flow of my words after a while and when they asked me for the fifth time how I'd got out of the house, I cracked and started to cry.

'Do we have to go over this again?' This was Luke. 'Ms Christensen has told you several times that she smashed a window. You must have seen it when you went to the house. Could we get to the point of all these questions? My client is tired and understandably upset.'

DI Cromer and his colleague exchanged a glance. There was a tension in the room. I thought we were getting to the nub of the problem.

In answer, DI Cromer slapped three photos on the table.

They were of Gavin. The first was a full-length shot of him lying on his left side by a tree, his body slightly curled round the trunk. There was something deeply peaceful about the scene. A stray beam of early-morning light had picked out the frost sparkling on the long blades of grass framing his dark hair. You couldn't see his face.

In the second photo, he'd been turned onto his back. The contrast was sharper on this photo, and the dark colours had melted into one, so that his body had disappeared into the grass and his face showed whiter than white against it. Except for the black mark on the left-hand side that looked as though a handful of his cheek and eye had been gouged out, leaving a black hole in its place.

Luke's eyes were fixed on the third photo. It was a close-up of Gavin's face. The black mark on its left-hand side wasn't a hole but a bruise centred on his eye and falling onto his cheek and then splitting off to trickle down to his jaw. It was spectacular even in black and white.

'We were wondering if you know how his face became so badly bruised,' DI Cromer said.

I turned to Luke. His face was set in calm lines, but I

guessed he was as close as he ever got to being rattled. I looked down at the damning photos. Maybe it was my imagination, but I thought that Gavin's mouth was curved in a small, secret smile. I ignored his body though and scoured its surroundings. Grass mainly. A few twigs and a couple of stones. Nothing else. Nothing out of the ordinary. Maybe, just maybe, they hadn't found it.

Luke started to ask DI Cromer for a few moments alone with his client but I interrupted him.

'You think I did that?' I said.

Luke put his hand on my arm. DI Cromer cleared his throat and addressed me directly. The tic in his left cheek twitched.

'Your husband went to his parents' house after he left you. He was distraught because you'd had a row and told him you were leaving. They calmed him down and he phoned you.'

I opened my mouth to deny this and DI Cromer stopped.

'Yes, Ms Christensen. Did you want to say something?'

I remembered Luke's instructions about waiting for a question and shook my head. He narrowed his eyes and continued.

'Mr Lyle's parents told us you'd both agreed he should return home to discuss things and he left. He'd had a couple of drinks so he told them he'd walk back. That was the last time they saw him.'

DI Cromer looked at me but Luke tapped my knee warningly. I kept quiet.

'Maybe the telephone conversation between the two of you wasn't as calm as Mr Lyle made it out to be,' DI Cromer went on. 'Maybe you were frightened. Maybe you decided to walk out and meet him. In the open, where you could run if he threatened you again. And maybe the discussion got heated. Maybe Mr Lyle became violent again.'

Luke's hand increased its pressure on my knee. I said nothing. DI Cromer smiled.

'No one would blame you if you fought back,' he said.

'Is that a question, DI Cromer?' Luke's voice was sharp. 'Because I don't like the way you've phrased it. *You* might not blame Ms Christensen, but she would be laying herself open to a charge of manslaughter.'

'Maybe he walked too fast,' I said, ignoring the look on Luke's face. 'He was stressed and upset. Maybe he had a heart attack and fell and hit his head on something. He had heart problems, you know?'

'Heart problems?'

'Yes. Check with his parents if you don't believe me.'

Gavin's heart. It hadn't stopped him attacking me but maybe it would save me now.

'It is common knowledge that Mr Lyle had heart problems,' Luke added.

'Well, it's an interesting idea and we'll check, of course. But it doesn't explain Mr Lyle's face.'

He picked up the third photo, the one with the dreadful bruise running down the side of Gavin's face, scrutinised it for a few seconds than pushed it towards me.

Luke cut straight in.

'I see from the photo that Mr Lyle fell by a tree. He might well have knocked his head on a branch as he tumbled.'

DI Cromer sighed. A long heavy sigh as though what he was about to say pained him.

'Nevertheless, there are still a couple of details we're confused about. The clothes you were wearing last night, Ms Christensen, are covered in mud. The path Mr Lyle would have taken from his parents' house goes through some very muddy ground.'

He paused.

'Is that another question?' Luke asked.

'How did your clothes get so muddy, Ms Christensen?'

'The ground outside the window I broke is very muddy. I slipped and fell as I climbed out.'

'I see. This is when you broke out because Mr Lyle had beaten you and locked you in. And, yes, that is a question.'

'Yes,' I said.

'I just want to be sure that we've understood the sequence of events correctly.'

'Gavin beat me,' I said. 'In our home. Before he left to go to his parents'. These injuries are not the result of a fight after he left his parents' house.'

'Let me put an alternative scenario to you. Let's agree for the moment that Mr Lyle attacked you when you told him you were leaving. It must have been dreadful for you. You clearly had no choice but to leave right away. So you were facing a new life, on your own, with little money and no home, having to start again from scratch. Of course, you'd have got something from a divorce, but it would have taken time and money to fight.'

He stopped. For effect? To provoke a reaction from me? I didn't know. And at that moment words were beyond me. The room narrowed down to DI Cromer's face. Luke, the other officer, the faint hiss of the ventilation, they all faded away. Nothing else existed except the story he was telling me in a voice that was now gentle and coaxing.

'It must have seemed very unfair. Whereas if Mr Lyle were to die, while walking – or maybe running – back to see you, upset, stressed, angry. All the things he was supposed to avoid. With him dead, you'd be in line for a large payout.

The insurance would take care of the mortgage and provide a healthy sum, not to mention the rest of Mr Lyle's money. So we wondered, Ms Christensen, whether, with all that in mind, you slipped on a coat and went out to meet your husband in the fields.'

He'd finished weaving his story and I was caught, held tight in its clear, shining threads.

'Ms Christensen.' DI Cromer voice was gentle.

And in the morass of half-truths, he'd spun, I suddenly remembered the lie Gavin had told that might rescue me. The thread that, if pulled, would make the whole structure unravel.

'You said he phoned me. How did he do that?' I said.

DI Cromer frowned.

'Gavin had my phone. Like I told you. He'd removed all the phones from the house. He could call me as much as he wanted but I wouldn't have been able to answer.' I paused. 'Maybe his parents are confused. Maybe he pretended he'd spoken to me to give himself a reason to come back. I don't know. The only thing I do know is that I didn't speak to him, and I didn't know he was on his way back. I didn't go out to meet him in the fields.'

DI Cromer's mouth grew tighter and tighter as I spoke.

'We'll take a break,' he announced. 'Interview suspended at 15:32 hours.'

They swept out of the room and it seemed to me they took their shredded story with them, leaving only a few strands behind to float down and disappear between the edges of the grey carpet tiles.

'They've gone to check what you told them.' Luke said. 'Just sit tight. I'll get us both a tea.'

He told me to hang on in there when he came back with the tea, then slipped out, clutching a packet of cigarettes. Did he smoke? I'd never smelled it on him. Or was it merely a handy excuse to avoid spending time with me and asking me questions he didn't want the answers to?

Half an hour later, DI Cromer returned. An uncomfortable half hour during which the chill in the room made me shiver and I lived and relived the events of the night before, until they became jumbled and confused, and I couldn't remember Gavin's face without the great bruise.

DI Cromer was alone this time.

'Mr Awuah,' he said. 'We're going to release Ms Christensen on police bail pending further enquiries.'

'I see.'

'We've found Ms Christensen's mobile, the house phones and assorted keys in Mr Lyle's car, but I'm sure you understand we need to check out the rest of her story. It's in her own interest.'

'It's fine,' I said, while inside I screamed at him to let me out of this horrible room.

'Will you go back to London?'

'Yes.'

They released me on police bail, told me to stay in the country, and report back in a week. Luke drove me back to the flat in London.

'Hopefully there'll be no more of this,' Luke said as he pulled into the garage under my flat. I noticed my car had already been taken away. 'I think they've thrown everything they had at you – so unless they turn up something new...'

The steel, I thought, they couldn't have found the steel. But what if they did? It would have my fingerprints on it and traces of Gavin. I couldn't think about it now.

'Thank you,' I said. 'Thank you for coming out for me. I didn't know who else to ask. I hope it isn't too awkward for you. Because of...'

'Ted's a good man.' Something about the way Luke emphasised Ted's name made me wonder if he thought Gavin wasn't. He switched off the car and the comforting purr of the engine stopped leaving a cold silence. He tapped his fingers on the dash. 'I'd recommend you don't talk about... about Gavin...'

'About Gavin hitting me?'

'It will be better for you if the... er, problems in your marriage aren't aired. They're nothing to do with Gavin's death. Best not to muddy the waters.'

This was undeniably true.

'OK. I'm not coming back to Surrey anyway. Not ever.'

He nodded as though he thought that was a good idea. 'You'll come back for the funeral?'

'No.'

'Obviously it's your decision but I'd recommend you do.'

The leather seat creaked as Luke shifted.

'All right.'

One last effort, I thought. One last pretence that my marriage had been all sweetness and light.

'I can't have anything to do with organising it though. Ted and Moira will have to do that. Please will you tell them, Luke?'

He looked doubtful.

'Please. Tell them I can't. Tell them it's beyond me. Because that's the truth. Tell them to let me know when and where and I'll be there.'

But it was Luke who told me. When he rang to tell me Gavin's body had been released. The post-mortem examination had shown he'd died of heart failure, but whether that was caused by the long QT or the head injury, they didn't know. The head injury could have been the result of a fall, but it was more consistent with a blow to the head. They'd found no weapon near him, but he could have staggered some distance afterwards. The investigation was still on-going.

I was free. For the moment.

I am free, I said to myself as I got ready to go to Gavin's funeral, layering foundation onto my face. Only the scar running red and angry through my eyebrow and the fading bruises showed what he'd done, and no one would see them beneath heavy make-up. I just had to get through the funeral, then wait for the police to give up, and my new life would begin.

But the police never closed the investigation. They called me in 'for a chat' a couple of times and all I could do was pray the steel never turned up.

31

Taxis had disappeared off the streets as quickly as the rainwater gushed out of drains. A group of us waited without much hope for a bus and watched as several, brimming with passengers, drove past, drenching us with their wake, until one was held up long enough by the thickening traffic for us to force ourselves on. Water ran off us and gathered in pools on the bus's floor sloshing from one side to the other as the bus went round a corner and sent a fountain of spray over the pavements and walls. Streams of rain softened the sharp edges of kerbs and buildings. Everything was dissolving into wet.

The other passengers were hugely cheerful now we were on the bus and chatting as people do when something out of the ordinary happens. I was silent though, willing the bus to forge on through the river the road had become. Waiting for the bus had stolen precious time.

As we inched closer to the hospital, the main roads filled with traffic diverted off the smaller side streets that overflowing drains had made impassable. The bus crawled, then ground to a halt. Their good humour evaporated as the passengers began to realise that this was more than a rainstorm. All the water that hadn't fallen since May was pouring out of the sky. People stared at the news on their phones and muttered reports of the heaviest rain for thirty years, six months' worth falling in an hour, flash flooding and so on.

I looked at my watch. It wasn't there. I was confused then understood. For a brief moment I'd forgotten where I was. Elizabeth's body had become less strange by the minute as the links between us strengthened. I rarely had to concentrate now to make her do what I wanted. Elizabeth didn't wear a watch but her phone told me it was nearly ten. I'd spent half an hour with Jonty. Half an hour waiting for a bus, and now half an hour creeping through the streets of south London. My time had been nibbled away. Only ninety minutes remained.

Fifteen minutes later I gave up on the bus. We hadn't moved for ten of them, and word had filtered through of crashed vehicles blocking roads slippery from the grease deposited during the long summer months.

According to Elizabeth's phone it was a twenty-minute walk to the hospital, but that didn't take into account the difficulty of walking through blinding rain, of sidestepping people rushing along with their heads down and avoiding huge puddles and streams. It was ten to eleven by the time I turned a corner, and the hospital's lights came into view.

Not far now. I flicked the rivulets of water running down my face out of my eyes.

The hospital disappeared. A black hole swallowed up the sky where it had been. I looked around. The lights were off everywhere. No street lights. No cracks of light shining out from the curtained windows of houses. Only the headlamps of the cars jammed solid in the road still shone. It was a power cut.

I thought of my body, kept alive by the ventilator pumping oxygen into its lungs. The hospital must have back-up power. Surely, all hospitals had back-up power? Fear caught at my breath and tightened the muscles between Elizabeth's ribs as I waited for the lights to come back on and I realised the connection between me and her body was almost complete. It had started to react to my emotions. I leant against a garden wall and tried not to panic.

Then a great cry seemed to penetrate the dark, calling to me in a rising wail, like the sound of a foghorn calling out over the sea, searching, searching for something in the rise and crash of the waves. A police car, siren blaring, pushed its way through the traffic. That was the noise I'd heard but for a moment I'd had the oddest idea that it was my body crying out for me to save it. To save myself.

Lights flickered. The hospital building reappeared, with fewer lights than before and dimmer, but a solid presence. I breathed a sigh of relief and launched myself off again, faster now, stomping through the water and not caring if I splashed the slow-movers cowering under umbrellas. Besides, it was bliss to choose to stride through puddles and leap over streaming gutters. Bliss to feel Elizabeth's body respond as if it were my own.

Hurry, hurry, hurry. The clock was ticking. I had to make it back to my body before Elizabeth woke and seized control of hers.

The entrance hall was crammed with people, green and shadowy in the emergency lighting. A huge crowd, all waiting. Some were chatting quietly, and some were listening to the receptionists explain that there would be a long delay before A&E reopened for non-emergencies, and no visitors would be allowed on the wards until full power was restored. A few complained but most were resigned. Some of them, the ones dripping carelessly over the floor and staring out through the doors and windows, had, I suspected, just come in to shelter from the rain.

The big clock over reception showed eleven.

I had no time. I had to get to Lucy.

I squeezed my way through the damp horde to the stairs at the side of the lifts, ducked down out of sight of reception, and started to walk up to the fifth floor. Water dripped off my coat and joined the puddles on the steps. I was drenched. No matter. As soon as I was out of view, I ran up the remaining flights of stairs.

I couldn't get into ICU. The power cut had stopped the night buzzer and the entry phone from working although I could see how busy it was through the window in the door. Nurses came in and out of the rooms lining the corridor, flinging the doors wide and leaving them to swing shut behind them, like a host of cuckoos in clocks striking midnight.

An orderly, pushing a trolley, came up behind me and hammered on the door until one of the nurses saw us and let us in, wedging the door open with a fire extinguisher.

I had no idea where my body was. I knew they'd moved me to a side room. But which one?

And then I saw Tilly. Standing outside one of the doors. A lone, still figure amidst the rush. A rock around which the current of nurses passed.

'Tilly?' I took her by the arm and shook her gently. She

seemed confused by the hubbub around her. 'It's me, Elizabeth. What's happening?'

'A power cut, I think.'

'I know. I saw it. But they've got some power back on now.'

The LED strip running down the centre of the ceiling gave enough light for the nurses to see where they were going.

'What happened?' I said again. 'Is Lucy all right?'

'The light went out and the pump stopped. I was trying to get to the door to call a nurse, when I heard a rustle. Lucy stretched her arms out towards me. I screamed for help, and Sean, the nurse who looks after her, came with a torch, but Lucy was still again.' She stopped and shivered, pulling her cardigan tight round her.

'And then?'

'And then they told me to leave.'

I seized the door handle, but the door was pulled away from me and Sean came out, his green scrubs crumpled and his hair escaping from one side of his ponytail.

'Lucy?' Tilly said.

'She's fine. The pump is on again. There was a problem with the back-up batteries.'

'But she moved,' Tilly said.

'Ms Christensen, it was very dark in there.'

'I'm sure. She held her arms out to me.'

Sean shot a quick glance up and down the corridor at the nurses scurrying in and out of the ward at the end.

'I need to check on everybody else. Lucy is fine for now. I'll come back and we'll talk once things have calmed down a little.'

Tilly edged towards the door to Lucy's room, her fists thrust into the pockets of her baggy cardigan.

'It would be better if you waited in the visitors' room.' Two nurses lugging a basket full of blankets strode between us, interrupting him. He waited with a patient smile as they passed. 'Until things have calmed down a bit. The water in the urn will still be hot, and your friend looks as though she could do with something warm to drink.' He gestured to me and to the water dripping relentlessly onto the floor from my coat. 'I'll ask one of the orderlies to fetch you a towel once we're back to normal.'

'You are sure Lucy is all right? I know that...' Tilly hesitated. 'That her life is probably limited but I...'

Sean turned to Tilly and bent over her, sheltering her from the surrounding chaos. 'Of course. Look, I promise you that whatever happens to Lucy, her end won't be like this. It will be calm and considered and you will be in charge.'

He turned and loped off up the corridor, stopping to admonish one of the younger nurses for running.

'He's so kind,' Tilly said. 'We should get out of their way. And you do look like you could do with drying off, Elizabeth.' She managed a faint smile.

I followed her, telling myself that eleven thirty was absolutely the earliest Elizabeth would start to wake up. *I still have time. I still have time.*

I hung my coat above a basin in the corner of the visitors' room and dried as much of me as I could with paper towels. Judging by the continuous clatter of feet outside, moving swiftly without running, the emergency was still going on.

We weren't alone. A scattering of other visitors, all with the same pinched look round their eyes and tightness round their mouths as Tilly, sat on the chairs that lined the walls of the dim room. Big comfortable armchairs. One woman in the far corner had gone to sleep. Nobody said anything.

I made tea for Tilly and me and watched the minute

hand of the clock tick round, Every jerk reminding me that time was running out.

'How was Lucy? Before all the panic, I mean.'

'No change.'

'Oh.'

We sipped our tea in silence, a bubble of quiet away from the constant movement outside. Some of the visitors sat with their heads back and eyes closed. Maybe they welcomed the moment of respite away from their vigils at someone's bedside. Maybe their exhaustion had robbed them of the will to do anything but wait. I was conscious that my fidgeting hands and shifting feet set me apart.

'Maybe I was wrong,' Tilly said all of a sudden, rousing the young woman curled up in the corner chair. 'Maybe Lucy didn't wake up. Maybe I dreamed it. I think I might have dozed off before the panic started. I remember telling Lucy about the rain and then not much...'

She drifted back into silence.

The clock hands reached eleven fifteen, and things sounded calmer outside. Fewer nurses hurried up and down the corridor, and voices could no longer be heard barking orders.

One of the nurses brought us some battery-operated tealights that flickered our shadows against the walls. 'Bit more cheerful,' she said.

I made a decision. In two minutes, I'd slip out and creep into Lucy's room. I'd tell Tilly I was going to the loo. And I wouldn't let anyone stop me.

'What are you doing here, Elizabeth?' Tilly said. 'Did you tell me you were coming?'

'I met up with a friend of Lucy's. He wanted to know how she was, and there wasn't much I could tell him, so I thought I'd come along and see for myself.'

'In all this rain?'

I shrugged. Ploughing through the storm to visit Lucy wasn't a very Elizabeth thing to do but I was too concerned by the time ticking away to concoct an excuse.

'It was kind of you, Elizabeth. People are kind. Moira phoned today. To find out how Lucy was doing. She wanted me to go and stay with them for a rest. Said she'd happily take over from me in the hospital, but I told her it wasn't necessary.'

I blocked out Tilly's voice and listened as the noises from the corridor died down. The ward door creaked shut and cut off the last voices. The hands of the clock clicked round another minute. Everything was quiet. I stood and muttered that I needed to pee and headed straight for Lucy's room but as I pushed the door open lights flickered and then snapped on, flooding the room with whiteness.

They were bright. Too bright. I blinked and stumbled.

The room and the corridor filled with the sound of machine alerts as the power surged through them. Nurses burst out of the ward doors and Sean pushed past me into Lucy's room. He gave me a quick glance as I followed him in then returned to staring at the dials on the machine by Lucy's bed and pressing buttons with agile fingers, muttering a checklist under his breath.

I bit my lip. If only he'd hurry up. I just needed a few minutes on my own.

It was chaos outside again. Doors opened and closed. Nurses called out to each other as they scurried between rooms.

'The power is supposed to come on in an orderly fashion,' Sean made a few rapid notes on the clipboard at the end of Lucy's bed, 'floor by floor. Ward by ward. Room by room up here. Telling us in advance. But it's come on in one fell swoop.'

Throughout it all, my chest, Lucy's chest, rose and fell in a calm-inducing rhythm, the ventilator pump whirred and as Sean switched off the alarms one by one, I started to breathe in time with it.

'All fine here now,' Sean said. 'I'll go and help elsewhere.' He left the room, and I counted to twenty and quietly shut the door after him.

It was time.

I hesitated for a few seconds.

Her body – my body – apart from the gentle rise and fall of her chest, was as still as a stone carving on the top of some medieval duke's grave and the face was as blank of emotion. A carved death mask whose stillness turned the features I knew so well into caricatures of themselves. The nose with its stumpy end and freckles more pronounced and the uneven scar twisting through an eyebrow more prominent than usual. I'd been away too long. It seemed like someone else's body. Someone I knew well, but not mine.

Its stillness worried me. Would my return wake it? Or would it continue slumbering, oblivious to life rushing past it outside? A sleeping beauty, with me trapped inside. Was I exchanging one trap for another? I didn't want to die. I so desperately didn't want to die. Fear tasted like acid in my mouth. I took a deep breath, forced myself to stop thinking and reached out to touch my skin.

The lights went out again.

The machines stopped.

Silence filled every corner of the room.

No reassuring lights blinked and winked. Nothing whirred. I held my breath and waited for the back-up batteries to kick in.

Nothing happened.

Outside, the noise started again. The second power cut, so soon after the first, had caused yet more chaos, and staff were shouting at each other.

I flung open the door and screamed into the pandemonium.

'It's not working. She's not breathing.'

Nurses poured past me, trying to avoid bumping into each other. I saw Sean and shouted at him.

'You've got to come back. The machine hasn't switched over. Please, please, come.'

He did. He frowned as he saw the unmoving body. He flung himself onto the floor, scrambled around under the bed, found a torch and threw it at me.

'Shine it onto the ventilator.'

My body was hooked up to so many different machines, I didn't know which one was the ventilator, but I shone it where he was looking. The light bounced off the dials and switches onto the bed with its motionless figure. My hands shook and I fought to keep them still, to keep the torch pointing in the right direction.

He dived down to a cupboard in the corner and pulled out a plastic bag, emptied its contents onto the bed and screwed and pushed different elements together. My eyes were fixed on Lucy's chest, willing it to rise and fall.

Sean said something sharp, and I looked up. He'd moved to the oxygen cylinder in the corner, but my torch had stayed lighting up the bed. I pointed it at him as he attached a tube, returned to the bed, tilted Lucy's chin up and her head backwards, put a mask onto her face and started hand-pumping oxygen into her. After a second her chest started to rise. I gave a little cry.

'One – one thousand. Two – two thousand. Three – three thousand. I'm Sean,' he said.

'Pardon?'

'I'm Sean. Five – five thousand.'

'I know. We've met.'

'I thought we had.'

'Elizabeth. I'm Elizabeth.'

'Well done, Elizabeth. Six – six thousand.' He squeezed again. 'Keep pointing that torch at her chest so I can see what's going on. And don't worry about my counting. I'm just making sure I don't over-ventilate. And if you could move to the door at the same time and get someone's attention that would be great. Tell them I'm having to use a BVM in here.'

'Blessed Virgin Mary?'

'A bag valve mask!'

I did better than that. I screamed for help until a tall lady, dressed in dark blue, marched down the corridor. The other nurses scurried out of her way. The ward sister, I guessed. She and Sean exchanged a series of incomprehensible questions and answers. Then she asked a question I did understand.

'How long was she without oxygen?'

He thought. 'Not long. When did the power go back off?'

'Eleven twenty-nine.'

He tilted his arm round to check his watch. 'Two minutes. Three minutes maximum.'

'Sure?'

'Yes. The BVM wasn't assembled, so it took a bit longer than it should.'

She raised her eyebrows.

A man in a brown overall appeared in the doorway.

'What happened, Mr Arncot?' the sister asked him.

He muttered something about procedures not being followed and power surges knocking systems out as they walked away together up the corridor.

'Power will be back on soon,' Sean said. 'Don't you worry. And this time they'll do it carefully. We'll be one of the first. As soon as it's sorted, I'll get someone to come and check the back-up batteries on this ventilator. Meanwhile, you grab that chair and bring it over here where you can sit down and keep the torch on her chest.'

I did as I was told.

'Will she be all right?' I asked.

'Yes,' Sean said.

'But she wasn't breathing.'

'We started with the BVM in time. It won't have done her any harm.'

His bony fingers squeezed and released the contraption in a regular rhythm.

'Are you sure?' It seemed little more than a plastic bag, a bottle, and some tubing. 'How does it work?'

I heard the wobble in my voice and I thought he did too because he started chatting while muttering his count under his breath. He explained how the mask worked. How it pumped oxygen into Lucy's lungs. How careful you had to be to make sure it went into her chest and not her stomach. That was why he'd tilted her chin and head back. Had I seen him do that? I nodded. And that was why he clamped the mask onto her face so that it made a seal with her skin.

'But what about the rest of the...' I nodded at the bank of monitors and machines that were attached to my body. None of them working.

'Nothing matters except the ventilator. The rest of the machinery simply lets us know she's doing fine. The one on your left with the cables attached to her chest shows her heartbeat, and the one attached to her finger monitors the oxygen levels in her blood. They have an alarm that tells us if anything is wrong. But you and I are here, and we can find out the old-fashioned way. Put your fingers round her wrist and you'll be able to feel her pulse beating.'

I picked up my wrist with Elizabeth's free hand and felt the beat of my heart sending blood surging steadily through my body. I felt Elizabeth's pulse beating, too. Faster than mine and out of time, and I slowed it until they matched. Then I moved my hand into hers.

It was strange to hold your own hand as if it was that of a stranger. Lucy's skin was cool and dry against Elizabeth's slightly sweaty palm. Then for a flash of a second, Elizabeth's hand was damp and warm in my fingers. I was aware of a slight confusion as to who was who and what was what.

And suddenly I had no more doubts. I was as determined to leave Elizabeth's body as I had been to flee the house the night Gavin locked me in.

Time had ticked away. Elizabeth would wake soon. It had to be now even though Sean was here. And, in any case, I could feel my body calling me. It was the strangest sensation. Like the tug of an ebbing wave dragging me out to sea. I shut my eyes against the too-bright light of the torch, blocked out Sean's muttering and the patter of rain against the window. It would be all right. Nothing that called me so strongly could be dead. My body was waiting for me. Waiting only for my consciousness to flow through it to wake up.

I relaxed and let the flow take me. Soon, it would all be over. Soon I'd be home. Soon...

Something seized me.

Elizabeth's body held me tight. Her flesh gripped me and wouldn't let go. The hours I'd spent embedding myself into every part of it had tied us together in a myriad of ways and as fast as I snapped one link, another one snaked into place.

Moments of struggle slid past until Sean's voice brought me back to the room.

I opened my eyes.

And looked into my face. Lucy's face. My body lay on the bed with Sean holding its head and pumping the air into its lungs, while I was still gripped tight by Elizabeth's body. I'd failed.

A head popped round the door. 'Power back on in thirty seconds, Sean,' the nurse said quietly. 'You'll be first as you're ventilating manually, so leave everything on and let us know once you're up and running.'

Why couldn't I transfer? It had been so easy before. Only the nurse's arrival had stopped it happening. Maybe it was because Sean was here. I didn't think so though. Last time I'd tried Elizabeth had been in control of her body. Hers was the presence tied into its blood and bones, its nerves and muscles – not mine. I had an awful feeling her body wouldn't let me go while I was its guiding force.

'Talk to Lucy,' Sean said to me. 'She must be bewildered at everything that's happened in the last few hours.'

But I couldn't speak. Something was stirring inside Elizabeth. Sparks of awakening were ticking along her nerves, and I'd lost control of her voice.

The lights flicked back on again. The life support machines bleeped and flashed again. Sean whirled round and pressed buttons, and the hiss and swoosh started as the pump took up its steady rhythm once more.

The nerves and muscles in Elizabeth's body grew obdurate and alien. I put the torch down on the bed and rested Elizabeth's hand on the bed. I could still make her body move, but I'd lost the fine control. Elizabeth was waking and stretching through her body to take it back.

One last try. Maybe I could ride the wave of her returning. Let her slowly waking presence push me out. I reached out with Elizabeth's hand and took mine, focused every bit of me on connecting with my body as the ties holding me inside Elizabeth were snapped one by one.

Shouting came down the corridor. Growing louder. Another head round the door. 'Are you ready yet, Sean?' the owner called, panic charging her voice with energy. 'Another battery's given out.' She left, giving the door a sharp pull behind her. It slammed shut.

Elizabeth woke. Her eyes – out of my control – darted round the room, flicking over the flashing machines and the recumbent body connected to them by a tangle of cables and tubes. She jerked her hand away from my hand and screamed.

Too soon. Too quick.

I was still trapped.

Elizabeth was wild. Every cell in her body flooded with adrenalin. She screamed again when Sean touched her, threw his hands off her shoulders and ran into the still dim corridor just as Tilly walked towards her, holding a couple of the flickering tea-lights. Shock whirled through Elizabeth, and she vomited dark brown tea all over the linoleum.

They kept her in overnight. Obviously. As far as they could see she'd had some kind of amnesiac seizure, because no matter how hard she tried, she could remember nothing since dozing off in the bar with Jonty. They scanned her brain, after a long wait while the hospital recovered from its crisis-ridden evening, but everything seemed fine. They admitted her for observation and to see a neurologist in the morning.

She didn't want to sleep. Of course not. Her mind was buzzing with shock, trying to remember what had happened, and she wasn't tired after the hours of unconsciousness the sleeping tablet had given her.

I was tired, though. And wrung out with utter despair. I'd come so close, only to be defeated right at the end. I would have wept if I'd had eyes. And cried out if I'd had a voice. But I had nothing.

32

I crashed and slept for a long time. It was probably the deepest sleep I'd had since the accident, and, when I woke, for a few moments I thought the last few days might have been nothing more than a nightmare.

They weren't.

I was still Elizabeth, dressed in the clothes she'd worn the day before, although they were still damp and sticking to her skin. We were in an office with windows overlooking the ward where she'd spent the night. She was listening to a nurse who was standing awkwardly hunched over a computer and peering through smudged glasses at the screen. The room was devoid of chairs.

Despair settled over me.

'So Dr Barton wants to see you again next week. I'll make you an appointment, and it will be in Neurology over the other side of the building. Not here.' She straightened her body and flexed her back before bending over the computer again. 'Wait a minute. I can't access your file.' She gave her glasses a quick polish with her sleeve and flicked her fringe to one side. 'I'll try again in a couple of minutes. Nothing's working as it should since last night. How are you feeling now?'

'Fine. A bit tired. I couldn't sleep.'

But she didn't feel fine. Unease festered. Her body was alert as though waiting for something to show itself. I thought that something might be me.

Elizabeth twitched as another nurse trudged in behind her and dumped a mass of paper on the desk. 'Serious Untoward Incident reports,' she said. 'Every machine has produced one. The ones that are working now, that is. A lot of non-essential systems are still offline.'

'Thanks,' the nurse muttered to her departing back. 'I'll file them in the bin. OK, let's try again.' She typed into the computer again, then wriggled her shoulders to ease the muscles.

A phone rang in Elizabeth's bag. She pulled it out, mouthed 'sorry' to the nurse who was staring at her screen and left the room.

'Hello,' she said.

'Mrs Lyle?'

'Yes.'

It was my phone. She'd answered *my* phone. She had my phone with her. Of course she did. She'd taken it, along with my purse, the first time she came to the hospital with Tilly. But who was calling Mrs Lyle? I hadn't used my married name since I moved into the shop.

'It's Mr Hunstan here. You rang for an appointment earlier this morning.'

'Yes, that's right.' Elizabeth spoke slowly.

'I could fit you in this afternoon. At one o'clock. Would that be possible?'

Elizabeth glanced at the clock in the ward. It was half past nine.

'Yes,' she said. 'That would be fine. I'll be there.'

She disconnected and turned the phone off.

Mr Hunstan. Who was Mr Hunstan? The name rang a bell. And then it came to me. He worked at the bank where I had my Mrs Lucy Lyle account and where the money from Gavin's estate currently waited. What was Elizabeth up to?

The nurse beckoned her back into the office as my thoughts raced.

'I understand why the system wouldn't let me book you an appointment now,' she said. 'There's a problem with your file. We can't seem to locate your records. It happens all the time since they centralised everything. Let's go through the information you gave us when you arrived and make sure there's not a mistake there that's stopped the system from recognising you.'

They went through all the details Elizabeth must have told them when she was admitted after the accident. All false except the address of my flat.

'NHS number?'

'Sorry. Never can remember it.'

'No one can, don't worry. Who's your GP?'

'Oh, what is his name? I've only just registered with him.'

The nurse smiled but I thought her brows creased faintly above her glasses.

'I've got it in my phone,' Elizabeth said. 'Give me a minute.'

She held the phone close to her body and tapped until Google supplied her with the name and address of a doctor's surgery in Greenwich.

The nurse took a note. 'I'll give them a call,' she said. 'And find out why you don't appear on our system.'

'Thanks. I'll pop up and see my friend while you're doing that?'

And she was out of the office before the nurse could reply.

For a moment, I had hope. Elizabeth was going to see my body and this time she was in full control of hers. She was enmeshed in its nerves and muscles leaving me a free agent, an unanchored spark floating at the edges of her subconscious. This time I could make the leap back home.

But Elizabeth veered away from the lifts in the entrance hall and strode out of the hospital instead. Dismay washed over me, and I felt Elizabeth hesitate. The prowler inside her stirred, and I tamped down my emotions. The time I'd spent in control of her seemed to have thinned the barrier between our feelings.

It was a bright day. The sun shone, reflecting off the water that covered the ground. It was truly a scene of two halves. Up above, blue sky and green trees, invigorated and waving in the breeze. Below, chaos, a mess of water running along roads and welling up from overflowing drains, grass drowned, and tidemarks of litter and mud everywhere.

But Elizabeth didn't stop to look. She took out her own phone and texted Reuben.

Have you got it?

Not yet.

Please. It's urgent.

All right. I'll go there this afternoon.

I'll meet you at the Stag and Horses afterwards.

OK.

3pm?

OK.

She shoved the phone back in her pocket and walked briskly away, only stopping to buy a beanie from a local shop and pull it down over her head, then caught the bus two stops away from the hospital.

For once the traffic was light, and the bus sped us away from the hospital. Away from my body. Away from picking my life back up again and towards whatever Elizabeth was planning to do. I was going to have to think of something to stop her.

33

Back in the flat, Elizabeth stripped off her damp clothes and showered. Then she sat in front of the large mirror above the table in her room and laid her make-up out on the table with the precision of a theatre nurse preparing for a complicated operation. She wound a towel round her head and stared at her face in the mirror, tracing the edge of her chin and the curve of her eyebrows. She hadn't shaped them for a few days.

Something about the ferocity of her concentration told me this was more than a simple touch-up.

First, she covered her face in foundation. A darker one than her normal skin tone. She smoothed and blended until it looked natural, then dusted pink over the top of her cheeks, ignoring her cheekbones. It changed her face, softening its flat planes and sharp edges.

She smiled. A strange smile. A forced smile. One that curved her lips and deepened the lines running from the corners of her nose to the corners of her mouth. She marked the lines with a brown pencil and added a light colour to make her cheeks seem fuller and rounder. Next, she attacked her nose, flattening it with the same combination of darker and lighter pencils. She made her eyes rounder and painted faint shadows beneath them, while deepening them in their sockets. She studied herself again and let her mouth sag and her head drop a little.

An altogether wearier and warier person gazed back at me from the mirror.

Finally, she chose two sharp-nibbed eyebrow pencils, again a darker brown and a lighter brown, and dotted them over her nose and upper cheeks, blotting the specks with her fingers. Freckles. She'd covered herself with freckles. Exactly like mine.

The smell of her creamy foundation was thick and heavy and turned her stomach over... or was it my own sick feeling as I began to realise what she was doing?

She reached into the box that had arrived the day before and unwrapped the new wig. Long and brown, and as she unrolled it and swooshed it in the air, I saw it was curly with ringlets that dissolved into frizz towards their ends.

How could I not have noticed before?

She laughed and ran her fingers through it, loosening the curls until it became untidy and natural. Her pulse quickened and a smile wrinkled the skin round her eyes. I remembered her fingering my hair in the cubicle in the hospital. She'd seemed to caress it. Had she been checking it over? Had the first glimmerings of her scheme to rob me arrived then? Because I was sure that was what this was all about.

She pulled a photo out of the drawer by her bed. It was a picture of me. A copy, I thought, taken on her phone, of the one from the article in the German magazine about me and other sculptors. The one that was blown up downstairs in the shop.

She stuck the picture to the mirror, bent her head into the wig and flung it back in a practised gesture so that it fell around her face. Side by side, the photo and the reflection of her made-up face now framed by a long, untidy mop of hair were the same person. By some cosmetic trickery she had transformed herself into me, and it only needed the brown contact lenses she slipped into her eyes to make the likeness nearly perfect. I, Lucy Christensen, stared through Elizabeth's eyes at the reflection of Elizabeth made up to look like Lucy Christensen.

The irony of it was lost on me.

Everything made sense now: the hunt for my passport; the appointment with Mr Hunstan; the draft contract from the solicitors; the bank account in the name of Charlotte Patricia Morgan. As if to confirm the truth of my suspicions, Elizabeth took my passport out of her bag, found my signature and copied it over and over again until she was sure the difference between our two hands was negligible.

She dressed herself in clothes she'd taken from my wardrobe. Even with flat boots on, she was tall, and my dress hung from her shoulders without touching her slender body, but the bank wouldn't know the difference. Mr Hunstan had only met me once, over a year ago. She added a thick and shapeless cardigan and an old handbag of mine into which she put some papers and my passport plus a few pounds. Then she inspected herself in the mirror, tweaked my hair and walked a few steps, dragging her feet a little and staring at the floor. Was that how she thought I moved? I supposed so.

She tiptoed down the stairs and froze in the hall outside the communicating door to the shop. Listening to Amy bustling around inside. Then she made a phone call on her mobile and the phone rang in the shop. Amy sighed and the stockroom door creaked as she went to answer it. Elizabeth hung up, slipped out of the front door into the alley, and hurried away. Unseen.

Elizabeth hesitated outside the main door to the bank as a breeze blew round her ankles. People picked their way round the debris from last night's storm, stepping over the pools that had gathered in every dip and hollow. Water still ran down the streets, draining into London's old underground rivers and tumbling down them towards the Thames.

Elizabeth checked herself in the glass revolving door as she entered and adopted a shorter stride and a slight hunch to her shoulders.

'I have an appointment,' she said to the cashier, 'with Mr Hunstan. I'm Mrs Lucy Lyle.'

This branch was one of the older ones that had escaped the slick shell of modernisation. Dark wood panelling lined the lower half of the walls and the square pillars dotted around the hall, but the upper half was white and soared up to ornate roof lights in the high ceiling, each looking as though they'd been cut out with a serrated pastry cutter. It could have been beautiful if the main floor hadn't been covered with a dirty, beige carpet and brown Formica furniture.

Not that Elizabeth really noticed. Her breathing was ragged beneath the loose dress and thick cardigan, and her fingernails dug into her thumbs one after the other. She wanted my money very badly. And I understood why. She was in a desperate situation and it was her only chance to escape. She was as trapped as I was, I thought, and, despite everything, I felt sorry for her.

I remembered Mr Hunstan when he appeared. Young

and grey-suited with interesting ties rather than a personality. Today's tie showed a narrow slice of a Van Gogh painting called *The Café Terrace* with tables and cobbles beneath a starry night sky.

Elizabeth had lucked out because Mr Hunstan wasn't someone who paid a lot of attention to people. I'd had a meeting with him when I'd opened the account. A formality, really. He'd tried to interest me in savings accounts and insurances, but he'd never turned his head from his computer screen for more than a few seconds at a time while he'd been talking.

He was more attentive to Elizabeth, though, than he'd been to me, pulling her out a chair in the cramped, windowless office and gazing at her from the other side of the desk, elbows resting and fingertips touching.

'What can I do for you, Mrs Lyle?'

'My husband died. Last year.' Elizabeth left a discreet pause for Mr Hunstan to look suitably shocked and mutter some awkward condolences then moved swiftly on. 'And I'm buying a property with the money he left me. It's the shop and flat I rent, and I need you to transfer the money to my solicitor.' She slid an envelope over the desk to him with hands that bore no trace of the nervousness I felt inside her. It contained the draft contract for the sale of the shop and flat emailed to me a couple of days ago.

'I have to go in and sign tomorrow,' she said, tapping her finger on the envelope. 'And then we'll exchange quickly because it's such a straightforward transaction – I live there already and there's no chain – and complete very shortly afterwards.'

She'd been leaps and jumps ahead of me all along. The purchase of the flat was the reason to transfer the money, because in these days of anti-money-laundering legislation you have to explain what you want to spend your own money on.

'I need to transfer the money to the solicitors in the next day or so,' Elizabeth continued. 'That's why I've come in, because I assumed I couldn't just call and do it.'

'No.' Mr Hunstan laughed. 'We'd need some verification.' He examined the contract Elizabeth had given him. 'Especially for this amount of money. Yes, indeed we would. You did well to come in and see me. We'll prepare all the paperwork now, and then you can just call me when you want the transfer actioned.'

'How long will it take to transfer?'

'Normally a couple of hours.'

The hairs rose on the back of Elizabeth's neck.

God, so quick. And so easy. After this meeting the money would only be a phone call away.

Mr Hunstan asked Elizabeth for my account details and brought them up on his computer screen. I watched him and listened to them both as they worked through all the stages necessary to process the payment. Elizabeth knew everything: account number, sort code, my date of birth, my passwords. She had all the paperwork he asked for. The contract for the sale. An electricity bill in my name with the shop address. My passport with its grainy photo that didn't look much like her but then it didn't look much like me. My birth certificate and Gavin's death certificate as well as the grant of probate that Ted had sent me some time ago and I guessed must have been in the pile of papers on my desk. She worked her magic on Mr Hunstan, flatteringly grateful for his help and listening intently to his patronising sales patter. Of course she'd like a quote for house insurance and, yes, she didn't know why she hadn't thought of moving the shop accounts to this bank.

'Your solicitor's bank details, please?' Mr Hunstan asked.

Elizabeth handed over a letter that appeared to have come from the solicitors but giving the details for Charlotte Patricia Morgan's account. The one that would be open as soon as Elizabeth produced ID for it. I knew banks rarely checked the name when they sent money. The papers were full of stories of frauds because of this. Mr Hunstan was nearly done. A few more swishes of his mouse and the printer in the corner whirred into life. He collected the documents.

'I'll need you to sign here, and here, and sign and date the last page.'

He leaned over her and marked little crosses on the paper as he spoke, and the smell of his citrus aftershave mingled with the rose air-freshener.

Elizabeth hesitated. She rolled the pen between her fingers and hesitated again. Her eyes flickered to my passport lying on Mr Hunstan's side of the desk. The signature worried her. Could she recreate it without the original in front of her?

Hope stirred my thoughts. She wasn't sure she could do it. Her fingers were soft and indecisive round the pen while her mind was elsewhere. Was this my moment? I slipped a little tentacle of myself into her body while Elizabeth was focused on the signature. A little nudge in the wrong direction, I thought, and her writing would be nothing like mine. My money would be safe. Tilly's house would be safe. Tilly would be safe.

Mr Hunstan straightened his tie and opened my passport, preparing to check her signature.

I wondered what he'd do when the signatures didn't match. There'd be a moment of disbelief. Maybe he'd ask her to do it again. And then, when it still didn't resemble mine, what? He'd get a colleague and they'd murmur outside his office. Maybe report it to someone higher up. The police would be called. How long would it take them to discover Elizabeth wasn't me?

My mind raced. They'd arrest her or at least ask her to come to the police station to answer some questions. Even if they let her out on bail, she wouldn't be able to go back to the flat. We'd be penniless and homeless together in London, trying to stay one step ahead of the people after her.

I couldn't let that happen. Not while I was trapped with her.

Elizabeth made a decision and I did, too. Her fingers tightened round the pen, but her grip was all wrong. I calmed myself and focused on nothing but those fingers and the cool hard handle of the pen. Her uncertainty made it easy to shift her grip. I couldn't take control completely. I didn't want whatever I'd woken inside her to notice me, so my touch was like a whisper of air blowing against her muscles. I signed my name. Three times I did it, each one easier than the last as her fingers learned the shapes of my signature. Afterwards, she pushed the documents over to Mr Hunstan and waited while he looked from my passport to the transfer document. Her body slid to the edge of the chair, and her hands grasped her bag. She would run if he queried it.

'Thank you very much, Mrs Lyle. I'll just photocopy your passport, and I can do you a copy of the funds transfer document, if you like?'

We stared at him. Neither of us sure what he meant.

'For your solicitors,' he said. 'So they know the funds are ready and just waiting for your call to transfer.'

'Yes, that's a good idea,' she said. The words came out strangely halting, and Mr Hunstan frowned, but she smiled and he left the room.

She let out a long, shuddering breath as soon as he shut the door and a little of the tension knotting the muscles in her shoulders relaxed.

I had to admire her. I'd never have had the nerve to do what she just had.

34

The pub where Elizabeth had arranged to meet Reuben looked as though it had seen better days. The dark paint on the outside was patchy and the windows were covered with out-of-date posters and strips of browned Sellotape, where even older ones had been ripped off. Elizabeth didn't go in. She sat on a bench in the square over the road, next to a bed of tired-looking shrubbery and roses, and fixed her eyes on the entrance.

The square was quiet, a little backwater away from the main roads, not on the way to anywhere. London was strange like that. One minute you could be pushing your way through people on a shop-lined road, deafened by the traffic noise, but if you took a couple of turnings off, you'd find a deserted pocket of streets and houses.

It wasn't pleasant though. The long summer had parched the bushes and last night's storm had stripped them of their yellow and brown leaves which now floated on the water-logged earth.

Elizabeth was jumpy. She kept checking the time on her

phone, until it was close to when she'd said she'd meet Reuben. Then she put it on silent, stood and hid herself behind a tree, peering through a gap where two branches met.

The quiet was broken by the put-put and rattle of a moped. It drove up to the pub and stopped outside. The rider kicked down the side stand, dismounted, and tugged the helmet from his head. Reuben.

But Elizabeth didn't move.

A van drew up alongside him and hid him from view.

A white van, not new, ten a penny in London, with a scratched and sun-bleached blue and green rectangular logo.

Elizabeth waited.

Doors slammed. The van drove off.

The pavement outside the pub was empty. Except for the moped, and the helmet rolling on the ground in a stream of water gushing into the drain on the corner. Its owner was nowhere. Reuben had disappeared. And I didn't think he'd have left the helmet in the gutter if he'd gone into the pub.

I felt the moment Elizabeth realised what happened. An electric shock ran through her nerves, and her ribcage trembled with the effort of breathing. But she didn't move.

I'd thought it was quiet before, but now even the little noises – the faint buzz of traffic and the sound of water trickling and gurgling everywhere, the occasional slam of a door and the burr of a mechanical saw somewhere behind the block of flats that loomed over the east side of the square – had stopped. As though the aftershock of Reuben's disappearance had passed through the square in an ever-widening circle and silenced everything.

Reuben had been snatched. In broad daylight. Without a scream. Without even a whimper. In less than a minute.

And it was undoubtedly Elizabeth's fault.

And she knew that because she started to cry silently with tears sliding down her cheeks and filling her nose until it ran. I knew she was thinking of Reuben, because memories of him rose through her head and burst open. Some I'd seen before: the train station; the late-night café. And some I'd lived through: his wonder at the murals in the Painted Hall and the quick smile he gave her when he agreed to get her passport. She stayed behind the tree, unmoving except for one hand that grasped a branch and squeezed it tight until a sharp spike pierced her palm.

She waited.

She stopped crying.

Her face dried in a sticky residue that cracked and itched but she didn't touch it. Life started up again. The background noises returned. A rat ran along the path and down a hole beneath a bush. Elizabeth slid a foot forward to take the first step towards the moped.

And froze.

A figure detached itself from the darkness of the porch leading into the pub. A man. He must have been leaning against the inside wall, sheltered from view by the half-open door. He ambled into the street, lit a cigarette, then lifted his head and swivelled a glare slowly round the whole square. Elizabeth stopped breathing. Slowly and smoothly, she slipped her foot back behind the tree and turned her head so she was completely obscured by the leaves.

And waited.

I thought I heard him speak. A few words whisked to us by a whisper of wind. Elizabeth risked a peek. He was talking on a mobile phone and, a few minutes later, the white van reappeared, stopped again, and must have picked him up because when it drove off he'd gone, and Reuben's helmet was no longer there.

Elizabeth waited.

A group of youngsters ran past us. A couple of curious glances at Elizabeth standing there so still, but their attention was on the ball they were kicking and an argument about someone called Kacey.

Still she waited.

An elderly man in a brown raincoat, clutching a rolled-up newspaper, lumbered out of the pub, crossed the road, saw the kids and their ball, muttered something sour and trudged away in the other direction.

Elizabeth took out her phone. Half an hour had passed since Reuben had arrived at the pub.

She waited until a couple hurried past us, deep in discussion as to which bus would get them to Marble Arch quickest. They gave Elizabeth a few curious glances as she peeled away from the tree and jogged alongside them to the road on the opposite side of the square to the Stag and Horses. Once there, Elizabeth stopped, tucked herself into the corner and sneaked a glance back over her shoulder.

Apart from Reuben's moped, the road outside the pub was still empty. She hesitated and took a couple of steps towards it. I screamed at her not to. I screamed at her to turn and get out of there. To go home. To do anything rather than walk across the square to Reuben's moped.

But Elizabeth was made of tougher stuff than me.

She examined her reflection in the dark window of a house on the corner. Despite the tear-smudged make-up, she still looked like me. Then she raised her head and strode across the square as though she owned it. I felt the terror prickling under her skin, but nothing showed. Nothing held her back.

She reached the moped, pulled the key out of the ignition and put it in a lock on the side. The seat popped up, revealing a bottle of water, a video game, and a brown envelope. She grabbed the envelope and walked swiftly away without a backward glance.

Once she was on a bus heading for Greenwich she cast a quick look inside the envelope and I caught a glimpse of a passport and a few official pieces of paper. Elizabeth smiled and thrust it deep into her bag.

She slowed as she approached the alley leading to my flat and I felt her fear flicker back into life. Her feelings were easier and easier for me to sense and I realised she was frightened all the time. It was an insistent strain of background music playing inside her. It waited for her round every corner and was the first thing she felt on waking, but now the fear was worse. It left a pungent trail I could taste in her blood.

She walked past the turning into the alley, darting a sharp look up it as she went. No one was there. No one hovered outside the shop waiting for her.

But she continued walking, then slipped up the narrow road that led to the waste ground at the back of my workshop, took out her keys and let herself in through the wooden door built into the big gates.

The yard was empty except for the bins and Tilly's car. The drain must have flooded at some point last night because tidemarks of scum, left behind as the water receded, stained the concrete paving, and the stench of something dank made Elizabeth grimace.

She removed the wig and scrubbed at the painted freckles on her nose. A quick glance in a pocket mirror showed her hair flat and dark with sweat against her scalp. Bald patches gleamed through. She slipped through the shop into the flat, giving Amy a quick wave.

We didn't stay long. A quick wash, a change of clothes –

jeans and a T-shirt this time, and the blonde wig she'd been wearing the afternoon of the accident. She grabbed my bag and the envelope and raced back out through the back of the shop. Then she took a train and the Northern Line to Gower Street and the bank where she'd opened an account online for Charlotte Patricia Morgan.

She made it before the bank closed. They had set up a dedicated desk for students bringing their papers in. Although it was late the queue was long and slow and full of students who didn't have the right papers but thought they could blag it. They couldn't, but it took time for the patient bank clerk to convince them. Time Elizabeth hated losing. She watched the clock on the wall and counted the number of students between her and the head of the queue.

The bank clerk, who'd stayed unruffled through the most outrageous claims by the youngsters before us, smiled when Elizabeth sat down. Smiled even more when she produced a tenancy agreement between Lucy Christensen and Charlotte Patricia Morgan and a copy of a recent electricity bill in my name. I didn't know when she'd created the tenancy agreement, but it would have been easy enough. Standard forms were available online. The electricity bill probably came from the landing table where I had a habit of stashing stuff before filing it in the bin. She passed over the passport from the brown envelope along with what looked like a birth certificate.

A quick glance at the passport photo and at Elizabeth sitting, with long hair, make-up free and unafraid, before her was all the clerk needed, and she smiled and handed the passport back, giving me a closer look.

The photo was Elizabeth. A younger Elizabeth who looked more like the Carly she had been. Of course. Charlotte Patricia Morgan. Charlotte. Nickname Carly. The passport wasn't a fake. Elizabeth was going to turn back into who she really was.

A few taps on the computer keyboard, a couple of swirls with the mouse, and the account was open.

'So can I pay money in now?' Elizabeth asked. 'Like my student loan?' she added quickly.

'Of course. The account is open. You just need to give the student loan company the sort code and account number. It will take a few days though for your debit card to come through.'

I felt Elizabeth's brain fire up.

'You'll send it to my Greenwich address?'

'Yes. It'll take between five to seven working days.'

'Could I pick it up from you here? I've had stuff go missing from my flat, you see.'

The clerk clicked away on the computer for a few seconds.

'No problem,' she said. 'But make sure you have ID with you.'

Elizabeth smiled, and for once there was nothing forced or calculating about it. Little pops of excitement exploded in her head, and brightened everything she saw as she left the bank.

She pulled my phone out of her bag and called Mr Hunstan. Everything was falling into place for her. But her run of luck faltered. Mr Hunstan was out of the office. He wouldn't be back today.

'Could anyone else help?'

'No,' Elizabeth said after a pause. 'No, that's fine. I'll call tomorrow. He will be in tomorrow, won't he?'

'Yes. I can confirm that.'

'Thank you.'

Her excitement drained away and tiredness replaced it.

For the first time today, she had nothing to do and nowhere to rush off to. She wandered for a while, letting the rush-hour crowds dictate where she went, and ended up in Euston station, carried there in the midst of people heading out of the centre of London and going home on the Tube or travelling further afield on the railways. Above their rushing heads, the black boards rippled with changing destinations. Crewe. Manchester. Glasgow. For an awful moment I thought she might buy a ticket and leave, but an image of Reuben, a memory of him standing hands on hips after he'd pushed the man preying on her when she first arrived rose in her head, and she turned abruptly and went to one of the cafés outside the concourse, sat down and ordered a coffee.

Her fingers tapped on her phone as she searched through airline websites, seeing what flights were available in the next few days. Then she browsed property websites, lingering over the details of remote rural properties and solid, stone-built houses in small market towns miles away from London. She was dreaming of her future. Planning her future as Charlotte Patricia Morgan. A future that was nearly hers. Only a phone call tomorrow morning and then a few days' wait.

I'd have to act tonight. The only problem was, I didn't know what I could do.

She emptied my bag on the table and laughed. She might be about to acquire a fortune, but she currently possessed twenty-three pounds and forty-eight pence. In all the rushing around she'd left the money Reuben had given her back at the flat. She'd have to go back to Greenwich. At least for tonight. For once I was in luck. If she'd had the money with her we'd be heading out of London already because I was as sure as anything that somebody somewhere was extracting every last bit of information about Elizabeth's whereabouts from Reuben. Elizabeth took a circuitous route back to south-east London while I chased ideas down dead ends and felt more and more desperate. I thought she was brave but stupid. I'd have gone somewhere else. Anywhere else. But I guessed she was counting on the fact that Reuben didn't know where she lived.

As she approached the alley to the flat, she joined a group of language students speaking halting English to each other and walked past, turning her head to peer up it. The alley was empty. Nevertheless, she circled round again, joined another group of people and slipped away from them and up the alley at the last moment.

She unlocked the front door to the flat and pushed it open quietly. Tilly's voice wafted down the stairs and Elizabeth froze, straining her ears to decipher the conversation then relaxed as she realised Tilly must be on the phone because her voice was interspersed only by silence.

She locked and bolted the door behind her. The door between the flat and the shop was ajar, although the shop was closed. Elizabeth crept through it and peeked out of the window through the display of masks. The alley was empty. The blood still thumping in her head subsided.

Tilly was in the kitchen, making dark brown tea with the ponderous movements of the very tired and speaking on the phone but there was a lilt of happiness in her voice that I hadn't heard since she'd arrived. The damp tea bag fell off the spoon and onto the floor as Elizabeth put her head round the door.

'Oh, Elizabeth,' she said, bending down and picking it up. 'I didn't hear you come in.' And then to the person on the other end of the phone. 'Sorry, Moira, just saying hello to Elizabeth.'

The hard lines of strain etched round Tilly's mouth had

eased and her eyes, although marked underneath with grey shadows, had a glimmer in them.

'It's great news,' she continued. 'Lucy's been different all day. Restless. She's lifted her arms a few times and her eyes flickered open once or twice, but I don't think she sees anything.' Tilly paused and listened, then shook her head. 'No, no. Not at all. The nurses only check on her every hour, so they've missed it. But yes, they think it's a good sign. A very good sign.'

She mouthed the word 'Moira' at Elizabeth and raised her eyebrows in an expression of mock despair as the voice at the end took over the conversation, but she was smiling. Her words started to make sense. My body was showing signs of life. Maybe my presence last night had dragged it out of its slow drift towards death and now it was searching for the presence it had briefly felt. How much longer would it wait for me before gliding away again? *Not long*, I thought.

'No, no, of course they haven't said that they're sure she'll wake up.' Tilly's voice sang with hope. 'But I can tell they think there's a much better chance.'

The shrill ring of the doorbell cut through her words. Elizabeth shot to the window and stared down into the alley outside the front door. It was the police.

'It's the police,' she said.

'Sorry, Moira, just give me a minute.' Tilly covered the phone with her hand. 'The police?'

'Yes.'

The doorbell rang again.

'Could you see what they want? I'll get rid of Moira.'

Elizabeth walked down the stairs slowly. Tilly's voice followed her. 'I must go, Moira. I've had a long day. I can hardly keep my eyes open.' She listened for a few seconds.

'No, no one's with Lucy, but she was much more settled when I left... Yes. Yes... Great news. Yes...'

Luke and two police officers were at the front door. One of them was Detective Inspector Cromer.

'Hello,' Elizabeth said. Wariness flooded her tone and for a moment I couldn't tell if it was hers or mine. It was becoming harder and harder to separate my emotions and hers.

'Good evening,' DI Cromer said. He gestured to Luke. 'Maybe you could explain, Mr Awuah?'

Luke nodded. 'You're Ms Christensen's flatmate, aren't you?' His raincoat was tightly belted round him and his face wore a polite smile, but I didn't think he was happy about being here.

'Yes.'

'I'm Luke Awuah, Ms Christensen's solicitor. These two police officers have a warrant to search the flat. As Ms Christensen is in hospital, they've had the courtesy to ask me to be present.'

So the moment I'd been dreading had arrived. There was only one thing they could have come for and it waited for them upstairs. Elizabeth didn't move.

'You have no choice,' Luke continued gently. 'It isn't anything to do with you, and I don't think it will take very long.'

Elizabeth opened the door wide, let them through and followed them as they marched up the stairs and into the kitchen. She had no time to warn Tilly who stumbled out of the kitchen, shock on her face and the phone still clamped to her ear as the second police officer pushed past her.

'Search warrant.' DI Cromer flashed an official-looking piece of paper at her. 'Please wait outside. We won't be a minute.'

'Moira,' Tilly said into the phone. 'The most extraordinary thing. The police are here.' She peered into the kitchen and then in a voice tinged with outrage, 'They're taking Lucy's set of knives.' She hung up.

And indeed they were. DI Cromer's glove-coated hands removed every piece of the set from the magnetic board on the wall and dropped them into individual plastic envelopes.

Elizabeth and I watched them in silence. I hoped the knives were all they'd take. That way Tilly wouldn't be in trouble.

'There should be a steel with the set,' DI Cromer said to Elizabeth. 'Has it always been missing?'

No. Please, no.

Elizabeth flinched as my reaction shook her. DI Cromer eyed her suspiciously.

'There's a steel,' she said. 'But Lucy keeps it in the drawer. That one.'

She gestured towards the drawer by the sink and waited while he rummaged through it and found the steel. It, too, went into a plastic envelope. DI Cromer muttered a few words of thanks and left.

'Why did they do that?' Tilly asked after they'd shut the front door behind them. 'What were they here for? And who are you?' This to Luke.

'Luke Awuah. Lucy's solicitor.'

'This is something to do with Lucy? But she's lying unconscious in hospital. Why would they want her knives?'

'For their enquiry into Gavin's death.'

Tilly ran her fingers through her hair, making it stick up in exclamation marks all over her head.

'I thought they'd decided he died from his heart condition. Whatever it was called.' She shook her head tiredly. I guessed she had too many other things on her mind to remember me asking her to buy the steel.

'The coroner's verdict was open. And so is the enquiry. Let's concentrate on getting Lucy better for now,' Luke said. 'I'll let you know if I hear anything.'

Tilly walked down the stairs with Luke while Elizabeth and I went into the kitchen and stared at the empty knife rack.

I felt sick. And I thought she felt it. She poured herself a glass of water and sipped at it. Through the window she watched the police car waiting at the end of the alley with DI Cromer and his colleague standing and chatting by it. She shrugged. It was nothing to do with her.

It was everything to do with me. And everything to do with what had happened the night Gavin died.

35

Most of what I told the police was the truth. I only lied by omission. I never told them exactly when the last time I saw Gavin was. I never told them about the last horrid unravelling of our marriage. They were too fixated on whether he'd phoned me or not to pin me down about our last meeting.

Gavin didn't phone me. That was absolutely true. He couldn't phone me. He'd removed all the phones. He lied to his parents and I don't know why. Although his decision to walk from his parents' house down to ours worries me. It was a thirty-minute walk in the cold but only a five-minute drive through back roads where the chances of meeting another car, let alone being stopped by the police were remote. And Gavin would normally have driven it. Despite the drink.

So I wondered if he was coming back to finish what he'd started. If he'd realised there was no escaping the consequences of what he'd done. After all, he couldn't keep me locked up for ever.

And if he'd told a story afterwards where he'd arrived home to find his wife, alerted by his phone call, already gone,

I don't think anyone would have questioned it. Thirty minutes was plenty of time for someone to decide to leave whereas five wasn't. And by the time someone realised I was missing...

I'll never know and I don't like to think about it.

I drove away from the house that night, exactly as I told the police, but I hadn't gone more than a few hundred yards when I realised I'd never get to London with my eye in the state it was. The blood had dripped through my eyebrow and encrusted the eyelashes. So, I stopped on the verge where the path across the fields met a quiet part of the road and fished around until I found a bottle of water and some tissues. I turned the inside light on and used the mirror to dab away the blood so outside was a dark blur, and I didn't see Gavin until he opened the passenger door and sat beside me, pulling the door shut with the clunk that echoed in my memories for months afterwards.

Shock thudded through my body. The bottle fell from my hands and emptied itself into my lap.

Instinct kicked in. I flung my door open and hurled myself out, but he grabbed at my legs. We fell out together, and my flailing hand met the steel still attached to the broken broom handle and rammed into the pocket in the door. I seized it as we tumbled into the mud.

Terror drove me to my feet first but as I turned to flee, his hand snaked out and grabbed my ankle. I was caught. I was trapped. I smashed the steel down on his head without thinking. The tape holding it to the broom handle gave away and it rolled into the dark. I didn't think it was much of a hit. It was enough to loosen his grip and I wrenched my ankle loose and tore away. I heard him swear and then his footsteps as he came after me.

I ran faster than I'd ever run before. My feet pounded the

dirt. Trees whipped lithe branches across my face and body, but I didn't care. He faltered by the stream, and I gained a few yards, but he was still close behind when we raced out of the woods that hid the field from the road and onto the empty grass. It was bright after the darkness under the trees. Street lamps weren't far away, and their orange light fought with the cold light of the moon. I remember smelling frost beginning to settle but still I ran.

I heard the moment Gavin stumbled but I kept on running. I ran and ran. Ran until I was sure the footsteps hitting the ground so close to my heels were no longer there, and then I dared to stop and look around.

I was alone in a field of whitening grass, its purity only broken by the black branches of the alders and their long, spiky moon shadows. The only sound was the breath tearing into my lungs.

I waited for him to appear, my eyes darting glances all around me and my lungs clawing oxygen from the cold air. But he never arrived. So I walked a long circuit back to the car, flitting from tree to tree and hiding behind a screen of shrubs when the verge I'd left the car on came into sight.

The car was still there, but there was no sign of Gavin.

I hid in the shrubs for a long time. The sweat of the run dried to a chill on my skin, and the frost froze my toes. The pain in my ribs and chest and arms, driven out by fear, seeped back in. I waited until I was sure Gavin wasn't there, and I limped towards the car.

The broom handle with its festoon of tape still lay on the ground. But the steel had gone. I guessed Gavin must have seized it as he came after me.

Should I have gone back to look for him? Maybe. But I never suspected I'd hurt him badly. And I only wanted to escape. I took the broom handle, drove to the flat, and threw it into a bin in the car park. When the police showed me the pictures of Gavin, I realised that my blow to his head had been devastating. I waited for them to brandish the steel with his skin and my fingerprints on it, but they never did.

The knowledge that I'd killed a man. That I was a murderer. That I might spend years locked away in prison and the rest of my life branded a criminal. It took a while to sink in. The weeks between Gavin's death and the funeral, I stayed holed up in the tiny studio flat in London, seeing no one other than the police when they called me in for another interview and reliving the last night of my marriage.

I told myself it was an accident. I told myself I was terrified. But nothing could forgive the moment when I'd smashed the steel into Gavin's head with as much force as I could muster. No holding back. There'd been no holding back. Guilt wrapped itself around me and dug its tendrils deep into my heart.

For months, I waited for the knock on the door, the phone call, the tap on the shoulder that would tell me the police had the evidence they needed. And now it had finally happened. The last act of the tragedy that was my marriage was about to play out, even though Gavin was already dead and his killer not far from it herself.

36

'Elizabeth,' Tilly said from the doorway into the hall. 'I'm shattered. I'm going to bed.'

Elizabeth touched the dark window. 'They're still parked at the end of the alley. The police, I mean.'

'I expect they'll go soon.' Tilly turned to go, then stopped abruptly and tapped her head. 'Amy left you a message. I nearly forgot. It's on the landing table.'

'Thanks. Was that Lucy you were talking about? To Moira?' Elizabeth asked.

'Yes. There's been a big change in her today. I'm feeling much more hopeful. Although she still can't breathe on her own.'

I thought how much I loved her. Tilly the steadfast. Tilly the true. Standing there in her old jeans and a T-shirt that had seen better days but clinging onto hope and fighting my corner in every way she could. If Elizabeth's plan succeeded, the future held nothing good for Tilly. Despair overwhelmed me and I felt it echo in Elizabeth's body. She twitched.

'It's as though she's looking for something,' Tilly added.

For me, I thought. *She's looking for me.* I was so close to her last night. I must have woken something in her. *Please*, I thought, *please, Tilly. Ask Elizabeth to go with you tomorrow. To give you a break. To be someone else to talk to Lucy.*

But Tilly trudged upstairs without another word.

Elizabeth sat for a while with her head in her hands. Lost in her thoughts. Then she filled a glass of water and headed towards the sitting room, picking up the note that Amy had left her on the way.

Elizabeth,

I've had a few phone calls for you today. Apparently you're not answering your phone. Is there a problem? Anyway: the hospital called twice. Could you ring Mrs Reynolds on 20 7143 9294 about your file? Jonty called, also twice. And someone called Reuben phoned for you. Wanted to check your mobile number because you weren't answering. I guess he got you because he never rang back.

Amy

Elizabeth stood like a statue with the note in her hand. Black specks whirled across her vision and her ears buzzed. She reached out a hand to steady herself against the table, and the note fell to the floor. With a sick feeling I remembered her telling Reuben how she was living with some dumb girl who sold masks. There weren't many mask shops in London and there was only one in Greenwich where she'd met Reuben. Was it Reuben who'd phoned? Somehow, I didn't think so.

She pulled her phone out of my bag. The screen told her she had several missed calls. Of course, she'd put it on silent while she waited outside the pub for Reuben.

She ran into the kitchen and pressed her face against the glass of the window so she could see right to the end of the alley. It was empty apart from the police car still parked on

the pavement. She stumbled into her bedroom and looked
out over the back. There was no one on the waste ground
behind the shop, as far as we could tell, for it was full of
shadows and places hidden by walls and trees.

Her eyes tore round the bedroom. She seized a black
sweatshirt, flung it on, and wrapped a black bandeau round
her head with shaky hands. Grabbed a belt pack and stuffed
Charlotte Patricia's passport and birth certificate, keys, her
purse and our phones into it.

A quick glance through the flat windows. Still nothing at
the back. Nor at the front. But the police car had finally
moved off.

And then her phone rang. She answered it, pressing the
phone hard against her ear, although she said nothing.

'Hello, Sophie,' a voice spoke. 'We're here waiting for
you. Why don't you come out? Save us having to come in and
get you.'

A couple of gentle taps on the front door stole up the
stairs. Tremors rippled up and down Elizabeth's body, her
knees gave way and she slid to the floor.

'It'd be better for you, you know.'

The voice was soft and sang with a foreign intonation,
although each word was clear and thoughtful and turned
Elizabeth's muscles to water. I knew the feeling. It was terror.
It was what I'd felt the night I fled from Gavin across the
fields. I felt it now. Felt the way it took control of Elizabeth's
body, screaming alarm into every nerve and cell. Felt it as
though her body was mine.

'We could tell Mr Petraitis that you came willingly,' the
voice continued. 'He'd be pleased about that.'

More knocking on the door.

But something about the name hardened Elizabeth's
trembling. She pulled the phone away from her ear, stared at

it for a couple of seconds, and cut the connection. Her fingers dug into the old carpet on the landing as the fright chemicals rushed through her veins.

More knocking.

Tilly appeared at the top of the stairs leading to my bedroom.

'Elizabeth. What are you doing? There's someone at the door. Have you fallen?' She ran down to the landing clutching her dressing gown round her. Her voice softened. 'Have you hurt yourself?'

Elizabeth shook her head.

'I'll go down and see who it is.'

'No!'

I couldn't tell which of us had spoken. It must have been Elizabeth, but the word had come from me as well.

The knocking became louder.

'Tilly.' Elizabeth dragged the words out of her body. 'Tilly,' she said again and took a deep breath and forced her body to stand. 'Go upstairs and lock yourself in. Call the police. Tell them it's urgent. Tell them someone's trying to break in.'

Tilly hesitated.

'They're after *me*,' Elizabeth said. Bitterness and fear infected her words. 'People I've pissed off. Pissed off badly. They won't hurt you, at least not straight away. Only when they can't find me. So call the police, Tilly. That's the only thing that will stop them.'

'But—'

'Call them. Now,' Elizabeth spat the words out.

Tilly picked up the phone and started dialling.

Elizabeth moved to the top of the stairs.

The knocking became a solid thwack. The sound of someone throwing themselves at the door. It would hold for a while but not for ever. She pressed her hands to her mouth and screamed silently into them, pouring out her horror, then moved down the stairs like a ghost, gliding slowly, noiselessly from step to step.

I knew what she was doing. It was what I would have done.

The only escape route was through the shop. There was a chance the men outside hadn't realised the shop and the flat were connected. They hadn't smashed the display window, which would have been the easiest way in. So, we were going through the shop and out the back, trusting the dark to keep us hidden.

She crouched at the bottom of the stairs. Eyes fixed on the front door with its old layers of paint breaking through the scratched black topcoat. A slender barrier protecting her from the men. Her hand clutched the cold metal knob of the door that led to the shop.

She knew what she had to do, but her body betrayed her and froze. The nearness of the men trapped her, paralysed her muscles and spun her thoughts into a never-ending spiral. Nothing good was going to happen if we stayed here. Without thinking, I slipped into the spaces her frozen presence had left. I soothed her jumping nerves, forced her to breathe and helped her ram steel into her muscles and bones.

Go for it, I whispered to her. *You can do it, girl. We can do it.*

The next thud punched the door and we didn't hesitate. We opened the shop door as the blow resounded, slipped through and sank onto the floor, pushing it shut with our feet.

And listened.

Silence.

The front door still held and, if they were looking inside the shop, they hadn't seen us.

We slithered across the floor, keeping below the bottom of the window. The shop was unlit and the street lights filled it with strange shapes and shadows cast by the masks. We were a shadow among shadows. No one called out. Their eyes were on the front door, shuddering with each blow. We crawled to the safety of the stockroom, stood and ran through it and through the studio into the yard.

And stopped.

Torchlight stabbed the night above the wooden gates, silhouetting the spikes on the top. Men were out on the waste ground. I heard their voices. Low and guttural. Men. Waiting for someone. Shining their torches over the windows of my flat above so that the rays bounced into the yard and onto the roof of Tilly's car.

We stepped back into the studio. Elizabeth's hands scrabbled along the table, her eyes darted around, searching for a hiding place, another way out. They lifted to the skylights. *No.* I told her, *no. They'll see you.* We were trapped.

Elizabeth's fear thinned the barrier between me and her thoughts. I felt her mind racing through the flat and the shop, desperately searching for an escape. Her body trembled with the effort.

Tilly's car.

I thought hard about Tilly's car. I thought hard about the big wooden gates.

I knew where the keys were. The keys to the back gate and the keys to Tilly's car. Elizabeth knew, too, but would she remember?

I took my memory of the moment Tilly arrived, when Amy reached up onto the shelf above the till, took the back gate keys from the box, and tossed them into Elizabeth's hands. Replayed it over and over again. Replayed Amy asking Tilly to leave the car keys with her. And prayed some part of it would reach Elizabeth.

Her body tightened – she'd got it. She slipped back into the stockroom and peered around the door into the shop.

Men stared through the window, cupping their hands round their faces to shut out the dim light from outside. They didn't see her. She was a black-clad figure, motionless in a dark doorway, but they would if she went into the shop to fetch the keys.

A body hit the front door of the flat with another sickening thud, followed by the noise of splintering. The door might hold but the frame was going. Shouts came from above. Some of the inhabitants of the flats in the alley had had enough. The battering on the door stopped and more faces appeared at the window.

Elizabeth flitted back into the stockroom. She whipped her head back and forth. A hunted animal seeking a hiding place. Somewhere to keep her attackers at bay until the last possible moment. Hoping the police would arrive first.

Her eyes fell on my desk. Albert Einstein stared back at her. A bald Albert Einstein with holes for eyes but otherwise perfect. The memory of Amy utterly disguised when she'd worn the mask opened in Elizabeth's head. She grabbed the mask and forced it on. With a cap on top and her body hidden by the greatcoat I kept behind the stockroom door for days when deliveries arrived in the rain, she stepped into the shop.

Torchlight shone through the shop window now. It ran slowly along the back wall, probing the dark corners of the doorway into the stockroom and fell on one of the masks in the Halloween display. An elongated white skull, screaming. The light stopped for a second and then moved on, passing over blood-stained ogres and dwarfish gremlins, sharp-fanged green-skinned aliens and a few grinning werewolves, before lingering over an array of classic Commedia dell'Arte masks. Long-nosed Zanni sneered back at the watching men, Arlecchino laughed at them while Pantalone glared through his bushy eyebrows.

The torch flew over the counter and passed over us, dazzling Elizabeth and then returned swiftly. I guessed the glint of her eyes had given us away.

She raised a hand to our eyes to shade them but slowly, as though she was an old man come down to see what the noise was, and walked to the till. Confused. Unsure. Pulling her wrinkled face into startled expressions. A little fearful but nothing extreme. For a long minute she stared at the men through the glass. The noise of Elizabeth's heart pounding filled her ears and then, with the light fixed on her, she lifted a hand and grasped the keys on the shelf above the till. She shuffled back to the stockroom, seeing her shadow loom on the back wall of the shop as the torch followed every inch of her progress.

At the doorway, she gave the men a last look, and I saw that the connecting door to the flat had swung ajar, disturbed, I guessed, by the thundering on the front door. It was only a matter of time before they noticed it.

Back in the stockroom and out of reach of the torches' searchlights, Elizabeth dropped the old man hobble and headed out. Behind us I heard shouts. They'd seen the connecting door. A few seconds later, we heard the shop window splinter.

The padlock holding the big gates closed was fiddly. Elizabeth's hands fumbled. Cold sweat against damp iron. The noise of glass cracking and shattering rose over the roof.

'Shit, shit, shit.'

And finally, the key turned, the padlock dropped, and

the chain slid off the gates. She was in the car in a flash, ignition on and away as the men poured through the studio door
behind her. The car shoved the gates open. Elizabeth flicked
the headlights on and floored the accelerator. Two men with
torches leaped out of the way and tumbled onto the ground.
Elizabeth forced the wheel round towards the exit. The tyres
sent a shower of gravel and mud up into the air, but we beat
the men to the exit, screeched down the lane, and onto the
main road. We'd got away.

On the other side of the road a van, parked illegally,
pulled off the pavement and followed us. A white van with a
scratched and sun-bleached green and blue logo. I glimpsed
it in the mirror and for a moment I thought Elizabeth, every
ounce of her concentration on the road ahead, hadn't seen it
but she gave a little moan and slammed her foot on the
accelerator.

37

The van caught up with us at one of the many traffic lights on the main road. Elizabeth jumped the red light and turned into one of the small streets amongst the new blocks of flats. It was a mistake. We'd driven into a cul-de-sac. She tried to reverse and escape but she was too late. The van appeared at the end of the street, blocking the exit. Too late she cut the headlights and drove in between two parked cars. Too late she thought about jumping out and running. She was caught. Trapped in the glare of their lights. Helpless as three men jumped out of the van and circled Tilly's car.

One of them wrenched the door open.

'Get out, old man,' he said.

She hesitated, not understanding, and then lifted a hand to touch her face. In the heat of her escape, she'd forgotten the clammy feel of the silicon against her skin. She was still Albert Einstein. She picked up the cap, fallen between the front seats, and placed it on her head, climbed out slowly and carefully, with the stiffness of old age, and watched while two of the men tore the car apart looking for her.

The other stood by Elizabeth, a hand gripping her shoulder. She watched and waited. I watched and waited. Fear rippled in and out of my thoughts, but every muscle in Elizabeth's body was poised to seize the moment and run. She only needed the man to relax his grip for a second.

His phone rang and she tensed, but his hand dug even harder into her shoulder as he answered it.

'We got the old man,' he said. 'But there's no one with him. She must have stayed behind.' He listened. 'No one got out, boss. We'd have seen.'

He clicked his fingers at the two others and jerked his head towards Elizabeth. They came over and each grabbed one of her arms while he walked away to continue the conversation.

Elizabeth kept her head down and out of the street light, but it caught her hands and she saw how slim and unlined they were. She buried them in the greatcoat's pockets.

The cul-de-sac was quiet. Far enough away from the high road for there to be no one passing through. The flats all had balconies overlooking the car park, and two days earlier there would have been people out on them enjoying the night-time coolness after the heat of the day, but the storm the previous evening had put paid to that.

All the same, I wanted her to scream. I wanted to scream. I wanted to vent my terror out into the night. Surely someone would hear. But Elizabeth stayed silent. Her voice, I thought. Her voice would give her away as surely as her hands did. She was right. Better to wait and hope the disguise would see her through.

She sneaked a glance at the two men, one on either side of her. I didn't like what she saw. They were big, their belts cinched tight under protruding bellies, but tough and muscled with it. And watchful, their grip on her arms unrelenting. But still Elizabeth prepared. She clenched and unclenched her toes inside her trainers, readying them for a chance to escape. A moment when she could break free and tear through the quiet streets to safety: a busy road, a bar, somewhere with people. None of it far away.

Number One man finished his call and sauntered back, sliding his mobile in the pocket of his skinny jeans and hitching them over his waist.

'He's coming over. We're to wait here.'

He wandered back to the car and ran his hands over the exposed metal floor of the boot, as though to convince himself no one could be hiding, then checked the ruins of the back seat.

A black car, long and sleek, nosed into the dead end and caught us in its headlights, casting our shadows down the walkways between the flats. It slid to a halt and the front door opened. A man stepped out, leaving the lights on and the engine purring. The clunk of the door shutting behind him echoed into the night, and a flicker of something nudged the edges of my thoughts: Gavin getting into the car beside me and slamming the door shut. The night he died. I shook the shred of memory away – this wasn't Gavin, although the fear was the same – and focused on the man walking towards us, his boots clicking on the pavement. The light caught his thin harsh features. Pale skin covered with a scattering of freckles, evenly distributed over his face. Symmetrical and expressionless until he came very close, when I saw that one eyelid was slightly lower than the other.

Something inside Elizabeth withered.

Number One man gestured to the car. 'See, boss, nothing.'

Elizabeth knew him. Elizabeth feared him. His arrival had unleashed a dark, gut-churning terror in her depths. And the fear had a name. Matis. His name was Matis. Matis Petraitis.

Matis cast a quick look at the car.

'Where is the girl?' His accent was less marked than the others. It was the voice on the phone.

'She must be back at the flat, boss?' Number One man said.

'No,' he said.

'She must have got out before you broke in.'

'She didn't,' Matis said. He grabbed Elizabeth by the arm. She stared at his feet. Black boots now framed with a thin layer of mud. 'You dropped her off somewhere, old man?'

Elizabeth shook her head slowly.

He put his hand under her chin and forced her head up. 'Lost your voice?'

She tried. She fixed her eyes on his nose, on the bony ridge separating his eyes. She coughed and said 'No.'

His eyes sharpened, then he laughed. 'Henrik, you are an idiot,' he said. And then something curt and guttural in a language I didn't understand. His hand tightened on Elizabeth, squeezing her chin until the mask slid up and over her mouth. He laughed again and spat at her. Smelling of stale cigarettes and sourness, the saliva trickled down onto Elizabeth's neck and disappeared into her sweatshirt.

'Not really an old man, then. Let's see who's underneath this.' He clicked his fingers at Henrik and muttered a few foreign words. Henrik handed him something small and black. He pressed a button and a blade shot out.

Elizabeth tried to speak but his hand gripped her jaw too tight. Not that it hurt. Nothing hurt. Right at this moment, fear of what was to come drove the pain away. Her legs gave way. He pushed her back against the car, holding her chin up so she faced the light, and ran the blade down the right side of the mask and then back up to her forehead and down the left side. The face of the mask fell.

'Hello, Sophie,' he said and flung her towards Henrik. She fell on the ground next to Tilly's car.

But she didn't give up. She forced her shaking muscles to roll her over and crouched. Even then her body thought it might escape. It kept her muscles tensed, pressing her fingers against the damp ground, like a runner ready to explode out of the starting blocks at the beginning of a race. A trickle of something ran into her eyebrows, but she didn't move.

Matis squatted down by her.

She flinched as he reached his hand out to her face. She couldn't help herself. But he only ripped the rest of the mask off. 'Not a very pretty mask,' he said. 'Not like your pretty, pretty wigs. Reuben told us about them, you know. Told us where you bought them. Told us if we went to your favourite wig shop they'd know where you'd had them delivered. Told us to look for a shop selling masks too. Poor Reuben. He didn't want to tell us, but I needed to find you. Wigs, Reuben told us, masks and Greenwich. And that your name was Elizabeth.'

The mention of Reuben seared an agony along her nerves. It almost undid her. Her rigid control slipped and her breath tore into gasping sobs.

'You killed my father, beautiful Sophie. You must have known I'd never give up until I found you.'

Matis smiled and straightened, casting a quick glance at the flats and the balconies, towering over the car park. He barked a couple of orders at the others. They seized Elizabeth and forced her towards the van. Too late she found her voice. The one she hadn't dared use before. She screamed. We screamed.

But only for a second. A fraction of a second. A clap of a shriek before a hand clamped over her mouth and nose, stifling her voice and her breath.

They bundled us into the back of the van. As though we were a sack of clothes. Slammed the doors shut as we tumbled over tools and tarpaulins and came to rest against the wheel arch. Elizabeth clung to it as we drove off and stared out of the back windows. At the outside. At the street lights flicking by and the sullen clouds crawling across the sky.

I didn't know what she was thinking. Maybe, like me, her brain was a blank, wiped clean of everything but the horror of what was going to happen to us. But I felt the fear as it picked away at the tendons tying her bones together.

The journey didn't take long. A few minutes at most.

They opened the back doors of the van and, beyond their black figures, I saw we were in a car park. Old and shabby and strewn with crates and boxes, its edges pierced by wild-flowers and weeds. One of the industrial units that ran along the side of Deptford Creek. I could hear water, but that was all. No one walked by. No cars drove past. No one was here but Elizabeth and the men gazing at her with dark, secretive faces.

38

They dragged Elizabeth out of the van. Her legs buckled as her feet met the ground, but she forced herself upright and stood facing the men. The three of them closed in at a nod from Matis, who stood slightly apart, leaning against the metal fence, his face in shadows.

There was no escape.

Stillness, heavy with threat and impending violence, clouded the air. Elizabeth remained motionless. The push and pull of her chest as the air glided in and out, so tiny as to be invisible.

The men waited. Only their eyes moved. Crawling over Elizabeth, brooding over her soft, white, unsullied, perfect skin. And in that moment of quiet, I prayed for it to be quick. For it to be over.

It was Matis who broke the stillness. 'Get on with it,' he said.

And it started.

The first punch smacked into her face. I saw it coming. The arm drawn back in preparation, the expression of deep, absorbing concentration, the moment when it released and shot towards us, powered by the weight of experience and muscle. It hit with a dull thud and knocked us back against the van. Knocked every thought out of us and numbed every feeling. Pain was a faraway thing, driven away by the shock reverberating through her flesh.

Elizabeth slid to the ground. Feet crunched on the loose stones as the men laughed. We stared up at them.

Suddenly, Gavin's face looked back down at me. The night shredded into confusion.

A fist on my cheek. A grunt. Another cracked into my ribs. So many fists. Blood on the fists. Blood on the carpet. A punch ground stones into my skin. Stones, not soft carpet. No blood on the carpet. *Where was I?*

Agony arrived. Elizabeth screamed. I was with Elizabeth. On the ground. With Elizabeth. Pain juddered her bones and raced through her like a whimpering animal desperately seeking an escape. I was Lucy. And I was Elizabeth. I was the dirty, battered heap of split skin and torn flesh, cracked bone and bruise, that was Elizabeth. I wanted to weep for her. Except I had no eyes. I wanted to reach out my arms and hold her close. But I had no arms. And no body to wrap around her.

All I could do was be with her. I didn't run. I didn't hide in a distant memory, pulling its edges round me like a child in bed curling under the duvet to escape a bad dream. No, I stayed. I bore witness. I noted each punch and kick. I would remember them. Each and every one of them. For Elizabeth.

And on and on it went. Their feet drove into us. Heavy-booted feet. Her body leapt and thumped with each kick. And curled around the agony bursting inside her. I felt her slip away. Down a great hole opening up in the centre of her. She slipped deeper and deeper away until the pain couldn't touch her. And I was glad. So glad for her.

The men stopped.

A break. A pause. A long moment of nothing stretching into peace.

Her body called out to me then, wanting me to fill the emptiness Elizabeth had left behind. But I stayed still and hard until it gave up and her blood slowed and the pain racing up and down her nerves faded.

Flashes penetrated her eyelids. They were taking photos.

Bastards.

I knew what the pictures would show. Images like my face in the mirror after Gavin beat me up. And anger flickered. For Elizabeth. But also for Lucy. Lucy who tried so hard. Lucy who never stood a chance.

Muttered voices. Orders barked in a language I didn't understand. Laughter.

They were mindless, evil thugs. I hated them. Elizabeth hadn't deserved this. No matter what she'd done. No one deserved this. Not even me. My anger grew and became a wave of fury breaking over me.

With the men.

With Gavin.

He was no better than them. He was a mindless evil thug. An egotistical bastard fulfilling his dark compulsions on my poor body and spirit. For the first time I saw him clearly, his true self unmasked, and the power of my rage swept everything else away. All the lingering vestiges of shame at what had happened to me. All the guilt at what I'd done to him. I didn't care if I'd killed him. I hoped I'd killed him. Because he would never have let me go. No more than the men who'd done this to Elizabeth would have. Our relationship would only ever have ended in the death of one of us.

And it had been Gavin. And I was glad.

And suddenly, more than anything, trapped in the battered shell of Elizabeth's body, I wanted to live. I wanted to walk away from the broken mess of the past. I wanted a future. I wanted time to do all the little things. Go bird-watching with Tilly. Visit Venice again. Have a proper conversation with Amy. And dig my fingers into clay to pull shapes out of it.

And I'd deal with the big things. I'd fight the police. Use Gavin's money to get a top-class lawyer. And even if the worst happened, I wouldn't go quietly. I'd shout my rage at the unfairness of it all until there wasn't a household that hadn't heard my name. Money can buy a lot of publicity.

And, I realised, I wanted Elizabeth to survive this too. She was a liar, a cheat, and a thief. But she'd been dealt a rough hand and made the best of it. She deserved more than this grubby, violent end in a scruffy car park. Somehow, I'd get us both out of this.

39

One of the men picked Elizabeth up and threw her over his shoulder, carrying her a few yards while I wondered what else they were going to do to her. Wondered what they had done to her, because the pain inside her told me the damage was terrible.

Hands lifted her body off his shoulders and hurled her forwards. For a few seconds she was a bunch of rags tumbling in the air and then she hit water with a great smack. The shock of it flung me into every nerve and cell of Elizabeth's body. Her arms and legs woke with my presence and jerked. All around was cold and dark, full of currents that swirled us this way and that, and dragged us into a rush of water racing away.

And then a great thwack.

We hit a wall. We were pinned to a wall, pushed tight against it by torrents of water rushing over her head and around her body. They thundered in her ears. Her lungs were bursting. Her blood screamed at me to breathe. I had to get her head out of the water. I forced her hands to reach out.

They clawed the stone, slippery with years of slime. Found something hanging. Soft, rubbery. Grabbed it and hauled us up.

Her head broke the surface. Her lungs gulped air. Water roared past. Her eyes cleared. We were plastered against one of the great stone stanchions supporting the footbridge over Deptford Creek, while the ebbing tide, swollen by the storm last night, tore past, heading for the Thames and the open sea. Southeast London drained past us as I forced Elizabeth's hand to cling to one of the rubber buffers draped over the stone to protect the sides of passing boats.

It wasn't long after high tide, because the surface of the flood-bloated waters was near the top of the stanchion. So near. I reached up to grab one of the blue metal uprights that held the footbridge in place. The relentless current snatched at her free hand, but I forced it up and into the gentle air and snapped her fingers round the metal. The effort knocked her legs away from the wall and the water saw its chance and seized them, dragging the lower half of her body towards the Thames.

Left hand gripped cold metal. Right hand dug into the slime-coated buffer and clutched the rubber beneath. The slippery rubber, slithering through fingers. Arm muscles, stretched beyond bearing, screamed at me.

I thought about letting go. Giving in to the water's urgent pull. We'd float away from the horror of what had happened. It would be peaceful out on the Thames. I would see the sky and the horizon punched through by the tower blocks lining its banks. I might be rescued by a river boat. Taken to a place of safety.

No, I wouldn't. No one would rescue me. No. The Thames would suck us into its depths, pour water into our lungs and roll our corpse along its bed until it caught on a tangle of twisted metal or sank deep into the mud.

The water roared around me. Rage roared through me. I was going to get out.

Let go of the buffer, I told Elizabeth's hand. *Let go. You must let go. Reach up. Grab the metal. Clamp it round.* Two hands on the metal would pull us out.

I let go.

And missed.

The current jerked us away. Only one hand on the metal held us and it was Elizabeth's hand with Elizabeth's muscles. Muscles, used for tapping on her phone and computer. Not my muscles, used to wrenching shapes out of clay. Her hand slipped but I forced it to tighten. I forced the muscles in her arm to haul us back. I flung her other arm out of the water and made it seize the metal upright too.

The racing current fought me every step of the way, but I was grit-filled and teeth-clenched determination and, inch by inch, I dragged Elizabeth's battered and bleeding body out of the water until we lay on the bridge and liquid streamed from us back into the dark water tearing downstream.

No one was around. The men had gone. Convinced no one could escape the raging creek. Least of all Elizabeth, unconscious, bloodied and broken.

We lay there while the night air, still warm despite last night's storm, dried her skin and drove the chill from her bones. Feeling returned. Pain returned. She started to bleed again. It was time to move. Time to get help. We stood and staggered, waking agony from wounds inside her that I couldn't see. Elizabeth flickered into wakefulness. Nothing more than a fluttering of butterfly wings before the pain pushed her away again, down into some part of her I couldn't reach. I was on my own.

One hundred and forty-three steps back to the car park. One hundred and forty-three steps, five falls and the fear that her body would collapse, and we'd bleed out on the path and die in this deserted and grubby backwater.

And the terror that the men might still be in the car park.

They weren't. It was empty. Scuffed and churned mud and gravel in one corner among broken grasses and wild-flowers showed where the beating had taken place, but the van was long gone. Only Tilly's car was there. They must have brought it with them rather than leaving it for someone to discover.

Something long and black caught my eye and I limped over. It was Elizabeth's belt bag, ripped off her body and left behind.

Elizabeth's phone was in it.

I levered her body onto a pile of old crates and wondered what to do. Who to call.

An ambulance? Elizabeth's body was weakening. Blood dripped from her clothes onto the ground, and the pain in her abdomen and back was an ever-tightening vice crushing her flesh. I laid her hand on her stomach and memories flared to life. The sound of vicious laughs overlaying the soft thud of a boot stamping on her stomach and feet kicking her as she lay curled round the agony. Something was badly broken inside.

Her phone rang.

It was Jonty.

'Elizabeth?' I could barely hear him over the background noise of shouts and running feet.

'Yes.'

Her voice worked. I could speak. Elizabeth must be so far away, so deeply unconscious that no whisper of her presence stopped her body obeying me. The words were mangled though. Elizabeth's mouth was cut and her tongue shredded by the sharp remnants of her teeth.

'Are you all right?' Jonty's voice was insistent.

'Yes.'

'I'm at the flat—' he started.

I drove my voice over him. 'Tilly. Is Tilly there? Is she OK?'

'She's shaken up but unhurt. The firemen got her out before the fire spread.'

'Fire?'

'Someone sprayed petrol all over the shop and set it alight. Luckily the police were already on their way. Elizabeth, what's going on? Where are you?'

But I didn't know what to say. It was too much to take in. The flat was on fire. To drive Elizabeth out, I guessed. Or kill her. They wouldn't have cared if she died.

'Tilly is definitely all right?'

'Yes, yes. She's very shocked. Do you want to speak to her? She's just talking to the police but—'

'No!'

I needed to think and do it fast.

'The police are there?' I asked.

'Everybody's here. The police. Firemen. Ambulances. Tilly was sure you'd got out but... Where are you, Elizabeth? I need to tell them you're OK.'

'No, Jonty. No. Wait.'

My thoughts raced, full of the shock of my flat on fire, the horror of what had been done to Elizabeth and the pain of her injuries that filtered through to me despite my efforts to block it. But one thought overrode them all.

We needed to get to hospital. My body was waiting for me there and Elizabeth needed urgent medical treatment.

An ambulance would take us to hospital and probably

the one where my body was as it was the nearest. But I'd be imprisoned there. In A&E. In an operating theatre. On a ward. I needed to be free to get back to my body. Tilly had said it was restless. I needed to get back. Before the emptiness overwhelmed it again and it withered and died.

'No, Jonty.' I fought to find a reason for him to keep silent. 'No one must know I'm alive. The people who did this, they'll come after me.' This was true. 'Please. Will you come and get me? Please, Jonty.'

It was very quiet where I was. In the background, a faint hum of traffic and the sound of water racing a short distance away in Deptford Creek. But nothing else. Except for the noises that came from the phone while I waited for Jonty's answer. Voices shouting, mainly. The occasional flare of a siren. A slap of rubber and feet running.

'Where are you?' he said.

'Not far away.'

'What does that mean?'

'Five- or ten-minute walk.'

'Tell me where and I'll come and get you.'

It was my turn to think.

'OK. But you've got to promise, you've got to swear you'll come on your own. And you won't breathe a word to anyone.' My voice started to break. I so wanted to trust him. I knew he'd have kept quiet for me but whether he would for Elizabeth was another question. 'It's quite safe, you know. So long as you tell no one.'

'Just tell me where you are.'

I did.

And I waited.

And watched the blood slip out of Elizabeth's wounds and thought about the blood leaking somewhere inside her and pooling in her abdomen.

Elizabeth woke. Completely, this time. She reached out into her body and pain overwhelmed her. She thinned into white-hot anguish, and her thoughts splintered into a thousand jagged needles. I still couldn't read them, but their anguish sped through her blood. I gripped her tight. Held her body still and cushioned the pain. She let me. She didn't fight but lay with me, entwining her presence with mine, present but quiescent. Her body gave a momentary shudder as she glanced around the car park and memories of the beating stirred in her. I blanketed them. We needed to stay strong.

By the time Jonty raced into the car park, Elizabeth's body was in trouble. Lack of blood was forcing her heart to beat faster and faster. The blood that lay round my feet in a black pool seeping over the mud. Jonty skidded to a halt as he surveyed the scene. Smuts stained his skin and the smell of smoke wafted over to me as his eyes opened wide in disbelief. He stretched out a hand.

'Don't touch me,' I said to him. 'I'm hurt. You need to take me to hospital.' I jerked my head towards Tilly's car. 'I'm beyond driving. The keys are in it. It'll be quick. The hospital's not far and I need it to be quick.'

Jonty ran to the car, chucked enough of the debris left by the men out of it to slide into the front seat, and drove it over to us. He had the sense to leave us alone to force Elizabeth's body in. It was agony for her, as was every minute of the drive. Every corner, every stop jolted harsh stabs of pain through her. She bore it. Contained it. As if she knew I was doing the best for both of us, and in her turn she fought to keep her body quiet and obedient.

But time was our enemy. It ate away at our strength. Our vision clouded and the night became a blur of yellow streaks and dark shadows. The journey seemed like hours. Like an interminable road trip across empty swathes of desert, where the days were hot and blinding with the sun, and at night a festival of stars chilled you to the bone. One minute sweat beaded Elizabeth's face and nausea made her feel dizzy, and the next, waves of cold iced her body and she shuddered.

The entrance to A&E was full of cars and taxis. Jonty swore. He stopped the car and leaped out. 'I'm going to get someone. Tell them you're badly hurt. Wait. I'll be as quick as I can.'

I tried to say OK but nothing came out of Elizabeth's mouth. Her body was failing and I'd lost control of the tiny muscles and nerves that made her speak. I lifted up her hand to signal OK. I could still do that. Her fingernails were blue. We were nearing the end. Elizabeth was still present but quiet and small. A glowing ember cooling into blackness.

Jonty disappeared.

I didn't want to die.

Elizabeth's body was shutting down but I didn't want to die.

I forced it back into life, opened the car door, swung her legs round, grabbed the top of the door to lever us up and out, and staggered away from A&E, away from the hustle and bustle of well-meaning nurses and porters, around the corner and into the street, to the main entrance to the hospital. Every step was a battle. Elizabeth helped. Helped me to transfer the weight of her shaking, sweating, panting body from one foot to the other.

The entrance hall was quiet at this time of night. The revolving glass doors were locked, but a side door let staff and the occasional late-night visitor in and out. The security guard, cocooned in the warm glow of the light above his desk, barely glanced up as they entered. Nevertheless I waited until he went into the room behind the counter and pushed the door open.

The clock above the lifts said two but, as I stumbled towards it, forcing Elizabeth's legs to move as fast as possible, its black hands blurred and melted. Elizabeth's heart beat a fast drum roll. Her vision darkened and buzzed. Her body screamed for us to stop. We staggered into the lift and slumped against its side as it took us up. I saw our reflection in the metal. A face. But only just. Blood oozed from one eye and her nose pointed to her left ear. Her mouth was mangled and cut, and when I opened it in horror, there was only darkness broken by a few remaining shards of teeth. Elizabeth whimpered, and I shut her eyes. Even the worst of my Hallowe'en masks was gentle in comparison to this.

The lift doors opened.

The fifth-floor landing was quiet and dim. The door to ICU was still wedged open by a fire extinguisher. The damage caused by the power cuts the night before unrepaired. Inside, the corridor was empty although light shone through the closed doors to the ward at the end.

No one appeared as we stumbled down to Lucy's room and opened the door. In the middle, my body, covered in a blue hospital sheet, waited for life to come back. Like Sleeping Beauty waiting for her prince's kiss to wake her. But no prince was going to save me. There were no princes. I'd learned that much. It was up to me. All I had to do was walk in, reach out and place Elizabeth's hands on my body. Her body was too weak to hold me back and, besides, Elizabeth was awake.

But something was wrong.

The noises were right. The bleeps of the monitors and the steady whoosh, suck and thump of the pump. Lines jagged across screens, rising and falling, green and safe. I checked the room. Ticking off the list of things that Sean had explained. Heart monitor, yes. Oxygen levels, fine.

Still something was wrong. I knew it.

The body in the bed. *So calm. So quiet.*

And then I got it.

Too calm, too quiet.

Too still.

My chest was still. No rise and fall. Nothing disturbed the draping of the blue sheet over me.

I moved towards my body. Its face was empty. Empty of fear. Empty of pain. Empty of life. Empty of plastic tubing.

It was dead.

I was too late.

Too late.

Time had run out.

No.

The No was a howl in our head. No sound came out of Elizabeth's mouth. Her body had no energy to spare for screaming. *Not now*, I wanted to cry out. *Not now when I finally knew I wanted to fight and win and live.*

Except the line of her heart still marched up and down across the screen. The pump breathed in and out and no alarms sounded. Nothing made sense.

Something bobbed against my foot. What was it? A balloon. A bright pink balloon. A little girl's birthday party balloon filling with air and nudging my leg. And then relaxing as the air went out and the rubber puckered into flatness. Someone had attached a balloon to Lucy's pump. Someone had taken it out of her mouth and used it to blow up a balloon.

I peered round as the door I'd left open behind me slowly closed. Someone stood there. Someone hiding.

It was Moira.

Plastered as flat against the wall as she could make herself.

Not a normal Moira though. Her hair was dishevelled, and her face was white with staring eyes. Her clothes were wrong, too. Her blouse was open, showing the cream lace of her slip and the electrodes taped to the skin above it. Their wires ran to Lucy's heart monitor. The wires on Moira's finger ran to the oxygen level monitor and round her arm was Lucy's blood pressure cuff. The machines were monitoring Moira, not my body.

Her hand gripped the tube and mask that had connected my body to the pump. I began to understand. She had removed them. She was killing my body and no one knew. I couldn't speak. I couldn't scream for help.

Moira spoke. 'Your face,' she said. 'My God. Your face.'

She shrank back into the corner of the room, as far away from me as the cables attaching her to the monitors would allow.

I turned back to my body.

Was I dead? How long had I been without oxygen? Maybe not too long. Tilly had said the nurses checked Lucy regularly.

There must be a call button. Where was the call button?

It too dangled from Moira's hand, shifting from side to side like the pendulum of a clock ticking my life away. No help from that.

Elizabeth's breath wheezed and gasped, snatching the precious, precious oxygen from the air and spraying droplets of blood over the bedclothes. Could I make it to the door? Open it and leave? Walk down the long corridor? Find a nurse? I didn't think so. Not even crawling. Anyway, what would I do when I found one? I couldn't speak.

No. I had to do something myself. And fast. No time. We had no time.

Think, Lucy, think.

Our eyes flicked round the room and came to rest on the bag valve mask that Sean had used the night of the power cut. It was where he'd left it. Coiled on top of the oxygen tank in the corner.

Elizabeth's hands were unsteady and bloody, and the valve on the oxygen tank was stiff but I opened it. I forced my mind to remember what Sean had done. I tilted my own jaw and head back and clamped the mask onto my face, curving Elizabeth's hand in the C shape like he had.

And squeezed the BVM.

My chest rose.

Moira laughed.

I squeezed again and then remembered Sean counting.

One – one thousand. Two – two thousand. Right up to six and then squeezed again. The sheet rose and fell, and I prayed some of the oxygen was flowing into my lungs rather than my stomach.

'She's dead,' Moira said. 'You're wasting your time. She's been without oxygen for hours.'

But I didn't believe her. She was lying. She'd have been long gone if my body was definitely dead. She was here because she wanted all hope of revival to be past before she replaced the monitors on my body and triggered the alarms that would bring the nurses running.

But at her words, Elizabeth's hands faltered. I forced them to grip and stared into my face, willing it to show some signs of life. Blood dripped from Elizabeth and landed on my skin. Vibrant, shocking. Red against its whiteness.

'She's dead,' Moira said and she laughed again. 'Finally.' Her voice changed into something syrupy and soft. '*Just a few minutes with my lovely daughter-in-law.* That's what I told the nurse. *Just a few minutes to share our memories of my darling boy.*

Elizabeth's legs gave way. We collapsed onto the bed. Elizabeth's body was close to death. I knew that. It had lost too much blood, and its heart couldn't beat fast enough to get oxygen to its dying cells. Only the combined efforts of Elizabeth and me kept it going. And only our combined efforts kept her hands squeezing the pump and forcing the oxygen into my lungs.

'I'm telling you she's dead.' Moira's voice throbbed with rage as she took a couple of steps towards me. 'She had to die. She killed Gavin. My lovely boy. She killed him. Did you know that, Elizabeth?' Her voice rose, and I prayed it might be loud enough to alert someone.

We couldn't speak. We could barely move. Elizabeth's body was shutting down, diverting the little blood remaining away from everything but the most essential organs.

'At first, I thought she only killed him with her cruelty. Stressed him so his heart failed. She knew it was weak. She knew that.' Moira neared. 'Stop doing that, Elizabeth.'

She reached out to grab us, and I turned Elizabeth's head and stared at her. Elizabeth's face was a horror, and Moira quailed and retreated. But the words still poured out of her mouth. She hated Lucy. And I was too late. On and on she went. But I let the words flow over me and blend into the swoosh of the useless pump and hum of the noise of the machines. Nothing mattered except keeping Elizabeth's hands pressing the seal of the mask tight on Lucy's face and forcing the precious oxygen into her.

'Selfish... I knew she was selfish. Right from the start.' Moira bit the words out. 'And thoughtless. But after Gavin's death, when she wouldn't talk to me, when she cut us both off, I began to think there was something odd about her behaviour. Not grief but something else. And the wound on his beautiful face. It bothered me. How did he get that? Tell me, Elizabeth, how do you think that happened? The police said it was probably a branch, when he fell. But I went to the tree and looked. I spent hours there but I couldn't find a branch that would have caused that bruise. Not without leaving scratches all over the rest of his face.'

I stared at my chest. It rose and fell. But that wasn't what I wanted to see. I wanted to see if my heart was beating. If it was taking the precious oxygen and pushing it to the corners of my body.

I took Elizabeth's hand off the mask while I repeated the count. *One-one thousand.* We grasped my wrist. *Two-two thousand.* Pressed Elizabeth's fingers against the soft skin, feeling for my pulse. *Three-three thousand.* Elizabeth's body was dying around me. I felt it failing. Blood dripped more slowly from her wounds, and her hands had little strength. *Four-four thousand.* Still no pulse in my wrist. I felt nothing.

Moira's words pierced the hum and whir of the useless machines in the room. She was mad. But her grief and madness gave her words a weird eloquence.

'So I looked for something else. Every day I looked. I walked round the fields where he died. Alone. All alone. I hunted through the woods. Ted said the police had combed the area, but they didn't look as hard as I did. No one but a mother would look as hard as I did. And then I found it. Fallen in the stream and hidden under the murky water all these months until this terrible drought dried everything out and I kicked the baked mud aside. A sharpening steel – Lucy's steel. A wedding present to her and my beautiful boy and burnt by her stupid carelessness.'

Five-five thousand. I couldn't feel a pulse. I was dead. No point continuing. Moira had told us the truth. Lucy was dead. A wave of grief passed through us, sucking away our last remaining flickers of energy. I lifted Elizabeth's fingers from Lucy's wrist. It was all over.

And as they left her skin, I felt a flicker. A brief tap against Elizabeth's fingertips. As light as a flower petal brushing Elizabeth's skin. So light I'd nearly missed it. *Six-six thousand*.

A pulse. My body was alive.

I grasped the pump and squeezed.

One – one thousand.

Should I try to slip into it – into my body? It would be the end for Elizabeth. I was sure of that. It was only the combination of the two of us, Elizabeth and me, keeping her body going.

Two – two thousand.

If I left Elizabeth who would pump oxygen into my lungs?

Three – three thousand.

If I left Elizabeth, who would stop Moira from killing me?

The eyes of the body in the bed flickered. My eyes flickered. And opened. But Moira didn't notice. Something reached out to me and the air in the room, charged with so much bitterness and grief, lightened.

'I showed the steel to Ted.' Moira never faltered. 'Told him it was Lucy's, and he took it to the police, but I wasn't sure they'd do anything. Besides, I wanted to deal with Lucy myself. I owed it to Gavin.' Her voice was calm now. Matter-of-fact. 'I'm sorry you were there, Elizabeth but I'd waited too long to miss my chance. Every afternoon, waiting for her to come out. I drove the car at Lucy, but you were in the way.'

For a second my counting faltered. *Moira had tried to kill me before*.

Lucy's hand lifted.

Moira's voice stopped.

Then the hand dropped, slipped off the bed and dangled at Elizabeth's knees.

'No,' Moira whispered, her voice full of hiss and poison. 'Will nothing kill her?'

I heard the scrape of metal as she picked up a chair and strode towards us, felt the rush of air as she started to slam it down.

I won't let this happen. I won't. I won't. I won't.

We reached deep down. Elizabeth and I. Together. We forced Elizabeth's body to stand and lean over my body, to shelter my body and take the blow. The chair smashed into us. Blood spattered the sheets and we fell, half on the bed and half sliding onto the floor. Moira bit back a scream of anger.

If only she would yell. If only we could speak. If only we could scream. If only a nurse would come in.

Moira raised the chair again, swinging it high above her head in a great circle. We could do nothing but watch her. Something had broken inside Elizabeth, and her strength was leaking away with the blood draining onto the floor. It was the end. Soon Moira's lungs would be the only ones tearing the oxygen from the air in this small room filled with grief and anger.

The chair reached the top of the arc. In a minute, it would crash down onto my body. The sensors stuck to Moira's chest heaved in and out with the force of her panting as she readied herself.

The sensors.

Elizabeth stirred. She reached into her body, forcing her

recalcitrant nerves and muscles to make one last effort. *We* reached into her body. And together we pushed it half up and raised an arm. It shook and trembled but we lifted it all the same. I loved Elizabeth at that moment. She never gave up. Even when there was no hope, she pushed on. And so did I. So would I. Always.

Our hand hit Moira's chest, grabbed the cables attaching the sensors and pulled them sharply. They dropped onto the floor. The chair crashed down on Elizabeth's head and we collapsed.

Alarms sounded.

Footsteps down the corridor.

The door opened.

Someone gasped... Then shouted... More voices.

Elizabeth and I tried to stand but couldn't. Her body sank against the bed. Something caressed her cheek. A hand? A nurse's hand?

No, it was my hand, lolling against the side of the bed where it had fallen. Skin touched skin.

Now would be a good time.

Warm skin touched skin that was chilling fast. Whose skin was whose? I was no longer sure. Except one of us was alive and the other was dying.

It was now or never.

I pressed Elizabeth's cold face into Lucy's hand. Lucy's flesh called me. But quietly. The hunger was less. Lucy was alive, but time had taken her a few steps further away from life.

Please, Lucy, I begged, *I need you to want me. I need you to fight for me.*

Because Elizabeth's body would not let go easily. And part of me had grown close to her. Parts of me were intertwined with her. Part of me didn't want to leave her. To abandon her.

Please, Elizabeth, I need you to let me go.

For a moment I hung between the two. Perfectly balanced.

I was neither Elizabeth nor Lucy.

I was both Lucy and Elizabeth.

And then Lucy called me. I felt Elizabeth give me a push, and I slipped into my body.

I was home.

EPILOGUE

North Denmark is very flat. We live in a white, upside-down house made of wood and full of light. A balcony wraps around the first-floor living room and kitchen. Even on days when the wind hurtles in from Sweden and the Baltic Sea, bending the trees sideways and scouring the long grass, even then, there's always a part of the balcony that's sheltered.

It was important because I had to be outside when we first moved here the year after I nearly died. I had to walk round and round, staring out over the plains, watching for cars or people coming down the narrow roads that criss-cross the flatness. And at night we had to sleep with the big sliding windows open, so I could raise my head when I woke and look out over the unbroken night.

The weeks passed.

It got a bit better.

I knew it would. I knew all I needed was time.

And when autumn arrived, Jonty persuaded me to stay indoors, although I still spent the first weeks wandering from room to room, checking the miles of wilderness through the windows.

It got even better.

And by my birthday in November, I was happy to snuggle up in front of the log burner with Talisker beside me and even laughed when I unwrapped the binoculars Jonty gave me as a present.

Walls no longer made me feel trapped, and as every day passed my subconscious became sure that no one was trying to capture me.

We celebrated my birthday, but we didn't celebrate the anniversary of my waking from the coma because neither of us could pinpoint the moment when it happened. I started breathing on my own that night in the hospital when Moira tried to kill me again, but waking fully was a slow process. It isn't how you think it is, you see. No Sleeping Beauty springing back to life on receipt of a kiss. The return of consciousness was a long and serpentine road, doubling back on itself and taking me off down strange paths that led to dead ends or disappeared. I had no sense of time. I didn't know the order of things. Nothing glued my life together. Yesterday could have been years ago and childhood memories felt like the present.

Dreams mingled with memories and then mingled with my half-sensed waking life, lying in bed, with either Jonty or Tilly sitting by me, holding my hand and talking. Always talking. Chatting about their day. About their hopes and fears. Reading me books and newspapers. Their words and my dreams took on shapes and sat with us, walked in and out of the room and sometimes dissolved the walls and showed me the beach I played on as a child on holiday or the walled garden from my favourite childhood book or the painted hall in the Old Royal Naval College in Greenwich.

But things got better. I got better. Time passed. I woke a little more, and over the next weeks I sorted through the fragments of consciousness, discarded the false, rearranged reality into some semblance of order and glued my life together again.

By then I knew everything. Jonty and Tilly had told me everything. During the weeks when I lay unconscious or half conscious and all they could do was talk and talk and talk.

They told me that Moira had tried to kill me twice. Ted said she'd been behaving strangely for a while, spending hours walking the fields where Gavin died. She was unlikely to face trial and had been sectioned and was now in a psychiatric hospital. And the police had returned the knives and steel to Luke. They were convinced that Moira, in her deranged state, had bought and marked the second steel in an effort to cast suspicion onto me. No trace of Gavin had been found on it and no fingerprints although that was hardly surprising given the length of time it had spent in the stream.

Tilly told me the strange story of the men coming to hunt out Elizabeth at the flat. She told me Elizabeth was dead. She died on the floor of my hospital room. No one knew why she'd gone there. No one knew who she was. But the police thought she was one of a horde of anonymous London sex workers who'd lost touch with her family and her life. In a way they were right, although Elizabeth was so much more than that.

I learned to use my body again.

I learned to move my hands.

I learned to talk.

I learned to walk.

It sounds so easy, listed like that, but it wasn't. Things about my body felt strange. My prolonged absence had created a rift and I'd grown accustomed to Elizabeth's body's ways. Even in the short time I'd been there. At times, the weakness of my body's unused muscles angered me, especially when I remembered the ordeal Elizabeth's body had withstood. It needed to try harder. But most of the time I knew it was doing the best it could and that some of the strangeness was because my mind was haunted by the pain Elizabeth and I had felt and a fear my bones would snap under my weight.

The police came to see me with questions about Elizabeth. No one had come forward to claim her. No friends. No family. No workplace had reported anyone of that name missing and all her possessions had been destroyed in the fire.

Did I know where she worked?

What had she told me about her past? Her background? Her family?

Did I have any idea why the men had come looking for her?

I'd have liked to tell the police everything I knew about her. To force them to acknowledge her life and hunt the men who ended it. But they'd never have believed me if I told them the truth. So I answered no and nothing and not much to everything, telling them what she'd told me when we first met and mentioning a friend called Reuben and her wigs, and a growing suspicion that she wasn't called Elizabeth Hughes. I hoped it might be enough to point them in the right direction. And they left, telling me to check any future flatmates more thoroughly, but satisfied with my answers. After all, I'd been in a coma while all this was playing out.

I was glad when they'd gone. I hoped I'd never have to talk to any police officers ever again. But I was sad to say goodbye to Amy. She came to see me several times, and we discussed all the things we'd never talked about before. My marriage. Her marriage, which had ended when the neighbours, disturbed yet again by the sound of her husband hitting her, had called the police and social services. Faced by the prospect of losing her children, she'd been forced to accept the reality of what was happening and leave him.

'Yes,' she said to me with the familiar firm look in her eyes. 'I was an abused wife. A battered wife. And for a time the weight of it nearly broke me.'

'I know,' I said. 'How did you...?'

'Recover?'

I nodded.

'Friends. Mainly friends. Who held my hand when I remembered all the bad times. Who told me it wasn't my fault and that he was a monster. Friends. And time. It takes time.'

I nodded again. Her husband had been an abuser, like mine. A monster. But she'd moved on. It didn't define her. It meant that she'd been unlucky. That was all.

She was moving to Kent, by the sea. She had friends who'd already made the move, and the fire in my flat had made her decide it was time to leave London.

I moved to Denmark. With Jonty. And carried on recovering.

And when Tilly came out to stay, I told them both everything. What had happened between me and Gavin and the days I'd spent trapped in Elizabeth's body.

With Elizabeth.

Watching Elizabeth's life.

They were kind, but they thought I'd imagined it, piecing together bits of what they'd said to me in hospital and spinning the rest of it from dreams and half-memories. And above all, from the sense of being trapped. Trapped by my comatose body. They didn't say the rest, but I knew they thought it. Trapped by my marriage. Trapped by Gavin. Trapped by what I'd done to him. The brain has a great need to make sense of things, they said. To create stories which explain our lives.

Maybe they were right. Tilly was sure, but from time to time Jonty scrutinised me from beneath his jutting eyebrows and I wondered if he remembered the strangeness of the conversations he'd had with Elizabeth. He'd told me about them while I was in a coma. Between them he and Tilly told me most of what had happened. Maybe they were right. Maybe I'd thought I was living it. Maybe my imagination had filled in the gaps. Tilly had read me endless newspaper stories. Anything to fill the silence, she said, and they were full of crimes and missing people and internet scams. Maybe they'd sparked dreams that I'd confused with reality.

I researched online to see what I could check.

There was no trace of Elizabeth. Nor of Reuben nor Sophie nor Charlotte Patricia.

I checked Gavin's money. It was still there, minus the amount used to pay the standing order to Tilly over the months I'd spent recovering. I called the bank to arrange for her to be paid back in full and I asked for Mr Hunstan thinking he'd be able to tell me if I'd been in to arrange a transfer to pay for the flat but I was told he'd left. Not just the branch, but the bank itself. And no, they didn't have a contact number for him. And when I asked if there might be a record of an unactioned transfer in their system, I was told it was unlikely after all this time. I left it at that.

My computer had been destroyed in the fire. Our phones had disappeared in the dash to the hospital. And by the time I was able to track down the solicitors for the flat, they were only interested in interrogating me about the fire. Exactly what I'd told them about wanting to buy the flat seemed unimportant to them, whereas who was responsible for the fire was paramount.

I gave up.

And anyway, I'd decided it didn't matter, because I had more important things to concentrate on, like finding out what I wanted to do and who I was. I went back to sculpting and made a series of heads. Each one was different. Each one belonged to a different time in my life. I called them Sunday, Monday and so on, but they weren't one week. They weren't even the same person and, although there were seven finished pieces, there were more that I destroyed. Each one was a memory of how I'd felt at different times. I just sat down and concentrated on that time and let my memories speak to my hands in the clay without interfering. It was a meditation, really. With the feel of the damp clay grounding me so my mind could run free without being overwhelmed by pain and grief and shame and guilt.

And, yes, of course it was therapeutic. It was a chance to acknowledge what had happened to me but remove the poison.

But I worked on the heads afterwards. Sculpture's not a magical process. It's hard work and planning and critical thinking wrapped round a tiny spark of something else. Inspiration? Creativity? Call it what you want. But it's nothing without the slog, without fighting through the moments when you want to abandon the piece, when it seems as though anything would be better than another day pushing clay around with minimal results.

Jonty says I learned determination while I was ill. He says the Lucy he knew in Venice would have taken twice as long to recover and never have produced such magnificent work.

Maybe he was right. About the determination, I mean. Not the magnificence of my work.

All I knew was that there was a small, hard core of grit inside me. It refused to be beaten. It refused to give in. It pushed me to take three more steps. To lift another five kilos. To chew my own food. To tell Jonty I wanted to go to Denmark with him. To go back every day to the studio and make the clay tell the story I wanted it to. To make my life tell the story I wanted to.

Maybe I'd learned determination.

Or maybe I'd had help. Maybe I was right when I thought I felt something of Elizabeth slip out of her dying body and follow me as I came home to Lucy. It would be just like her to seize the chance for more life.

Who knew? But, if she had, she was a benign presence. Occasionally, when I felt weak, something seemed to pour steel into my resolve. I thought it was her. And, on bright breezy days, when I ran through the wind-whipped grasses on the dunes and danced beneath the scudding clouds, I felt delight bubble through me and rise into the swirling air. And I was sure the delight was hers.

A LETTER FROM THE AUTHOR

Dear reader,

Huge thanks for reading *Her*, I hope you loved reading about Lucy and Elizabeth and their strange journey as much as I loved writing about them. If you want to join other readers in hearing all about my new releases and bonus content, you can sign up for my newsletters.

www.jane-jesmond.com/contact

www.stormpublishing.co/jane-jesmond

If you enjoyed this book and could spare a few moments to leave a review that would be hugely appreciated. Even a short review can make all the difference in encouraging a reader to discover my books for the first time. But, please, don't give any plot twists away! Thank you so much!

The idea for *Her* arrived in my head out of nowhere and possessed me until I managed to get the first draft of the story written. I had such a clear sense of Lucy and Elizabeth – two women trying to deal with difficult experiences in their own different ways – and how I could interlink their lives that I was desperate to write it. *Her* touches on issues that are important to me but my main reason for writing the book was to share their stories with you.

Thanks again for being part of this amazing journey with

me and I hope you'll stay in touch – I have so many more
stories and ideas to entertain you with!

Jane

www.jane-jesmond.com

 facebook.com/JaneJesmondAuthor
twitter.com/AuthorJJesmond
instagram.com/authorjanejesmond

ACKNOWLEDGMENTS

First and foremost, a huge thank you to Kathryn Taussig and Oliver Rhodes at Storm, my publishers, for being so excited about *Her* when they first read the book. I was bowled over by their enthusiasm and have loved working with them and the rest of the team at Storm. Thank you Melissa Boyce-Hurd, Anna McKerrow, Liz Hurst, Liz Hatherell, and Lisa Horton for the stunning cover. The version of *Her* that you have read owes a great deal to Kathryn Taussig's suggestions and insight.

I wrote an early version of *Her* several years ago during a particularly low point in my writing journey. However I was very lucky to be part of a supportive group of writer friends. Some of them read *Her* and their advice made it into a much better book. All of them were encouraging. So thank you from the bottom of my heart to William Angelo, Jules Ironside, Shell Bromley, Martin Gilbert, Sandra Davies, Janette Owen, Lorraine Wilson, Fiona Erskine, Matthew Willis, Philippa East, Katharine Hetzel, Karen Ginnane, Jonathan Crowe, Thea Burgess and the ever-wonderful Debi Alper.

Thank you to Amanda Preston, my agent, at LBA Books for her support and advice.

Thank you to Michelle Kiedron for putting me right on the policing aspects of *Her*. Any remaining mistakes are entirely my fault.

Thank you to my sister, Nikki, and the rest of my family

and friends for letting me take my writing seriously and to my husband, Alex, for everything.